Servants of the Wind

ISBN: 1-4196-2836-4
ISBN-13: 978-1419628368
Library of Congress Control Number: 2007900710

Visit www.booksurge.com to order additional copies.

JOHN FERRY

SERVANTS OF THE WIND

2007

Servants of the Wind

TABLE OF CONTENTS

IN APPRECIATION…

I would like to express my sincere thanks to all of the people who have helped and supported me in the writing of *Servants of the Wind.* I especially want to thank Sue (Suzie) Curtin for allowing me to serialize my tale, then titled "Heritage," in the *Valley Voice* weekly newspaper over a period of fifteen months. If it feels as if the Old Veteran actually sat down with folks every Sunday for more than a year, it is because he really did, with a loyal circle of readers that included Tommy, Gary, and Ike, and the Wilson twins, and many, many more. I want to thank Chase Putnam for the help and support he has always provided, and for all the wonderful coversations over the years, a few of which even encompass a serious topic. Thanks to Galen Wilson, who knows James Miller better than anyone else alive, and without whose favorable comments I would approach the publication of "Servants" with an amateur's trepidation. Jedediah Mannis, with a special connection to the Miller family through marriage, was instrumental in getting James's letters published, and I also thank him for all his hard work. Thanks to Abigail Skinner of the Warren County Historical Society, who signed on late but has been a gem of an editor and cheerleader. And last but most of all, thanks to my wife Mary for her tireless reading and rereading and constructive comments from the beginning of our travel through time.

"Servants Of The Wind" Is Dedicated To My Parents, Lloyd And Joan Ferry And To My Wife Mary's Father And Mother, William And Theresa Schumann. When My Parents Met In 1942, My Father Was An Artilleryman With The 29th Infantry Division, And Mother Was A British Lass From Brighton Who Had Lost Her First Fiancé When HMS Courageous Was Torpedoed In 1939. It Took Courage To Fall In Love And Hope For The Future In Those Days, But Their Courage And Hope Prevailed And They Were Married For 55 Years. Dad Passed Away In March 1998, And Mother In February 2006.

Mary's Parents Met In Massachusetts, Before Pearl Harbor. Her Father, As A Platoon Leader In The 37th Tank Battalion, Was Severely Wounded In The Saar In December 1944, But Survived, And He And Theresa Raised A Family Of Four Boys And Three Girls On A Farm On Miller Hill. Theresa Passed Away Much Too Soon, In January 1992, But Bill Is Still With Us, 87 Years Young As Of This Writing.

Our Heroes Often Purchase Their Fame With Their Deaths. Our Parents, Having Survived Their War, Will Be Remembered For Their Lives, Nobly Lived, And The Life They Gave To Us, Their Children.

October 2006

PROLOGUE

***

This story is a partnership, an alliance of people from the past and the present. It is a novel only in as much as the craft of the novelist is called upon to stitch together a rich fabric of diaries, letters, reminiscences, and the regimental history of the 111th Pennsylvania Veteran Volunteer Infantry, all to create a tapestry of living, breathing American heroes fighting to save a nation during the American Civil War.

The first members of the partnership are no longer alive. They are James T. Miller and George A. Cobham. The story centers around these two men who became "Servants of the Wind," heroes in the fight to save the Union. They moved in entirely different circles, but both were one hundred percent Americans. The son of Scottish immigrants, James Miller never became rich or famous, but his civil war letters were donated to the William L. Clements Library at the University of Michigan, Ann Arbor. George Cobham was descended from English nobility, enjoyed a certain amount of privilege and distinction, and earned a bit of fame. His letters are preserved by the Warren County, Pennsylvania, Historical Society.

And then there is Susan Miller, James Miller's wife.

"...I remember my Grandma Susan. She was real old and real little. She kissed us when we came and kissed us when we went. She subsisted on rye whiskey rather than food--little sips at a time. The sugar which crystallized on the bottle wall she gave to us as candy when I visited her. She always sat in a rocking chair by the side window. The walk from her door to the road was lined with flowers, blooming from early spring 'til late fall." [1]

The above quote is the only firsthand information we have on James and Susan Miller. Susan's granddaughter, Edith Miller Gunnell, was an elderly lady herself when she was interviewed in 1985.

The living members of the partnership are, first, historian Galen Wilson, who as Manuscript Curator at the Clements Library became acquainted with James Miller through the collection of his letters. He became captivated with James's uncompromising patriotism and courage, and vowed to share him with the world. James Miller's letters, edited by Galen Wilson and Jed Mannis, were published by the University of Tennessee Press, under the title "Bound To Be A Soldier." The second member is this author. My in-laws owned the farm where James had grown to manhood. My lifelong interest in the Civil War and military matters, and a twenty-three year career in the United States Marine Corps and United States Army, melds perfectly with respect for fellow soldiers of long ago.

The first call for volunteers, put out after the bloodless bombardment of Fort Sumter in April 1861, suffered no lack of response. President Abraham Lincoln asked for 75,000; he could have easily gotten triple the number. Throughout the North and South, men and boys responded enthusiastically, in patriotic fervor, and in blissful ignorance of what war was all about. Actually, nobody could have known, for this struggle, the first of the "modern" wars, saw a meeting of passion and technology which would change the way men looked at war forever.

From April of 1861, throughout the long, hot summer, James Miller and George Cobham stayed at home. James tended his crops on a small farm he rented near Titusville, Pennsylvania. If he wrote any letters during this time, they have not been found. We can only speculate why this man, thirty-one years old, with a wife and three children, waited until after the Battle of Bull Run, when it was becoming apparent that the war would be longer and harder than anyone had imagined, before getting involved. It seems James needed something more than adventure for a reason. He waited until it became a life or death matter for the country before enlisting in the 111th Pennsylvania Volunteer Infantry Regiment. When he finally got in on it, he gave it everything he had.

Bull Run changed everything. George Cobham signed up three days after the battle. He was instrumental in recruiting three companies of the 111th Pennsylvania, and was rewarded with a commission as lieutenant colonel, second in command of the regiment.

James Miller and George Cobham may seem less real to many people because they lived and died way back when, before television, before automobiles, before anyone alive today was even born. Possibly their uncompromising patriotism, their enduring stamina, and their determination will make them seem larger than life and, therefore, less real; but the visions who peer at us from the history books and the dusty files in historical societies were real people. If this book has a goal other than to share a group of remarkable men living in historic times, it would be to breathe life into history, to expand the horizons of its readers with the realization that we have much in common with our forebears. As you get to know them, those stiff, stern faces will seem to soften and relax a little. Their clothing will even seem to be a little less archaic. Their dreams and hopes were not so different from ours. The dreams they had for their country were realized beyond their wildest imagination...

Other dreams were destined to be smashed by the momentous events of 1861-1865, four years when the United States teetered on the edge of self-destruction, only to emerge stronger than ever, ready to assume leadership on the world stage. How did they do it, those sturdy souls of long ago, who fought with bloody passion on both sides? They endured unbelievable hardships, and destroyed each other by the thousands, only to meet for decades afterward to shake hands across those stone walls and leveling trenches that they had once risked death to take, or keep. These pages may contain a few answers for those who search.

Our Civil War veterans have long since departed from us. The people who knew them are getting on in years, and even then they were very young and the veterans very old. What if we could have gathered around a veteran's rocking chair in the winter of his years and heard it all? Perhaps it would have gone something like the story you are about to experience. I'll see you later, on the other end of this tale.

John Ferry
Farmington Township, Pennsylvania
Autumn, 2006

CHAPTER ONE
FARMINGTON, PENNSYLVANIA

Our neighbors in the northwestern part of Warren County can remember an old man who lived down the road who used to tell stories. Yes, he was old—over ninety, they say—a tough old codger with a dribble of tobacco juice on his chin and a jug from which he'd take a nip now and then, and make a face.

He was a veteran of our civil war—the ***"War o' th' Rebellion,"*** as he called it. His bad habits, two of which were just alluded to, were frowned upon by proper society, but it is supposed that he got away with them by being the oldest man in the township. He wasn't feeble in mind, body, or spirit. There was a gleam—no, a glint—in his eye, which took fire when he talked of the old days, of battles, sorrows, and heroes. Days that were even then fast being forgotten as time stole them away.

But OH! the stories he told! Most were true, but when that glint became a twinkle they'd know they were being taken in. He had a way of seeming to make time melt away. With a proud, strong voice he'd take them back there, and they would seem to live it with him, all over again, as the people, places, and events became real.

Miller Hill Road is paved now, but he could remember when it wasn't. The road climbs south out of Lander, known as Farmington Center in 1861. Lander was named after General Frederick W. Lander, who died of pneumonia in March 1862. Pneumonia was once a common complication after a gunshot wound.

You have probably never heard of Farmington Center, or Miller Hill, or General Lander. Time was, though, when not many folks had heard of Gettysburg, or Missionary Ridge, or U.S. Grant. Or George Cobham. Or James Miller.

James Miller. The road and the hill are named for his family. In the mid-nineteenth century, Robert Miller and his wife, Janet, raised a family of five sons and two daughters up there on a ninety-acre farm, and James was their oldest. This writer has often walked the fields where he tilled and plowed. We've never met, of course—at least not in this world, but we know each other very well, and his story, the story of the servants of the wind, is a story which needs to be told. And nobody told it better than the old veteran. This is how he told it, all those years ago.

That first session was billed as a community picnic. Folks young and old came from all over and they sat out on his front porch, him in a rocking chair he had made himself, with a crock of "refreshment" by his side, older folks on benches and chairs and the kids on the floor with their hands clasped around their knees. Tommy and Suzie were there, sitting close together as usual. Gary claimed the rain barrel, and would sit there most Sundays, whittling on a stick and seeming like he wasn't paying attention. Ike was there, and Shorty and Roy and the Wilson twins. Those eight were the faithful. Others would come and go, and it would always be a chore to fill them in on what had happened since the last time. He told them all to get comfortable. They had finally persuaded him to tell his story, and he warned them it would be a long haul...

***

THE OLD VETERAN

I was born on September 14, 1844, so I'll be ninety-two this year. All those events I'm about to recollect for you took place more than seventy years ago. I know young folks never understand about time until they are no longer young, but whether you understand or not, I have to say that those days seem just like yesterday to me. Except for aches and pains and wrinkles, and legs that ain't as steady as they used to be, I feel the same now as I did back then.

As I go along, you may wonder how I know all the things I'm talking about. Well, I'll be straight: I don't. Not one hundred percent. Oh, when it comes to the story of the "War o' the Rebellion," I know that well enough, and of course lots of times I was *there* and ought to know, if anybody would; and over the years I've talked to lots of folks about what happened back then, but in those few occasions said or done by other folks behind closed doors...well, you'll just have to remember that I'm telling a story—a story as true to life as can be, but a story nonetheless. I'll try to tell it in ways that you'll understand, you being young and all...

Which brings me to my command of the King's English: It seems to me that I have always been too busy learning about life to get much of an education. I did not have much schooling, and I must say I was an indifferent student when I did attend, but I would imagine that by now I have heard every word in the English language. Some I did not understand, some I do not care to use, and some I say when I shouldn't, but they are all here, tucked away in my thick skull someplace, and some of them will blurt out in my story. It's like an old timer, a veteran of the Mexican War, told me one time, "Consarn it, I know a lot, if I could only think of it!"

So I talk plain, but I dig up a fifty-cent word once in a while to add color. As I go along, I want you to ***listen.*** Listen to my voice as I peel away a century as if it was nothing (which is so, in the grand scheme of the universe) and listen to James as he sits cross-legged by the campfire with a scrap of paper and a stub of pencil in his hand. Listen to Susan as she writes with a feverish child on her lap. They were—they are—as real as today's newspaper headline.

So here goes:

Imagine, if you will, an old photograph of a farm, rutted driveway curving past the house to the barn. It is late spring, the trees captured in full foliage, but all is black and white and gray.

Slowly the picture becomes more than a picture. The black leaves gradually become dark green, and move slowly in the breeze that often blows up here on the hill when folks down in Warren are suffering from the still, sultry heat of a Pennsylvania summer. The house is clapboard white, the barn a brownish red. Cows and horses graze in the greening grass, and beyond the pasture a man with a team of horses and a plow is turning up fresh brown earth. It is a warm, late spring day in the year of 1861.

***

JAMES AND SUSAN

A horseman trots down the road and turns in the drive where a woman, Susan Miller, age thirty-two is busily hoeing between the freshly planted vegetable rows. Susan was a little wisp of a woman, but she had grit. Comes to looking for a wife, a man could do no better than to find another Susan Ann Main Miller a-waiting on her front porch swing. Time I'm done telling this story, you'll know what I mean, so I'll leave it go at that for now.

The visitor was Charlie Lyon, who the books'll tell you was the fourteenth man from Warren County to enlist in the struggle for the Union. Charlie was near twenty-five then, but he was as boisterous and exuberant as any two-year colt. A fine fella, that Charlie.

Susan would remember that day. It was years later when she told me about it, but she remembered it was a bright May day, and she remembered Charlie was barefoot, and he wore a soldier blue jacket over his farmer overalls, and she remembered the dress she was wearing. It was plain homespun cotton, and she wore a bonnet to shield her from the mid-day sun. Her hair, usually done up in a bun, hung loosely around a face that I thought was rather pretty. Susan would have blushed if somebody'd told her that. Other than maybe James, I don't know that anybody ever did.

She looked up from her hoeing as she heard hoof beats in the driveway. Charlie reined up, being careful not to let his old horse, Sally, step into the vegetable rows. "Where's Jim, Miz Miller?" he asked urgent-like. "I've got to talk to him again."

Susan motioned past the barn. "He's out plowing on the ridge field, Charlie, but I'm surprised to see you here. He made it fair clear to you last time that he's staying put."

"Yes, but—aww, goldangit—excuse me, Miz Miller, for speakin' so—excuse me, ma'am." He nudged his bare heels into the horse's flanks and trotted away.

Susan, somewhat distracted, went back to her gardening. Just then, her mother-in-law, Janet Miller, came out on the back porch. Says she, "Wasn't that Charlie Lyon? All in a rush, I see."

"Yes, it was Charlie, come to see James again."

Ol' Miz Miller sighed. "Oh, I wish he wouldn't come around."

"Why, Mother Miller! Charlie's a nice boy," said Susan.

"All the same. Charlie has some crazy notions about this war. I don't like him talking to James."

"James is a man full grown. He knows his own mind."

"All the same, daughter, all the same..." Her worried expression made James's mother look older than her sixty years.

And Susan remembered a strange feeling, of her heart skipping a beat, as Charlie galloped across the field toward her husband.

One night, as we sat around a campfire somewhere in Virginia, James told me about Charlie and about Charlie's last-ditch attempt to sign him up. Charlie remembered the day pretty well, too. James and his father, Robert senior, were working the field together, taking turns plowing and loading the stoneboat with the numerous rocks that turned up from a field only just cleared. James was thirty-one years old in 1861. Thick black hair topped a broad face, a face capable of much expression; intelligent, piercing eyes, the jaw square and firm with a short beard. He was of medium build, perfectly adaptable to the outdoor life of a farmer—or a soldier. He moved with an easy stride across the rough furrows where his father had reined in his team of workhorses. His father was a short and stocky Scotsman with a fringe of whiskers along his jaw line, and only just starting to show his threescore rounds about the sun.

James said, "I'll take a turn, Pa. Fetch yourself some shade yonder." He turned at the faint sound of a voice drifting across the fields. Charlie was coming, pushing old Sally hard. James smiled to himself, because he knew right off the purpose of the visit.

"Halloo, halloo, Jim!" Charlie was calling as the horse picked its way over the furrows. He reined to a stop, slipped a foot over the horse's neck, and bounded to the ground.

"Hello, Charlie," James said amiably. "A good morning to you. And the answer is still no."

"Aw, goldangit, Jim. I guess you know what I want." Charlie scuffed a grass-topped clod with his bare toe and thrust his hands deep in his pockets. He nodded to James's father. "Mornin', Mister Miller." The older man nodded in reply.

James folded his arms and smiled at the younger man. "I sure do. You want me to leave the farm and go with you to shoot rebels. I told you Wednesday last that this whole ruckus is foolish business and I want no part in it."

"But Jim," Charlie pleaded, "They're looking for more men for the sharpshooters, and I told Cap'n Allen how you can shoot and, oh Jim, you've just GOT to come along!"

James took a bandanna from his hip pocket and wiped the sweat from his face. "Charlie," he said wearily, "Charlie, it just ain't for me. I told you that. Maybe ten, twelve years ago, when I was young and foolish—and single—I'd have done it, but now what do I say to a wife and three youngsters?"

Charlie waved his arms and did a sort of a full-circle pirouette. "Say you'll be back before the leaves fall! Jim, it'll be a grand time! It'll be a lark! A chance to see some country and be paid for it, and to show those traitors that they've made the mistake of their lives!"

James put his hand on Charlie's shoulder. "A lark, hey? Sorry, but I've got a farm to run. My larking days are over. I got no time to be running about the country playing at soldiering. All this tom-fool marching and beating on drums down at the courthouse and over at Marshtown is for you young, single fellas. Not for me."

Charlie went from exasperation to disappointment. "It's serious bizness, Jim. The country needs you."

"No, it don't. There's more than enough young tomcats like you and your Captain Allen to do the job."

"Wa-al, if you say so, Jim, but you're missing the chance of a lifetime. I just thought you'd like to be in on it before it's over." As Charlie seen he wasn't getting nowhere, he brightened up. "Sattidy next we leave. Will you be down to the center to see us off?"

James picked up the reins from the plow handle. "Sure I will, Charlie. Wouldn't miss it."

With a shake of the reins the team lurched forward. Charlie ambled alongside the plow. "Can you imagine, Jim? All the way to Washington, D.C. Why, that's halfway to Californy..."

Mr. Miller stood with his hands on his hips watching the two of them move away, Charlie chattering on and James nodding now and then. Then he ambled to the shade of a lonesome chestnut tree, where the water jug was waiting.

***

GEORGE AND ANNE

Well, there you are. I wondered if you'd come back to pass some time with an old man. How's that wart on your toe, Suzie? It'll go away if you soak it in stump water, you know. All right, enough about your toe. I promised I'd tell you about my Colonel George. You know, he was one of the best men who ever lived...

Well sir, a gentleman by the name of Roy Stone had raised the Warren Guards—the company that Charlie had enlisted in—but then he came up with the idea of another company and a scheme to take it off to war. So, he turned the command over to Harrison Allen, a local lawyer turned soldier, and in no time at all he had enlisted a seventy-five man outfit that he called the Raftsman's Guards. His plan was to float down the Allegheny all the way to Pittsburgh, and then to take the train to Harrisburg. The plan was novel, but well suited to the rough crowd of lumberjacks and river roughnecks he had recruited from the hills of Scandia and the valleys of Kinzua.

They departed Warren on May the 20th, 1861. Warren's old six-pounder cannon roared in salute as the Raftsmen made ready to slip away from the riverbank to begin their voyage to Pittsburgh. The crowd on the riverbank had grown to more than a thousand souls waving and wishing Godspeed to this first unit to leave for the Seat of War, as we called it. The men clambered aboard eight large rafts and, yelling and cheering, they pushed off. The Stars and Stripes flew from each raft, snapping in the breeze. Boys cavorted in the mud of the riverbank, dogs barked, women cried, and the sun sparkled across the rippling waters of the Allegheny.

Among the crowd were George Cobham and his wife, Anne. George was about thirty-five, handsome, bright, and ambitious. He had had a pretty good education as an engineer, at Allegheny College in Meadville, Pennsylvania, and had a bright future there in Warren. His wife was real pretty and vivacious and a lot younger than George. I do believe George spoilt her. There was nothing he wouldn't do for her.

"Oh, George, what a time to be alive! Have you ever seen anything so grand?" She fluttered her little white lace kerchief at Captain Stone, handsome in his blue uniform and posing grandly at the stern of his raft. All the other boys had uniform suits homemade for them by the ladies of Warren, but Stone was fully decked out. He answered with a courtly bow and then blew a kiss to the blushing young ladies who lined the bank both upstream and down.

George saluted Stone and company with a touch of his fingers to his hat as he took Anne's hand and stepped away from the railing. As he pushed his way through the thinning crowd he said, "Hell's to pay, Annie. We'd best cheer now, for we may be crying later."

"Oh, George, don't be an old poop. My father says he'll bet the job will be done before the troops have done their ninety days."

"I hope Mr. Page is right, I truly do—" He was interrupted by a darkly handsome man, also in a new blue uniform, emerging from the crowd and proffering a hand, it seemed, not to George but to Annie.

"Why, George, Anne! Good to see you. What a grand spectacle, eh?"

"Why, that's exactly what I said, CAPTAIN Allen. Grand—"

"So Stone beat you to it, eh, Harrison?"

"Oh, it's for show, George. Roy Stone is great for show. Ten days and the Warren Guards leave, on YOUR railroad, and I'll bet we may yet beat him to Washington."

"Well, best of luck to you, old boy," said George, about to take their leave.

"Say, there's still room for another bold savant, George. I'd juggle my roster to make room for you."

"I don't think so, Harrison. Too many pressing matters at present. Perhaps later."

"Ah, but it's the early bird who gets the glory, George...my proverb for the occasion. My goodness, it's hot for a May afternoon. What say we skip across the street to the Carver House for something cold?"

"Why, we'd—"

George interrupted her. "We'd best not, Harrison. I was about to drop Annie at her father's and then go out by Youngsville to check one of my bridges."

Allen laughed. "If you built it, George, it's certainly not going to fall down. Perhaps..." For a moment there he might have offered to escort Anne home while George went to check on his ol' railroad bridge, but he thought better of the idea and said, "Oh well, some other time. We must get together before I go south. Goodbye, George. Anne, adieu." He bowed and bounded up to street level and headed across the muddy thoroughfare.

"Oh, George, why couldn't we have had a lemonade with Cap'n Allen? He's such fun and next week he'll be gone." She put her hand to her cheek. "P'raps we'll never see him again."

"Oh, he'll be back. If I know Harrison, he'll be back."

***

BULL RUN

From April to July of '61 a host of regiments descended on Washington, D.C., and soon the cry was "On to Richmond," the reb capital. I had joined up at first chance, so I was there too, a-chomping at the bit in one of them fancy New York Zouave ninety day regiments, with our tasseled fezzes, natty embroidered short jackets and red baggy pantaloons. Couldn't wait to "see the elephant," as the saying went. I should explain that expression, because you'll hear it more than once. See, back then folks didn't travel much, so when the circus came to town all the younguns flocked to see the elephant, something they had never seen before. Battle was something we'd all never experienced before, so it was compared with seeing the elephant for the first time.

Anyway, our commander was General Irwin McDowell, and everybody wanted him to advance on a Confederate army based around Manassas, Virginia, behind a little creek called Bull Run. McDowell's problem was that we didn't have an iota of discipline, or organization, even at regimental level. No higher organizations, like brigades, had been formed on anything except paper, neither. The country demanded action, but McDowell, as a professional soldier, knew that combat would be totally beyond our capabilities for some time to come.

No matter. The army was forced by pressure from the public, the newspapers, and the politicians to advance, and we fought a battle along that little creek.

So I seen the elephant. Seen boys shot, blown to bits. Seen fellas I thought was the bravest of the brave whimper and cry like babies—and run. My, did we run! That battle sobered us all. Everybody expected we'd win, and many civilians, including congressmen, senators, and foreign diplomats, had followed along behind the army and sat down with their picnic baskets to watch the battle. When it all fell apart, some troops stampeded back toward Washington, and artillery caissons thundered along the road neck and neck with civilian buggies. A letter written by one of the boys to the folks in Warren County was published in the *Warren Mail,* one of our two weekly local newspapers: "If we was scared we was in big company," he said. He got that right. When my regiment's time was up I was one of those who hit the road. Ninety days was enough for me.

To James Miller, and others, the news of the Bull Run defeat was devastating. Throughout history, there have been those people who will not be stirred simply by the rattle of drums or sabers. Their common traits are strength, common sense, and steadiness. Now, suddenly, they saw beyond the glitter and the falderal, and what they saw was a nation in dire peril.

***

JOHN FERRY

DUTY

George Cobham strolled around his small office, fingering the knickknacks on the mantelpiece and gazing at the pictures he'd hung to dress up the drab walls. He looked at the empty valise by his desk, sighed, and commenced to his work, which was to fill the valise with a few papers and personal items he'd rather not leave for others. On this day he was packing it all up. He laughed to himself. "All up, or all in."

His assistant's voice from the outer office heralded a visitor. "Good morning, Mr. Wells."

"Yes, yes, I'm sure. Is George in?"

"Yes sir, he is, I'll—"

"Never mind. I'll announce myself." Caleb Wells entered the office, his round face flushed and sweating in the August heat, his rotund body puffing from his climb up the stairs. "George Cobham, I rushed over here as soon as I heard..."

"Well, good morning, Caleb. What have you heard?"

Wells dropped into the nearest chair. "Just say it's not so, George. It can't be. You're too smart."

"What is it, Caleb? Calm down before you swoon."

Wells mopped his brow. "Of all the foolishness. Two young fellows down at the livery just told me that you were recruiting a company to take off to the war."

Cobham smiled and playfully poked a finger at Wells's lapel. "Why, Caleb, a man of substance as yourself, taking the word of a liveryman. The idea! A company?"

Wells laughed. "Oh, they gave me such a start. I should have—"

"Actually, I'm recruiting THREE companies, Caleb. George Cobham is about gone for to be a soldier."

Disbelief clouded Wells's face, and he puffed up like a toad. "You can't be serious! George, you have outright lost your mind!"

"Oh, come, it's not as bad as all that. In fact, I finally know exactly what I'm doing."

"George, George, George," said Caleb in a pleading, whiny voice. "It's a war! People get killed in wars."

"Caleb, I'm touched. Such concern."

"And the money! George, the money we could make! Why, with your enterprise and influence, there's no limit."

"Ah, that's more like my old Caleb."

"Money, George. Colonel Drake's oil well is the beginning of a colossal enterprise. Fuel oil and lubricants. The government will pay handsomely for every drop we can get out of the ground. And lumber! And cattle and hogs! Why, George, why?"

"Caleb, this, simply put, is something I have to do."

"It's the shoulder straps, isn't it? They'll make you an officer and you'll be able to prance around the ladies."

"Come on, Caleb, You know me better than that. My wife might have something to say about it, too. I'd rather be a rear rank private than see these United States go to ruin."

"Power, then. Glory! Excitement!"

"Didn't you hear what I just said? Caleb, don't assume that everyone is driven by the same values as yours. The country is tearing itself apart."

"The country be hanged! As Horace Greeley says, let the erring sisters go in peace."

"I don't ask you to understand. You, being you, can't. Since Sumter I've watched all the frantic, hysterical goings on as Allen and Kane and Stone and all the rest have pulled to all the points of the compass, all scrambling to get into their glorious little war, meantime letting Dan Sickles steal the Tidioute Rifles from under their noses up into his New York brigade. I even recall you making some rabble-rousing remarks at the courthouse rally. Now I can see it's going to be a big, bloody war—for survival. I've decided to use all my enterprise and persuasion and influence to enlist a body of sober, serious men for the long haul. If I'd come to this decision six months ago and persuaded others to approach this rationally, intelligently, in an organized fashion, we'd have had our own Warren County regiment. What a regiment that would have been, eh?"

Wells waved a stubby finger. "Hang your regiment. This will be your ruin, mark my words."

"Aren't you going to wish me luck?"

"I don't wish you luck. I wish you to come to your senses."

Cobham walked to the window and pulled the curtain aside. "Look out the window, Caleb. What do you see?"

"I see the Allegheny River and dusty old Water Street," Caleb snapped. "What of it?"

"A boat on that river was once able to float all the way to New Orleans in peace. Now there are armed traitors from Kentucky on down stopping the commerce YOU put such store in. And the children there by the Hickory Street corner, by the Carver House—what kind of life will they know if we let those men have their way?"

Wells groaned, "Let others do it, George. What will it matter to have one soldier less?"

"It matters to me! It matters to me... At night, when I can't sleep, it matters. In the day, when I see some boy who's never been south past Barnes kissing his mother goodbye, not knowing when, or whether ever, he'll see her again, it matters."

Wells moved to the door and stood there a minute. Finally he said, "Good day, George." And he was gone. It would be a long time before ol' Caleb understood what George had said.

George Cobham went back to filling his valise.

***

MILITARY PARADE

Despair was short-lived. For the steady ones, and even for many of those who had seen war as a romantic adventure, reality began to replace some notions of what war was all about. All over the country, rallies and parades were held to rejuvenate the martial spirit, and Farmington Center took the lead in those parts.

Now by this time James had long since struck out on his own. He had rented a little hardscrabble farm down in Southwest Township, which as its name indicates, is in the southwest corner of the county, near thirty miles from the homestead on Miller Hill and just a few miles north of Titusville, where the big oil discovery happened. Come planting and harvest time, though, he and Susan would come up to help out. It was also an opportunity to get some of his sparse equipment repaired, and that was mainly what brought them all to town on the day of the big rally. Well, it was all wrote up in the *Warren Mail*, edition of August the 24th, 1861:

MILITARY PARADE IN FARMINGTON!

The loyal citizens of Farmington Center and vicinity, anxious to revive the military feeling in their midst and to be prepared for any demand of the government upon them, made preparations for a kind of military picnic on Friday of last week.

The Sugar Grove Company, Capt. Anderson; the Busti Company, Capt. Martin, and the Pine Grove Company, Capt. Sloan; were invited to meet the Farmington Company, Capt. Niles, at the Corners. These companies, not all of them quite full, arrived there about 11 o'clock. The peoples of that township with those of Busti, Sugar Grove, Pine Grove, and other sections came in unexpectedly large numbers till there were at least 1,000 present. After drilling some time much to their own credit and the satisfaction of the spectators many of who we presume had never seen so much of a military demonstration and many others who had not for several years, the companies were marched to the dinner prepared by the ladies in the unfinished Methodist church. It was a capital place and capital dinner reflecting much credit on the hospitable people of Farmington. Though brought in from all sections in picnic style, it seemed to lack nothing that the appetite could demand. We only repeat the opinion of all who were free to express themselves on the subject, when we declare it the best and most nicely arranged dinner we have seen on such an occasion. And though twice as many came as were expected, yet was there enough for all and some to spare. Really we guess Farmington is a good place for a young man, true to the Union, to look for a wife. Where so much good cooking is done by the mothers their good looking girls must know something about it!

After the dinner and further military exercises, they marched to the stand, made of a wagon in the shade of the church, where the meeting was called to order by friend Curtis, Esq., and short stirring and patriotic speeches were made by L. D. Wetmore, Esq., of Warren, Rev. Mr. Shattuck, Congregational Minister of Farmington, Rev. Mr. Marsh, Methodist Minister of Sugar Grove, and Mr. Cowan...

...The music was capital, several of the old fifers and drummers of our "General training" memory taking a part. The companies, though none of them entirely full, acquitted themselves well, going through the exercises from "file right" to the "double-quick" with a zeal and energy which showed their hearts to be in the work of preserving the glorious Union, "peaceably if we can, forcibly if we must."

It wasn't mentioned, but Captain Harrison Allen was there, home on leave to do a little speechifying to pick up a few recruits for his regiment.

James and Susan stood at the edge of the crowd as Cap'n Allen drew cheer after cheer from the gathering as he appealed for enlistments. "Ladies and gentlemen, friends, neighbors—and soldiers! It is inspiring to see so many patriotic citizens gathered to support our cause. Make no mistake, this war is for union, for the survival of our country, the United States of America! The fervor with which we responded to Mr. Lincoln's call, while admirable, must now be replaced with determination.

"The battle fought lately in Virginia at Manassas has taught us that restoration of the Union will be no easy task. The sunshine soldiers—and I was one of these—are being replaced by new regiments dedicated to the long task before us.

"I am here today to appeal to those sturdy young men of this community who have not yet answered the call. The Warren Guards are determined, experienced comrades beside whom you can march with confidence. I know I will.

"I assure you I will be here for some time—I don't want to miss out on all this good food and the company of the fair ladies of your community. I will be available to answer your questions and take your names down as enlistments in this splendid regiment."

The crowd gathered around as he finished his speech. "Them captain's bars look mighty good on you, Harrison!" hollered a man in the crowd.

Allen had all that posturing and rhetorical stuff down pat but he was just a little too frank in his reply. "I intend for them to be general's stars before this fuss is over, my friend. A keg of ale to those who join us! What say you, boys?"

His invite prompted a surge of thirsty patriots, but with that "leetle incident," I had Captain Allen so well sized up that I never afterward had to change my opinion of him.

James's brother, Bob Jr., and his friend Paul Brown listened for a moment and then joined James and Susan at the edge of the crowd. James was impassively watching and listening.

Susan said, "James, are you ready to go?"

"In a minute, Susan."

"I'll be over at the buggy."

James nodded. As Susan walked away a man left the crowd, gnawing on a chicken bone. His name was Arch Goodin, a neighbor of James's from Southwest, widely despised throughout the county as a man with no moral fiber, no ethics, no redeeming qualities a-tall.

He nudged Miller with an elbow. “Sleep in the mud, eating bad food, folks shooting at you, disease! Not for me, I’ll tell you! Or for you, eh, Miller? Eh, Brown? Eh? Eh?” He walked away laughing and chomping on his chicken bone.

Paul and Robert traded disgusted glances. “C’mon Paul,” said Bob. “I think I just lost my appetite for any more of this. That chicken bone was probably cockfightin’ for him just last week.” They headed for the general store.

James listened as the band launched into a tinny version of “Rally ‘Round the Flag.” He was alone now, alone as the crowd, taken by the enthusiasm of the moment, joined in the music. James found himself taking a step toward the recruiting officer; then he turned and hurried away. But, almost... almost...

The family was gathered around the wagon down the road from the church. Missus Miller was already sitting in the high seat; Paul and Bob sat on the tailgate.

Bob said, “Oh, there you are, James. When you didn’t come right along I thought maybe you were a-going to enlist.”

His ma turned quickly in her seat. “Oh, Robert, how could you say such a thing!”

“Oh, Ma...”

“Oh, don’t make light of it. The idea! My boys.”

“Come now, Mother,” said Mr. Miller. “Calm yourself. Nobody’s enlisting.”

“Well, don’t. None of you! Don’t even think of it. It’ll be over soon. They don’t need you. Let us head up the hill. I feel faint.”

“Yes, Mother. We’ll go. Calm yourself.” He glanced at James and patted his stomach. “Supper at six, if you have room.”

“Directly, Pa. I have to pick up the plowshare at the smith’s and we’ll be along.”

Mr. Miller climbed up on the wagon, took up the reins, and clucked to the horses. “Ho, Jim, Bet! Let’s go!” The wagon creaked around and lurched toward the hill road. Paul and Robert, dangling their legs off the tailgate of the wagon, waved and began their usual horseplay.

Susan looked up at her husband's stern face. He seemed to be looking at something a mile away. "You thought of it, didn't you?"

James answered reluctantly. "Yes. I even took a step..."

"James, I know this is tormenting you. Whatever you decide, it must be what is right in your heart and mind. Not your mother's, or even me and the children."

"Susan—"

"We'd manage, James. Whatever God wills, we'd manage."

James mused, rather to himself, "Well, if I did enlist, it wouldn't be with a traveling military medicine show and circus such as Cap'n Allen runs, and the militia will never do nothing but parade, but I heard that fella Cobham talking sense when I was in Warren with your pa—" He stopped himself short. "We'd best get over to the smith's." He turned away, not noticing the tear Susan hastily wiped from the corner of her eye.

Behind them the music blared and the crowd sang.

CHAPTER TWO
THREE YEARS, OR FOR THE WAR

Come up on the porch and sit. I was hoping you'd come, because it's time to tell you how we all got together for the great adventure, and the great tragedy, of our lives.

Had they cared to notice, folks traveling the road between Titusville and Warren over the next two weeks would have seen the same sight every evening after the chores got done: James sitting on his porch, puffing on a pipe, reading and rereading the Bull Run accounts and the editorializing that stemmed from the defeat and the dire predictions of what it all meant for the country.

James did a lot of thinking on those late summer days. He remembered back to a day in the '50s, just after he had took on the farm. He was walking in the woods a few rods back from the road which meandered up from Titusville, past his place and on north toward Youngsville and Warren and points north. The sound of a voice from the road drew his attention, and he saw a wagon coming to a stop on the roadside.

"Hurry up, boy," the voice was saying. "It's a terrible chance we're taking, stopping like this, but I don't want you soiling my rig." Through the leaves James recognized the Reverend Mister Burroughs on the seat, and then, popping out from under the canvas in the back, came a black lad of about mid-teens. Stepping partly into the bushes he opened the flap of his misshapen overalls and commenced to water the weeds on the roadside. When the boy was done he looked up, and James was almost certain he was seen, because the boy's mouth dropped open and his eyes became as big as saucers. In a flash, he was tumbling back under the canvas, and the reverend was snapping the reins and moving on. James concluded that he had just witnessed an unscheduled stop on the Underground Railroad.

He wouldn't have thought much of it—he knew of the secret smuggling of runaways from the South to Canada and supported the notion, even though he was not personally involved—if it were not for another incident about a week or so later.

This time he was setting posts for a fence between his field and the road when he heard the rattle of wheels on the hard-packed road and the clip-clop of horses. Looking up, he saw an expensive looking rig, drawn by a matched pair of chestnut geldings, and two well-mounted outriders. Four men rode in the carriage, all dressed as gentlemen. They stopped in the road and one of the men rode over to him.

The man sat tall in the saddle. He seemed to be about James's age, with a darkly handsome face shaded by a broad-brimmed hat. He nodded a greeting, and with a drawl strange to these parts, bid James a good day. He did not dismount.

"And a good day to you, sir," James said pleasantly. He smiled, and so did the stranger. The men in the wagon, though, looked to be all business, serious and menacing. James noticed the barrel of a shotgun propped up by the back seat, and seen that the mounted men had revolvers in their belts.

"You look as if you've come a long way."

"All the way from Fauquier County, Virginia," said the stranger. "How far is it to the next town, my friend?"

"Well, the next town of any size is Youngsville, about fifteen mile up the road," replied James. "Is that where you fellas are headed?"

The stranger smiled. "We're headed wherever the trail takes us, my friend. By the bye, do you know a man by the name of Goodin? Arch Goodin?"

An uneasiness come over James, like he'd just taken a step into a dark world he did not know. He found his grip tightening on the sledge in his hand, but his voice was cool and calm. "Sure. Arch lives about halfway to Youngsville, a little place on the right of the road, with a carved rooster hanging off the porch. You won't miss it."

"Seen any strange darkies around here lately?" asked the stranger. The smile was still there, but the eyes seemed colder.

James was not a man looking for trouble, but he seemed to be dealing with men who were. That's why he surprised himself with his answer.

"There are no darkies at all around here," he said coolly. "We do our own work."

The stranger's smile seemed thinner. He shifted in the saddle and scanned the surroundings, the open space in the woods that was only now starting to look like a farm. "I see," he said. "And a fine job you do, too. Good day, my friend."

James nodded as the Virginian pulled on the reins and took the horse back into the roadway.

"Let's go, Clayton," said one of the men in the carriage. "We're wasting our time around here." With spurs and a snap of the reins they pulled out, leaving James there by the road. The whole thing left him with the shakes, not out of fear, but out of loathing for the whole idea of men hunting men. And his neighbor, Archie, that poor excuse for a human being, evidently was in league with them. Archie was such a snake-in-the-grass, that that was the only possibility.

Now, sitting on his porch, he remembered. His whole notion of the traitors to the Union was embodied in his memory of the Virginians, the syrupy southern drawl, the condescending politeness, the cool, cultured arrogance. The war would be a contest of the manhood of the North—Yankee ingenuity and stubbornness—against these men of the South, with their violent frontier passions, their notions of class and superiority. A mighty wind was going to blow, and somebody would be knocked down.

Yes, James was doing a lot of thinking and most likely a sight more praying about what he himself was to do about it. I opine that what made that coming war so hard fought was that so many folks on both sides of the Mason-Dixon felt a personal responsibility to take action to make things right. Anyway, somewhere in those two weeks he reached a decision.

Having moved to Southwest, James and Susan didn't go to church in Farmington very often, but a special occasion brought them there in early October. The Methodist church, site of the big picnic that was wrote up in the *Warren Mail* back in August, was finally finished and they dedicated it to the service of the Lord on an Indian Summer Sunday. Reverend Burroughs, the same what was a conductor on the Underground Railroad, ran the service. He spoke of a building of wood and stone, and a church of flesh and blood, of the Holy Spirit filling the building as it was built, and the partnership with the faithful who would worship there. After the sermon, they sang "Faith of Our Fathers," and then the reverend recognized James Miller, who had asked to speak.

James stood up, and the words that he thought would be hard to come by just come natural to his tongue. "Yes, Reverend, I have something to say," says James. "I grew up here, and even though we have put down roots at the other end of the county, I still consider you folks to be my neighbors. After many months the Lord has finally shown me the way, and we will need your prayers, my wife and children especially.

"Starting back in April, I've seen this country torn up by war. Bull Run showed me that what I thought was going to be easy, is not going to be so easy. Those people down south are not going to be brought back into the Union except by the sword and the gun.

"This country has been generous to me and to my family. My father and mother brought me to America, away from poverty and famine in Scotland. The United States gives us freedom, land to farm, a good life. It is the greatest of all nations.

"I am a Christian, and the Bible says 'thou shalt not kill.' But I am also a citizen, and I owe all that I am to this country. Now, in my country's hour of need, I as a man cannot sit home and let others pay the debt that I owe.

"Mr. Cobham of Warren is helping to raise a new regiment, to start forming up in Erie at the end of the month. I am going to join that regiment. I don't know what the future holds. I hope to take care of this business and come home safe to my family. If the Lord wills otherwise, then His will be done.

I ask for your prayers for my wife and children, and also for my mother, for this decision grieves her deeply. That is all I have to say."

The next week James Miller hiked up to Warren with a neighbor boy name of Washington White and they both signed up with Cobham's outfit. They became servants of that mighty wind.

October's frosts had turned the leaves all shades of red and orange and yellow, and there was a hint of winter in the air on the day James packed a few possessions in a gunnysack, swung it over his shoulder, and walked out into the dooryard to gaze up the road. All over the county—indeed, across the American landscape for these last six months—men were walking away from everything near and dear to them for the purpose of fighting for something at once much larger than themselves and also identical with themselves.

"Warsh and his pa are due any minute. Guess we'd best say our goodbyes, family." Susan followed him holding ten-month-old Johnny. Robbie, age two and Ellen, three, had clustered by the gate, not really understanding but sensing that something very momentous and sad was happening. Ellen took a halting step toward her father, her face screwed up in an effort not to cry. James scooped her up into his arms and gathered his wife and baby to him.

"Cornbread and ham and spring water are in the one sack there, James. It should do you until the army starts feeding you." Susan said it so matter-of-fact that a fool could tell she was forcing it. There was a tautness to her voice, and her upper lip was stretched tight on her teeth. Without realizing she was doing it she stroked his sleeve as she gazed into them dark eyes of his.

"Thank you kindly, Susan. I'll make it last." James wasn't no good actor, either. His voice wasn't never that husky before.

They hugged, the four of them in a tight circle of love. Then James noticed Robbie, standing alone and apart, head bowed. He lowered Ellen to the ground, took a knee in front of his son, and held him gently by the shoulders.

"Countin' on you, boy," James said. Your ma will need your help to keep ol' Bossie fed and to gather in the apples."

"Pa, why you goin' away today? Can't you go tomorrow?"

"Sorry, son. It has to be today, but I promise, I'll be back directly."

"Well, I kin help, if it's not for long."

"That's my boy." The clop-clop sound of hooves on the hard-packed road came to them, and James gave Robbie a little squeeze and stood up. He kissed Susan, swept up his bag, and started through the gate, noticing its awkward angle. "Always meant to fix this," he mumbled as he tried to push it straight, but then he realized that things undone weren't going to get done for a long time. With a wave he turned and walked to the waiting wagon. Washington White climbed to the back and made room for James to sit beside him.

My sentiments in those days were the same as James: That George Cobham made sense. He got me to go along, and that should have took some doing. Well, it really didn't. I was passing through Warren, having "seen the elephant" at Bull Run in July, when I read that a Mr. Cobham was raising a three-year regiment and needed a few more men. I say I was "passing through" but really I was just a-wandering and a-wondering what to do about this mess my country had got itself into. I tell you, true, I had half a notion to go 'way out west and not come back until the war was over, but something in me led me instead to the recruiting office.

Anyway, fall of 1861, it was, me and James Miller and near a thousand other fellers enlisted in the 111th Pennsylvania Infantry. Was they glad to have me! There wasn't but a few had ever smelt powder before, so they figured I could do 'em some good.

Our commander was Colonel Matthew Schlaudecker, with George Cobham second in command as lieutenant colonel. Our major was Tom Walker, from Erie. Camp Reed was right close by the shores of Lake Erie. I probably could have picked a better spot to lay up in, what with the north wind howling across that lake all winter, but I couldn't have picked a better regiment. "Soldiers True," Adjutant Boyle called us in his book, and we were. [2]

But to my mind, the truest of all was James Miller...

We entered by the gate, never again to leave camp except on pass or for maneuverings. The wind was blowing across the Camp Reed parade field, gusting up little tornadoes of dust and blowing scraps and leaves around as it practiced for its later howling. We were marched up to a sergeant sitting behind a field table.

"What's your name, soldier?"

"Miller, Sergeant."

"Your full name, man! And speak up!"

"Private James T. Miller, Sergeant!"

"'At's better. Miller. Company B. Move on. Next man."

"Private Young, Sir!"

"Don't call me sir! I'm a sergeant! I work for a living! What's your FULL name, sonny?"

That was November the 2nd, 1861. I was the next man in line, and I also went to Company B. Over the next three years I got to know James Miller as well as I'd know a brother. And, I'll tell you, there was one hell of a man.

Camp Reed was where the 111th Pennsylvania went from being a collection of a thousand of the roughest set of fellers you ever saw to being one of the finest regiments ever to come down the pike. "Sober, serious men," George Cobham had told ol' Caleb Wells. Well, we was serious, but sober mostly only when the army wouldn't let us buy it or make it. The colonel never said he was rounding up a bunch of Sunday school teachers, although come to think of it, we had a few of those, too.

Here's a piece of James's first letter home, or at least the first we know of, wrote on November the 13th, 1861, to his father:

"...I have had a furlough and have been home six days. I came back on Monday and I suppose it is the last time I shall have the privilege, as they are quite strict with the men. Still, I like soldiering full as well as I expected to, only the boys are very rough and profane. I did all I could to arrange business; still, I had to leave it unfinished and I want you to do the best you can to arrange matters so as to save all you can for Susan and the children. There is some talk of marching orders next week, but I do not think there is much prospect of an immediate move. Still, they move at any moment..." [3]

The first time I met James's wife, Susan, was when she came up to Camp Reed for a visit. It was a nice fall day, not cold at all, and a group of us went for a walk on the beach: Five of us boys, and James and Susan. We each tried to outdo the other in being chivalrous and considerate to this lady, but finally the most thoughtful one of us (and it probably wasn't me) suggested that we withdraw to give them some time to themselves.

We sat on a bluff and enjoyed the clear sky and the view of the lake. James and Susan walked on up the beach, holding hands. Still after all these years I can vividly picture them, two small figures far down by the lake shore. They tossed bread crumbs to the seagulls and watched them soar and dive around them. James skipped rocks out into the water. They would walk to the edge of the water and then run back laughing as the waves lapped in. It would be their last time together for a long time.

***

CALVIN BLANCHARD

During the three months we were there at Camp Reed we kept gaining men. One came in sometime in January of '62, although at the time he was more a wet-nosed boy than a man. His name was Calvin Blanchard. As far as I know he's still alive, out in Californy.

Calvin lived south of Warren, between Sheffield and Barnes. On January 10th, 1862, he took his rifle and went out to see if he could get a deer—slopped around in the rain and sleet all day and got home, cold and tuckered, after his mother had washed the supper dishes.

Calvin pulled up a chair to the kitchen table. Miz Blanchard bustled around the kitchen, plopping a spoonful of cold mashed potatoes and fatback on a plate, all the while reminding Calvin how inconsiderate he was.

"I work hard to set a decent meal on the table, seems to me the least you could do is be here to eat it, Calvin. And, lordy, son, look what your feet are doing to my clean floor."

Calvin swiped a towel off the cabinet and went to mopping water and mud with it.

"Oh, my word! Calvin, that's a clean towel. Can't you—I declare, son, the older you get the less brains you show me."

"Ma," says Calvin, "I'm sixteen and a half, and my brains are telling me I've had a bad day. I'm wet and I'm tired and all I seen of deer today was tails a-goin' away."

"Serves you right. Chasin' round the woods all day while your father cuts logs. Wants you to split 'em for stove wood tomorrow." Sarcastic, she added, "If you have the time."

Calvin slowly laid his fork down and looked up at her. "If I'd of shot a deer we'd have the meat and you'd be happy. Ma, I told you, I'm plumb tired. Cain't you rake me over the coals some other time?

"Don't you get smart with me, young man!"

"Ain't gettin' smart. I jes' want to eat this here grub in peace and go to bed."

"Grub is it? I'll tell you, until you change the way you talk and act, if you want peace you're going to have to look for it somewheres else."

"Whaddya mean by that?"

"You know what I mean. If you can't do better, you can get out!"

Calvin stood up, knocking the chair over. "Well, maybe I'll just do that!" He started to leave then thought better about going to the loft with no supper and hooked a hunk of meat from his plate. Then he went to his blankets and commenced to doing a heap of thinking.

Next day, Saturday the 11th, he cut wood all day until supper time. After supper he changed clothes and walked down to Barnes where he stayed overnight with his three sisters, Pert, Martha, and Emily. They all went to meeting Sunday night, and then Calvin started out on his big adventure.

The bitter cold stung his cheeks and made him catch his breath as he stepped out of the meeting house. Still, his mind was made up. It was fifteen miles to Warren. It was 9 p.m.

He passed his house, four miles on the road to Warren, at 10:30. It was very cold, and the road was icy.

He reached the Allegheny River at the Glade Ferry about 1 a.m. There by the riverbank was Ziegler's shack. Ziegler was the ferryman. Not a light showed, but Mr. Ziegler had to be there; he always was. The river was high, the ice running strong. After crossing the river there at Glade, it was still two miles more to the courthouse, where the recruiting office was. Calvin knocked on Ziegler's door and got a muttered curse in reply, and a widening glow as a lantern was lit.

"Why, you look froze to the bone, Calvin," said Ziegler as he pulled Calvin over to the potbelly stove. "Do you know what time it is? What in thee tarnation brings you out on a night like this?"

Calvin shivered. "Gotta cross, Mr. Ziegler. Gotta be at the courthouse when it opens. I'm enlisting today."

"The hell you say. Enlistin' are ye? Does yer pa know?"

"No, he don't—not yet. But it don't matter."

"You younguns. No more sense than a gone goose. Calvin, in the first place, hain't takin' nobody across; way the ice is running it hain't safe. No, you just hunker up on the day bed there, and head on home in the daylight..."

"Mind's made up, Mr. Ziegler."

"...An' second of all, you're too young an' small to enlist. I don't even bleeve they'll take you."

"Yes they will too! Your son Henry enlisted and he ain't much older or bigger than me."

"Calvin Blanchard, I just ain't up to arguin' at after one in the morning."

"Me either. If you won't take me over, let me have a rowboat and I'll go it alone."

"Yes, and drown yourself and I would lose a boat."

"All right, if I can't get across here I will walk down this side of the river and cross on the rail bridge."

"You are a stubborn rapscallion, Calvin." Ziegler slowly sat down on his bed and pulled his boots over by his feet. "So you want to go jine up with George Cobham and his boys. If it were anybody else I'd tan your hide and haul you home myself."

"You mean you'll take me?"

"First I'm going to make us some coffee, to thaw out those bones of yours, and then I will," Ziegler grumbled, "but they'll probably throw you back, like the little fish you are, and I'm counting on that, too."

It was said that Mr. Ziegler made the best coffee ever served on the banks of the Allegheny. He served it up with a chunk of cornbread and a slice of bacon, all the while making little innocent comments that were engineered to cast doubt into a less determined mind. Calvin just let them breeze on by. Then, having failed at psychological warfare, Mr. Z showed that he was good at his day job. He snaked that boat across between the whirling ice chunks without much ado. Calvin climbed out and turned to the ferryman.

"How much, Mr. Ziegler?"

"It's on the house, Calvin, though I have to tell you, anybody asks where you're going, I'm bound to tell 'em."

"Fair enough, Mr. Ziegler. I'll say hello to Henry for you." Calvin waved and set out up the muddy road. Ziegler shook his head and turned to tackle the river again. Reckon he made it.

The sun was coming up, bringing the barren stump-covered hills that lined the valley into focus, as Calvin reached the courthouse. The stoker had just arrived to fill the big furnace in the basement, and let him in to wait for the recruiting office to open.

It was the same thing all over again. He was too young, too little.

Calvin certainly had a way of stating his case: "Look here, sir. If you don't enlist me I'm just going to hoof it up to Erie, and look up the company in barracks, and enlist there."

"How you gonna get there, boy?"

"I just told you. I'll walk! I've already walked fifteen mile since last night."

Well, the officer and the sergeant exchanged glances, each one's expression pretty much telling the other that they had a determined kid on their hands, and who were they to turn down a warm body who wanted to go to war for Uncle Abe?

"Face the flag, raise your right hand, and repeat after me, son."

Calvin's heart like to bust out of his chest as he 'bout faced and faced Old Glory. Within a few minutes he had swore in, signed his name, and was headed for the train depot with a ticket in his hand for Erie. [4]

***

CAMP REED

"Look at that'n," said Washington White as he pulled a swab from the barrel of the old musket he was cleaning. James laid down a half-blacked shoe and looked up the company street.

The fella we seen was Calvin Blanchard, but he looked more scarecrow than soldier. His uniform hung on him like a Sibley tent on a fence post, arms and legs too long, pants cuffs scuffing in the mud as he slogged along.

Warsh snickered. "He gots to take two steps afore his uniform moves one. Hey, sonny, does yer mother know you're out?"

Calvin scowled and spun toward us. "You talkin' to me?"

"Yes I am, little fella."

"Well, now, you're a big one. How tall are you?"

Warsh drew himself up to full height. "Six-two," says he.

"I didn't know they piled it that high for old Abe." Suddenly Calvin broke out in a big ol' grin. "Name's Calvin. What's yours?"

Warsh didn't know if he'd made a fight or a friend. Figuring he would only be paid to fight rebels, he smiled and stuck out a hand. "George Washington White. Welcome to the outfit."

We were all equals, 'cept for a few with a high opinion of themselves and, of course, the officers. We were ready to tolerate anybody until seeing the elephant would separate the men from the pups.

Even the next day, when Calvin would faint at dress parade.

Just as we were shaking hands all around and sizing each other up, the bullhorn voice of our company commander interrupted. "Blanchard, front and center! You have a visitor." Captain Pierce was coming down from the headquarters building with a civilian in tow.

"Uh-oh. That's my dad," said Calvin, his forlorn statement made all the more so by his appearance.

"Your pa's come to take you home, Private Blanchard."

"Can he do that, sir? I mean, I swore an oath, and a man ought to hold up to an oath, oughtn't he?"

Pierce chuckled. "He tells me you ain't even seventeen, son, so he sure can." Mr. Blanchard stood by with his hat in his hand and a plaintive, screwed up look on his craggy old face.

"Pa, I guess you could take me, me bein' under age and all, but I do wish you wouldn't. I'll just run off again, first chance I get."

"Son, why don't you give it a year or two? Your mother's worried sick and sorry she put you up to this."

"Shucks, ain't her fault. I sassed her and she set me straight. Ain't no hard feelings, but in a year this war'll probably be all over and I'll have missed my chance."

Cap Pierce interrupted. "Ahem...Mr. Blanchard, let me talk to you for a minute." He motioned the old man aside and the two of them jawed for a spell, and we had no idea what deals were being made. Finally Blanchard strolled back over to his boy.

"Well, I reckon it's a question of whether you're a kid that ought to be tanned for running off or a man who knows his mind and...I reckon, seeing all the folks you've had to buffalo to get this far, maybe if you want to try soldiering for a while, you should do it."

Calvin grinned. "Thanks, Pa."

His father fumbled through a vest pocket. "Here's a couple of dollars to tide you over until the army pays you..." his voice trailed off and he pulled a big kerchief from another pocket and wiped a hasty swath across his face and blew his nose. Cap Pierce said, "Blanchard, maybe you can take your father down to the mess for a cup of—"

Mr. Blanchard waved him off. "No, no, thank you kindly, but that's all right. There's a train back to Warren I've got to catch. That was your fare money I just gave you, Calvin." He and Calvin shook hands and Mr. Blanchard was not to see his son again for two years.

The next day was that fainting spell I mentioned awhile back. First time on dress parade, and Calvin just up and keeled over in ranks. The captain had me and James Miller drag him over to the side until he could get away.

"Calvin," says the cap'n, all fatherly, "Maybe we could find a place for you as a drummer in the drum corps."

Calvin came to as if somebody had throwed a bucketful of smelling salts on him. "No! I mean, No, sir! I'm going to carry a gun. I, uh. . .my knapsack straps are too tight, that's all. That's why I got dizzy."

"But your father..."

"Aha! That's what you and him were scheming about. No sir, Cap'n Pierce, sir. I'm going to carry a gun, and I'm going to be the damnedest soldier you ever saw!"

We had a lot of 'em

We were lucky to have Colonel Schlaudecker for a commander. His military experience over in Prussia or wherever he came from ensured that we would have a solid foundation of training and discipline if the government gave him the time to drill it into us. That winter, it seemed we had all the time in the world.

We drilled all week, but Sundays were pretty easy. We'd have a company inspection in the morning and a dress parade in the afternoon, but the rest of the day was ours. Religious services were a problem when the weather was bad, because there wasn't a building in the camp big enough to hold but a portion of us. Our chaplain was Professor Williams, of Meadville.

Our barracks were comfortable, but when the boys were all in it was all noise and commotion, and as James said in a letter, from a religious point of view it was a hard place to live. In spite of a double guard, some of the boys would slip into Erie and get most gloriously drunk. Then they would come back and make it miserable for us who were just trying to get some sleep. Nobody is more inconsiderate than a happy drunk.

***

IN HONOR OF DONELSON

On February 17th they lined us up and marched us into Erie in honor of a victory down in Tennessee. Seems an Illinois general captured Fort Donelson, a reb stronghold on the Cumberland River, scooping up fifteen thousand prisoners. That general was all business. When the enemy asked for terms, expecting some kind of chivalrous reply, he wrote back that there were no terms except unconditional surrender, and that he proposed to move immediately on their trenches if they didn't go along. The newspapers had a field day with that "Unconditional Surrender" talk. It matched his initials: U.S. Grant.

We didn't mind celebrating. We were in the midst of a long, dreary winter, being either bored to death or drilled to death alternately by degrees, and we needed some good news. As we marched—if that's what you call wading through mud halfway up your knickers—our field officers, on horseback, picked their way through the fields alongside the road. Colonel Cobham, on his high-spirited Billy, a fine looking horse, was not five feet away to my right. Then there was Major Walker, then Colonel Schlaudecker. Actually, Schlaudecker was from Bavaria, and he was drilling us well, even if we sometimes didn't understand his lingo.

"Dis Grant, he iss making a name vor himself," Colonel Schlaudecker was saying.

"Yes, another nail driven in the southern coffin," replied Major Walker. "Every time we have a success I fear that there will be less chance of our ever striking a blow."

"It iss a long way from dis vort—Donaldson, is it?—to New Orleans, Major. I sink ve vill see our share off donder und blitzen."

"What do you think, George? Are we going to see Mister Elephant, or are we not?"

Colonel Cobham replied, "It's what I've enlisted to do, Major..."

(Now, Colonel Cobham had been commissioned by the state on July 1st, been seriously soldiering since the first of November, and had a federal commission less than a month old. Still, from what I seen, he was developing military savvy built on common sense and the mental discipline of a trained engineer. Something about Tom Walker didn't sit right with me, and, I suspect, not with Cobham, neither. Little patronizing remarks like this last were part of it, and the way the maje seemed to sulk when Cobham took command in Schlaudecker's absence, and the supposed-to-be-humorous remarks about George's two companies of country bumpkins from down Warren way. Hmph! As if Erie was ever kin to Londontown! And then there was Major Tom's frequent references to all his political friends. It all told that while the major was probably plenty brave enough, he was plenty brass, too, and would bear watching out for.)

The colonel continued, "...But I'll have no regrets if all these boys go home live and whole to their wives and mothers."

And I thought, "Well said, Colonel George." Later on some of the boys expressed a disappointment that Cobham hadn't come back with some fire-eating reply, but after all, they was just boys, and hadn't none of them smelt powder yet.

"Amen," said Colonel S. "War ist a great abenteuer vor dem that liff to talk about it."

So we went to Erie, and the bands played and the guns roared out a salute, and then we hiked home to Camp Reed, with mud to our knees but joy in our hearts.

Camp Reed, February the 19th, 1862:

"...was glad to hear that Father's health was so good but was sorry to hear that Mother's was so feeble. I got a letter from Susan the night before last, and she wrote that she and the children were all well, and that Ellen said she was coming to Erie and would lick them all if they did not let her Pa come home.

...I want you to tell Robert that I think he might write a letter to me. He scolded like fun because I did not answer his letter and it is now some four or five weeks since I wrote to him. I should think he might find time to write to me if he tried very hard. But then, I suppose the girls take up a good share of his time...

...John writes that Mother fretted a good deal about me and I wish she would not do it, for I feel that the cause in which I am enlisted is one of the most just and holy that mortal man ever engaged in. I have faith that I shall live to see the Stars and Stripes float over our whole country. And I hope to see the British lion well licked for his insolence this last winter. I think that if I live and have my health until the day of vengeance comes—as come it will, I hope and trust—I think I know of one that will help to wipe out the insult in the best blood of Britain, for I think that when we get this war settled and get a breathing spell, we will be able to give John Bull such a flogging as he never got." [5]

About John Bull and Company, across the pond: I don't know if you know how close we came to having a real shooting war with Great Britain. An over-enthusiastic navy captain of ours had snagged a couple of Confederate emissaries off the British mail steamer *Trent* on the high seas, setting up a crisis which the wise Abe Lincoln only defused by having the emissaries let go. Oh, how some people howled about that, but if we had gone to war against England again, I would speculate that the South would have gained its independence in the outcome. No use speculating in things that did not come about, I reckon. As far as James's remarks go, you have to remember that he was a Scot and had the blood of William Wallace, Robert the Bruce, and Rob Roy in his veins.

***

TO THE SEAT OF WAR

Well, now, you're just in time for to get on the train to leave good ol' Erie for the Sunny South. All aboard!

We finally got our marching orders to leave Erie on February 24, 1862. We were delayed a day while the railroad collected enough cars to hold us all, but finally at ten o'clock on February the 25th we left Camp Reed and marched to the city, up State Street, past Brown's Hotel to the Cleveland Railroad depot. The regimental band playing "The Girl I Left Behind Me" marched at the front of the column. A huge crowd of citizens was waiting for us at the depot. They presented our Colonel Schlaudecker a beautiful new sword and belt, and we had to listen to a lot of speechifying. Everybody was anxious to shake our hands but we kept a cordon out to hold them off.

Later on, when it come time for families and friends to say their private goodbyes, they let 'em through. Old men, some with tears, came up to grasp the colonel's hand and say, "Goodbye, Colonel. God bless you, bring my boys safe home again," and this was when I learned it was true about the feelings women have for men in uniform. More than a few kisses were gave out where you didn't know her name and she didn't know yours. At one o'clock the band struck up "Dixie," the colonel commanded "Forward March" and we loaded on the cars. We started off amid the thundering of the cannon, the hurrahs of the men, and the tears of the ladies. All in all, it was as good a send-off as we could have wished. [6]

Until I started soldiering with the 111th, I had never seen a big ocean like Lake Erie. Seemed like an ocean to me, anyways, since you couldn't see the other side. Canada, I supposed. In the fall it had been bright, light blue, calm as you please behind the reds and yellows of the autumn leaves. Peaceful.

Now we were headed for Cleveland. The lake was off to our right the whole short autumn afternoon. Froze over, it was gray until dusk, when the sun set and sent beams of all the colors of the rainbow across the silvery ice. We was headed west, which was strange to young Cal Blanchard.

After the excitement of the sendoff, and gazing at the countryside rushing by at ten-fifteen miles an hour for a couple hours, Calvin was gazing sleepily at the sunset.

"Ain't Washington east and south of us? Here we are headed west."

James chuckled to himself, remembering Charlie's geography. "Halfway to Californy..."

Says I, "Mebbe it's just to fool the reb spies in Erie on where the mighty 111th is gonna hit the scene."

Calvin perked up at the thought of spies in our midst. "Gosh, do you think so?"

"Naw, really it's jest the way the rails run. We'll double back from Cleveland, down to Pittsburgh, and acrost the Alleghenies to Harrisburg. I don't figure we'll hit Harrisburg until day after t'marra, but still it beats walking."

We made Cleveland by seven o clock that night, had supper, and they added another engine to the train. I had noticed that we hadn't been making very good time with only one. The clickety-clack had a mesmerizing effect, and one by one, except for a noisy poker game at the front of the car, we dropped off to our dreams. With dreams of home, dreams of the future, specters of fear and loneliness already starting to raise their ugly heads, we rattled on through the night and passed through Pittsburgh by six the next morning. It beat walking, yes, but it still seemed to take forever to get over the mountains.

We arrived safe and sound in Harrisburg the next morning. We unloaded from the train and formed up in front of the United States Hotel, where all the ladies were put up—oh, yes, many officers brought their wives. Cobham's wife, Annie, a pretty little gal, was there as well as Mrs. Schlaudecker and others. From there we marched to Camp Curtin, which was on an elevation maybe about a half-mile from the city. We passed the 54th Pennsylvania Regiment going the other direction on their way to Washington.

The next two days was all business. They issued us our muskets, which turned out to be inferior Belgian rifles, imported to fill the need until our own factories could make enough U.S. models. These guns was heavy to tote, the hammer spring was so poorly tempered that sometimes you would have to cock the hammer and pull the trigger two-three times before they would go off. When they did fire, they kicked like a goddam mule.

We had expected, or hoped, to draw our own Springfield model, or at least the Enfield. Imported from England, Enfields turned out not to be as easy to keep in condition as the U.S. Springfield, but there wasn't that much difference between them. Enfields were .577 caliber, while the Springfield was a .58 caliber. You could interchange the ammunition between the two, but at the risk of jamming a .58 caliber minie ball in the slightly smaller bore of the Enfield, especially after it fouled.

I suppose I should explain things once in a while or you'll just sit there and pretend you know what I'm talking about. A minie, for instance, wasn't a ball at all. It was a conical bullet, made of soft lead, hollow in the base. It was invented by a French fella, Captain Minie, who figured out that if the bullet was loaded small and then expanded when you shot it, it would load easier and take the rifling better when fired. It was a devilish invention, making rifles that was deadly accurate out past a quarter-mile and a slug that would do a lot of damage, especially if it hit bone.

But I digress, as they say. For a time, we would have to make do with the Belgians. The regiment got sixty thousand cartridges for our new rifles, all our camp equipments, bayonets, tents, new pantaloons, and shoes. We now were well dressed, well equipped, well fed and ready for bear, and on Saturday morning we marched down to the state capitol to get our regimental flag from Governor Curtin. [7]

Nothing much impressed me about Harrisburg except the capitol building itself. From it there was a quite a view of the Susquehanna River. We marched right up to the steps of the Capitol, a thousand men in mass, officers out front, on a crisp, sunny day with a hint of spring in the air. The governor commenced to make a speech. Seemed like the entire State Legislature had come out to see us, and there was officers of other regiments, private citizens, old gray-bearded men with their hats off and tears rolling down their cheeks. Governor Curtin was in earnest. Ain't many politicians I ever respected as much as him. He spoke about how the state was going to take care of the soldiers' families, and when he handed the flag to Colonel Schlaudecker he told him to bring it back with honor, or not come back at all. Put me in mind of my schooling and learning about the Spartans of Greece of 2,000 years ago, where the warriors' mothers told them to come back with their shields or on them. Carried home on them dead, they meant. I figured Governor Curtin had also read about the Spartans.

As the governor continued on, his words sending a shiver of pride through every man in the ranks, I noticed an official looking chap go up to Colonel Cobham and tap him on the shoulder. They bowed their heads together for a minute and then Cobham nodded and saluted. The very moment the governor finished his speech and the colors were in Colonel Schlaudecker's hands, Cobham was at his side, and then Schlaudecker nodded, and turned around and give the commands which faced us to the right and started us in column to the rail depot. Orders were for us to be in Baltimore before midnight.

As soon as we crossed the Mason-Dixon you could see the difference. As Colonel Cobham put it, everything looked like war, all the bridges guarded, nothing belonging to the army left unguarded. I had been down this way some eight months before, when it wasn't known which way Maryland would jump. Turned out, she didn't jump. She was held in the Union by some heavy-handed—you might say unconstitutional—methods, but it had had to be done. Abe done a lot of strong-arm diplomacy and old-fashioned arm twisting to keep the border states of Maryland, Kentucky, and Missouri in the Union, and Baltimore was a hotbed of secesh sympathies. Troops headed for Washington had to pass through Baltimore, and due to the incomplete railroad system, had to march through the city between train terminals. One of the first regiments, a outfit from Massachusetts, was attacked by a mob while in transit, and people got killed.

We arrived in Baltimore two hours early but we didn't get to our assigned post until rather late in the day and, even though there were officers and sergeants to assign us to barracks by companies, it was way after midnight before we turned in. I'll tell you, it is fun for a thousand tired men to set up housekeeping in a strange place in the middle of the night. Colonel Schlaudecker, Colonel Cobham, and Major Walker had to go see our commanding generals first thing in the morning, so they probably got less sleep than we did. Daylight came mighty quick.

And it's getting late. See you next Sunday? Yes, Tommy, we'll be getting into the "shootin' war" in a little bit. Maybe then you'll pay attention.

CHAPTER THREE
BALTIMORE

Like Charlie said, we were going to see the world and get paid for it. We started off with Baltimore. Any of you ever been to Baltimore? It's a nice enough town, nothing special, I s'pose, but it was a wonderment back then to all them boys who had never been off the farm.

Guard duty is one of the necessary evils of a soldier's life. It must be done, in fair weather or foul, day or night, and so it has its varying degrees of hardship. Take guard duty at regimental headquarters, for instance. It certainly had its advantages, such as having the opportunity to pick up news firsthand on what was to be done with us, and maybe to get a close-up look at the ladies that the officers brought along. 'Course, there was some that wasn't much to look at, but some were very fine. The disadvantages were that you had to take extra care to black your shoes, press that uniform, and wear everything just so. And if you made a mistake, you usually did it in front of God and everybody.

So it was with mixed feelings that I shouldered my new Belgian musket and took post at the entrance to the McKim mansion, about ten yards from the front porch steps. From top to bottom, my uniform consisted of a fancy "Hardee Hat" which had a high crown and a brim turned up on one side. It looked first-rate but it was not a too practical head-piece for field work. I wore a new three-button dark-blue sack coat of wool, and sky-blue trousers of the same material. I had on brogan shoes with cleats on the heels to save wear and tear on the leather soles. My cap box (in front of my right hip) and bayonet (hung rather to the rear on my left side) were strung on a wide leather belt with a "US" buckle. My cartridge box with room for forty cartridges (they only gave me five that day) was slung on a wide leather strap across my chest from left shoulder to right side, and was held in place by the belt being over the strap. The belt and cartridge box, taken together, were called our "leathers," just so you'll know for future reference. In addition to that, my quart-canteen was slung across from right shoulder to left side. It had been quite a while since I had had all them traps on at the same time, WITH the gun, AND bullets, and I felt real pugnacious.

The McKim mansion was an impressive house, built in southern plantation style. It had belonged to the mayor of Baltimore, but he had taken too active a part in the ruckus when regiments first tried to pass through the city on their way to Washington. So, neither he nor his estate had been treated too kindly by the military. I don't know for sure where the mayor was by then—probably someplace with iron bars between him and freedom, or maybe he lit out for southern Dixie—but his house was now headquarters, Camp McKim.

And the grounds was now military to the core. All the fences were gone. All the trees, except for a row of locusts in front of the mansion, had been cut down for firewood. Other trees, shrubs, orchards, and such had all been rooted out and burned to make a parade ground. Big two-story barracks housing the troops had been built enclosing a three-hundred-foot square in the yard, and the biggest flag I ever seen flew over it all.

A band was playing bon voyage for the 17th Massachusetts as it formed up in the square. The 17th was about to march out of camp on its way to reinforce McClellan's Army of the Potomac. It was a stirring sight, combining this display of armed might, a thousand determined looking boys from the "Abolition State," with the pomp and pageantry of the occasion. I stuck out my chest and stood about two inches taller.

My special orders were to make sure any person entering was there on official business before passing them in to the adjutant, old Major Boyle. As I took my post I looked up to see Colonel Cobham seated on the balcony with his feet up and a writing pad in his lap. But he wasn't writing right then. He was gazing out over the city of Baltimore. Not that we would get to do any sightseeing to speak of, but the colonel was looking out over quite a beautiful city, with paved streets, gaslights, monuments—and a Yankee fort on every hill. We now occupied one of those forts.

There were four other camps in the city with eight or ten thousand troops, with the guns of Fort McHenry, Federal Hill, and Potter's Hill bearing on the city from three different directions. What secessionists there were in Baltimore dared not say their souls were their own, to quote a certain James T. Miller.

The notes of a little Beethoven piece came tinkling out the open French doors behind the colonel. The story had gone around camp of the delivery of a hired piano for Missus Colonel Cobham. The piano was in tune, but her playing needed work. The colonel looked down and noticed me and give me a little friendly nod, to which I replied by bringing my musket up to "present arms," and then he smiled and touched his fingers to his temple in a little salute. I went about my business, but couldn't help but overhear them:

"George, can we go for a ride tomorrow?" Her voice, coming from somewhere inside, was more melodious than the tune she had been playing.

"Mm-mm, possibly late in the day, Anne. You know Colonel S. will never let up in his training regimen."

There was a rustle of skirts as she joined him on the balcony. "Yes, but you work so hard. I should think he owes you a little time off."

"I work hard for my own account, Annie—and the regiment's."

"What if I should ask him—"

The colonel interrupted. "Not on your life, my sweet."

"Yes, but Major Walker gets whole days away and his wife isn't even here." (I detected a slight gasp of prurient curiosity.) "What do you suppose he does with his time?"

"I can't imagine. And it's none of my business—or yours."

"Well, I simply must have a ride out and away from here. When I ride the grounds the men do nothing but gape—and I could name a few officers, too."

"Well, I can't blame them, but if you want me to shoot a few privates and send the offending officers home, or vice versa, just say the word."

"Oh, George, I'm serious."

"Well, don't be. As you said once, long ago and far away, this is a great time to be alive." Then I reckon he remembered me, and where they were, and he got up and they left the balcony. I heard the French doors close.

Although duty had put me in that location, and I would have looked unmilitary and ridiculous if I had plugged my ears, I blushed and felt like a peeping Tom. And about here I believe I will take my narrative in a different direction.

Our quarters were new construction after a pattern that has not changed much since: Sleeping quarters on the second floor, and the kitchen and mess on the first floor. Part of the education for becoming manly soldiers for the Union was to learn how to scrub and sweep and mop and make up your bed. We kept everything clean and tidy, better than most folks do their houses. Compared to conditions other armies were enduring about then, we had it pretty good.

And they finally paid us, from enlistment up to January 1st, so Uncle Sam still owed us two months' pay. He would always be behind in paying what he owed but it was probably planned as an outlet for those soldiers who always needed something to complain about. The men with families crowded the express office to get money back home, but the single or irresponsible fellers started throwing it away, gambling or buying worthless items from all the peddlers who laid siege to the camp. In a short time everybody would be broke again.

I got to see our generals several times during our stay in Baltimore, usually with us sweating in the ranks and them riding by on their horses, or with them sitting their horses, looking every inch the generals, and us marching by in the dust or mud. General Dix, our division commander, was about fifty, a rather small, natty looking gentleman. General Duryea commanded our brigade. He was Colonel Cobham's age—mid-thirties—and a good looking fellow, a soldier, and a gentleman. He had started out as colonel of the 7th New York Regiment.

The most important thing General Duryea had to say, as far as affecting us directly, was that our officers were to take a written examination on all they knew about soldiering—from the officer point of view—and those who could not toe the mark would be sent home. I was glad to see that, for there were not a few officers who thought all you needed was a loud voice and no pity for the men. There were more than a few pale shoulder straps when they heard that piece of news, and we started putting up wagers on who would be going home, and hoping a few, a certain few, would fail, and on the other hand hoping the best for our more favored leaders. As it turned out, we lost only three or four from the regiment, but one of them was our Captain Pierce, who had a good heart but little aptitude for the business at hand. Actually, on learning that he had failed, he resigned rather than be embarrassed. Lieutenant W.J. Alexander took over the company and was promoted to captain.

Well, Colonel Schlaudecker had reported our arrival in accordance with orders, and got instructions from the generals: Stay put until further orders. Very important to keep a strong force around Baltimore, in case of reverses at the front. Continue to drill. (Thank you, Lord, as if we needed more of that!)

We drilled according to "Hardee's Tactics." It was a manual, put out by a fellow whose name, of course, was Hardee. He was an officer in the Regular Army who ended up going south when the big split up came, and became a general in the Confederate Army. I am sure many of our volunteer officers, who were expected to go from civilian life to being tactical experts almost overnight, suspected Mister Hardee of writing an unfathomable book just to confuse us Yankees while he was now down south explaining everything in plain English. Later on, "Casey's Tactics" came out, but it was just Hardee's with a Yankee's name on the cover. Both books started with the "School of the Soldier," prescribing in painful detail how you marched, carried, and fired your musket. It graduated to the "School of the Company" which told officers how to put their companies through all the gyrations necessary to go from column into line, maneuver, and fire. Most learned, but the process was painful.

Along about March 7th General Dix ordered the whole division to muster at Fort McHenry. Yes, you've heard of Fort McHenry. It was the place where Francis Scott Key wrote "The Star-Spangled Banner." We formed up in light marching order and marched the four miles to the fort. This time the historical occasion was a hanging.

We went to witness the execution of a man who had shot his second lieutenant. I reckon General Dix wanted us all to see what military justice and martial law was all about, the lesson being that this will happen to you if you shoot your second lieutenant. It was an important lesson, because at that stage of the game most second lieutenants were so stupid and worthless that a man might almost figure it to be justifiable homicide if he were to plug one. I'm kidding, of course. Half-kidding, anyways.

Now, hangings are not pleasant. James said he never wanted to see another, and I had to agree with him. However, our disdain seemed to be in the minority. In addition to a pretty much captive audience of five thousand or so soldiers, there were also probably two thousand civilians who turned out to see the show. I suspect the crowd may have had a majority of secessionist Marylanders who were always glad to see a Yankee die, no matter if it was by rope or bullet.

It was quite a spectacular occasion, I must say. There was seven regiments of infantry, one cavalry regiment, and a battery of light artillery and two batteries of heavy artillery. That was the most troops we had ever seen gathered in one place. We admired the fancy red trappings of the artillerymen. The cavalry had had their horses long enough to set 'em easy, and the horses was all sleek and glossy, not at all resembling the wretched steeds that they would be after a few weeks of campaigning. We formed three sides of a square, facing in towards the gallows.

They drove the prisoner and his coffin up in a wagon, and he had a minister with him. He appeared firm and cool as they led him out and up the steps. A drum roll, the dropping of the trap, and that was it. Game to the last, he was said to have died easy. [8] The hike back to Camp McKim was a mite more somber than the march out.

And on that somber note, we'll end it for this week.

Now there, Tommy. You're only somber because school starts in a few weeks. Compared to that, a hanging probably wouldn't bother you a whit.

Camp McKim, Baltimore, MD, March the 8th, 1862

"...The officers are very strict with us here. No privates go out of the camp and the boys do not run the guards here, for their rifles are loaded with ball cartridges and they have orders to shoot anyone who does not stop when hailed three times. The only time I have been on guard here, I stood at the main entrance and one of our captains and two of his friends came in and did not stop when I hailed them. Just as I had brought my gun to my face to fire, they stopped and the corporal of the guard went out and passed them in.

...It is evident that we have gotten into a slave state from the number of Negroes to be seen in the streets, and the despairing look that most of them have.

...There is not as much war news here as there was at Erie. I expect that the nearer we get to the seat of war the less we shall hear of it." [9]

I've always wondered if James would have shot those fellows at the gate!

We were out drilling on a Monday morning a few days after the hanging when at about ten o'clock we got orders to return to camp. Two companies, ours and Company F, were picked to guard the government property at Camp Hoffman, which was being vacated by the 5th Maryland Regiment ordered to Virginia, and we had to be at that camp, three miles away, in a hour.

Our officers came up with a plan and passed orders as we hustled back to the barracks, and once we got there all was a flurry of hurry as we packed our knapsacks and formed up for the march.

We double-timed all the way, in formation, and made it with a few minutes to spare. We were winded but still game. General Dix dropped by that afternoon to commend us on our performance. It is by small tests such as these that you can measure the potential of an outfit. There was no wasted motion, no contradiction of orders, just coordinated actions of two companies which had become military machines.

Camp Hoffman, Baltimore, MD, March the 13th, 1862

"There was a great deal of rejoicing on account of the victory in Arkansas, and if I am not mistaken, the rebels will find that when Fremont gets in among them, they will have to run faster than they have yet if they are to keep out of his clutches, for I believe him to be..."
10

Well, the rest of that letter is missing. The battle in Arkansas referred to was Pea Ridge or Elkhorn Tavern, depending on your allegiance. I should tell you that "Fremont" is General John Charles Fremont, the famous "Pathfinder" of the West. History did not give Fremont the high marks that James Miller did. Fremont was about to be sent east to try his luck against Stonewall Jackson. Any bets on how *that* turns out?

Camp Hoffman, March the 18th, 1862

"I have been here most three weeks and I have not been outside of the guards except when the company has marched out for drill, but the Colonel has given orders that two men out of each company shall have leave to go into the city from nine till one o'clock each day so I shall have a chance to see a little of the city after a while, that is, if we don't move from here before my turn comes. And I do not see any prospect of our ever moving from here.

This city is completely in the power of the government, for our guns command every house and from what I hear from the loyal citizens,

nothing but the strong arm of the government kept the city and state from going with the rest of the rebels. There is the least business going on here that I ever saw, but the people think when the Baltimore and Ohio Railroad gets in running order, which I think will be in two weeks, it will partially restore the business prosperity of the city.

We have good news tonight from Burnside: the capture of New Berne by his forces. The work of crushing the rebellion goes bravely on, and I think if McClellan moves according to his promise, the rebels will find Virginia too hot to hold before long.

From what I can learn, the Western Division of our glorious army means to leave them no place of retreat to come to in that direction.

Tell Rachel that I am much obliged to her for her letter and especially for the news she sent about Susan, for I have not heard a word from her since I left Erie until I got her Rachel's letter....I don't know but my becoming a soldier will spoil me for work when I get home for I am as fat and lazy as you please. I only have just enough of exercise to make me have good health, and if it was not for my wife and children, I should be as contented as I ever was in my life." [11]

With the coming of April, with battles and rumors of battles heard of from every quarter, successes on all fronts, we began to feel that we would never go any farther south. The good news was counterproductive, making us all feel in good spirits but despairing of ever trying our luck in defense of the old flag.

Some of the battles were being fought over in the Shenandoah Valley, not over a hundred miles from Baltimore. Our next excitement was late in March when some reb prisoners, taken by Shields's division during the Battle of Kernstown, were shipped to Baltimore. We had no way of knowing that that battle, which we won, was the ominous first step taken by Stonewall Jackson to kick us out of the Shenandoah Valley and scare the hell out of the government.

Anyway, the prisoners were housed temporarily in the new jail (built, I believe, to replace a jail which fared badly in the excitement of 1861) and here we had a recipe for trouble: A few hundred fair-haired boys from Virginia locked up in a jail surrounded by a population whose most vocal element was all on their side. They quickly became a cause celebré for Baltimore's would-be rebels. Cause celebré? Well, that's French for getting so wrapped up in a notion that you are only cured if a soldier or policeman beats you over the head. I hope the country never sees the like of it again. The secesh started kicking up such a fuss about the prisoners being housed in a ***jail***, of all places, that General Dix decided to move the prisoners to a better spot.

The 111th got the job of escorting the prisoners from the Baltimore jail to Fort Delaware, which sets on an island in the middle of Delaware Bay. Four companies, over three hundred men, were to escort them from the jail to the wharf, and then each of our ten companies were ordered to send eight men to accompany them on the boat ride to the fort. James and I got volunteered as two of the eight from our company. Before going, we all got a long lecture on behaving ourselves and acting like soldiers regardless of provocations. It turned out to be a timely lecture.

When we got to the jail it seemed that the secessionists had turned out in full force for the occasion. The majority of the crowd was women, female pulchritude from all the classes and levels of Baltimore society. About all they had in common besides their southern loyalties was that they wasn't none of them acting like ladies right then. As we marched in they spat at us and shrieked and called us names using words that I did not know women had ever heard, and it was all mixed with God Bless the Virginians and hurrahs for Jeff Davis.

We formed a hollow square formation in front of the jail, facing out toward the hostiles. "Attention Battalion!" cried Colonel Cobham in a loud ringing voice, and there was one sound as heels came together. "Fix—bayonets!" and a chilling clatter as near two feet of cold pointed steel were affixed to the muzzles of our muskets. As we went through the maneuvering by the numbers you could see the crowd calm down. Our show of discipline and training seemed to make them think twice about trying anything, even though there were five of them to our one.

One of the women came tauntingly close to our line of bayonets, cussing a blue streak. She had a small southern flag sewed across her ample bosom. Warsh White muttered, "You had better warch out, madam. We have been training for some time in storming breastworks." That brought a chuckle from those that heard him, and went some toward relieving the strain of the moment.

After the way had been cleared to the jail entrance our company went in to escort the mayor and the prisoners out. We lined the corridors as they marched out between us, and then followed them to the outside.

As they emerged into the sunshine a great roar came up from the crowd. Most of the men in the crowd kept still, letting the women raise hell. The idea, of course, was to antagonize us into bayoneting a few women so they could say what brutes we were. Two men did get a little rowdy and the police hit them over the head (thus curing their "cause celebré") and snatched them up and hauled them away. Slowly, with the prisoners enclosed within our square and the crowd taunting us from without, we made our way to the wharf.

Once we got to the wharf the pressure was off. Our eighty-man detail and the prisoners loaded aboard a chartered schooner and cast off while the rest of the regiment hiked back to Camp McKim. Most of our country boys had never took a boat ride so there were both blue and gray, with a common skin color of seasick green, hanging over the rail before we had gone too far out of the harbor.

Most of the rebs were Virginia Irish. Nothing more peculiar than an Irish brogue with a southern accent. They were good enough fellers, who said they were better off as prisoners than as soldiers, but they still predicted the South would win in the end.

We got to the fort, some forty miles below Philadelphia, in good time, and we stayed long enough to eat supper and tour the place, which was not completed yet, and only sixty guns were mounted. The finished plan called for two hundred guns.

Camp McKim, April the 2nd, 1862:

"I never thought that I should feel like shooting a woman, but if our officers had given us orders to fire, I would have shot some of the women of Baltimore if I could have held my gun steady enough.

(Fort Delaware) is built after the plan of the castle of San Juan de Ulloa in Mexico. The walls are some forty feet high and from four to ten feet thick, and are built of blue granite. The casements are of the best brick I ever saw. The fort is so arranged that they raise some twelve feet of water in the moat which surrounds the fort on all sides, the only entrance being over two wooden bridges which in case of an attack should be blown up in an instant..." [12]

That fort, with the investment of all those guns and fine quality masonry, never fired a shot in anger. It served as a prisoner of war camp for the whole war.

***

FOOLISHNESS

And now for another word about our rifle muskets. Hah! Sounds like I'm gonna try to sell you one.

The muzzle-loading single shot musket was adopted by the government because they were cheap, there weren't many parts to break, and any fool could be taught to load and shoot one. There were a few drawbacks, however.

One was that it was impossible to tell at a glance if it was loaded. Of course it would be a good clue if you saw a percussion cap under the hammer, but even then it might only be capped but not loaded with powder and ball. The only way to see was to drop a ramrod down the barrel. If it sprang back with a metallic ring the gun was not loaded; if the ramrod went "thunk" then you most likely had a charge in there.

Just a couple of years ago, back in September of 1934, there was a famous singer—I believe he was one of those "crooners" that are all the rage with the young folks. Russ Columbo, his name was, was accidentally killed by an old single-shot percussion pistol that had been loaded for a hundred or so years. A photographer friend was fooling with it and held a lit match over the touchhole, and there went a talented young man who was killed in one of the most freakish accidents I ever heard of.

Anyway, another drawback, related to the first, was that except by firing it was not easy to unload a musket. To draw the bullet out you screwed a coiled attachment called a worm onto your ramrod and twisted it in the barrel until the worm dug into the soft lead bullet, then you drew the bullet out and dumped the powder.

So there we were living in downtown Baltimore, and firing the rifle just to clear it was not an option. We had to use the tedious method I just told you. I'm telling you all this so you'll understand what I'm about to relate:

Like James said, guard duty there in Baltimore was serious business. Many of our neighbors were inclined to do us harm if they could, so our guards were ready to defend themselves. Usually fellers going off guard would swap guns with their relief, but sometimes not. That "sometimes not" led to a very sad incident which taught bitter lessons.

On that day, we had just come off the field from squad drill and our arms were stacked in a neat row along the company line. Three muskets, linked together by the bayonets, formed a stack, and any spares were leaned against the three. With a ten-minute break before platoon drill, we lounged behind our stacks in the shade of one of the few trees left standing. James and I had just lit our pipes.

A ripple of laughter came from the circle that generally formed around Washington White during down time. Warsh was tall and gangly and funny, always quick with a joke, and I reckon half the boys in the company figured him as their best friend. This time he was doing his Johnny Reb character.

"Now, I want y'all to git out'n my state. Leave me and my niggers alone," Warsh drawled, "or I'll sic the houns on y'all."

Charlie Lobdell fooled back: "We et all your hounds, Reb. What'll you do now?"

"I'll just have to shoot y'all," replied Warsh. "Shoot y'all and feed you to the hawgs."

"Hell, we et your hogs before we et your hounds, Reb."

"You won't shoot us if we shoot you first, Reb," said a boy named Hultberg, and he pulled a rifle, a "leaner," off a stack.

"Say, what's your name, Reb?" said one of the boys.

Warsh drawled it out: Gawge Warshin'ton White." (Laughter)

How could you be a low-down reb traitor with a name like George Washington? Air you shore that's yor name?"

"That's White." (Laughter)

"So you're gonna shoot us all down?"

"That's White." (More laughs)

"Not if we shoot you first." Hultberg flicked a cap from his pouch to the musket, and me and James exchanged looks of "this ain't funny no more." James made a half move toward the boys as Hultberg pulled the trigger from the hip, expecting to hear only the snap of a cap, but—

"BANGGG!"

Warsh White let out a howl of pain as he spun and fell to the ground. For a second everybody froze in dead silence, then all was commotion.

"Oh! Oh! Oh! My arm! My arm!" Warsh writhed on the ground as men stared at the first bullet wounding most of them had ever seen.

Blood spurted from just above Warsh's left elbow. James propped him up. "His arm's broke," he muttered as he wrapped his kerchief tight around it. "Couple you boys help me get him to Doc Stewart."

By then our officers and sergeants had descended on us. Without thinking I had grabbed the musket from Hultberg, as if by doing so I could take back what had just happened.

"Who fired that shot?" demanded Lieutenant Warner. He seen the rifle in my hand. "Was it you?"

"No, sir," Hultberg sobbed. "It was me. I done it. I'd swear my rifle wasn't loaded."

Lobdell said, "That wasn't your rifle. It's mine. I didn't unload it when I come off guard."

Both of the boys were carted off to see the captain. The accident brought a ripple of new rules and guidelines from regiment on how and when rifles were loaded, inspected, when you could handle one, and most specially that you never pointed a gun at another person unless you meant business. A hard lesson learned, the most basic rule in gun safety.

April 2nd, 1862 (continued)

"...We had a sad accident in our company last Friday morning. Some of the boys were fooling with their guns when Charles Lobdell's gun went off. The ball broke Washington White's arm between the shoulder and elbow. It was the left arm and the Doctor thought he would have to cut it off but they think they will be able to save his arm now. I went to the hospital last night and sat up with him; he is as comfortable as could be expected. And as I have had no sleep last night you will please excuse all blunders." [13]

Such foolishness. Such waste. It is unavoidable in war that we should kill and wound some of our own—happens in every war—but when that gun went off and I seen Warsh go down I couldn't believe it. He and James was as close as brothers, and that bullet broke up a close set. James spent most of his off-time with Warsh until we left Baltimore.

Now, as this story goes on, I'm bound to tell you about a lot of gruesome things, and a major part of that will be the number of arms and legs that the sawbones will lop off. And you may wonder why. Remember what I said about what a minie ball did to bone? Medical science was pretty primitive back then, and there just wasn't too many answers other than cutting off the offended limb. The doctors didn't enjoy doing it, to be sure, and in the beginning they tried to avoid the practice, but lockjaw would usually set in and the patient would die. He would have his arm or his leg, but he would be dead. Sadly, that's what happened to Warsh

White. They tried to save his arm, and he ended up dying on May 10th, 1862. He is buried in a cemetery on the right-hand side of the road as you ride north from James's old place. [14]

***

MUSIC

As I think of it, it seems to me that the War of the Rebellion was about the most musical war ever fought. You have probably heard of Julia Ward Howe. I saw her once. She was a pioneer for women's rights—a rather outlandish notion back then. Freeing the Africans was one thing; freeing our women was quite another. She was also an abolitionist, a poet, and an author. She wrote the "Battle Hymn of the Republic." Way she came to do that, in case you have not heard the story, was that she was visiting our camps, seeing the great armed host gathering to do battle on the Potomac, and happened to be sitting by her window when a regiment marched by. They were singing "John Brown's Body," based on the tune of an old southern camp meeting song. The words were those of soldiers, morbid and fatalistic, but she listened, thought, and wrote a poem, which was set to the music and published in the *Atlantic Monthly.* The song became immensely popular at once, and unlike so many songs back then which were personal and moving at the time but have since been forgotten, the Battle Hymn lives on. I am not surprised that it has stood the test of time. Made me feel like I was in church whenever I heard it—and on the march, with two-three thousand voices lifting it up, well, just let me say, it was inspiring.

To begin with, each regiment was authorized to have a band, and most had one. In July of '62 the War Department, in its wisdom, decreed that bands were to be disbanded, as it were, but some outfits figured out ways to get around the regulations and still have one. The bandsmen were discharged, reenlisted as infantry or whatever, and then detailed back to the band. Bands and music were important to morale. The desk generals in Washington did not understand that. Also, when the music was mostly the bass provided by cannons and muskets, the bandsmen would lay down their horns and become stretcher bearers. They shared the same dangers as we did, sometimes without weapons to defend themselves.

There were bands and there was field music. There was a difference. Field musicians was provided for in the regulations. They were the buglers, drummers, and fifers whose particular tunes and beats regulated our daily activities, from reveille to tattoo, and provided signals on the battlefield. The long roll of the drum especially, was the ominous call to form for battle.

And then there were bugles. Bugles helped keep order, both in camp and on the battle field; there were bugle calls for everything. I recollect a certain general, old Dan Butterfield his name was, and he would end up for a while commanding a division in our corps in 1864. Well, he had a brigade down on the Peninsula with McClellan at about this present time, and one night he decided that the call for telling his men to put out the fires and go to bed was not, well, "restful" enough. So he called his bugler over, whistled a few notes that came to mind, and had the bugler play them. The call caught on, and soon all the brigades in the army were using it. His men thought the notes were saying their commander's name: Dan-Dan-Dan Butterfield-Butterfield-Butter-field.

Today we call it "Taps."

I do not recollect the date, but late in the spring I had the measles and was sent to the hospital at Little York, Pennsylvania. I thought at the time it was the most beautiful country I ever saw, and Little York had the most pretty girls...

***

FIT TO FIGHT

'Scuse me for moving a little slow today. I helped Fred with his threshing yesterday, and I'm a little sore today. A day pitching wheat straw pales next to what we had to do back during the war, but then again I was a lot younger than ninety-two! I had a good time last week at the reunion of the 111th Pennsylvania. I won three dollars playing poker. Each time we get together there are less and less of us. It will be seventy-five years this fall since we joined up in Erie. My, how time flies.

Kind of sad, though: Seeing men that was once the most ferocious fighters in the world now reduced to drooling in our soup. Eyesight so bad you can play your cards face-up and still bluff. Not but a corporal's guard left, fewer every year. Having enlisted at such a tender age, I'm one of the "youngest," but pretty soon, well, pretty soon the 111th will finally lose a battle.

When I first joined the army I thought I was in pretty good shape. I had always done hard physical labor, outdoors mostly, and considered myself a hardy individual—until we got to Baltimore, that is. As our leaders were making soldiers out of us, they were also working us up to be first class athletes. We started with "short" runs, the whole regiment of us, carrying rifles but not much else. Early on, we would end up toward the end of the run with our lungs about to burst, legs and arms like wood, praying to see the main gate again. As time went on, we progressed to light marching order, then with knapsacks, the runs getting longer and longer. Soon we were going on for miles, day or night, sometimes clattering through the streets of Baltimore at five o'clock in the morning, waking the whole neighborhood, especially the dogs. How they did carry on! I can still hear the sound of our steel-tapped brogans echoing off the cobblestones, and the howl of a thousand dogs...

As he built the Army of the Potomac, McClellan had come up with a special bayonet drill, which we were required to master, designed to impart aggressiveness and confidence to us: Thrust, parry, guard against cavalry, smash, jab, and on and on, until we thought our arms would fall off. At first. Soon our arms was built up just like our legs and lungs.

Folks have always been amazed at the hardship we were able to put up with. Well, look at it thisaway: Many, many thousands of men were enlisted into the army during the war, but maybe one in five (my estimation, with no facts at all to back it up) was able to last it out. You can build up the physique of a man, but I believe that the ability to withstand the rigors of campaigning is something *born* into a man—being able to sleep outside on the ground for weeks at a time, all the while feeling just as well as if you had slept in a bed, with but little sleep, poor grub, toil, and danger all around. Some had it, and some didn't. James had it; I did, too. Maybe twenty or thirty out of a hundred were that way. Others, once you got them out in the field, just wilted like violets in the hot sun, and that would take out the first third of us within a month. Others did their best, but they was always coming down with this or that ailment.

CHAPTER FOUR
A WAR OF HER OWN

One of the great things about storytelling is that you can travel through great pieces of time and space in the wink of an eye. Here I'm about to whisk you back to Pennsylvania to see how Susan and the family is faring through all of this.

Now, us soldiers had our songs to inspire us, and danger and hardship was a tonic for determined men. Beats me, though, how Susan Miller stood it. Songs like "Weeping Sad and Lonely" and "The Vacant Chair" were not calculated to inspire. Oh, the songs back then! As bad as things were, I do not now understand why we would subject ourselves to the sadness that poured out in some of our music.

Alone, Susan and the children lived on that rented farm in Southwest Township, north of Titusville. I wish I could tell you more about her life on that farm. She was always lonely, always looking for James's letters, which a kindly old neighbor would fetch up from the Garland post office. The daily dread of bad news from the battlefield would tax her fortitude. She was fighting a war of her own on that hardscrabble ridge.

The date is April 5th, 1862, in a little log house south of Grand Valley.

Little Robbie stopped by the kitchen table on his way out the door. "What are you doing, Ma?"

Susan buttoned his coat and stroked his hair. "I'm going to write a letter to Grandma and Grandpa Miller."

"When I get to be big I'm going to write to them, too." And off he went, out of her arms and off to fight imagined rebels in the thicket by the road.

Susan, with a wistful smile, watched him go. Ellen was visiting at Grandpa Main's, Johnny was sleeping soundly—finally—in his little bunk near the fire. The house was quiet, and through a window she could see a faint hint of green in the thicket. Spring was here, after a long, hard, lonely winter, and summer dawning. Ah, summer, summer...

She welcomed it, and she dreaded it. Summer meant no more battles with the cold and wind, chopping ice to get water for cooking and washing. Hanging out the laundry would now be a breezy pleasure instead of a dreaded chore.

But summer meant good weather for campaigns and battles. James had said the weather in Maryland was already as warm as Pennsylvania's June days. Susan didn't know much of army life and fighting, but her sense told her that dry roads meant movement and greater chances of armies colliding and blood being spilt. James wrote that he was afraid this McClellan would end it all before the 111th could prove its mettle. If only...if only he would. She picked up the pen:

April 5th, 1862

Dear Father and Mother

It is with pleasure I now sit down to write to you, for I know you must be anxious to hear from us all. My health is good. Ellen and Robert are well. The baby took a relapse last Sunday, and Tuesday afternoon I thought he was dying. His feet swelled and his hands lay helpless wherever I put them. The fever left him very low and weak, but he began to recover and is gaining strength. The doctor thinks he will get well if he don't take any cold nor eat too much. I have received a letter this week from James. He was well and his company had got back to Camp McKim. Mother, do not grieve for your absent son. I feel firm in the faith that he will return home to his family and friends before next fall. He wrote for me to go up there and get the money that he sent to me and see Father and Mother but I dare not take little Johnny out this spring if he gets well. His lungs are so diseased. He coughs very hard. I have kept a fire night and day for more than three weeks; but my wood lasts well. I hope this finds you all well. I should like to see you all. Robert says when he gets to be a big boy he will write to Grandpa and Grandma Miller. Write soon. My love to all.

Susan A Miller [15]

She fought her war with no glory, no books about it in the library, and only a precious few of her letters was saved.

But some were saved, including the one we just read. It arrived up on Miller Hill a few days later, and Mr. Miller was reading it when Missus Miller came into the sitting room. She was feeling poorly, had lost weight and especially her vitality, all since the last October. That was about the time James had joined the army. She dropped herself into a chair at the table next to her husband. Mr. Miller patted her hand.

"Here's a letter from Susan for us, Mother. Johnny is some better, and she mentions James..."

"Does she say when he's a-comin' home?"

In his soft Scottish brogue Mr. Miller says, "Oh, Mother, dinna greet so. He's in Baltimore, for heaven's sake, not the Barbary Coast."

"That fight in Tennessee, Robert. All those boys..." She started to cry, big tears rolling down her pale cheeks.

He held her. "It'll be all right, Mother. God will protect. It'll be all right."

That battle she mentions was Shiloh. You'll see when I tell you about it later that its outcome would have upset anybody, but especially those fearing for their loved ones.

It strikes me that I have been remiss in not giving you a rundown on who all those loved ones were back on the home front. James wrote to them all from time to time.

James was the oldest of the Miller boys. Back home was Susan with Robbie, Ellen, and little Johnny. The other brothers were William with his wife, Harriet, and a little boy; John and his wife, Cordelia; and Robert and Joseph, still single. Joe was just about the handsomest young man I ever met. James's sisters were, first, Jane, who was married to George Henry Cramer. G.H. developed an opinion about the war that ran square against James's convictions. He was an anti-war Democrat, and it led to sparks, some smoldering letters anyway, later on. They had a son, Seymour. James's other sister was Rachel, who was married to Bill West, and they also had a little boy. That's the lot. All those boys stayed civilian except James and brother Bob.

***

BAPTISM OF FIRE

I see you boys are certainly getting fidgety about when I'm going to get to the fighting. That is nothing compared to how we felt in the spring of '62. All over the country there was fighting aplenty, but we just sat there in Baltimore, and just about gave up on ever being used. You see that feeling in James's writing. We need not have worried.

We were lucky even if we didn't know it. All that drill, much as we hated it, would be the saving grace of the regiment more than once, and contributed to our success and the reputation we built. Believe it or not—and I'll mention some examples later on—some outfits went right straight from muster to the battlefield and got shot to pieces before they knew which end of a musket was up. That's pretty much what happened to my old outfit at Bull Run, one of the many, in that battle.

Also believe it or not, we finally got Mister Hardee's book figured out. By May, not only our officers, but most any of our smarter privates could give the commands and then execute the movements for even the most complicated maneuvers. The hollow square formation was made basically to protect against cavalry rather than mad Baltimorians. We got so we could form into it so fast that we could sometimes shut our colonel outside of it, which was always a joke on him as long as we promised not to do it if the Black Horse Cavalry came at us.

Camp McKim, April the 16th, 1862

"The picture on the first side of this sheet is a true representation of our camp. Our company is on the left of the regiment. It is considered one of the posts of honor, but we have the most marching of any of the companies on regimental drill--and our drill is quite severe. We go out for squad drill at eight o'clock in the morning which lasts till half past nine. Then at ten we have company drill till half past eleven, and at two o'clock we go out for regimental drill which lasts generally until after six, which makes us feel quite tired when night comes. But our colonel appears to be determined to make soldiers of us in fact as well as name. I do not think our regiment will ever smell powder in earnest, but if we do, I think we will not give our friends any reason to blush for our behavior before the rebels (if we ever meet them and only have half a chance for our lives).

There is a great deal of uneasiness to hear from Yorktown. I think if the rebels only stand up to the rack like men, we shall have the great battle of the war there. If our troops are victorious, the backbone of the rebellion will be broken.

I think if you keep on studying law and reading Brown's writing, you will get so that you can't read your own writing when it gets cold, for I did not recognize the last letter as your writing until I saw your name at the bottom. I am very much obliged to you for the stamps you sent, for we have not got our pay yet, and I don't know when we shall, but I hope before long, for money is as scarce in our camp as hens' teeth." [16]

That letter was to brother Bob. He was studying law under Judge Brown, of Warren. The next was to sister Jane and good old G.H. Cramer.

Camp McKim, Baltimore, MD, April the 17th, 1862

"...But I don't have any reason to find fault for I have better and easier times than I expected to. The company I have is very rough and profane which is the worst I have to contend with. There is a rumor in camp today that our regiment is going into tents and that they are going to make a hospital of our barracks, but I am inclined to think it is only a rumor.

The weather has been very warm here for the last two or three days. It is as warm today here as it is generally in the forepart of June in your part of Pennsylvania, and our thick woolen coats and pants are quite uncomfortable. We have got new dress coats and pants. They are a great deal better than the first ones we got. The coats are a dark blue and the pants are a sky blue. They look first rate, I think. I hope they won't give us any more clothes for we have more than we can carry now.

I was not surprised at hearing that Louisa Foster was sick after getting married. I think that like enough she will feel worse than that before she has been Mrs. Golding a year. At least, old maids have a habit of having dropsy after getting married—but it generally falls in their arms. I hope it will be the case with her because I think she would like it to be so." [17]

That Louisa Foster must have been some prize. You know, there's a cemetery named after her up in Farmington. Or her kin, more likely.

***

BAPTISM OF FIRE

Our stay in Baltimore was pleasant enough—good quarters, a little excitement with the locals, a hanging, but nothing lasts forever. As the regiment drilled in Baltimore the war was heating up, pulling us toward it, away from drill and police duty.

On April 6th, out west, the rebels pulled a surprise attack on our army at Pittsburg Landing, Tennessee, which also became known as the Battle of Shiloh. U.S. Grant commanded an army of some forty thousand men and he was about to be joined by near as many more under General Don Carlos Buell. The reb general, Albert Sidney Johnston, decided to hit Grant before Buell got up, and he caught Grant napping. He came close to driving all the Yankees into the Tennessee River, but Grant held on, with a lot of help from a division commander by the name of William Tecumseh Sherman. From then on, Grant and Sherman was a team. The next day Buell's army was on the ground, and then the combined force gave the rebs a decisive licking. What was ominous for the future was that, bad as we thought Bull Run had been, Shiloh produced more than five times the losses at Bull Run, even though there was not much difference in the numbers of men engaged in the two battles, at least on the first day. Both the northern and southern armies were almost totally untrained and unseasoned. Early on, we and the Johnnies were beginning to display a talent for mutual destruction.

Johnston did not live to see the end of the battle. A bullet nicked an artery in his leg and he bled to death. Johnston was a heroic and gallant fool (in my humble opinion) as he must have known he had a bootful of blood but kept going on. A tourniquet, which would have saved his life, was in his pocket.

There in Virginia and Maryland we thought we had the rebs on the ropes, too. Little Mac—that's what we called McClellan—had took an army of about 100,000 men by water down to the peninsula southeast of Richmond. That's where all those troops were going that James mentioned as passing through Baltimore. There were battles at places like Williamsburg, and Yorktown of Revolutionary War fame, and a hundred scattered skirmishes as our boys advanced. The rebs, until they could pull in more troops from all across the southland, could do nothing but retreat. But they always did it at the last minute, after Mac had made all manner of painstaking preparations, digging in siege batteries, building roads, bridging swamps. He was scientific and methodical, and he was so-o-o-o slow. He intended to use the shiny instrument he had fashioned and named the Army of the Potomac without getting it all nicked up in battle. The irony turned out to be that in trying to spare his men he probably lost at least two or three chances to end the war about three years early and save thousands of lives. But I keep getting ahead of myself. Pardon me for that.

Anyway, Mac had got within five miles of Richmond when General Joseph E. Johnston (no relation to Albert Sidney) decided he had enough men and the Yanks was close enough. He attacked on the last day of

May, scaring the devil out of McClellan but not accomplishing much except his own wounding. Joe Johnston went down, stricken by bullets and shrapnel, wounds that would keep him out of action for about a year. First Albert Sidney gets rubbed out and then Joseph E. gets shot up, and I do believe if I had been a Confederate general at that time and my name had happened to be Johnston I would have gone home and hid under my bed!

We should have saved all that metal that we threw at Joe Johnston, on account of President Jeff Davis replaced him with another unknown by the name of Robert E. Lee and, as they say, the rest is history. At the time, though, things looked promising for the Union.

Now, the way we got involved with all this was because, in the Shenandoah Valley, things had not gone our way a-tall.

All told, we probably had sixty-seventy thousand men, maybe more, scattered all over northern Virginia and Maryland. A lot of those troops were scheduled to go down to McClellan's army. Davis and Lee knew that if all of us ever got together, that area of the Confederacy would never stand a chance, so they put together a little army under Thomas Jonathan Jackson, an eccentric former mathematics professor better known as "Stonewall" and gave him the mission of, as Jackson put it, "to 'mystify' us." That he did. Three separate Union armies, under Fremont, Banks, and McDowell, were out-marched, out-thought, and outfought. Finally, the government pulled out all the stops, setting in motion the chain of events that forced the 111th to keep its appointment with destiny.

If I sound melodramatic, it is intentional.

It was while I was admiring the young ladies of Little York that the regiment finally got its marching orders. I wish I could've been there because from what I heard later the orders were received by the boys with much whooping and hollering, and the colonel gave an inspirational little speech, and it was just about the most exciting time since the Erie sendoff. That day, Sunday, May 24th, they loaded on the cars and set out for Harper's Ferry.

Anybody who has ever been in the army has heard the term, "hurry up and wait." After packing up and leaving camp in a swirl of dust, the regiment found themselves plodding along the tracks like on a slow boat to China. I'll bet the man driving the train had southern sympathies. We often found that a cocked pistol in the engineer's ear was good for five or ten miles per hour more speed. But I don't know in this case; I wasn't there, don't you see.

We needed to hurry. Banks was defeated at Winchester on May 25th, and was forced to retreat toward Martinsburg, away from Harper's Ferry and Washington.

Well, the twentieth century seems to be passing Harper's Ferry by, but in 1862 it was an important place. The Baltimore and Ohio Railroad passed through there (still does, I suppose) and there was a canal, which was still a going concern back then. Harper's Ferry sat at the northern end of the Shenandoah Valley, a natural route for anybody trying to invade Maryland. There had been an arsenal there, the one John Brown raided, but the rebs had taken all the gun-making machinery down south and, what they couldn't move, they wrecked.

Harper's Ferry, Virginia, May the 27th, 1862

"...The country along the road from here to Baltimore is very poor and rough. Until we got to the ferry, it was not scenic, but here it is majestically beautiful. The Potomac and the Shenandoah are very rocky and the mountains are rugged and sublime..." [18]

Young John Boyle, in our regimental history, writes about the whole regiment pitching their Hardee Hats ("hated tiles," he called them) into the Potomac as it arrived at Harper's Ferry. From then on, until at least late 1863, most everybody wore the forage cap, the jaunty little tilted forward headgear made of wool with a leather bill in front.

The regiment tried to push on through Harper's Ferry to Winchester, but met the 1st District of Columbia Regiment on a train coming our way on a one-way track. Their major would not go back, so the 111th pulled back to the Ferry and unloaded.

At first there was not much standing in Jackson's way if he wanted to capture Harper's Ferry again, just our regiment and two or three others. It was very suspenseful, and the gloom and doomers in our crowd predicted straight passage from Baltimore to a prison camp. The boys gamely formed column and set out on foot for Winchester, but they met the tattered flotsam of Banks's army coming back in forlorn retreat. Those fellers were mighty shook up, I'll tell you. They had all kinds of wild tales. Later on, we learned to discount the lurid stories that defeated men had to tell, but this was all new, and the boys hung on their every word.

Before we march out of Harper's Ferry for our first smell of powder, I think I should tell you something about artillery. Just like our muskets, artillery was almost all muzzle-loading. There were a few breechloaders, mainly Whitworths, imported from England, but their only real advantage, besides you didn't have to step out in front of the gun to load it, was their range. About the only ammunition they fired was a solid bolt, which made a fearsome screech as it flew overhead. At Gettysburg, Confederate Whitworths were able to fire all the way from Oak Hill to Little Round Top.

Also just like muskets, artillery guns were either rifled or smoothbore. The rifles were more accurate and longer range, but rifled field pieces were only about a three-inch bore so their shells were not all that deadly. Oh, if they hit you direct, you were certainly dead, but their shell fragments were rather few and far between.

The best smoothbore—maybe the best field piece in the war—was the Napoleon gun howitzer. Just like the minie ball, it was invented in France. It was a twelve-pounder, with a 4.62-inch bore, and with a maw that big it could spew some deadly projectiles. It fired solid shot, which was a non-exploding ball of iron, good for wrecking guns and wagons; it fired shell and spherical case which was set to explode a certain number of seconds after being fired, or on impact, and it fired canister, which was a giant shotgun round, sending dozens of iron slugs spraying into the enemy at close range. In hot, close fights, gunners would fire double or triple canister. Most artillery rounds were more a detriment to morale than a real casualty producer, but a Napoleon firing canister was the deadliest proposition on the battlefield.

All right, forward—march!

Harper's Ferry, June the 1st, 1862

"...Well, the next morning after I wrote to Robert, (*May 28th*) our regiment and two pieces of artillery and about four hundred cavalry started on a scout after the enemy. When our advance got about four miles, we found the rebels' pickets which we drove in after a smart skirmish. Our cannon threw a few shells among the enemy's advance and one company of our regiment was sent out from the main body to skirmish with the enemy's pickets but they (the rebels) fell back with the loss of two killed. Our loss was two wounded—they belonged to the cavalry and were wounded in a charge on the enemy. We then

resumed our line of march with the cavalry in front and followed the rebs to Charlestown, a place about two-thirds as large as Warren. It has quite a historic reputation as the place of the trial and execution of John Brown." [19]

Camp in the woods near Winchester, VA, June the 5th, 1862

"...We found the enemy pickets two miles in front of the main body which was situated to the south of Charlestown. Our skirmishers and artillery drove them rapidly, and our regiment followed them through the town where we got orders to halt and eat our dinner. Our cavalry was sent out to find the rebels and just as we got our dinner eaten, the cavalry were driven in on the run and we got orders to fall into line, and our cannon commenced to throw shell at the enemy. Two deserters that came in said that the second shell our boys threw at them killed and wounded fourteen. They commenced immediately to shell us in turn but made very bad shots for they fired as much as forty shells at us and only hurt two of our men--and we were in plain sight and not over a mile from them. But as our orders were to fight only just enough to make them show their force, as soon as we had done that our colonel gave the order to retreat. As our company was the rear guard, we stood still until the rest of the regiment got past us, and the rebels' shot and shell flung over and around us. But although it was the first time that any of us ever smelled powder in earnest, not a man flinched, but stood as cool as if they had been on drill. When the order came to march, the men fell into their places and marched as steady as they ever did. Some of the other companies got broken up a bit and threw away their blankets and haversacks.

Although our company was in the rear of all the rest, there was scarcely a man that threw away a thing and a good many of them brought in blankets that the others had thrown away. Not a man of our company was hurt and only two in the regiment, but the cavalry lost two killed and three wounded and had one captain and nine men taken prisoners by the rebels....

...The night that our regiment crossed to the Maryland side of the river our company was sent on picket duty and was the last company to come in in the morning. The rebels were as thick as blackberries in August, and there was a rumor that we were cut off and all made prisoners. Our colonel paid us the compliment to say that he would rather lose any two other companies in the regiment than ours..." [20]

Well, so far, so good. The regiment had been thoroughly trained, and it had just come through a nearly bloodless baptism of fire, just enough ruckus to get the boys accustomed to the sights and sounds of battle, to "make their eyes stick out," as James wrote once. Reinforcements came in over the next several days, "hand over hand," as James said, and on Tuesday, June 2nd, we were ready to move south in force.

When I got sick, I thought I had The Typhoid. I was mortified when it turned out to be measles, which I considered to be a kid's disease, but then I felt better, in a perverse way, when half the regiment came down with the same malady. Perverse, because back then people died from measles and other diseases which are pretty much run-of-the-mill, or even forgotten, these days.

Anyway, I survived. I caught up with the regiment just as it marched out of Harper's Ferry, at about four in the afternoon on that Tuesday. Our order to march seemed to be a signal to Mother Nature to let loose a torrent of rain that would last for days. In spite of the rain, the boys were just full of themselves over the excitement, and the way everybody had praised their first performance under fire. They just couldn't wait to go it again.

There was some ten regiments of us, and twenty pieces of artillery, on this march to retake Winchester. We marched all day in the rain. The next day we made eight miles, and still the rain came down.

As we hiked along that muddy road up the valley, General Sigel, our division commander, rode by with his staff.

James says, "Don't that look like Billy, Colonel Cobham's horse?"

"Where?" says Calvin.

"Why, the one the general's riding," replies James.

"Well, I swan! Durned if it ain't Billy. Been promoted to General's Horse." About that time the colonel came footing it alongside the ranks. Calvin, who never knew when was a good time to keep his mouth shut, says, "Sell your horse, Colonel?"

The colonel, looking a little sheepish, muttered, "No, I've just loaned him to the general a while."

The colonel's striker, George Osgood, told me later that the general had taken a liking to Billy and asked the loan of the horse, and colonel had been pleased to do him a temporary favor, but then he got an airy message from the general that he, Sigel, wished to buy the horse, to which the colonel quickly replied that Billy was not for sale. But the outset was that Cobham was on foot for a while, in some miserable weather, on our first campaign.

Now, I didn't know the particulars of why General Sigel found himself without a horse in the first place. I had not heard tell of any horses getting killed under him in battle, and so concluded that he had trouble managing his affairs. If so, how would he be at managing an army, especially against the likes of Stonewall Jackson! Sigel did not command us for long, and we later counted ourselves as fortunate. Troops he commanded came in for a big share of hard luck, both during his command and afterward. I'll refer to this a few times later on.

About midnight, with the rain still coming down, we halted for the night. Colonel Cobham walked up to this big house nigh the road and knocked on the door, polite as you please, and could he come in for the night. That snooty Virginian slammed the door right in his face, and that's when he called me over. "My knocking on the door didn't seem to do any good," says he. "How about you try this time—with the butt of your musket." Which I did, and it ended up that Cobham, Colonel Schlaudecker, and some of the other officers got to sleep under a roof that wet night, though they had to sleep on the floor. Most of us had no choice but to sleep in the road, or the fields, with no tents or blankets.

June 5th found us four miles from Winchester. It was still raining.

If Jackson had chose to take us on we probably would have been badly whipped, because we were all green regiments, thrown together in a new division under a General Saxton, who we had never heard of before.

Our higher ups thought that Jackson was trapped, being so far north with Fremont coming in behind him, but Jackson pulled out, marched his men hard up the valley, and got away after a little scrap with Fremont. By the time we closed in on Winchester we found ourselves batting at thin air.

See there, Ike? I told you we'd get to see the elephant this week. Grant you, it was a mighty small elephant, but it was a miracle how we got eased into the business of war so we could learn on the job without getting killed first.

Right then, early June of '62, Winchester, Virginia, was an unhealthy place. The late battle had left a lot of dead horses and fresh graves all over the place, and Jackson's boys had camped thereabouts for a spell, leaving quite a mess. I forget how many times that town changed hands during the war. For the time being, we held it, and we just made camp while our leaders tried to figure out what to do next and, due to the mess, I do believe, half the regiment came down with the dysentery.

Four miles southwest of Winchester, camp in the field, June the 12th

"We have been in this camp for a week and I don't hear anything about when we shall move from here. We marched in the rain for two days to get here and I guess our general found it was no use to try to catch Jackson, for he marched his men on half rations as far in one day as we could in two and a half. We have news from Fremont eight miles beyond Harrisonburg, and it seems that Jackson got the worst of the battle although he fought under cover of woods and on ground of his own choosing. And as that fight was some sixty miles from us, and happened five days ago, our chances of a fight with Jackson are very slim.

Our division is under the command of General Sigel. The prestige of his name makes him popular with the men, but to my notion he does not look much the General. He appears to be a man of some thirty-five years of age, with light sandy hair and whiskers, and a thin, pale, boyish face. Still, the expression of his mouth and eyes indicate firmness and determination of character. Our brigade is composed of our regiment and the 102nd New York, the 3rd Maryland, the 109th Pennsylvania, and the 1st District of Columbia Volunteers, and Reynolds's New York Battery of six pieces of six-pounder rifled cannon. But we do not number more than thirty-five hundred effective men. Our Brigadier General is James Cooper of Maryland." [21]

The smell of wood smoke always reminds me of the war. Bacon frying in the pan, salt pork sizzling on a ramrod. During the big encampments along the Rappahannock in '63 the air was always smoky. Everybody developed the camp cough. Figure a hundred thousand men and a campfire to every squad or so, that's a lot of smoke. That many fires also burned up huge tracts of trees in nothing flat. For a time during and after the war parts of Virginia and elsewhere were as bald as your Uncle Harold. At first, although there was orders against it, we just burned all the fences we found, because the wood was dry and burned easy, and was, well, handy.

Well, sir, here we were in the field, away from barracks and garrison spit and polish. Some of the boys that had shone in that kind of business were no great shakes as field soldiers. On the other hand, some of the types that were always getting in trouble for one thing or another while in barracks really came into their own when we got down to the real business of soldiering. Seems that, for all our training in tactics and maneuvers, the one thing we should have spent more study time on was field living. We learned the hard way.

One thing the army did to make things harder was to issue us all sorts of traps. Lugged along with all the personal stuff that a body felt he just could not live without, the first time he packed his knapsack, it all made a load that would kill a mule. Then, when we threw it away to strip down to only what was essential, the quartermaster made us pay for it. Took it right out of our pay.

For another thing, we had to learn how to cook. As I recall, each company only had a half-dozen pails and nine or ten basins for all the cooking, and at first we had no cooks to speak of. As time went on there surfaced a few fellows who showed themselves to be no good at killing people with guns, so they were made cooks instead.

What we ate could've killed as quick as anything else we put up with. The regulation ration was one thing, what we actually got was another. Hard rations on a campaign was salt pork, hardtack, and coffee. Everybody has heard of hardtack, a thick, hard cracker. If the crackers were fresh, they weren't half-bad, but as they got older they got harder. Sometimes to soften our crackers we would soak them in bacon grease. Think about that on your stomach! Tasted good that way, though.

Oh, and beans sometimes. Say what you want about beans and snicker, but they was one of the things that was good for us. We'd bury a pot in the evening in hot coals and they'd be ready for breakfast. Umm-umm good. The good old army bean.

We all lost weight. From 170 pounds I lost twenty, and never got 'em back. I've weighed the same for about seventy years. James lost twenty-three pounds, but what was left of us was all wire and grit.

Camp Sigel, two miles from Strausburg, July the 3rd

"... I have been enlisted over eight months and in that time I have only had about one month of what can be called hard service. There has not been more than two weeks that need have been hard if it had

not been for the rascally quartermasters and commissaries who robbed us of our rations or at least that part of them that the men relished, and for two weeks we were reduced to salt bacon, crackers that were as hard as Pharaoh's heart, and coffee. And in that time we were on the march in the rain, sleeping on the wet ground, and going into a limestone country where the water is as hard as it can be. Between the hard water, the marching and sleeping in the rain, and the robbing us of our rations, it made plumb one-half of our regiment sick with the dysentery. But after two weeks of that kind of work, General Sigel sent for the quartermasters and told them plainly that if they either could not or would not do their duty and furnish the men their rations, he would find men that would, and since that time we have fared better.

...You wanted to know if we had anything comfortable to eat. Well, according to what I think are your notions of comfort, I should say we did not, but when we are well and especially when our appetites are sharpened by a hard march we lay hold of our coffee, hard bread, and boiled beef or pork with as keen a relish as though the quality was a good deal better." [22]

***

THE ARMY OF VIRGINIA

Jackson had beat all comers—Fremont, Banks, and McDowell—one at a time, and that was the problem. Short of Washington, where Lincoln was trying his hand at generalship—with poor results—there was nobody in overall charge of those separate little armies, who could have brought them all together to beat Jackson.

Abe Lincoln was no fool. Sooner or later he had figured out what Jackson was trying to do, which was to beat the scattered Yankee forces one at a time, in the meantime keeping the government rattled and reluctant to send any more troops to McClellan, but the problem was he couldn't do anything about it by pulling wires from Washington.

His answer to the problem was to reach out west, where we had a few generals, some of who I already mentioned, who were seeming to get things done. He picked Major General John Pope to take command of the new "Army of Virginia," made up of the troops scattered from West Virginia to Winchester (where we were) to Fredericksburg. Pope had had a bloodless success in capturing Island Number Ten on the Mississippi

River. The fact that the fort on the island was taken by engineering skills and other people's initiative rather than by fighting—or a great deal of generalship on Pope's part—was missed. General Pope was a winner, and that was all that mattered. He was also a bully, a braggart, a self-promoter, and a conceited ass, and events proved him to be totally bereft of any tactical or strategic sense. Other than that, he warn't a bad general.

But at the time Pope took command, he sounded pretty good to us. He spoke of attacking, of having no mercy on anyone, military or civilian, who supported the rebellion. In a way, he was ahead of his time. In the middle of 1862 there was still a place for chivalry and going easy on the other fellow if he was down but not out.

Lincoln also brought in a general to replace McClellan as overall commander. Little Mac had his hands full down by Richmond, so Henry Wager Halleck was put in charge at Washington. That's how it turned out, anyway. Halleck was a book soldier, nicknamed "Old Brains" by those who knew him well, and he had no inclination to take the field to command anything. Halleck took over the job of Washington Wire Puller from Lincoln, with no better success. It just put another layer in the hierarchy between Lincoln and the men who worked for him. It also upset our little napoleon, McClellan, who had become a legend in his own mind and considered any lessening of his authority as a potential disaster for the country.

Scarcely hiding his contempt for Halleck's office mentality, Pope said his headquarters would be in the saddle, which caused some comedian among us to say that Pope was putting his headquarters where his hindquarters should be. That joke is seventy years old but I still chuckle over it.

Jackson had "mystified" us, and then toward the end of June he vanished, to reappear with Lee down at Richmond. The showdown took place from June 25th to July 1st, 1862. Robert E. Lee reorganized the army he had inherited from the wounded Joe Johnston, brought Jackson down from the Shenandoah, and attacked. For a week he tried to destroy McClellan's army, but never quite pulled it off, thanks in large part to some splendid fighting by the Pennsylvania Reserves, the division which Charlie Lyon's outfit was assigned to. The result of this battle—actually it was a series of battles—was something we would see more than once, with several other commanders: McClellan, as a man, was thoroughly beaten, personally intimidated by Lee, although his army still had lots of fight left in it, and could have quickly resumed the offensive if the commander had had the gumption to do so. But it was not to be. McClellan pulled everybody back into a fortified camp on the north bank of the James River and cried out for reinforcements before he would advance again.

Lee would not wait for that. Some of the things John Pope said, such as about making war on civilians, and unrestricted foraging and so on, had upset General Lee, and he told Jackson he wanted Pope "suppressed." Jackson went first and then, shortly afterward, leaving a skeleton force to shadow McClellan, Lee began shifting the main force of his army north against Pope, hoping to destroy Pope before the Union could bring another concentration to bear on him. All that I'm relating here is recited with the benefit of years of hindsight, not only by me but by battalions of historians. The thing to remember about what I just said is that when I say "destroy Pope" I'm saying "destroy me, Calvin, James Miller, Colonel Cobham, and the other fifty-sixty thousand soldiers in the Army of Virginia." In other words, think of it in personal, human terms, rather than of us as pieces in some gigantic game of chess.

CHAPTER FIVE
WAR IN EARNEST

I just got me a store-bought rocking chair. My first project the first time I retired was to whittle out that old rocker out there on the porch. That was in 1911 when I was only sixty-seven. Since then, I keep retiring, find myself still alive the morning after, and so go out and get another job.

We had mustered between nine hundred and a thousand men when we left Baltimore but, right away, as soon as we started experiencing the hardships of field service, we started leaking men to the rear, to the hospitals and cemeteries. We done a heap of marching that first summer, that wore down a lot of good men. Other armies fought battles that dwarfed that little spat at Bull Run, but our regiment just marched, from Harper's Ferry down the Shenandoah, across the Blue Ridge into Northern Virginia, up and down, up and down.

July 3rd continued

"...I know no more about where we are going or what we are going to do than you, and I don't care much, but hope it will be to bring us nearer to the foe. I believe it would be the best thing that could happen for our men in this brigade that are partly sick and a good deal discouraged. Bringing them into close proximity to our foe, the excitement would cure them twice as fast as the doctor can.

By the by, the doctor is hated worst of any man in the regiment. But he and I are on first rate terms and ever since I have been in the service I never have been unwell and gone to him for to be excused from doing duty but he has done it without finding a bit of fault. I think you are too harsh in regard to the care that the sick and wounded get in the hospitals. It may be true in regard to some of them, but I had a good chance to see the care that the sick and wounded got in Baltimore and I don't think that if they had been at home they would have gotten any better care than they did there..." [23]

This next is a snippet of a letter that Susan wrote to Ma and Pa Miller. Paper being in short supply, James used the backside of it for a letter home in August. Folks would send letters around to James that they got from Susan, and vice-versa, so that's how he got a hold of it. Since there are not many letters from Susan I thought I'd read it to you:

Susan, to Mr. and Mrs. Miller, July 26th, 1862

...As I had no chance to send my letter to Garland until today, I thought I would open it and write to you that I have just received a letter from James. It was wrote the eleventh of July, Camp in the field, four miles from Warrenton, Virginia. He wrote that he was in good health and spirits. They did not leave their old camp until the 6th of July and had been on the march ever since. But the men was gaining in health and strength very fast...[24]

When I was talking about campfires and wood smoke I mentioned that there was orders against burning fence rails. There was also orders against picking apples off trees in the orchards alongside the road, or doing any damage to private property. All those rules made the boys in blue pretty mad. It seemed to us that we were coddling a population that was traitors to our government. General John Pope felt the same way.

Camp near Washington, Rappahannock Co., July the 26th, 1862

"...since General Pope has given orders that a stop be put to the guarding of rebels' property and allowing us to levy on the enemy the soldiers begin to think that we are going to have war in earnest and that we are to be supported by the Government...No false notions of mercy are to save the scoundrels that have caused this war...If the powers at Washington only continue in the good work that they have commenced since the repulse of the army at Richmond I shall think that the lesson though a severe and bloody one was the best thing that could have happened to the country...I wish that the North would raise five hundred thousand men and teach the rebels that we have the power and disposition to crush this rebellion and the effect will be to make France and England know and respect us.

There is a rumor that Stonewall Jackson is at Gordonsville with thirty to sixty thousand men. It is said that he intends to try the mettle of Pope and his army and let him come I say...

Our men are in good health and spirits and anxious to measure their strength with Jackson at any time that he may feel disposed to give us an opportunity...

...if the rebels feel like getting possession of this part of the state they can try us on at their earliest convenience and the sooner the better...

In regard to the stamps I got seven from John and that is all I have got since we left Baltimore with the exception of the three that you sent me and I am very sorry that I have not got them. I can't get only once in a while. Once in camp I have known the boys to offer as high as ten cents apiece for stamps and could not get them at that and I could not get a single stamp some of the time since I have been in Virginia if I had given twenty- five cents for it and some of the time I have written as high as eight or ten letters a week but I am very sorry to say that I have not got more than half as many as I have written and worse than all the rest I have not got a letter from Susan since the first of July and she said that she had not got a letter from me since the first of June and what the reason is I can't tell for I have written a letter every week since I left Baltimore to her. Your letters come better and in less time than any other ones that I get.

We got two months' pay some ten days ago and I sent ten dollars to Susan in a letter. The sutler Mr. Caughey was going to Erie and I put the money in a letter and sent it by him to Erie and he said that he would put it in the Post Office in Erie. I want you to write to Susan and tell her that I have done the best I could to get a letter to her and I want her to keep on writing for maybe I will get one of them after a while...

The Westfield Cavalry are mounted and ordered to active service. They are stationed some six miles from here. Lieutenant Spencer of Co. D was up to see them and he told me that he saw Harm Cooper and a good many of the other boys but it is almost impossible to get a pass to leave the camp of our own brigade or I would try and go to see them. I was on picket duty the day that they passed our camp. I saw the regiment but I did not know what regiment it was until the next day.

PS if you conclude to enlist and have to take a private's position it would be my advise to you to join some of the regiments now in the field for you will learn a great deal faster than you can in a new regiment." [25]

Who was the Westfield Cavalry, you ask? Well, now, for one reason or another, a lot of boys from Warren County ended up in New York regiments. The Westfield was part of the 9th New York Cavalry, which was a good regiment, as far as cavalry goes. All right, it was a damned good regiment. Anyway, a bunch of the boys over Sugar Grove way, which is only about two mile from the state line, decided to ride their way to glory, and PA wasn't raising any cavalry thereabouts, so they jumped the line and formed a company in the 9th. Good men, every one.

Colonel Cobham was one of the good men felled by the trials of active campaigning. The Typhoid got him sometime in July and we had to do without him for nearly four months while he went back to Warren to recuperate. Colonel Schlaudecker followed shortly after, never to return. Major Tom Walker took temporary command and would bring us through our first all-out fight.

We all felt pretty much as James did: Let them come. Let them try US on for size. Jackson had about twenty-five thousand men. More times than not, when James gave an estimate in his letters about men engaged, or men shot, he turned out to be pretty close. His estimation of various generals was more prone to miscalculation, at least as far as history's final verdict is concerned.

Pope was ready to fight; so were we. Say what you will about his brag and bluster, he had made us believe that we really were going to lick the Johnnies. We could have, too, if it were not for the sad, simple fact that Pope was playing out of his league, in over his head, and that dark forces—and I mean in Union blue rather than in butternut and gray—were conspiring against him. McClellan, upset that the government was recalling his army to northern Virginia, dallied in transferring troops to Pope, and some of his commanders that did report to Pope did their best to thwart his plans, such as they were.

We were now in the Second Corps, Army of Virginia, under General Nathaniel Banks. Long before we had got shuffled into his corps, Banks had come in second to Jackson several times already. In fact, the rebs had captured so much material from Banks that they called him "Commissary Banks."

Anyway, on August 8th our cavalry reported the rebels coming north across the Rapidan River. Pope ordered Banks to move south from Culpeper and block Jackson until the rest of the army could come up.

True to form, Pope was caught at a bad time. There was us, eight thousand strong, supported by Ricketts' division, with maybe six thousand more. Ricketts was a part of McDowell's Corps—the same McDowell who had lost at Bull Run the year before and nobody had ever forgot. Whether he deserved the censure or not, many of us didn't trust him. He was the only professional corps commander in Pope's army; the others, Sigel and Banks, being "political generals." While you may not understand what that means right now, it will become clearer as the war goes on. I don't want my account to wander at this time.

It was a bad time because, even with Ricketts, we would be outnumbered almost two to one. Without him: three to one. Bless me, of course we did not know that at the time. Perception after the fact is always pure, as they say. But Pope was not disposed so as to cover unexpected problems such as eight thousand of us against 25,000 of them with no help in sight. Sigel, the Horse Borrower, had just dragged his uh—corps—into Culpeper without rations and so could not be counted on for two days. The rest of McDowell's corps was even farther away.

We left our camps at Culpeper on August 8th on a forced march. It was scorching hot and dusty. That night I lay on the ground with my cartridge box for a pillow, and slept so soundly that, though a horse that had been tied near tramped the shoulder strap of my cartridge box into the ground, it did not awaken me. [26]

I guess Banks decided that he had had enough lickings and was determined to thrash Jackson as quickly as possible, maybe to beat his vanguard troops before the tail could come up. Instead of staying defensive, he attacked. "The elephant" lived on Cedar Mountain. He came down to see us on August 9th.

The noise of battle has changed some in seventy years, I reckon. The modern, smaller caliber bullet, sent on its way by powerful smokeless powder, snaps like electricity as it goes by the ear; with each improvement the bullet has gotten smaller and goes faster. When you read of the crash of musketry, or when we old-timers talk of bullets buzzing around our heads, it ain't just talk. The report of a black powder musket is not ka-boom! like the newfangled Springfield bolt-action or the trusty Krag; it is an earsplitting crash, which when magnified and multiplied by the thousands, makes the goldangest racket you ever heard. And them big old minnies, buzzing through the air, reminded me of nothing so much as a big old dragonfly in summer. A feller who fought in the big war, back in 1917, told me once of being in the path of a "friendly" .50-caliber machine gun fired from about three miles away, and the sound he described was a lot like that of a .58 minie at two hundred yards.

Sights are as different as the sounds. Instead of crawling along, or ducking from ditch to stump, like they do now, we stood in ranks, dressed on our flags. A line of battle was usually two ranks of soldiers—privates and corporals—the rear rank about an arm's width behind the front rank, each man able to touch elbows with the fellers to the left and right. Behind the two ranks was the file closers, the sergeants and lieutenants. The only officers up front were the captains. When everybody was ordered to fire at once, the rear rank would shoot over the right shoulders of the men in front. You'd yell "coming over" and lightly rest your left forearm on his shoulder and blaze away.

Seems quaint and silly now—and deafening, I reckon—but there was reasons for the system. Single-shot muskets, spread out thin, could not muster enough firepower to influence a situation, so we had to bunch up to deliver our fire in volume. It is interesting that a modern squad with clip-fed weapons spreads out about as wide as our regiment did, and in emptying their guns sends out about the same number of bullets as one of our regimental volleys.

Breechloaders and repeaters were available, but the conservative and narrow-minded desk generals thought they would waste ammunition, so they went for the old reliable muzzle loader. I believe the war would have not lasted half as long if repeating Henry and Spencer rifles had been chose over the Springfield and Enfield muzzle loaders, because the South could never have matched our firepower and the North's ability to manufacture such guns. Later in the war, when some of our units did have them, they usually had things all their own way in a battle, not only in firepower but also in being able to spread out so that shooting at them was not like shooting at the broad side of a barn. Their losses was mostly always light.

Our flags were not only important to the tactical system but, as symbols of what we were fighting for, whether our state or our country, they soon became as dear to us as life itself. Each volunteer regiment carried both the state and national colors. Early on, there was even guidons for the companies, but they were mostly tossed away in the infantry. We would rather die than let those shot-riddled rags touch the ground or, worse, be lost to the enemy. That's where the tradition started of never letting Old Glory touch the ground.

And so it was with those sights and sounds and sentiments that the 111th went into its first big fight. We called it the Battle of Cedar Mountain; the rebs called it Slaughter Mountain, and as such it proved to the 111th. Major Walker was in command of the regiment; Brigadier General Prince commanded the brigade, made up of our regiment plus the 3rd Maryland, 102nd New York, 109th Pennsylvania, and a consolidated battalion of the 8th and 12th U.S. Regulars. Brigadier General Augur commanded the division.

Camp near Culpeper, Va Aug the 13th 1862

"...the enthusiastic dream of my Boyhood, a battle field in all its glorious pomp and stern reality, opened to our view. Artillery and ammunition wagons were scattered in seeming confusion over the field and the dark lines of infantry were marching and countermarching in all directions. Just as our brigade got its position in a Cornfield on the left of our line the battle commenced in earnest with a heavy fire of artillery on both sides and our brigade was ordered farther to the right to support our artillery..." [27]

We laid behind one of our batteries for what seemed like hours as our artillery fought their artillery, and we were innocent bystanders. The ground shook under our bellies as the big guns banged away, and the bad part was that shells aimed at our battery often overshot and landed amongst us. It was surprising that we lost very few men from the shelling.

As this is intended as personal reminiscences, I will relate a little incident that took place as we were lying there. I was in the rear rank and the man in front of me was not very popular with the boys of the company. You'll remember him. His name was Hultberg. I saw a lowse about the size of a kernel of wheat crawling up his back and I called attention to it by saying, "We'll soon be in it now, boys, Andy is deploying his skirmishers." There was no love lost between us and Andy. He had a brother that we all liked, and when the brother was killed at the Battle of Peach Tree Creek, Georgia, Andy was taken prisoner. When he was exchanged and returned to the company, Calvin said to him, "What a pity it is that it's not Charley that comes back to us." [28] Andy was such a scoundrel that you couldn't hurt his feelings.

Finally it was our turn. As we dressed our ranks, Captain Pitcher of the regulars stepped out in front of his battalion, which was alongside of us. "Men," he says, "you are about to meet the enemy in battle for the first time. You are in the presence of volunteer troops. Every man of you should set a regular soldier's example to these men. You are REGULARS! Don't forget that."

We heard that speech plainly. Humphh! Regular army uppity-ups, I recall thinking.

Major Walker heard it too. He steps out, and in a loud, clear voice, says, "Men of the 111th: You have heard Captain Pitcher's soldierly words to his battalion. I want to say to you as you go into this fight, that as they remember they are regulars, so you are to remember that you are **volunteers**, and while you can load and fire a musket you must not allow regular soldiers, the enemy, or anyone else to outfight you! Do you hear?" We let out a cheer and stepped forward proudly.

Here I was again. I capped my musket on command and listened to the "Thwack!" "Thud!" "Thwack!" as bullets commenced to strike down comrades all around me. I had sworn off all this over a year earlier and for a moment I cursed myself for ever listening to George Cobham. I thought to myself: "Sure, these other fellows are leaning into the harness. They don't know what to expect, whereas I have seen the elephant, and I know how fearsome he is." I took a furtive glance to the rear, to the imagined safety of the cool green woods behind us. I thought of looking for a woodchuck hole for to step in, so as to break my leg and get myself excused from this business...

Then I espied James, jaw set tight, eyes taking everything in, and he give me a little nod, which compliment I returned, and we commenced to advance. All through the war, seemed like I'd always have the jitters until the first time I fired my gun, and then I'd settle down to business.

Our whole line went in. Off to the right one of our brigades hit part of Jackson's celebrated division, including the Stonewall Brigade in person, and, believe it or not, caved it in. They say Jackson was beside himself. A rout of his troops was not an everyday occurrence and he waded in like a common brigadier, rallying and inspiring, urging up his reserves, and soon he got things turned back around.

We advanced slowly and methodically across an open cornfield and traded blow for blow. We fired and screamed our defiance and cursed like madmen. Curses, curses, curses! For Johnny Reb. For the hot sun and the thick smoke. For the worthless muskets we forced to the work. We shot up our basic supply of ammunition, though our shoulders ached from the mule kick they give us, and we cried with exasperation at the times the hammer didn't fire the cap. I think I could give a more detailed account of this fight if I had not been distracted by the malfunctions of that Belgian boat-anchor called a musket!

The racket intensified off to the right and soon we seen our boys coming back, at first in twos and threes, and later the whole battle line surged back, until we of the 111th found ourselves all alone in that field.

We had no choice but to follow suit, to keep from being flanked, but we did it in the same style as our advance, slow and methodical, never breaking ranks, delivering right smart volleys that kept the Johnnies at a standoff. Right then, I knew the mettle of this 111th Pennsylvania was of the very finest kind. We rarely did anything that got much space in the newspapers, but it was because we never did anything for show. Yankees to the core, we would stick to anything as long as there was a fair prospect of it paying off, and all that drill was redeeming itself. We finally made cover, minus about ninety-five of us killed and wounded, and we only had maybe 350 men in the fight to start with.

The first sight I saw on entering the woods was Calvin lying on the ground, a bloody mess amongst the leaves and ferns. I was distressed, don't you think I wasn't, but not near as distressed as Calvin.

I knelt beside him as the line continued on. "Oh, Calvin," I says, "don't tell me they got you too!"

"Oh, those lily-livered, cold-hearted cowards," says Calvin in a voice surprisingly strong for a dead man.

"Who, the Johnnies?"

"No, no, no! It's them damned stretcher bearers. They got me this far and dumped me. Took off for the rear. Said I was too far gone and not worth saving."

"Where you hit?" I said as I knelt by him.

"They said I was shot through the body," Calvin replied. His blouse was pulled open in front, and he poked his finger into his chest, about as careless and nonchalant as others would be in showing off a new tattoo. "See, it goes in here, and they told me it came out the back. But, partner,

I don't feel near as bad as I would expect to with such a terrible wound. See to it, will you?"

I pulled his blouse away and hiked up his underwear shirt. The bullet had gone in all right, an inch or two above his first ribs, but there was a wide, ugly purple line under his hide, around under his armpit to near his shoulder blade, where another hole showed where the bullet had gone on its merry way. Minies did strange, unpredictable things. This one had traveled halfway around Calvin and, except for blood and pain, did not seem to have caused much damage. Then I noticed his cartridge box lying beside him. The eagle shield, a heavy three-inch brass and lead disk that is mounted on the cartridge box strap where it crosses the chest, was bent nearly in two from deflecting a bullet.

Just then some shave-tail lieutenant come along and was about to whack me with the flat of his sword for shamming. "Get along, thar," he says. "Leave the wounded for the stretcher bearers."

I was not in the mood for this youngster. "Them stretcher bearers are to hell and gone, and you can go there too, Lieutenant," says I. "Or, better yet, take an arm and a leg of this feller and help me get him back." The Looey was about to backtalk me when I says, "Give a hand or s'help me I'll tell the Maje about the time you went to Miss Lettie's in Baltimore." This was all bluff on my part. Miss Lettie's was an off-limits whorehouse which was very popular with young officers. I figured this kid would have had to have gone at least once. He must have, for he took an arm and a leg without another murmur.

We reached the ambulance wagons just as they were about to depart. It was curious that the infantry that had done all the fighting were not much fazed that I could tell, while the rear echelon boys were a pretty scared set. I made sure that a surgeon understood what had happened to Calvin before I went back to the regiment.

Poor Calvin. He was on his way to the rear, to the tranquility of Alexandria or Washington, if he survived. He would have to endure a long ride in a springless ambulance wagon, sharing it with maybe a half-dozen other poor unfortunates. Pain and infection and damned poor grub, and sometimes not much of it, would kill some of the occupants of that wagon.

But as it turned out, Calvin made it to Alexandria and, when convalescent, transferred to Emory Hospital in Washington, D.C.

James wrote several letters describing Cedar Mountain. I'll pick a few interesting parts. I want you to notice something though, something new: With these letters written after our first fight, you start to see references to the grumblers at home, to the folks who wanted the war to end on any terms. People at home did the complaining while we did the fighting. They were starting to disappoint us, but we were determined not to disappoint them. What follows is the fragment of James's letter, undated, that was on the back of Susan's note I read to you a while back. Don't know when exactly he wrote it, or who it was to.

"The battle was on the 9th, and on the morning of the 11th the rebels sent a flag of truce asking for leave to bury their dead. Jackson commanded in person. Banks was our general commanding until the fight was over, when Pope arrived on the field...We were ordered back to Culpepper yesterday. What it means I don't know, but I think that it will be another long march and another fight. Paper is scarce here and I have used a part of an old letter that Susan sent to Father." [29]

Aug the 13th 1862 continued

"...General McDowell was ordered to reinforce us with ten thousand men but as is usual with him he did not come in time to help us any and it is rumored in camp that Pope has ordered McDowell under arrest but whether it is so or not I don't know but I hope it is true for I think he has blundered enough in this war to entitle him to be hung at least half a dozen times and I hope he will get what he deserves.

...The predominant feeling with me after the first fire or two was revenge seeing comrades fall around me. I thought more about revenging them than I did of being hit myself.

Our regiment behaved first rate and obeyed every order that was given. Our Brigadier General Prince is missing and there is but one member of his staff but what was either killed or wounded. Our Division General Augur was slightly wounded. General Banks was hurt by a cavalry man running against him. Brigadier General Geary lost an arm." [30]

Camp near Culpeper, Va Aug the 17th 1862

"I will simply say that I was not as much excited under fire as I expected to be...You can't have any idea the amount of fire and showers of bullets that flew around us. It seemed as though they could not help

but hit every one of us for they came on all sides of us and I could feel the wind from several as they passed my face and head and one of our boys was shot on my right that stood not more than a foot and a half from me. He was shot through the face and the bullet that hit him must have passed within four inches of my nose and I have no doubt but that there were at least a dozen bullets that passed within that distance of my head. I lost my belt that holds my bayonet and cap box and I think it was shot off but I don't know for certain. Charles Lobdell was wounded in the hip. He was the only one in our Company that was hurt that you knew. We had four wounded and one killed in our Company... The third day after the battle our division which was the worst cut up of any was ordered back to Culpeper and we have been doing nothing but rest since.

The troops in this army have unbounded Confidence in Pope but none at all in McDowell. In regard to McClellan I think that Stanton and McDowell are all to blame for McClellan not taking Richmond and I hope that Halleck will give him half a chance and I think he will prove that he is not only a good general but one of the best that the world ever saw.

...I do hope that some of the grumblers in that Country will have to shoulder their guns and take the chances of a soldier's life and I think that when they march through the mud and through the rain and sleep in the mud and wet grass for four or five days and have nothing to eat but hard bread stinking pork no tea or coffee or sugar and at another time marching in the dust and hot sun of VA for three days and fight on the last and see their comrades shot down by their sides I think they would not find so much fault with the government and if they would heartily support the government the war would be over soon.

Tell Mother not to fret about me for I shall not be killed until my time comes." [31]

Culpeper, Va Aug the 17th, 1862

"...If you or any of the rest of the boys in that neighborhood conclude to volunteer I should like to have them come and join this regiment. I can't help but think that the boys who are volunteering are foolish to join the new regiments, for they will have to endure the monotony of drilling for three or four months. If they would join the old regiments they would learn as much in four weeks in them as they

can in four months in the new ones...Give my love to George Henry and Jane and tell them that they may think it is hard times there, but if they could only come to Virginia and see the desolation that is here—farms of 1,000 acres stripped of all their fences in a single day and all the wheat, oats, and hay on the same farm taken, and every one of the horses and fat cattle taken. The only way that the owners can get anything in payment is to prove that they are Union men...

Since I left Harper's Ferry, I have not seen twenty able-bodied young men for the rebels have driven them all into the army. I think it is a pity if the loyal North can not make as large sacrifices to support the Constitution and the laws as the rebels can to destroy them.

...Virginia will not recover from the effects of this war in one hundred years if the war should close now, and if the war should continue six months longer, two-thirds of the inhabitants will be in a starving condition. And I don't care if they are, for they have themselves to blame for this war and its consequences. Secesh as the most of them are, they say that our soldiers are gentlemen when compared to the soldiers of Jackson.

Tell George Henry that if it is his luck to come here and stay as long as I have that he will be more of an abolitionist than any person could make him believe to be possible.

...I believe that I only echo the universal opinion of the army when I call McClellan the Prince of Generals. I believe that he will yet vindicate his claim to be considered the greatest general of modern times." [32]

No, Pope did not have McDowell arrested; no, General Geary did not lose an arm; and no, McClellan was not America's answer to Napoleon. As we started moving away from Cedar Mountain we were about as used up as an outfit could get. The corps was a frazzle, with nearly one-third either on that long, painful journey to the hospitals or dumped into graves on the battlefield. Still, we had got the fight we wanted, and had showed what we could do, given a fair chance. Morale was up, but our numbers were down. We were in need of everything, from shoes to decent food, to reinforcements. And just when we were most in need, Jackson cut around to our rear, burned our supply depots, and cut us off from reinforcements. Damned if he didn't.

Due to our cut up condition we were not called on to participate at the Second Battle of Bull Run, or Second Manassas, as the Johnnies called it. You may notice that a lot of our battles have two names. There was a tendency for us to name battles after landmarks, such as Bull Run, or Antietam (Creek) while the Johnnies, being from the locale, named them more often after their towns, such as Manassas, or Sharpsburg. Anyway, James called it on the mark when he wrote that we were in almost continuous retreat after Cedar Mountain.

Since the war I have been able to make sense of most of our meanderings through Virginia and elsewhere, but at the time we just plain gave up trying to figure out what was going on. Lee outgeneraled Pope and got him going in circles and I'll leave it to you to look up other accounts for details. Not that I couldn't do it, mind you, but I get so exasperated when I even think about it, let alone try to put it into words.

The campaign was over by the beginning of September. It was a disaster for us. James would get it half right: Near twenty thousand boys in blue bit the dust, but the rebs probably lost no more than twelve thousand. It took almost two years before somebody (Grant was his name) figured out that, although it was grim business, the Union could stand that kind of arithmetic better than the Confederacy could. At the time, though, even if somebody had come up with that theory, he would have probably been ignored, or locked up. But things were pretty blue, no matter how you measured it.

We soon found ourselves back in the defenses around Washington. Pope was transferred out to Minnesota to fight Indians, which was more his speed. There was a lot of mutual abuse and blame amongst the higher ups for the way things had turned out, and it started almost as soon as the last shots of the campaign were fired in a miserable little battle fought in rain and thunder and lightning at a place called Chantilly. It was Lee's last attempt to cut off our retreat to Washington. I remember Chantilly as notable only because the army had two division commanders, Phil Kearney and Isaac Stevens, killed within the space of a half-hour. A few court-martials were instigated which eventually led to the ruination of some careers, but while our side wasted time trying to spread the blame around, Lee's Army of Northern Virginia followed up the victory by marching into Maryland. His target: Harrisburg. Or maybe Baltimore. Or Philadelphia. Who knew?

There was only one man who could save the bacon right then. Sadly, he had said and done a few things which in no small part had caused the Union to be in the current mess, but no other general had the talent to rally and reorganize us, and no other general had the—what's the word? Yes, charisma, no other way to describe it—the charisma that led the rank and file of the Army of the Potomac into an extreme case of hero worship. We would follow this man anywhere, and if he had flaws, we overlooked them, every one.

MCCLELLAN!

The name rolled like a tidal wave through our march columns, our bivouacs, and the forts around Washington. Hats would fly in the air and heartfelt cheers met him wherever he would go. God, we loved that man! He had a way about him, the way his horse pranced and the way he tossed that jaunty salute to the rank and file as he cantered by. More importantly right then, he was also an organizational genius. Somehow, in the space of a very few days, he got us sorted out, fed us, got us some shoes and such, and set out after Lee.

In the case of the 111th Pennsylvania, we found ourselves indebted to Major Tom Walker, our acting commander while George Cobham recuperated from The Typhoid back in Warren. It was all about those cursed Belgian muskets. Major Tom, he was quite a talker, and he did not hesitate to use his skills when necessary to get what we—or he—wanted. Way I heard it, he took advantage of some little praise handed out by one of our senior generals to say that a grand regiment such as us deserved better guns than them damned Belgians and, well, to make a long story short, the next day several wagons came rolling into camp with crates of .577-caliber Enfield rifles.

Nothing short of a thirty day leave for all hands could have had the positive effect on morale that those rifles had. Walking through camp, you'd notice fellas sitting with their rifles, running their hands over the polished wood of the stocks or the blue-steel barrels, or working the hammer and trigger. Getting those rifles was the last step in turning a bunch of Pennsylvania farm boys, schoolteachers, and shopkeepers into warriors, with weapons worthy of them—and their foe.

I came to nickname my rifle "Old Reliable." I carried it all through the war, except for a spell in the fall of '64, which I'll tell you about when the time comes. That's it hanging over the mantle there, and I can still drive tacks with it.

Of course, all these events happened years and years ago. I'm pretty sharp for ninety-two, but even I can't remember everything. In recollecting, I am aided by these letters which I read from from time to time—ninety or so letters saved from the time we enlisted until, well, don't let me get ahead of myself. Old James wrote letters during the Antietam campaign, for sure he did, but for some reason the Antietam letters were not saved. I don't know why, but I can guess: Could be that he described such sights and scenes from the battle that the family could not bear to save them, possibly for the sake of his mother, who was practically crazy from fear and prostrated every time her son went into a fight. She went into a tizzy after James sent home the gory details of Cedar Mountain and here the next month was a battle even worse. But whatever the reason, it's a shame, because what a battle that was!

CHAPTER SIX
THE BATTLE OF ANTIETAM

Now, I'm going to tell you about Antietam from my point of view, but before I do, I'm going to share a letter with you which James wrote in the summer of '63. By then we'd been in lots of scrapes, but I'm almost positive that James was thinking about Antietam when he wrote about battle to his brother, William. These are James's words. Not me nor anybody else takes credit for what he said so well...

June 6, 1863

"...In regard to the danger I have passed through, that part is very pleasant. It is not the danger a soldier has passed that bothers him; it is the danger still to be met that he fears. If you could only be with us around our camp fires after a fight, and listen to the accounts of the hairbreadth escapes that are told, and hear the loud laughs that greet each one's experiences, and see the gay, reckless, careless way in which they are told, you would think that we were the happiest set of men you ever saw. But if you should go with us to the battle field and see those that are so gay, their faces pale and their nerves trembling, and see anxiety on every countenance almost bordering on fear, you would be very apt to think we were all a set of cowardly poltroons—this picture to be taken just before the fight begins and the enemy is in sight, and the dull ominous silence that generally takes place before the battle begins. And then as the skirmishers are deployed to the front and you begin to hear the sharp irregular crack of their rifles, and to see the puffs of white smoke that tell where the foe are, and anon to hear the deep sharp sound of the cannon and listen to the screaming whistling of the bursting shells, and then to see the solid columns of the foe advance in plain sight, every man seeming to step as proudly and steadily as if on parade, and even while the artillery tears large gaps in their line, still on they come, hardly faltering for a moment. Now look at our line, and you will see those men that one half hour ago were pale

and trembling, and now just as the musketry begins, to see the same men pale still but no trembling now. Instead, see the firm compressed lips, the eye fixed and precise and bloodshot, the muscles rigid, the veins corrugated and knotted, looking more like fiends than men. And after the battle has raged for some time and comrades are lying thick around, and then as the soul-stirring order comes to charge, then away we into the very jaws of death and never for one moment faltering, but yelling like devils up to the mouths of the cannon...

...And then to hear the wild triumphant cheer, and within a few hours to see the same men passing over the battle field with the kindness and tenderness of a woman, helping friends or foes as the case may be. And by the time you have seen this, you will begin to think that a soldier has as many characters as a cat is said to have lives. But still I hope it will not be your luck to tread the rough life of a soldier..." [33]

And that's the way it was, and the way it always will be. Like I said if given the chance to contemplate while marching to battle, I would daydream about finding a chuckhole to step into, to break a leg so as to avoid the danger. I never did it, of course, but the sentiment was there. Yet while in battle or if thrust suddenly into a matter of life or death, I hardly remember being afraid. Soldiers of nowadays and of other wars would have to be honest enough to say they felt the same, and I'll bet they did.

Camp in the field three miles from Washington, September the 5th, 1862

"On the night of the 19th of August, we broke up our camp at Culpepper and commenced retreating toward the Rappahannock and since that time we have retreated almost every day.

The 6th: I had just got this much written when the order came to fall in, and we were marched to the Potomac and up the river for two or three miles in plain sight of the capitol, and crossed at the aqueduct bridge to Georgetown. We marched to the northeast some five miles. Where we are going I don't know or care.

The day after we left Culpepper and crossed the Rappahannock, the rebels drove in our pickets. The next day they appeared in force and tried to drive us from our position but failed. The following morning there was a severe artillery fight. We had a battery planted on the rebel side of the river and the rebels tried to take it, but the shell case shot came too thick for them and they fell back. Tried three times in all of which they failed, and the last charge (which was a most determined one on their part) brought on the most terrific artillery fire from our side that I ever heard. We opened some thirty guns on them. They were four lines deep of infantry and they marched in good order across an open field but when they got near enough for tin case shot to be effective, our guns tore them all to pieces. Our battery was the Fourth Maine. It seemed as though every shot that they threw tore gaps from twenty to thirty feet wide in their lines and it came so hot that they could not stand it, and broke and run for the woods. They were busy for five hours picking up their dead and wounded; their loss in that affair was ten to our one. That is the only fight that we saw.

As near as I can learn, our loss in the last two weeks is not far from twenty thousand in killed, wounded and prisoners and the loss of the rebels must have been greater than ours. Joel Gardiner was wounded in the leg and arm severely but not fatally." [34]

***

MARYLAND

Lee was in Maryland, somewhere around Frederick, and soon we found ourselves on roads north of the Potomac, headed northwest. A strange command we were. We had been bled white at Cedar Mountain, and to give us enough men the government sent our corps a bunch of brand-new, green regiments. Some of the new regiments were bigger than the old brigades, and we were like a man going into battle wearing odd boots: one too small and the other too big. And the new regiments were of the kind I mentioned a while ago—straight from mustering in to the service. Some of those boys had never fired a gun before, and probably thought Hardee's Tactics was a book on social manners.

Camp in the field near Rockville, MD September the 8th, 1862

"...We have had a great deal of very hard marching since I wrote to you before, having marched near one hundred miles in the last two weeks. There is a report that the rebels have crossed the Potomac and hold Poolesville in force, and that is some fifteen miles in front of us. We are lying here in line of battle but when we will move or which way, I neither know nor care, for we have marched and countermarched so much lately that we don't care where we go or what we do. I hope

that the rebels will cross the river for I think that we can fight them to better advantage in Maryland than we could in Virginia. But I don't think that they will be foolish enough to let us cut them off from their supplies as we shall surely do if they attempt to march on Baltimore. And that makes me think that they are only trying to excite us by their movement on Poolesville...Give my love to all enquiring friends and accept a large share for yourself and wife." [35]

Like James said, where we were going we neither knew nor cared. The big picture was unknown to us, but nobody hesitated to speculate around the campfire on what the possibilities were. As we neared Frederick our cavalry was chasing their rear guard out of town, so we moved in.

Try to judge for yourself what it would be like to camp in a field that had been recently vacated by ten thousand used-up enemy soldiers and all their horses and mules. They had tore out most all the fences for firewood and everywhere was their waste and litter. You will recollect we had occupied an old Confederate campground down at Winchester two months earlier and it was right afterwards that half of us had come down with the dysentery. I reckon we—what was left of us—was a hardier lot by now, because the present unsanitary situation turned out to have no ill effects.

It was there in one of those fields not far from ours that a couple of chaps from our corps made a famous discovery. Seems two boys from the 27th Indiana Infantry, First Sergeant John Ploss and Corporal Bart Mitchell, went to scrape the debris away to make them an overnight home in a fence corner when one of them picked up two-three segars wrapped in paper. As they stretched out to take their brogans off and light a pipe it was the segars that piqued their interest at first, Confederate tobacca being in high demand with us, but by and by Corporal Mitchell took to reading the paper they had been wrapped in.

It started off with "Special Orders Number 191, Army of Northern Virginia." It went on to mention names that had already become legend with us. Names like D.H. Hill, Longstreet, Jackson, Lee...

And of a sudden they forgot the segars.

They went to regiment, regiment went to brigade, brigade went to division, and presently the paper was in the hands of General McClellan himself. To top that, there happened to be at headquarters an officer who could authenticate the handwriting of Colonel Chilton, the reb officer who had wrote out the order.

The order gave the location of every division in Lee's army and what each was to do for the next few days. It was as if Mac had been privileged to sit in on Lee's most recent strategy session, and he was thrilled. "Here is a paper," he said, "with which if I cannot whip Bobby Lee, I will be willing to go home."

Somebody would remember you said that, general. Rarely has a general ever been given such a gift. I'm not so sure that Little Mac deserved it, but we did—and the country did, too. Funny thing. Nobody ever figured out how those orders came to be wrapped around those segars and then lost; and for sure no reb ever admitted to losing them.

With uncharacteristic confidence—and speed—born of his knowledge of Lee's situation, McClellan soon had us back on the road, now headed west toward South Mountain. If you ever get to Maryland, the views are still there. All that would be missing would be our long blue snaking columns topped with rifle barrels glittering like silver in the sun. From miles away you could see the breeze billowing the dust, unfurling our flags from their staffs. Up ahead rose the heights of South Mountain and some other minor ridges. From those heights the Johnnies were watching us come on. In later years they remembered us, "terrible as an army with banners," and the pageantry of their enemy spread out before them.

Robert E. Lee had crossed the Potomac River with less than fifty thousand men. They have been described as the flower of his army, the cream of the crop, but what they were, when you get right down to it, was the hard cinder of the Army of Northern Virginia. The weak ones—and the cowards—either could not or would not keep up, and they limped along the roads in Lee's wake, a hemorrhage of fighting men that could prove fatal when push come to shove. Lee was testing his soldiers to the limit of human endurance in the hope of winning the war in 1862.

Incredible, McClellan still thought he was outnumbered and outgunned. See, the one piece of information which "Special Orders Number 191" did not give was the strength of all those Confederate divisions. McClellan for some reason figured them at about twelve thousand apiece, instead of five thousand each, tops.

We who lived in the real world of death and misery plainly saw the signs of an enemy in dire straits: Alongside the road, cobs of green corn gnawed bare of every kernel—by men, not horses; dead and broken-down mules and horses, pieces of worn-out harness; shoes with soles totally gone, and bloodstained footprints in the macadam road thereafter; now and then a straggler so exhausted that he didn't care if we shot him or not, long as we first gave him a mouthful of hardtack and a slug of coffee. The one thing that might have bothered me, had I thought of it at all, is that to my best recollection I did not see a single abandoned musket along that entire road from Frederick to South Mountain.

When we reached the mountaintop there were muskets aplenty, but usually their recent owners lay beside them, stone dead. An undermanned Confederate division had been given the job of delaying us until Lee could complete his programme, which included the capture of Harper's Ferry, a town familiar to us as the place where we had entered the war. With Lee's characteristic steel nerve he persisted in gobbling up the garrison—supplies, field pieces, and ten thousand men—while these dead Johnnies on South Mountain had bought him the time. McClellan crowed about the Battle of South Mountain being a great victory over Lee's army, but we only met a piece of it there. On our side, another first-class bit of fighting by the Pennsylvania Reserves—Mister Charles Lyon, Esquire, and friends—had carried the day.

Meanwhile, old Calvin had tired of hospital life. Although his wound had not fully healed he wanted to get back with us, but the surgeon in charge would not give his consent. So on the 12th of September, when they were sending a squad to the front, he slipped in among them and went out the gate. He knew the army was in Maryland, and by the daily papers he had kept posted where the different commands were.

Calvin stayed with the party he had started with that day, but as our corps was nearer and on another road, he left them and started out alone on the morning of the 13th. He soon fell in with a squad of new recruits going to Company F of the 111th. One of the new recruits was a man named Howard. He had a brother in Company F who was with the company from the first. They were a fine party of young men from Erie and Crawford counties. They all asked Calvin a lot of questions about how it felt going into battle, but young Howard's questions had a special urgency. He told Calvin that he knew he would be killed if he went into a battle. [36]

We were all delighted to see Calvin when he sauntered into the light of our campfire on the night of September 14th. He was a good present for my 18th birthday. The thirteen new recruits were a welcome addition to our strength, but Calvin was family.

Next morning, we found ourselves with a new corps commander by the name of Major General Joseph K. Mansfield. He was about sixty years old, white-bearded and rather fat. General Banks had been left back at Washington in command of the garrison that the government always insisted that we leave there when we took to the field. For several days General Williams, the commander of our First Division, had led the corps, but Mansfield had begged for a corps command and they gave us to him. We never got to know him, but he seemed a nice enough old man, and extremely happy to finally get a field command at a time when most men his age were at home bouncing grandchildren on their knees.

I have never understood why Lee decided to make a stand at Antietam, but then again neither has anyone else, really. It was, I guess, just not in his combative, quietly belligerent nature to back down from a fight. So, although he was initially outnumbered four to one, he calmly deployed what troops he had and waited—for Jackson to bring the other half of the army up from Harper's Ferry, and for McClellan to get the ponderous Army of the Potomac set up on the east side of Antietam Creek. There was not a reason in the world why McClellan could not have attacked before Jackson arrived, and even when Jackson came up, the odds were two to one in our favor.

But Little Mac could not attack just yet. He needed everything to be just so. It was as if he had pulled out his book on Napoleon's tactics and intended to emulate the great commander to a "T," which would guarantee a win. He had been compared to Napoleon, and must have felt obliged to play it thataway.

His plan came right out of Napoleon's book: Hit the flanks of the enemy, make them to shift forces from their center, weakening and disorganizing it. Then, at the decisive moment, Napoleon would throw in the Imperial Guard, his crack troops, which would bust through the center and win the battle. McClellan's "crack troops" were his veterans from the campaign down at Richmond, some 25,000 men of the Fifth and Sixth Corps. Later, he even massed our cavalry in the center, just as Napoleon would have done, ready to ram through and saber down the Johnnies as they fled. The plan for the cavalry was based on looking at a map and from looking at the ground from almost a mile away. In reality, from the creek to Sharpsburg, the ground was a washboard of knobby hills and gullies that would have worn the cavalry down even if they had not been resisted.

Using Napoleon's theories, McClellan once again ran afoul of reality. He sent the First Corps, under Fighting Joe Hooker, across the Antietam late on the afternoon of the 16th to get ready to hit Lee's left at first light the next day, as a part of the Grand Plan. The First Corps contained three divisions, of which one was the Pennsylvania Reserves. The Reserves straightaway ran into Hood's Texas Brigade, and there was some bitter fighting in a woodlot called the East Woods. All Mac had done was telegraph his punch, and Lee and Jackson were assured where the first blow would fall, and got ready to meet it.

We ended up fording Antietam Creek at about midnight. It was rainy, with an eerie fog in the low ground. By two a.m. we were where they wanted us: about a mile to the left rear of the First Corps. We were not allowed any fires. (Theory, again; they knew where we were.) We wrapped up in soggy blankets on boggy ground and, if you were lucky, and had no thought of what first light would bring, you got maybe three hours of sleep.

Not many slept. Somehow we could tell it wasn't going to be just another battle. Something on the night wind, tinged with a sprinkling rain, told us that. Greater than the feeling a man always has when he knows the next day is going to bring fighting and dying, a heap of us went through the night and marched at sunup with a swolled-up feeling in our chests, telling us this could be it: The last one. Bobby Lee had shot his bolt, give us a hard time all summer, but now we could finish it, and be home in time to finish the harvest.

But the harvest on that field, of lives and legs and arms, of bodies forever maimed and mangled, would be the only harvest we would know that year, and indeed all that would be served at the soldier's table, from then on until 1865.

***

THE BLOODIEST DAY

As I went into battle on September 17, 1862, I would have gladly died that day, because I thought we were about to win the war, or more to the point, end it. When I did not die, and it finally sunk in that there would be many more days of battle ahead, I changed my philosophy: I was no longer prepared to die. Not that I became a coward or any such—in fact, I doubt if my philosophical turn had any major effect on my later conduct. It was just that after we wasted that bloody day I was determined to stay to the end—to survive—until that invisible day, far out in the smoke, when it would all be over.

We rose at dawn and moved forward without breakfast. Attempts to brew coffee were doomed to failure, because the woods was wet and there was no time. Already by six a.m. rolling volleys of musketry echoed through the woods and fields. General Mansfield seemed to be everywhere, being energetic enough for any younger man but actually interfering too much in the doings of regiments and brigades. It was obvious that he was new to this corps commander business, and that he wanted to put in a solid performance without leaving too much to chance. He was concerned about all the green regiments that we had with us now, and prescribed cumbersome, unwieldy formations to get us into the fight.

It was as he was leading one of those green regiments up to put it in line at the edge of the East Woods that a Confederate line loosed a volley that put a bullet in the old general's gut. He was helped off his horse and carried to the rear, where he later died. With his wounding, we ceased to fight as a corps and presently it was every brigade for itself, pulled this way and that by the ebb and flow of the battle. Still, some of those brigades managed to do some pretty impressive things.

When it was our turn, we of the 111th cleared the East Woods, that shattered woodlot carpeted with the dead and dying, both ours and theirs. We were part of the Second Brigade of Greene's Division, commanded by Colonel Henry Stainrook, the other regiments of the brigade being the 3rd Maryland and 102nd New York. We went from "companies closed in mass," which was a totally useless formation from which hardly anybody could shoot, into line of battle, and then we could get down to business. We went into that battle the strongest regiment in the brigade, with 13 officers and 230 muskets.

Our first volley from our new Enfields was something to behold. A spontaneous cheer went up and we advanced steadily. We volleyed, we fired by file, we fired at will, and stepped over our fallen comrades as we pushed forward. Major Walker spun like a top and went down, and I thought the worst, but he got right back up, limping from a flesh wound in his foot. The commander of Company B, Captain Corrigan, fell early, shot through the head.

James shouts, over the tumult, "It's almost laughable to remember that we were afraid we wouldn't get in on this!" "Yes," says I, "har-har." Just then a bullet went "Twanggg" and James looked down to see a scrap of leather where his bayonet scabbard used to be. "This is pretty hot," he gulped, but then he reloaded and fired as if nothing had happened.

We were aimed for high ground to the left of the Dunker Church, whose whitewash shone out against the dark green of the West Woods—another, bigger, woodlot. Between us and the high ground was rolling fields of corn and plowed ground, with but a few particles of cover.

In no time at all our sixty rounds of ammunition was about used up, and then we halted while they brought up more. As we lay down just before reaching the crest of a low hill, a clatter set up behind us that we could hear over the other battle sounds. We looked back to see a full battery coming up at a gallop. Hampton's Battery F, Pennsylvania Light Artillery.

When I seen that sight, it made me wish I was in the artillery: Four, 3-inch ordnance rifles, each drawn by caissons with six horses, with ammunition limbers following, with pennants and guidons a-flying, spattering dirt and striking sparks off the limestone outcrops as they thundered up. Around our right flank they swung, from rear to front, pity the poor infantry who got in their way. The guns skittered sideways in the turn, and in no time at all the four of them were unlimbered on the crest and lashing out with shell and solid shot at the distant wood line. The rest of the division artillery, Knap's and Cothran's batteries, went into action off to our right, their smoke turning day to night. All this while we were being issued another sixty rounds of kill seed.

While we were lying there, the new recruit, Howard, took a drink of water from his canteen. One of the boys asked for a drink and then another wanted a drink, when James Miller spoke up and said, "Don't drink all the man's water, you ought to have water of your own." And Howard said, "Drink it, boys, it will never do me any good." Just then Captain Hampton of the battery said, "For God's sake, Colonel, bring up your support!" 'Course, we didn't have a colonel right then, just poor Major Tom stumping around with a bootful of blood, swearing like a trooper and holding us to our work. He ordered us up and we met the enemy with fixed bayonets at the guns and at a range of fifty yards we poured in a volley that, combined with canister from the guns, literally tore the Johnnies apart. Just as we had raised up in line, young Howard was instantly killed. Calvin looked down at the poor boy, ripped the paper on a cartridge with his teeth, and as he poured the powder and rammed the ball he muttered, "I've always contended that it is more pride than bravery that makes men fight." [37] Calvin was barely seventeen years old right then.

We was in the thick of it, I'll tell you. We druv them rebs back again a quarter of a mile or so, changed front to the right, charged and druv them from a line of rifle pits, across the turnpike, past the little white Dunker Church, and when about fifty yards past the church I seen Calvin go down again. That boy was just a magnet for minie balls.

We held our own in the West Wood for some two hours, even as units to the left and right of us were shattered and stampeded by counterattacks. Finally, same story as Cedar Mountain, we had to withdraw because we were practically alone. We didn't run—don't blush for us—we just backed off, stubborn-like, a-shootin' all the time. It was all confusion and blood and smoke, there in the pretty landscape of western Maryland.

As we pulled back past the church, three wounded members of the regiment had Calvin on a blanket, trying to carry him back. Lieutenant Woeltge, Company I, wounded in the thigh; Sergeant George Head, Company D, slightly wounded; and Corporal George Oliver, wounded in the arm, had laid him in the shade of the church, but when the rebs began to shell it they started to carry him back out of range. I could only note that the blanket was already soaked with Calvin's blood, and concluded his luck, as well as his blood, had run out. This time I could not leave the ranks; there was much more hot work ahead.

Somewhere around dusk I saw George Head and he told me that they had set Calvin down between two oak tree roots at about 2 p.m. and left him there. The tree was between the picket lines; there was no way to get to him. I grieved for my friend, though he was but a cipher on that dreadful day. Out of 243 officers and men we lost twenty-six killed and seventy-six wounded. More than a dozen were missing, but a few, like Sergeant Head, turned up later in the day.

Like I said, the Johnny Rebs had been in pitiful shape: ragged, barefoot, wore down by marching and no other rations than what they could pick from the trees 'n fields as they marched. But they had kept their muskets clean and they knew how to use them. Never was they in worse shape except right before the end in '65. Never was our chance of ending the war in a single day greater. And the 111th had been right in the middle of it, and done better than most. Charlie Lyon's Pennsylvania division lost half its men, while ours only lost one out of three. Charlie come through all right, though. So'd James.

The next day, there was Bobby Lee, waiting to see if we would attack again, but we didn't, so he pulled out and, based on that, everybody figgered we'd won. And based on that, Old Abe issued his Emancipation Proclamation, setting the Negroes free. Like I said, what a battle that was!

On the day after that, an attempt to cross the Potomac in pursuit was turned back with disastrous results for the regiments involved, and that was enough for Little Mac.

Our "victory" had a unique price tag. September 17th, 1862, still stands as the bloodiest day in American history, [38] and I say again that we lost so many and killed so many of the enemy because of we were convinced that one more violent day would end it. Antietam was to be our Armageddon, and the war would be over.

McClellan's plan would have worked—in fact, given the odds, ANY sensible plan would've worked—if only he and his senior generals had tried as hard as the privates in the ranks. On the Confederate side, by late afternoon, General Longstreet was holding his staff's horses while they worked an abandoned cannon. Division commander D.H. Hill was taking up a musket and fighting like a common private. On our side, 15,000 men of our Fifth Corps were waiting for the word to go in and end it. The word never came. They, the generals, never appreciated the stuff of which we were made.

One of the benefits of growing very old is that you don't have to drink to forget. I've been meaning to thank Tommy's friend Gary for his kind words and faithful attendance at these sessions. Says he wants to be a soldier when he grows up. Well, there ain't no money in it, but he'll have first crack at the next war, which ought to be coming along in five or ten years.

Well, sir, the battle is over, and we spend the next two days caring for our wounded and burying the dead. We had given no thought to the carnage while the battle had raged, but now that it was over we could think of nothing else, because it was all around us. It would be too tedious to detail the painful sights of that dismal battlefield, but there was a new way of letting the civilian world know what real war—or at least the aftermath—was like. A picture is worth a thousand words, they say…

Yep, it was photography. Pioneers like Matthew Brady were putting darkrooms on wheels and sending them where the action was. Making a photograph was a slow process at first, and I only know of one picture, of an artillery battery near Fredericksburg, that was taken in action. For the new science of photography, where the subject had to stay perfectly still, dead bodies were perfect subjects. Brady's assistant, Alexander Gardner, showed up at Antietam right after the battle and took a series of pictures that were put on display at Brady's New York City studio the next month. All of the bodies were Confederate, sprawled where they had fell, in the West Woods, in the Sunken Road, near the Dunker Church, along the Hagerstown Pike, hundreds and hundreds of them. One visitor to the gallery wrote, "If [Brady] has not brought bodies and laid them in our dooryards, he has done something very like it."

Later on, after other battles, there would be accusations that the photographers actually "posed" the dead bodies, but Antietam was the genuine article. Among all those pictures of dead soldiers was a particularly poignant study of a noble white horse, dead in an upright kneeling position.

We turned our backs to all of that on the 19th of September, not pursuing the enemy but sidling down our side of the Potomac to Harper's Ferry. Lee had captured it, cleaned it out of anything militarily usable, and then give it back to us. We reoccupied the town and the mountains that surrounded it on all sides, and there we sat.

The president came up to visit the army shortly after the battle, with lots of congratulations for all of us. Mac promised him that we would soon be going after Lee, but for six weeks we would stay along the line of the Potomac. If the country was stunned by the carnage of Antietam, McClellan, never the most aggressive of generals, was practically paralyzed. His beloved Army of the Potomac, the shiny instrument that he had forged and led into the history books, was battered, dented, and covered with blood.

***

SMOKETOWN

Do you know who Clara Barton was? Well, I had the honor of meeting her while she was earning her fame.

We took care of our own. Sometime after the first of October, Major Walker got word that a few of our boys were ready to leave the hospital back near the Antietam battlefield. Seventeen miles was a far piece to walk for someone just out of the hospital, so he emptied a regimental baggage wagon and got up a detail to go pick them up. It was me, Sergeant Alexander, and the driver, John Wesley Culver.

Sergeant Alexander was a no-nonsense noncom. I respected him, but he didn't have many friends. Wesley was a different story. He was, I believe, the tallest man in the regiment, and we called him J.W. Legs Almighty Culver. He was a good fellow.

Anyway, the three of us with a four-horse army wagon made the trip back to that fateful field of Antietam, which had not improved with age, especially in the vapors it gave off.

Smoketown Hospital, north of the battlefield, was row on row of white conical canvas tents. I recall the smell of wood smoke and death, a growing graveyard alongside the tents as the wounded succumbed, even as the doctors worked around the clock to save them. Since we were not in any special hurry, we decided to visit some of the other wounded boys, to see what we could do for our friends. During his visit, President Lincoln had done the same, spending as much of his time with the wounded as he had with his generals. We appreciated that.

After we had wandered around for awhile, I recall J.W. greeting me and the sergeant at the end of a row of tents with a broad grin on his face. Says he, "Follow me, boys, and see what I found." Three tents down the row he showed us in and there in the first bed was a very peaked looking lad who was getting well versed with hospital routine.

It was Calvin! Next to him was George Peters, who had been shot through the chest and also written off. Both of them had been reported dead or dying in the papers, but here they were. We had quite a reunion right there, and Calvin told his story in his usual colorful way:

***

CALVIN'S STORY

"Yes, I thought I was a goner, too. The boys set me down between two roots with my back against an oak tree, and left me there. Several

parties gathering up the wounded looked me over and passed on, no doubt thinking I wasn't worth trying to save.

"I remained all night in the position they had left me. About sundown a soldier came along with a haversack of green apples and I asked him for some and ate a couple, which did not add to my comfort during the night. The wound bled freely until the accumulated blood stopped it. In the morning a surgeon came along and stopped and looked me over, took some white powder from a vial and put it on my tongue, took a syringe and injected some liquid into the wound, and left me. In an hour or so an ambulance came and took me to one of the field hospitals. I was very weak from loss of blood, and dressing the wound was very painful, but the wound seems to be healing rapidly. It won't be but a few days until I'll be getting around somehow.

"George Peters, there, he was shot clear through the body in the right breast. His wound became fly blown and yesterday the surgeons pulled a silk cord through the wound to remove the maggots.

"And, boys, who should come to visit us a few days ago but President and Missus Lincoln. He was tall and sad looking, even though he was doing his best to cheer us up. He kneeled down by my bunk and took my hand, asked where I was wounded and what my regiment was and such, and when I told him he said, "Ah, Pennsylvania. Another of Governor Curtin's brave soldier boys. I see many of them here." Mrs. Lincoln looked at me and said, "So young, so young..." [39]

He would have went on for hours. Once you got Calvin talking, especially if you encouraged him, it was hard to shut him up, but about that time one of the nurses came by.

Now, most of the nurses were men—not many women could put up with the conditions in field hospitals—but this one was a honest to goodness female! She was a pleasant-looking matronly lady with a gentle smile, but she was evidently all business when it came to her patients.

"Now you boys shush, right now," she said. "Private Blanchard and the others in this tent need their rest."

I said, as I took my hat off in the presence of a lady for the first time in about a year, "All respects, ma'am, it was Private Blanchard doing all the talking."

She smiled and said, "That does not surprise me. He has been talking since they carried him in here. Now, Calvin, shush! Please give it a rest."

Calvin, meekly but with an affectionate grin, said, "Yes, Miz Barton."

We bid our goodbyes and filed out as orderly as we could. Seeing Calvin and George alive had cheered us up considerable—even Sergeant Alexander was buoyant—and we practically skipped back to camp. We almost forgot to take the wounded fellows with us!

Nurse Clara wore a dress with a sleeve torn by a bullet that had nearly missed her during the battle and killed the boy she was working on. She never patched the hole.

***

EMANCIPATION

War and politics. One and the same sometimes. I believe some great philosopher said something like that once, so don't give me credit for saying it again.

Politics was saying, on the one hand, that the separate states had a right to go their own way if they had a mind to; on the other, Abe's politics was saying no they couldn't, and we went to war over that difference of opinion. Sum it up by saying me and James went to war because the country was a-going to hell.

But after a year or so Abe saw that politics wasn't enough—that there was more to it, a moral issue that made all the politics of no account. The real question was whether or not does any human being have the right to literally own another human being. Those who sought to abolish slavery held that no matter how humane individual slave owners could claim they treated their "property" the system was immoral.

Now the leaders of Europe, 'specially England and France, thought southern gentry to be fine folk, aristocrats like themselves, overlooking that they ate grub raised by their slaves, off fine china washed and polished by their mammies, and the southern cotton that Europe bought was the product of the unpaid toil of a million black hands.

The rebs figured that Europe needed their cotton and that sooner or later old Abe's blockade would backfire and foreign governments would force the North to come to terms.

Abe seen that southern strategy working, after a fashion, so he took up pen and paper and wrote out one of the most decisive documents ever wrote. He called it the Emancipation Proclamation, and as of January the one, 1863, it said, all the slaves were to be free.

It was like he was telling everybody, all them European monarchs, all his political opponents, if you are for southern independence you are also for slavery, and shame on you if you are! He turned a political issue into a moral one, and vice versa. The proclamation was at once everything and nothing. Among other things it meant that every slave owner technically was thousands of dollars poorer of a sudden.

But it was nothing at all if we didn't win. Abe Lincoln framed the Emancipation Proclamation during the summer of 1862, but the war was going badly. He needed a victory, so that the proclamation would not look like the last desperate gasp of a losing cause.

Antietam would be that victory.

CHAPTER SEVEN
LOW POINT

I recollect the day George Cobham reported back to duty: October 22nd, 1862.

Antietam had been fought five weeks earlier. There were only ninety men in our ranks out of the thousand we had enrolled only a year earlier. Things looked dark for us. There was talk about consolidating us with another Pennsylvania regiment, which is always a sad fate for a proud unit. To accent the state of affairs, we were stationed on Loudoun Heights, at that time one of the most desolate places you could imagine between Arizona and the Sahara Desert. It was a high mountain overlooking Harper's Ferry. (The view was fine. Not just the autumn countryside, but the view of mile after mile of tents housing our army.) The 111th was practically isolated with only a very steep, rugged two-mile road—I should say, mule path—to the top. The ground was one complete bed of stone and rocks. The brush on the mountain had all been cut, and later it had all burned, making one of the blackest and most dismal places I ever seen. The wind blew ceaselessly up here, covering everything and everybody with dust and ashes.

So we looked more like a convention of chimney sweeps than anything else as we, what was left of us, came out to greet him. I will never forget his doleful look when he climbed down from his panting, borrowed steed and took a look around. I thought he was about to cry. Then the boys brought Billy, the colonel's own horse, over from the picket rope, and when the horse nuzzled his master's face and give a pitiful little nicker it looked like everybody else would cry, too. It was the most "human" thing I ever saw an animal do.

When the colonel had taken ill and went home to recover only a couple months earlier, we had still mustered at least five hundred men. Now some companies had some trouble getting enough men together for a decent poker game. Now that I think about it, this was THE miserable low point of our military existence; so bad that it was almost funny.

But life went on, and somehow we survived the consolidation axe. We, some of us, got assigned provost duty down in the town itself. So it was that we had what we first considered to be a once in a lifetime opportunity to have the Army of the Potomac pass in review before us. What happened was that McClellan finally got going, and almost the whole army was to pass through Harper's Ferry on its way back to the war.

At first it was novel and inspiring. Starting at two in the morning on October 31st, regiment after regiment passed over the pontoon bridge that spanned the Shenandoah River and marched up the valley on the opposite side of Loudoun Heights.

We started out hallooing and cheering our various states' regiments, especially them that had made a name for themselves, and the ones that were from close to home. We saw Berdan's U.S. Sharpshooters, all dressed in forest green uniforms. We had heard a great deal about them and were disappointed in their appearance—they were the dirtiest and worst drilled set of men I ever saw. One of their men, on hearing our comments, said, "Jings! I was chose by how I can shoot, not how good I comb my h'ar!" That fetched a chuckle from us. We envied their superior rifles: Sharps patent breechloader rifles, with adjustable sights and double-trigger set locks. Colonel Cobham swore he even saw a regiment from California, but I didn't notice it, and have since never seen a California outfit on any of the battle rolls of our eastern army. The new regiments made quite a contrast to the remnants of the old ones, with bright new uniforms, arms, and accouterments, and most were two or three times the size of the old ones.

The 83rd Pennsylvania marched past. They were mainly from Erie, Crawford, and Warren counties, and so we saw not a few familiar faces. Our colonel recognized their colonel, Strong Vincent of Erie, and rode a ways with him, exchanging pleasantries. The 83rd was just as depleted as we was, with a flag so full of bullet holes that we wondered what held it together. 'Course, ours wasn't in much better shape.

The best looking regiment was the 19th Maine, near one thousand strong, healthy looking fellers, and scarcely a man under six feet tall. Colonel Cobham murmured as they marched past, "I can't help but think how few of them will in all probability ever see Maine again." I had a wistful, mournful thought of the green hills of Warren County when he said that.

And so it went on, an unbroken column of men, horses, wagons, and artillery pieces, passing along until, by the next day, it was tiresome to see them pass. We ended up leaning on our muskets, or searching for a seat to take our ease, as our senses were dulled to the repetitious pomp and pageantry of war.

Late that day it was our turn to march out, but we had only marched a few miles when they turned us around and brought us back to the Ferry, where we were to stay as a garrison. I'll tell you, as we marched back it was difficult for us to stifle our cheers of joy over our good fortune, as we saw it. While the rest of the army marched away to fate and glory, we were permitted to take our ease in the familiar environs of Harper's Ferry.

In the early part of November, Calvin Blanchard and George Peters ran away from Smoketown Hospital in their hospital clothes and hoofed it down the tow path of the Sharpsburg and Georgetown Canal to Harper's Ferry. By twos and threes, the regiment was starting to regain strength, but we still only mustered 125 out of almost the thousand who had been with us when we first saw Harper's Ferry at the end of May.

It was at about this time that James's kid brother Bob joined the army. Harrison Allen had recovered from his illness, raised another company in Warren, and ended up commanding the new regiment, the 151st Pennsylvania Infantry. Notice the regimental numbers: the 83rd, 111th, and now the 151st. Each higher regimental number represents at least a thousand Pennsylvanians putting on a uniform and taking a rifle in their hands. A roster was in the *Warren Mail* newspaper on October 25, 1862. Among the ninety or so Warren County volunteers were fifteen young men from Farmington, including Frank Lyon, Charlie's brother; John and James Stanton; George Merchant; Paul Brown, and, of course, young Bob Miller. Their orderly sergeant, or first sergeant as they were also called, was old Judge Lott, who was well past fifty. Lottsville, over toward the west side of the county, is named after him and his kin.

You may wonder why, when our regiment and many others was down to a corporal's guard, that they made new regiments instead of just sending the men to us. Such a system would have made a great deal of sense. Like James said, the men would have learned faster when assigned to an old regiment. At Antietam the strawfoot regiments suffered a high percentage of the overall losses. Well, it was politics again. New regiments meant that all the state governors would be in the position to reward loyal supporters by making them majors and colonels and such. It was just another form of political patronage, pure and simple.

But we did get a few good laughs out of letters that James got from his brother Bob, who by then was learning the art of soldiering with his regiment up at Camp Russell near Harrisburg.

We fervently hoped that we would stay at the Ferry until the end of the war, but we knew that could not be. Sooner or later, they'd need us. Not that we were on vacation, mind. Harper's Ferry was the main supply depot for McClellan but it was a shambles. When the rebs had captured the place in September they had taken or destroyed everything of value. The Potomac railroad bridge had been burned two or three times, but it had been rebuilt, and four or five trains came in, heavily loaded, each day.

Two of our boys were taken prisoner while on picket on November 5th. We saw rebs most every day, but we weren't marching or fighting. That suited us. Detached from the regiment, we did six hours of provost guard duty each day, from six to nine, morning and evening, so as James said we had all night to sleep and most all day to play. The food was good for a change, and we slept under a roof, while the rest of the regiment was in tents, and the weather was turning cold…

***

GOODBYE, LITTLE MAC

Harper's Ferry Nov the 12th

"There is a good deal of excitement among both privates and officers in regard to the removal of McClellan from the post of commander of this army. Everyone is dissatisfied with it. I hope it may be all for the best, but one thing is certain: although we consider Burnside a good general, he has not the confidence of the men in his ability to command a large army that Little Mac had. In fact, there is no man in the army that the men have as much faith in as they have in McClellan." [40]

Well, you heard it here first, folks. As James reports, General McClellan got the sack, but he don't say why. McClellan--well, I told you about him enough, I suppose. He was finally sacked for wanting too much and doing too little with it. For instance, there was the exchange of correspondence toward the end when McClellan wrote to the War

Department about needing more horses for the cavalry, because what he had was worn out. Lincoln replied, "You will pardon me for asking what your cavalry has done lately that would wear out anything???" When you get that kind of sarcasm from the boss, you have to know the end is near.

Like I told you, the men in the ranks fairly idolized McClellan. Yours truly too, I suppose. He had built the army up from nothing and made soldiers of us all. He gave us such a sense of ***belonging*** that it has never faded, even after all these years, and will not die until the last of us is in his grave.

We the army, both enlisted and officers, were so attached to McClellan that Lincoln had to take our sentiments into account when he finally decided that Mac had to go. For good. Abe was genuinely for good reason concerned that if he tried to fire Our General he would find the entire Army of the Potomac on his doorstep next morning. If the military took over the country, the great experiment in democracy would be over. More than a war would be lost.

He sent General Buckingham, a staff officer in the Inspector General's office, down from Washington with the necessary orders, but Buckingham was first to go to Burnside and get assurance that he would take the command. If Burnside refused, Buckingham was to go back to Washington with the orders still in his pocket, and I don't know what Abe's next move would have been. Don't know, because it all went smoothly.

Burnside took the job—reluctantly. Any notions about the army bringing down the government turned out to be just reckless campfire talk, for which a few brash officers got canned. And, most important, McClellan was enough of a patriot to see the damage that would have been done and to shy from it. He packed his bags, there were some emotional farewells, and Mac rode out of our camps, but not out of our hearts, forever.

***

BURNSIDE

Hmm-mmm...Ambrose Burnside. Sounds like the name of somebody you picked on in school. He wore these big mutton-chop whiskers that not quite met at his chin. Sideburns got their name from Burnside. His claim to fame lies in the whiskers department rather than in military skill.

Burnside was a strange chap. He was modest—for good reason, as it turned out. Commanding a brigade, he had fought well at First Bull Run. He had scored a considerable success for the Union down in North Carolina early in '62, carving out a bridgehead in the New Bern area that would become a thorn in the side of the Confederacy throughout the war and end up being a factor in its demise. With all that went on out west and here in Virginia, the South never could muster the strength to yank out that thorn. I believe James wrote about all this in one of his Baltimore letters. Taking New Bern was a comparatively small-scale affair that pioneered combined operations betwixt the army and the navy, and Burnside was good at this particular kind of work, an executive and coordinator *par excellance.*

A real battle was another matter. At Antietam he had dallied down on the far end of the battle line, taking hours to take a bridge over a creek that was easily waded in most places, and then getting his corps stampeded in the last Confederate counterattack of the day. Obviously, it was in spite of all this that Lincoln gave the Army of the Potomac to him. The reasons for the promotion were that Burnside was not ambitious or "political" and he was the only general handy that could claim even a small success. So, hello, General Burnside and hello, Fredericksburg.

Fredericksburg is on the south bank of the Rappahannock River. It changed hands many times in the early course of the war, the Rappahannock becoming the real dividing line between Union and Confederate territory. Burnside took over the army, put on a burst of un-McClellan speed, and soon had most of the army lined up across from Fredericksburg while half of Lee's army (Jackson's half) was still in the Shenandoah Valley, with us keeping a nervous eye on it. It was a matter of quickly crossing the river and overwhelming Longstreet's half, then attending to Jackson.

What do you need for to cross a river? Book says you need a bridge. Later in the war, in the Carolinas, we crossed over rivers on bridges made of cracker boxes if we had to. Burnside, though, he had these big pontoon bridges that he ordered to meet him at the Rappahannock. And he waited for them to show up. Well, due to mud and faulty staff work, they were delayed—for weeks. And the army sat there and waited for them, while the Confederates united their army, dug trenches and rifle pits and gun positions, and waited for the attack.

This is where Burnside fell short. His mind wasn't fast enough to change the plan once it went sour. He finally got his pontoons, crossed his army over, and attacked the well-fortified rebel army on December 12, 1862. The results were predictable. In his next letter, James calls it a slaughter.

And us? The only thing we did, early in December, was to make a heavy reconnaissance into the Shenandoah.

Calvin had just rejoined the regiment and was supposed to remain in camp but he persuaded the captain to let him go along. We went in light marching order, but still it was too much for him and he was permitted to ride in the headquarters wagon. He wasn't so poorly that he couldn't do a little foraging on the side, so that he and Wesley Culver invited me and James over and we had fried chicken for supper.

Three or four inches of snow fell the next day. We were without blankets. We went into camp in a cornfield where the corn was in the shock, took rails for firewood, and made a lean-to of rails and covered it with cornstalks. We all bunked together, huddled together spoon fashion for warmth. Calvin had such a pain in his hip, where he had been wounded the last time, that he couldn't lay in one position very long and when he had to turn over he called out "spoon whop" and everyone had to turn over at the same time. In language more forceful than elegant we told him to go to hell or at least go sleep somewheres else. From then on he was called Spoony when not on duty. Even Colonel Cobham sometimes called him Spoony. [41]

We had been sent on scout to see if Jackson was still in the valley. He was, but "Just leaving, thank you." His rear guard evacuated Winchester as we came in, so that town changed hands again for the umpteenth time. A cold and miserable hike it was, and after four days and nights of hardship we were glad to pull back to the relative comforts of Harper's Ferry.

A week later we were on the march for Fredericksburg. The battle was fought while we were moving, about the third day or so, so it must have been an afterthought to have us rejoin the main army. Even in the best of seasons it would have been impossible to move from the Ferry to the Rappahannock in three days—and this was certainly not the best of seasons. It got cold, it started to rain, and all those Virginia roads became seas of mud.

There's another old joke about a veteran who was asked if he had ever been through Virginia, and he says, "Yes, in a number of places." James described it very well: Guns and wagons sunk in the gooey red Virginia clay like they were going to pop through and come out in China. Slogging in that mud exhausted men and animals before they had gone three miles.

Camp in the woods, five miles south of Fairfax Courthouse, Va. Dec the 22nd, 1862

"...for nine days we were on the march. The first night we stayed near the village of Hillsborough, passing through a very pleasant and I should think a rich farming country. The next day we went three miles beyond Leesburg which is a place of some two thousand inhabitants. The place has a dilapidated, neglected appearance, but that is the case with all the towns in Virginia that I have seen. The country was for most of the way on the second day's march, through a rich wheat and corn valley. If it could only have the benefit of Northern culture, it would be a perfect paradise for farming. The third day we went some eight miles in the forenoon and encamped at a place called Gum Spring and stayed, and the next day we went to Fairfax Court House. Our route after we got some eight miles from Leesburg passed though a very pretty country but I think that the soil is very poor and cold....

We have had the worst time for grub on this march that we ever had; for the first time since I have been a soldier, I have been hungry and had nothing to eat...Since we got here, we have had enough to eat (such as it is). The country from here as far as we went was the poorest I have seen in the state and as poor as I ever saw in my life. The roads were the most horrible, muddy ones I ever saw, and in plenty of places the wagons were dragging on the axles...

What do you civilians think of your favorite General Burnside? I think after the fight or, more properly, slaughter, at Fredericksburg, the less we have of such generalship the better for us. I feel the most discouraged I have been since being in the army

P.S. I got a letter from Susan dated December the 9th. She said that she was bothered to find fodder for her cows. I would like to have some of the boys go and get them and keep them through the winter

if they can, and sell one of them if possible. I will pay them for it if I live to come home. I am afraid that if she tries to keep them that they will die before spring. If you get someone to keep them, I shall be very thankful..." [42]

The Union Army withdrew from the frozen bloody fields in front of the Confederate positions at Fredericksburg. Most of the troops were pulled back to the north bank of the Rappahannock, but Burnside left a bridgehead force on the south side, holding Fredericksburg itself, just in case he ever wanted to make the attack again over that ground. Brr-rr, what a thought! The carnage had been awful; the aftermath was obscene: During a truce, the frozen, naked bodies were piled into trenches scratched in the icy earth. They, the dead, were naked because the Johnnies had crawled out in the dark and taken their clothing and equipment. You have to be philosophical about that as the Johnnies needed those warm overcoats, and the former wearers did not need them anymore.

With the last shots fired by our rear guard the fighting ended in the east for the year 1862. It had been a terrible year. As 1863 come in, a lot of us got to feeling that it would be a year of decision, one way or the other. If the new year would not bring victory, it would at least show who would win.

In many ways, that winter in Virginia was the most enjoyable of my army experience. Although there were a few diversions to interrupt our slumber, we basically went into winter quarters after we caught up with the rest of the army. I forget exactly when, but the army came out with these little tents—we called them dog tents—some time in later '62. Pup tents, same thing. Well, for field use they replaced the big old cumbersome Sibley tents that required wagons to haul and three men and a boy to put up. With a dog tent, you carried half and your bunkie carried half, and you buttoned it together to make a passable abode for most weather. We only put up Sibleys if we expected to stay in one place for a while.

Permanent winter quarters required something a little more substantial. If living in a log cabin made you presidential material, there were hundreds of thousands of candidates in those days. We built them, chopping and notching the logs, making chimneys of mud and sticks and barrels, topping them with our shelter tent canvas. It was hard work, but healthy, and it filled the hours with activity as we strove to put a roof over our heads. Usually it was four men to a hut, and with a committee like that creativity and ingenuity knew no bounds. On some general's whim our camp might be moved—and it was, more than once—but we would go to work with a will at our new address and in a surprisingly short time we would be set up for housekeeping.

We also drilled and built fortifications. There was very little grousing as we dug and chopped. For one thing, it was healthy exercise, better then sitting around, for another it was better to be safe than sorry, and for another (not that we knew it), we were perfecting techniques that would be put to good use later on. We and the enemy had discovered that standing up in an open field and blazing away at each other was damned foolish business to be avoided if possible. The way I see it, first the rebs discovered it, and then us enlisted Yankees discovered it, and finally our officers got it through their thick heads. General Geary was one of the more enlightened of our officers. We dug trenches in places where we were no more likely to be attacked than if we had been on the moon.

Camp near Union Mills, Va Dec the 28th, 1862

"Yesterday, I heard that Brother's regiment was here and I got a pass to come here to see him. I am sorry to say that I found him quite sick with typhoid fever, but I think that he will get along without much danger in a few days. Still, it seemed very hard to find him sick after not seeing him for more than a year. But he was pleased to see me and you may bet that he was not more so than I...

I think that Robert will have as good care as is possible under the circumstances. I had quite a visit with the colonel, Harrison Allen, and he gave Robert a very good name. It is a very good regiment. They have learned very fast and I think they will give a good account of themselves if they are called upon to defend their flag...

I find that William Carr is well and so are all the rest of the men in his company that I know." [43]

James's words about the potential of Bob's regiment, the 151st Pennsylvania Volunteers, was quite an accurate—I might say uncanny—prediction.

Camp in the woods near Fairfax Station, Va Jan the 4th

"I am lying on the ground in a Sibley tent without fire and my paper spread on Mother Earth, but still things are not so bad as they might be. If they will only let us stay here and not keep us on the run,

we will get along bully. You have no doubt seen the letter I wrote to Father on the 28th of last month from Union Mills in which I told him of Brother Robert's sickness. I left him on the 30th and he was considerably better than he had been. Have not heard from him since I left him, but think he will get along after a while, though it will be some time before he is fit for duty. I left camp to go and see Robert on the afternoon of the 27th and the same night at ten o'clock our Division were marched to meet the rebel cavalry under Stuart, Fitzhugh Lee, and Hampton. The next day they had a slight skirmish with them, but the rebs thought discretion the better part of valor and run as fast as their horses could carry them.

The box of things that the folks were kind enough to send to me I have not got yet, but still hope I may soon, for it would come good to me now. But if I don't get it, I will do the best I can without it, and if I only have the good luck to have as good health as I have had so far, I shall get along very well. Whether I get the box or not, I shall be very thankful to you and the rest of the folks for sending it." [44]

The shooting stopped for a spell, but the war went on. In Virginia we fought against boredom and discouragement. Discouragement the worst ever. With two years of war, none of us dared to guess when it would all end. Problems at home took their toll, too.

***

THE HOME FRONT

Nov 24th, 1862

"...If you do go to see Susan this coming winter, I want you to do the best you can to cheer and encourage her, for she must have a lonesome, terrible time of it. Worse than all the rest is Johnny being sick so long. Must be a terrible trial and how she stands the fatigue of taking care of him is more than I can understand. I want you and the rest of our folks to write her often for it will help greatly to cheer her, to think that my folks pay some attention to her. For my sake I want you all to be as kind as you can to her and the children, which I am sure you all will be. The thought of them makes me often feel lonesome and homesick—if it were not for them, I should like being a soldier first rate.

George Henry appears to think that the Democratic victories in the state elections this fall will have the effect to shorten the war. I hope it may, but for the life of me, I can't see how it is a-going to do it and I know that the rebels that we take prisoner tell us with an air of triumph that we are getting divided among ourselves. They point to the Democratic majorities for proof and are very much tickled about it. You can tell as well as I can whether that will have a tendency to shorten the war." [45]

Recounting the horrors of the battle and the hardships of the march challenges my powers of description, but I feel even more unequal to the task of doing justice to Susan's life in those days. In fact, it cannot be done. No storyteller, no writer, no novelist, has yet captured the private misery, the gnawing foreboding, the constant drudgery, endured by Susan and the other million "Girls We Left Behind Us."

We lost an officer that winter, as well out of the war as if he had been killed or wounded or taken prisoner. Captain Langworthy, a good man, had a wife that was, as James said, "...not true to her conjugal vows" and had got herself a baby. Susan told me of Langworthy's visit when I dropped by to see her in 1882. She put up with a lot of lonely winters in those days, with callers few. Having a visitor was a real event, remembered long after all the other days had faded to a blur. She remembered the captain's pain, and his stuttering manner of talking. It went something like what I am about to relate:

January in Southwest Township. When it gets cold up there, the air is like brittle glass, and the world turns gray. Slate sky, the bare scraggly limbs of the thicket, the crusted snow where the sun, being always low in the sky, shoots its pale rays across the dead fields. All gray, all gray.

But a rose streak told of the setting sun as Susan stepped out into the silent world, catching her breath as the icy stillness wrapped around her. She chopped doggedly at the icy layer on top of the water barrel and dipped a kettleful for the house. Every noise sounded like flint on steel.

She heard the sound of horseshoes striking the frozen road with bell-like clarity. Peering, she saw a solitary somber figure on horseback round the curve in the road. Clad in an army overcoat of light blue, he rode slowly, head down, up to the picket gate. For a split moment she dared to hope it was James, but no such miracle. She recognized the rider, finally, as he swung wearily down from his horse.

"Why, it's Captain Langworthy," she exclaimed, with a cheeriness she did not feel—not so much because of her own situation but because she had heard rumors of the reason behind the captain's leave.

The captain took her hand as he stepped onto the porch. "Mrs. Miller. It's…ah…good to see you…ah…I hope I've not come at a bad time."

"Oh, no, Captain. Please do come in. It is so seldom that we have callers up here, that there is never a bad time to receive one."

"Good, good," he said as they entered the house. "I expect I'll trod up your floor…ah…so I'll stay here by the door."

"No, no, come by the fire! You must be froze. I could get you some tea." She set the kettle on the woodstove. Robert was doing lessons on a slate board at the table, Ellen was in the loft, playing quietly with her rag dolls, and Johnny was coughing fitfully in his little bed in the corner. The room was neat and tidy but dark, not much relieved by the light of a single lantern which glowed over the center of the table.

Captain Langworthy removed his gloves and held his hands over the stove. "I…ah…promised the men that I would call on as many of their families as I could during my short stay, to reassure them of their men's welfare..."

"I appreciate your calling, Captain."

"...but I make a special point of stopping here, ma'am. I wish to tell you…ah…how much I thoroughly admire your husband. He is a good man and a good soldier. He deserves the support and loyalty which you give..." He made a vague motioning reference to their surroundings. "This must be very difficult for you."

"It is. But what cannot be helped must be endured," she said in a resigned way.

"Would that my wife could have had half the loyalty that you—" He caught himself up short. "I'm sorry. A true gentleman would not discuss such things as where that statement may lead."

"My sympathies go with you, Captain Langworthy. I know it would be impossible now for you not to condemn her, but she is young and the pressures of the world nowadays would have been impossible for us to imagine a few short years ago."

"Quite, quite," agreed the captain as he hastily brushed a glove across a cheek where a tear may have formed. He stood stiffly. "You must forgive me, but I'll take that tea at a later time. I had hoped to stop at the cemetery and see Washington White's grave, and I am spending the night at his parents' house."

Susan escorted him to the door. "I should like to give you a small package to take to James if it would be no trouble. When do you return?"

"The twentieth. I would be glad to return in a day or two to pick it up—and have that cup of tea."

"It will be ready."

"Goodbye, Mrs. Miller. God bless you."

"The same to you, Captain."

He opened the door and was gone.

***

Susan to Robert and Janet Miller, January 10th, 1863

Dear Parents,

I received your kind and welcome letter last Sunday and was glad to hear that Mother was no worse. I wish I could see her. I get so lonesome and discouraged that I hardly know what to do with myself. We are all well except Johnny—he is quite sick. Dr. Wilson from Neilsburg was here yesterday. He said that Johnny had bronchitis. He thought he could help him and left medicine for him. The first dose was a pill of calomel. He took six doses of physic oil and pills before it had any effect. I was quite alarmed about him—he is very pale and poor. The doctor said I must not take him out in less than three or four weeks providing he got better.

I watch him very close night and day. The doctor thought he would have sinking spells, but he has not had any yet. My sister is with me. I have not heard from James since I wrote to Jane. I shall look for a letter on Monday. I wish he was at home to help me take care of Johnny, but I suppose he can't come this winter. If he lives to come home when the war is done, I shall be thankful.

Captain Langworthy is at home; he is going back the 20th. He came rather unexpectedly. In regard to the money, I have thirteen dollars yet, and it will last me some time. If George Henry and Jane come down as I hope they may, if you could get one pound of tea and ten ditto of sugar and send down by them, it would greatly oblige me and would answer in place of the money.

Give my love to all and write soon.

Affectionately, Your daughter,

Susan Ann Miller [46]

I wonder how many times it was in those years that she said such as that: "I shall look for a letter Monday."

Besides the loneliness and boredom, both at home and there in the army, there was the battles against sickness waged that winter. The 111th, the two hundred fifty men or so that remained out of the original thousand, was a hardy lot by then, but other regiments were not so fortunate. The 151st Pennsylvania, Rob's regiment, was wracked by all the diseases in the catalogue. Sickness would end up taking out more than half of the regiment. Sometimes God will work in mysterious ways, however. Another regiment, namely the 20th Maine, was quarantined that spring due to a smallpox epidemic and missed the Battle of Chancellorsville. Their reprieve from losing men in that battle may have been their saving grace when they would be tasked to hold a rocky hill at Gettysburg.

Well, you may have an idea by now of how much the Miller parents, especially Missus Miller, worried about their sons. Her illness was probably a true example of a psychological worry contributing to a physical downfall. Anyway, when they got the news that Rob was down with The Typhoid they wrote him off as having both feet in the grave, and nothing reassuring from Virginia could convince them otherwise. Rob's friend, Sergeant Paul Brown, was asked to send the body home. Paul replied, and I quote, "I will try to do all that lies in my power to comply with your wishes but to say the least of this matter posable he is not agoing to dy at present he is doing first rate." The whole matter reminds me of what Mark Twain had to say when the newspapers reported his passing: "The report of my death is an exaggeration."

Camp in the woods near Fairfax Station, Va Jan the 15th, 1863

"You say that the weather is very unsteady there. Here this has been the most pleasant winter weather I ever saw by all odds. In fact, it has seemed like pleasant October weather a great deal more than it has like December. Last night it rained which makes it quite unpleasant around camp this morning.

...I wrote a letter to you from Union Mills the first time I went to see Robert. Last Saturday I went the second time and he was as well as I expected to find him. He has had a very hard run of typhoid fever, but I think he has passed the crisis and is gaining strength slowly. If he were not to catch any cold he will get along after a while though it will be some time before he will be fit for duty. He has been over four

weeks confined to his bed but he seemed in first-rate spirits and he told me that he had not been homesick a bit. The first time I was down to see him was at the time of Stuart's raid. I stayed with him three days and in that time the rebels were hovering on the lines and his regiment was about one-half of them on picket and the rest were under arms the most of the time. But it did not seem to excite Robert a bit; in fact, not half as much as it did me, for I did not know whether the boys would stand fire or not. I felt it would not do for me to run, and I could not relish the idea of being taken prisoner. But they did not come in any force and since that time we have not had any excitement.

I was pleased to hear that you had taken the old cow, for from what Susan wrote, I began to think that the chances were that some of them would starve. I have very little confidence in Father Main's ability to winter the heifer and red cow. I expect it will cost me more to winter the two than they are worth before I get through with him, but be that as it may I will trust luck. The last letter I got from her, Susan, the youngest boy was worse and no prospect of his ever being any better, and she said that she was a-going to go to her father's to stay until the child got better or worse. Under the circumstances, I can't say anything against it, but I don't like the arrangement at all if it could be helped..." [47]

With the ringing in of 1863, the Emancipation Proclamation went into effect, and ending slavery finally became an official goal of the war. Some folks were in favor of the proclamation, and some weren't, and it was a strange document when you think about it. For one thing, it did NOT free the slaves in states that had NOT seceded from the Union. For another, it did not actually free a single slave in any place where the Union Army was not physically there, on the ground, in control. With the ebb and flow of coming campaigns, some slaves were freed and then enslaved again a half-dozen times as we came and went. I'd imagine some wore themselves out celebrating all the time.

So it was all up to the army. As pleasant as it was to sit still and enjoy the October-like weather, which was about to change, we were not doing a thing toward winning the war; so, in the midst of winter, we embarked on another campaign. In the history books, stuck in the middle of a succession of campaigns with heroic names like Antietam, Chancellorsville, and Gettysburg, there is an ugly thing that went down in history as "Mud March." James described it in a letter to the folks:

Camp in the woods near Aquia Creek, Va Jan the 28th/63

"...In the first place, my health is good and has been so, notwithstanding the fatigue and exposure of the last two weeks. It has been the worst march that we have had since being in Virginia. We started from Fairfax on the 18th with the weather cold and the roads in good condition. For two days it continued so. On the night of the 20th it commenced to rain and it has hardly stopped since. The roads are in the most horrible state and it took hard work to get four miles in a day. I never saw half so many horses and mules dead in the road on any march as I saw on this last one. We had nothing but our shelter tents to protect us from the storms at night, and taken all together, it was as nasty and unpleasant a time as could be well imagined. It was no uncommon sight to see from fifty to sixty baggage wagons and half as many artillery wagons and caissons stuck in the mud and all in sight at the same time. Quite often, I saw from six to ten teams hitched to one wagon and even then it took the help of as many men to move it. On the roads in your country, Old Jim and Bet would have drawn the load easy, but the soil is a tough quicksand clay, and often, the wagons were in the mud until the hubs were all out of sight. But all things human have an end, and after six days of terrible labor, we got through to here." [48]

Burnside was determined to make up for Fredericksburg, and all his senior generals advised against going up against the rebs dug in behind the town. The wonder is that he had to be talked out of it, when any fool second-grader would have seen the stupidity of trying that trick again.

So he came up with a plan that he should have tried out in December. He decided to make a short move to the right, upriver from Lee's army, and cross the river where we would be almost unopposed. It was a good idea, and his replacement would end up doing almost the same thing in May. The problem was, Burnside picked the wrong time of the year to try it. Rain, snow, and sleet fell in abundance, and the entire army wound up stuck in the mud.

Well, sir, with that farce being the last straw, Burnside gave up. He went back to his old Ninth Corps with the blessing of Lincoln and the War Department, and Fighting Joe Hooker took command of the Army of the Potomac.

James goes on:

"...We heard that Burnside is superseded and Hooker had taken the command. If so, I don't know what will come next, and it don't make much difference, for it seems to me that the government is determined not to let us do anything. They keep moving our generals so, that I wonder that the men do not get more discouraged than they are..." [49]

Yup, Burn said, I don't want to be boss of the Army of the Potomac no more. It's just ain't workin' out.

CHAPTER EIGHT
ALL QUIET ON THE RAPPAHANNOCK

About here, before things start popping in the spring campaign of '63, I suppose I need to give you an idea of what was the larger goings on, both in Virginia and all along the front to the Mississippi. Might take some back-tracking. I haven't told you much about the western armies since Shiloh, which was back in April of '62.

Grant. Well, Grant, he was in the doghouse awhile after Shiloh. True to his present and future form, Grant had stood firm there, chewing unlighted segars to bits while he calmly patched together a battle line enough to stop Sidney Johnston and G.T. Beauregard. But the bottom fact was, he had been caught unawares and generals are always supposed to be up on things.

Took a while, but Grant finally got top command again in western Tennessee and along the Mississippi down to Vicksburg. That was partly because many of his fellow generals went on to bigger things. Halleck came east. I told you about him, and John Pope, too. Up like a rocket and down like a stick against Robert E. Lee. I wonder what would of happened if Grant had been brought east back then instead of Pope...

Well, out in the west the Johnnies lashed out with their own invasions and attacks at the same time that Lee came across the Potomac and we fought Antietam. Sounds like it was all planned and coordinated, but it wasn't. It just all happened to happen at the same time.

The rebs invaded Kentucky in the fall of '62. Two smallish armies, under Generals Kirby Smith and Braxton Bragg, went tearing north from Knoxville and Chattanooga, scaring the hell out of the loyal citizens of Kentucky and also those of Ohio, who found themselves digging trenches on their own side of the river, just in case. (They were never used.) The Union Army of the Ohio, under General Don Carlos Buell, gave chase all the way to Louisville.

Bragg and Smith were independent of each other. With an overall commander, like Lee was in Virginia, they might have accomplished something, but each had his own plan and seemed to be worried more about what the other was doing than about the Yankees. The only battle to speak of happened at a place called Perryville. It was dry there in Kentucky, and the battle was over water holes rather than points of strategy. The rebs finally pulled back into Tennessee, and a potentially decisive campaign died on the vine.

They tried to invade western Tennessee. Forces under Grant were strung out across northern Mississippi, and nasty little battles were fought at places you probably never heard of, like Corinth and Iuka. In the end, Grant's men stayed put, and the rebs pulled back deeper into Mississippi.

One of Grant's generals, a brilliant and quirky feller by the name of William Rosecrans, distinguished himself at Corinth, and in the fall Lincoln hired him to replace Buell. Rosecrans took his army, renamed the Army of the Cumberland, down to Murfreesboro, Tennessee, and them and Bragg fought a battle that began on New Year's Eve, 1862, and ended on January 2nd, 1863. The battle was hard-fought, with over ten thousand men (twenty-five percent) lost on each side, and in the end Bragg retreated deeper into Tennessee. Like most battles it had two names; the rebs called it Murfreesboro, we called it Stone's River.

It was at about this point in our military career that we became stevedores. Our brigade was parked closest to Aquia Creek landing, where supply ships came down the bay to us. From the landing a railroad was put in commission to Falmouth, where most of the army was concentrated. We spent long hours unloading ships and loading supplies on at least twelve trains a day, but at least it kept us busy.

I'm going to breeze through a few of James's winter letters with you this afternoon. He had some interesting things to say, and there wasn't much else going on except to get ready for the spring campaign.

Camp near Aquia Creek, Va, Feb the 6th 63

"...There are not more than 150 effective men left of us, but what are left, are ready and willing to do our whole duty to our country. As far as mortal men can, so far will the 111th P.V. do their full share of putting down this most accursed and unprovoked rebellion. If there ever was a causeless resistance to legal and legitimate authority, this war is it--resistance without the least provocation in the world. I do hope that Old Abe's Emancipation Proclamation will have universal

success, for as far as I can see, there is not other cause for this war but slavery and the sooner it is done, the better for us...

...The 9th Army Corps has been ordered to Fortress Monroe. As that is the old Corps of Burnside's, I think he is a-going to take the command in North Carolina again." [50]

Camp in the woods near Aquia Creek, Va Feb the 12

"...I think that you all have been somewhat needlessly alarmed about [Robert.] *He has been quite sick yet not very dangerously so, and he told me that his head had not been a bit affected--not so much as to give him a headache. The whole tendency of his fever was to congestion of the bowels. I think from what I could see and hear the last time I saw him there is but very little danger. He will get along without any trouble, only it will be some time before he will be fit for duty. That is all I am afraid of--that he will attempt doing duty before he is able to stand the fatigue. I told him that he must be careful of that and I hope he will, for there are a great many men that are ruined by trying to do their duty before they are able to.*

Our Corps is consolidated with the Eleventh Corps under the command of General Sigel, and forms the reserve. We are encamped about one mile from the landing. Some of our regiment are doing guard duty along the railroad and some of them are kept busy loading stores on the cars to supply the army at Falmouth..." [51]

Camp near Aquia Creek, Va Feb the 18th

"...I was sorry to hear that Mother had been sick. I am afraid that she helps to make herself unwell by fretting about her boys that are in the army. If I knew of anything to write that would prevent her from doing so, I would gladly do it but I have written and said everything that I know...

We have a very nice camp, our shanties being warm and dry, thanks to our industry. There is a shanty for every four men; we have a good floor in ours and a nice little fireplace. Although it is very stormy today (a mixture of snow and rain) I am warm and dry and as comfortable and contented as is possible for a man to be in the army, away from the endearments of family and friends. If I never had anything worse to do than we have here I would like to be a soldier very well, but a soldier's life is a succession of extremes--first a long period of inactivity followed by a time when all his energies both mental and physical are taxed to the utmost.

I was sorry to hear that Harm Cooper was dead. Poor fellow--the last time I saw him, which was a few days after the Battle of Cedar Mountain, he looked as healthy and hearty as a buck, and now poor fellow, he has gone to his long home where this accursed war is sending so many thousands of our bravest and our best. But then such is the fate of war.

You seem to think that the war will be closed next summer. Well, I sincerely hope it may, that is if it can be honorably settled. But if it is to be a dishonorable one, I would rather that it would last for the next five years than that it should be closed to suit the opinion of the rebel sympathizers in the North. If the so-called Democrats force us to make a disgraceful peace they will deserve the curses of every lover of his country, and if this war is unsuccessful, the traitors in the North will be more to blame than all the rebs in the South...

I think that if the Democrats in the North are successful in their efforts to close this war, they will have another--only a worse one--in less than ten years. And if I live to get home safe, the Democrats may do their own fighting in the next war unless I am drafted.

...You can tell all the friends that I am heartily in favor of old Abe Lincoln's policy of freeing the niggers." [52]

Camp near Aquia Creek, Va Feb the 25th 63

"*...Was glad to hear that George Henry and Jane had started to see Susan for I know a visit from any of my folks would do her a great deal of good. Poor girl--she must have a terribly lonesome and fatiguing time with the children. They are sick so much of the time. I was pleased to hear that you had sent her some money for her funds which must be getting low. We got two months' pay since we came to Aquia, but I had to throw away so much clothing during the forced marches and retreats of last summer, and had to draw new clothing in place of what I was ordered to throw away, that I overdrew my share of clothing to the amount of $15.95, and had to settle the account at the last pay day. That, with what I owed the sutler, took the whole of the two months' pay so that I had none to send her. But we have the promise of getting four months' pay next month and if we do I will try and send some to Susan...*

Warren Foster has resigned his commission, been honorably discharged, and gone home. What his object is, I can't tell--I don't

believe he can get the same amount of pay for anything he can do at home. But then I guess he didn't relish the fatigues and exposures of a soldier's life. Well, I for one am glad he has gone for he has been trying to get out of the service a good while and has at last succeeded..." [53]

Camp near Aquia Creek Va March the 3rd

"...Lieutenant Colonel Cobham has got his commission as Colonel and I think he is one of the best of men, both as an officer and a citizen. He is just as mild, affable, sociable, and gentlemanly now as he was in Warren. Still, he is a strict disciplinarian and when the occasion requires it he can put on as much style as anybody. But to see him around the Camp when not in the discharge of his official duties, he is so quiet you would think he was a visitor and not the commander..." [54]

I suppose possibly you think our system of electing our officers and noncoms was a curious way of doing business. Well, it worked better than you might expect, at least in the long run.

At first we tended to vote for people we liked: fellers who were personable, agreeable, and easy-going. So, our officers tended to be: personable, agreeable, and easy-going. Discipline suffered accordingly. After all, if Captain So-and-So threw Private Such 'n Such into the stockade for some infraction, then Such 'n Such might not vote for So-and-So the next time around.

Later on, after we "saw the elephant," we judged our leaders by a new set of rules. If Officer A (Old So-and-So) was a fine, sociable fella who knew not a whit about leading men into combat, he would lose out to Officer B, the man who, in a fair and honest way, made you toe the mark, who might not have been the most agreeable campfire companion but knew how to extricate from possibly murderous situations on the field of battle. Cool nerves, keen eye, decisiveness. Those qualities got MY vote.

We found ourselves in the winter of '63 in a quandary. The issue was not as clear-cut as the imaginary situations I just exampled to you. We had two fine officers wanting to command the regiment: George Cobham and Tom Walker.

Now, Cobham never personally politicked for the position except by doing the best job he could in his position. Since May of '62, except when The Typhoid laid him low in August and September, he had for all intents and purposes been the commander of the regiment, due to Schlaudecker's poor health or temporary elevation to brigade command most of the time.

Tom Walker, on the other hand, had led us at Cedar Mountain and Antietam and we knew he was a brave and capable officer. He was also extremely ambitious. Being from the Big City of Erie, he had more connections and influence than did George Cobham, and he did not hesitate to use all his resources to try to get command of the 111th. That winter he took three leaves of absence to go to Harrisburg to lobby Governor Curtin to appoint him colonel. He also invested in a five-gallon keg of whiskey come election time in the regiment.

Well, I drank the major's whiskey but voted for George Cobham. The results of the election were not binding on the governor, and the outset was that Cobham got the eagle insignia of full colonel. Major Tom was rather crestfallen over the whole matter, but he got over it and did his duty as second in command. His opportunity to command would come again, far down the road.

James T. Miller also got a promotion during the spring reorganization. Sometimes it seemed as if the louder and rowdier men got noticed and promoted over the quiet solid types (like James) who just did the job without a lot of bitching and complaining, so it was refreshing to see him get promoted to corporal. Fifth corporal was a long ways from being "General of the Army," being as how there was only six corporals to a full company, but I thought it was the least due him. He never missed a day of duty, always was counted present on the morning report, and was one of the steadiest men I ever knew. When I heard of his promotion, while he was off visiting Charlie Todd in the 145th Pennsylvania, I drew a new sack coat in his size and sewed his corporal stripes on with my own hands, and presented it to him on his return. As for me, I was just as happy remaining a private.

I'm taking a train to visit my niece down near Atlanta over the holidays. A lot of my comrades are still in Georgia; the most of them are in the Marietta Cemetery. I'm going to visit them, too.

***

A NEW YEAR

For those who weren't here when I started my yarn, it was on a hot day around the 4th of July that we all got together on my front porch to share some lemonade and tall tales. Well, I shouldn't say "tall tales" as the most of it is true: The way it was for us in the 111th Pennsylvania Volunteers in the field, and the way it was for the folks who stayed home. Anyway, we moved indoors here by the fireplace around the end of October, and popcorn, hot cider, and coffee became the menu. I look forward to moving out on the porch again when the weather permits. Here we are in a new year, 1863, in my tale also and we still have a long way to go. Here's hoping that you don't run out of patience and I don't run out of time. If you know what I mean.

If you missed some of these talks, there's a young feller been sitting off by himself at every session, a-trying to write down all I say. Says he's a-going to write a book someday. Whilst I was down in Atlanta the town was all abuzz about a book a lady by the name of Mitchell had wrote about Atlanta during the war. It just won a Pulitzer Prize, and the rumor is they're a-going to make it a talking picture.

If the old Southern way of life is gone with the wind, and that wind was the northern army grinding relentlessly on, regardless of defeats and incompetent generals, then my comrades and I were the servants of that wind. Servants of the Wind, the North's answer to Miz Mitchell's bodacious book...

So, at the beginning of '63 you had Bragg and Rosecrans facing each other in Tennessee, and Grant moving down the Mississippi to attack Vicksburg. In Virginia, Hooker had almost 140,000 men getting ready to go for Lee, who would have only sixty thousand men with him at the end of April. With odds like that, how could we lose?

Camp near Aquia Creek, Va March the 2nd

"...I am glad to be able to say that my health is good and I hope that it may continue for judging by my experience the past week, I don't want to be sick any more in the army. I have been just sick enough to be cross and feel mean and feel that I could not do my duty. But I am better today and able to do duty. Lazy as I am, I would rather do duty every day than be on the sick list. And speaking of being lazy, you can have not the least idea of how lazy we are getting. I don't think there is any danger of our ever dying for we are too lazy to draw our last breath...

Billy Scranton of Martin's company that went from Busti in the Westfield Cavalry was here to see me the other day. His regiment is

stationed some six miles from here. He looks tough and hearty as a bear and seems to feel first-rate. I guess that their regiment like ours has seen a good deal of harsh service since they got their horses, for they have been doing picket and scouting duty all the time. For some three months they were in the brigade of General Stabel of Sigel's Corps, and the little Dutch general kept his cavalry on the jump. But the Westfield Cavalry have been detached from Stabel's Brigade and attached to the command of General Pleasanton, and are recruiting their horses at present.

...Let me know whether Warren Foster is at home and how he gets along. I think it will come awkward for him to go to work again since for the last 18 months I don't believe all our work put together--except marching--would amount to one week's work. And I would not wonder if he should be somewhat arbitrary and consequential for he has not known what it is to be contradicted in so long. But I must do him the justice to say that he was quite popular with his company." [55]

Camp near Aquia Creek, Va March the 10th 63

"...On the seventh instant I got a pass and went to see the 145th Pennsylvania Volunteers, the regiment that Charley Todd is in. I found him well but he does not look strong enough to bear the hardship and privation incident to the life of a soldier. Still, he seemed to be cheerful and contented. He is cook for the Adjutant and Lieutenant Finch--the second lieutenant of Company E and the son of Thomas Finch of Freehold Township. He came out as third sergeant but as near as I can find out, the Battle of Fredericksburg took the starch out of a good many of the feather-bed officers and on one pretense or another, a good many of them have gone home. That, with the number that were killed, has made room for a good many of the non-commissioned officers. The regiment is encamped on a hill something like two miles from Fredericksburg in plain sight of the battlefield. It is some ten miles from here and the troops are encamped thickly all the way. In the whole distance, I did not see a single camp that would compare with that of our regiment in regard to cleanliness and beauty of location.

Our regiment was very highly complimented in a general order from the commanding General Hooker and we are the more proud of it because ours is the only Pennsylvania regiment that was mentioned with praise. You can find the order in the New York Herald on the fifth or sixth ultimo.

...Please to let me know what the Copperhead Democrats of that section think of the Conscription Law. I for one am heartily in favor of its full and stringent enforcement. I do sincerely hope that they will fill up the old regiments to a war footing and let the secesh sympathizers in the North howl if they want to." [56]

We had some diversion on the 17th of March. Early in the morning we were startled by brisk firing. We were ordered out and formed in line of battle only to learn a little later it was the Irish Brigade celebrating St. Patrick's Day.

It was during this spring that we came into our own as a regiment. We finally established who we were, to ourselves and the rest of the army. The 111th was the only regiment from Pennsylvania to pass the stiff government inspection that spring. We got mentioned in the papers, and due to our good showing we were authorized to send on furlough one more enlisted man and one more officer than previously authorized. That is doing pretty well, I think. As Colonel Cobham said one day, there were some regiments who were stopped from sending anybody on furlough and had to recall their officers, due to their sorry state of affairs. By far the most regiments were not mentioned one way or the other, which showed the most to be middling, as he put it. [57]

It had been a very pleasant winter. We fixed up our camp to be the nicest in the division, if not the army. We laid out regular company streets, covered with fine white gravel and sand, which was swept every morning. The entrance to the camp was through a twelve-foot-wide arch of pine boughs with the regimental number on top of it, and in front of the headquarters tent we flew a twenty-five-by-forty-foot garrison flag.

So we built our little log huts and laid out our company streets and drilled the days away, and chaffed each other as soldiers do, but a measure of boredom was unavoidable. Being bored, we groused over things that wouldn't have bothered us much in other circumstances. Them with families found themselves homesicker than usual. With the Johnnies out of sight beyond the river, the only enemies that evidenced themselves was those that whispered through the newspapers and letters from home. How demoralizing it was to endure all the hardships of soldiering on behalf of your country and its citizens, only to see some of those fine folks doubt the wisdom and justice of the cause. We never got so mad at the enemy as we did at the Copperheads.

James, especially.

Camp near Aquia Creek, Va March the 28th, 1863

"Inspections and reviews are the order of the day. We have had no less than six within the last three weeks and one of them by General Hooker in person. He paid us the compliment to say that ours was the best Corps in the army. Our regiment has been transferred from the Third to the Second Brigade. Our present brigade is composed entirely of Pennsylvanians. There are five regiments of us stationed in line from right to left as follows: the 29th, 109th, 111th, 120th, and 124th, so you can see that we are in the center. Our Brigadier General is Kane, the old lieutenant colonel of the Bucktails. I think he will keep us busy and if there is any chance he will get us where we will get some of our heads broke. But never mind--it is a soldier's business to fight and I am confident that if we have anything like a fair chance we will give the rebels such a meeting that they will have no wish to renew the acquaintance.

...I think that General Hooker means mischief. As far as I can judge, he is a smart man and a good officer and I believe he can and will flog the rebels under Lee. And if he does, they will stay whipped. I don't believe he will commit the terrible blunder of McClellan after the Battle of Antietam and lay still, letting the rebels slip away from him when he could have crushed them just as well as not. Still, I would like to have seen Little Mac be let alone. But with us soldiers we don't care so much who commands--just that we win.

Now in regard to the letter you wrote asking about the Copperheads. I did not intend to name any personalities but if the coat fits any of my friends they can wear it if they choose. But I would fain believe that none of my relatives have done or will do anything to deserve the name of traitor. How I can call any man or set of men anything else but traitors who are doing all they can to embarrass the government in its efforts to crush this most causeless and damnable rebellion is more than I can see. In my opinion, the Democrats of the Vallandigham-Wood-and-Cox School have done more to dishearten the army and prolong the war than ten times their number could have done if they had been in the rebel army. But I am glad to see a great many of the best of the leaders of the old Democratic Party have stood by the President from the first--for instance, Johnson of Tennessee, Holt of Kentucky,

and Dickerson and Dix of New York. It makes me feel pr that such men as John Van Buren, James Brady, and Judge Daly of New York City are leaving such men as Fernando Wood to lead the Copperheads while they wheel gallantly into the line of the supporters of the President and keep step to the music of the Union..." [58]

I intend to go on with that letter, but I just thought I would make sure you knew what James was talking about. I was a lad of eighteen, and not much into politics, while James was over thirty and mightily interested in what was making the war tick—or misfire, take your pick. Lots of times I fought just for the hell of it, but James was out to save the Union with every shot he took. Copperheads took their name from the Indian-head pennies they wore for identification amongst themselves. It is coincidental but a fitting irony that Copperheads were also snakes. Clement Vallandigham was the leader of the snakes. If I can figure out a way one of these Sundays to make politics exciting, I'll tell you more about ol' Clement, and Fernando and Mr. Cox. Don't hold your breath, though.

This here next continues a letter that I read you part of last Sunday. The subject is conscription. The government was forced to resort to a draft when less and less men and boys were anxious to take a chance on getting their heads blowed off or their health ruined in order to save the Union.

Well, we drafted during the Great War, in 1917, and most went along with it, but in 1863 it was a brand-new idea, and was met with opposition. Some of that opposition was awful violent. It is probably hard for you to imagine a Napoleon cannon firing down the streets of New York City, but it happened in the summer of 1863. Ugly mobs set fires, including torching an orphanage for Negro children, and people were murdered in the streets.

I'll mention the draft and its abuses later, but just now I will say that part of the Conscription Act said that if a man paid three hundred dollars he could be exempted, or he could hire a substitute for that price. It just meant that a man with money could avoid the draft, while the poor man would have to go. The exemption money was used for enlistment and reenlistment bonuses to those who volunteered. Opponents said that Uncle Sam was tampering with states rights by conscripting the men direct.

"...I just think that we must have more men, although I don't like the 300 dollar part of the Conscription Act. Still, the rest of the bill I do like first-rate. In regard to the violations of states' rights, if the country was at peace it would then be worthwhile to think about them, but when the nation is engaged in a death struggle with traitors I think the end justifies the means. In regard to the classing of men over 35, I know that men over that age are not half as quick to learn their duty as younger men and that they do not stand the fatigues of a soldier's life is very evident to anyone with half an eye who has seen troops on a long, hard march. If, as you say, there is not a man in that town who will come if they can raise the 300 dollars, it shows an amount of cowardice I did not think existed anywhere in the North much less in that township. With all I have endured for the last year, I would far rather take my chance for the next two than to have the rebels succeed. The men of Farmington can do as they think best but as for me, I intend to do my duty to my country every time and die (if die I must)--so that no person can tell the truth and say I ever flinched, and so that my wife will never mourn her husband nor my children their father nor my parents their son as a coward. It is my opinion that before you and I die, if we live to be seventy the time will come when the Copperheads will be disgraced and hated as much as the Tories of the Revolution are now."

Camp near Aquia Creek, March the 30th

"...Nothing but the dull, heavy hum of preparation for the terrible struggle with the foe...

Our regiment never was in as good fighting trim as it is at present. Although there is but a handful of us left--some 250--I am confident we will not disgrace our friends or belie the reputation we honestly gained on the bloody field of Cedar Mountain and Antietam. I think that there never was a commander of this army that had the confidence of the whole army to the same degree that Hooker has and I expect he will give us a chance to see the elephant before long.

If it were not for the miserable Copperhead traitors at the North, I should have nothing to fear as to the result. But to think that we have left our families and all the endearments and pleasures of home and friends; and cheerfully endured all the fatigues, privations, and dangers of a soldier's lot; and after all we have suffered and endured in this war to have those mean, low-lived, cowardly traitors and scoundrels that are afraid to take their muskets and come help us crush the rebels, to have them (the meanest part of God's creation) do everything in their power to dishearten us and encourage the enemies of our flag and country, trying like midnight assassins to stab us in the back, is maddening. Curses loud and deep go from thousands of brave men every day. If the traitors keep on I should not wonder to see the time when after this war is over our own strong arms will take vengeance on those cowardly skunks that are a disgrace to our country..." [59]

***

THE WHITE STARS

Well, spring came at last. The roads dried out, and the great Fighting Joe Hooker would lead us, a big army, more than double the size of Lee's, in a campaign designed to cut Lee off and destroy him. James's brother Bob got better and he rejoined his regiment just before the battle, but Bob's commander, Colonel Harrison Allen, went home on leave. It was getting so that you didn't have to be a genius to figure that if Allen was a-going home it meant that we were about to fight another big one.

I believe it was Napoleon that said, "Give me enough ribbon and I can conquer the world." What he was referring to was the remarkable effect that medals and distinctive insignia can have on a unit, helping to build what the French called *"esprit de corps."* Our "esprit" got a big boost when Joe Hooker took some steps which basically had a practical purpose. When he was in the Third Corps, he and General Kearney—the same General Kearney that got snuffed in the thunderstorm at Chantilly—they devised a badge for their corps so that they could distinguish their men during a battle. I guess there had been an embarrassing moment when Hooker commenced to give orders to a regiment and then found out they did not belong to him. Well, now Joe had himself the whole army, so he gave each corps a distinctive badge. Our corps, now officially the Twelfth Army Corps, was given the star. In each corps the first division's patch was red; the second division's was white; the third division's was blue. That's how we became the White Star Division— Second Division, Twelfth Army Corps. When we formed up, we looked like five thousand blue-suited deputy sheriffs. We became mighty proud and possessive of our corps badges. One of the major bones of contention when units got reorganized the next year was the men not willing to give up their old corps insignia, so they got to keep it even though their corps was defunct. General Slocum commanded the corps; General Williams commanded First Division; General Geary commanded Second Division; we did not have a third division until 1864.

The Army of the Potomac was made up of seven infantry corps, each with its own badge. Commanders changed for one reason or another, but the basic organization stayed the same through the spring and summer of 1863. You might be interested in what become of the corps commanders by September, so I'll mention them all again later. The First Corps (disc, or circle) was under John Reynolds. Allen's 151st Pennsylvania was in this corps. The Second Corps (trefoil shamrock, or the club card suit) was under Darius Couch and included the 145th Pennsylvania with cousin Charley Todd. The Third Corps (diamond) was under Dan Sickles and the Tidioute Rifles was in the Excelsior Brigade in this corps. The Fifth (Maltese Cross) under George Meade included the 83rd Pennsylvania—and the 20th Maine. The Sixth (Saint Andrew's Cross) under John Sedgwick included the 49th New York, the McKelvey brothers' regiment which James will mention shortly. The Eleventh (crescent moon) under Oliver Howard, included the 154th New York, out of Chautauqua County; and our Twelfth Corps under Henry Slocum rounded out the infantry roster. The cavalry, heretofore scattered amongst the various infantry corps, was finally organized as a corps in its own right, of three divisions all under George Stoneman. One of the cavalry brigades got a new commander after Chancellorsville, a hot-shot boy general by the name of George Armstrong Custer. The 9th New York, with our Sugar Grove comrades of the Westfield Cavalry, wound up in Devin's brigade of John Buford's cavalry division, which opened the ball at the Battle of Gettysburg.

You may notice that I did not mention Charlie and the Pennsylvania Reserves. After Fredericksburg they were pulled out and sent back to Washington for a well-deserved rest. They had been shot up in every battle they even got near to.

Lee's army was organized into two big corps, under Stonewall Jackson and James Longstreet, but Longstreet, with two divisions, was sent down to Suffolk, Virginia, early in the spring. That left Lee with a little over sixty thousand men. Jackson had four divisions, and Lee directly commanded the two of Longstreet's divisions which were still with the army. For some incredible reason Longstreet was not recalled in time to be at Chancellorsville. I think he enjoyed having an independent command and dragged his feet in coming back. No blame was placed on anyone because it all turned out all right for the rebs, but as Wellington said about Waterloo, Chancellorsville was a near-run thing, only won by Lee's sheer audacity. If they had lost for want of men, Longstreet, the Confederate War Department, and Lee himself would have had to answer for it. Now, if I was writing a novel I should be criticized for giving away beforehand the results of the coming battle, but you probably know your history well enough to know what the outcome was, and, sorry to say, I can't change it.

Hooker also improved our medical services, tightened up on desertions by shooting an unfortunate few as examples and other less awful measures such as not permitting civilian clothing to be sent to his army. Food was better and there was more of it. The one thing which he did not tighten up on—and some said he actually encouraged it—was the small army of painted ladies which had set up shop in the area and seemed to decamp when we did and show up at our destination before we arrived. They was styled "Hooker's Army," and over time became simply "hookers." And so another item entered the all-American lexicon.

Abe Lincoln came down to see us several times this spring. That homely looking man, gangly even on a horse, trotted along the ranks with Hooker and the glittering entourage of officers and strap-hangers. He peered into our faces, seeming to be both looking for the answers and trying to instill the determination it would take to to conquer our foe. Sometimes after the formal review he would pass by again on his own, often with son Tad trotting along with him mounted on a spirited little pony. Old Abe would ride close to the front ranks with his hand down so that the men could reach out and touch him. In my estimation that spring was when a bond was sealed between our president and the Army of the Potomac.

I trust he peered into Hooker's face the same way, for it was there that the ultimate answers would lie. We wanted to win very badly—so much so that if we did not win the fault had to lie someplace else. I felt it in my bones as I watched the day-to-day doings of our regiment. There was a new quiet confidence there. A consuming desire...a consuming desire to prevail, no matter what.

Camp near Aquia Creek, Va April the 16th

"...Three days since we got orders to be ready to march and judging from all appearances we are to have a busy time and a hard march for we were ordered to pack five days' rations of hard bread in our knapsacks, three days' rations of hard bread in our haversacks, and pork to last us three days; and to have beef cattle enough for five days which we are to drive with us on the hoof. When we get our eight days' ration of bread, sugar, coffee, and salt; sixty rounds of ammunition; our clothes and guns--the load that each man has to carry will weigh forty pounds. So you can see that all we lack of being pack mules is a little in the length of ears.

...When we shall move now I can't tell, but there is a rumor in camp this morning that we are to go tomorrow. Well, I don't care how quick, for I don't see any prospect but what we have got to fight the rebels, and the quicker the better...

Conrad Rowland of Farmington who belongs to Baldwin's company (which is doing provost duty in Washington) has been in our camp for the last three days. He is a-going back today...

We have not got our pay yet and the men are quite uneasy and fretful at the delay. I thought we would get our pay sure before we moved and I would have been glad if we had so that I could have sent some home. But there is every prospect of our being disappointed and after we start on a march there is no telling when we will be paid. Under the circumstances, I want you to furnish Susan with what money you can or at least enough to keep her along until I can send her some.

...Don't get uneasy if you should hear of a battle and not happen to hear from me quite as soon as you expect. I may possibly be hit, but I never felt more confident of coming home safe and sound after the war than I do this morning. Of one thing you may be positive and that is if I ever do come back, I shall come "man fashion" and be able to look all honest men in the face and say truthfully that I for one have endeavored to do my duty every time..." [60]

CHAPTER NINE
CHANCELLORSVILLE

Well, Chancellorsville. Now there was one hell of a fight. You may or may not know that Chancellorsville was the battle which Stephen Crane featured in his novel, *The Red Badge of Courage.*

As soon as the buds came out on the trees that spring the rumors started to fly about when we was to go for the Johnnies. Now, the news from home was starting to make us a little mad. More and more folks were talking about giving up the war as a bad idea. Long casualty lists were starting to evaporate the patriotism of the people, I guess.

There was maybe a time when ending it could have been acceptable to most, but there came an unheralded day, I guess it had to be in 1862, when a sentiment was born amongst us that all the good men and true who had died would not die to no purpose, the day when we who bore the burden knew that we could not put it down. Who knows when that day was, the day when we as an army, as a people, as a nation, crossed an invisible line and there was no turning back.

We came up with a resolution that spring of our common purpose as a regiment, to fight, to win the war, and quit only then. We were fighting men, getting real good at our new trade, but we came up with that resolution as citizens of these here United States. It was published in the *Warren Mail* to let everybody at home, including the croakers who thought the war had gone sour, know that the men who were doing the fighting and would do the dying were intent on sticking with Abe Lincoln.

In mid-April the signs began to multiply that our vacation was about to end. All our extra traps that we could not carry were packed up and stored, and the commissary and ordnance folks loaded us down with eight days rations of coffee, sugar, and hardtack and three days rations of salt pork, and sixty rounds of ammunition to the man. An immense number of beef cattle, enough for five days more rations, was herded in. We packed up and awaited the order to march.

Camp near Aquia Creek, Va April the 17th 63

"...So we have lain for the last four days with knapsacks packed, ready to jump at any minute but as yet we have not got orders to move. How long we will stay I can't tell but I think not long. The load each man will have to carry will be full forty pounds--enough for a mule, let alone a man. But never mind; we are willing to be made jackasses of if it will help to crush this cursed rebellion...

I don't know anything about where we are a-going to, or what we are intended to do, but there is a general impression here that when the ball fairly opens, there will be plenty of music and some hard dancing. The weather is lousy and threatens rain. The day after we got ready to move it rained all day as hard as it could pour down, and it must have raised the Rappahannock a good deal...

Got a letter from Susan dated on the fifth instant...She said that she had moved back on the hill which pleased me very much, for in my opinion, be it ever so homely, there is no place like home. We have not got our pay yet and I don't know when we shall. In two weeks there will be six months' pay due us and some six weeks ago the papers stated that Secretary Chase had furnished the Paymaster General with funds sufficient to pay all the troops up to the first of March. But we don't get it yet.

In regard to the preamble and resolutions printed in the Mail: I am glad to hear that you have seen them for I can assure that they were adopted without a single dissenting voice. The only fault I heard found with them was that they were not severe enough on the Copperheads. If you hear any of the sympathizers with the rebels saying that this army is disheartened or demoralized, or even willing to hear of peace on any other than honorable terms, you can tell them from me that they are either liars or fools for I can assure you the army is loyal to the core. "
[61]

(Ten days later we were still waiting the call, but the good news was that they finally paid us.)

Aquia Creek, Va April the 27th

"...As we were paid last night, I intend to send 30 dollars to you by express and I want you to send it to Susan as soon as you can. As

I shall start the money today, in all probability it will be in Warren before you get this.

I have not seen Robert yet but I have seen some of the company that are in the hospital and amongst them are Paul Brown, Dan Porter, John McManus, one of the Slys, and George Merchant. They all say that Rob seems to feel very well and the sick ones are all doing as well as I could expect." [62]

I was at Chancellorsville, fighting alongsidc James Miller, Calvin Blanchard, and all the rest, under our brave colonel, George Cobham. Our brigadier was General Kane, the organizer of the famous 13th Pennsylvania Bucktails. He was from our part of Pennsylvania, the town of Kane being in the next county east of Warren, and Company D of the Bucktails was from Warren. They was the Raftsman's Guards. You may recall the sendoff in Warren back in May of '61. You may also recall who commanded Company D if you were paying attention. It was Roy Stone, a lowly captain back then, who James will mention as now being in command of a brigade.

I must tell you the story of that brigade. Stone got the idea that if a regiment of Bucktails was a good idea, why not a whole brigade, so he went back to Pennsylvania to recruit it. He didn't get as many men as he would have liked—enthusiasm for glory was waning—but he did well enough. He was made a brigadier-general and he had himself a Bucktail Brigade in the First Corps.

But in recruiting this brigade Stone got into one hell of a row with our General Kane. Kane had the notion that there was only one Bucktail Regiment—the one he had raised—and as if he had the patent or copyright on the name, he raised quite a fuss about it. To keep straight between the original Bucktails and this come-lately outfit, we called Stone's boys the "Bogus Bucktails" but they were as good an outfit what ever came down the pike.

General Kane was a very small man, but he was a scrapper, as we used to say. He had been wounded several times in previous battles. On the 2nd of May our regiment was sent forward into the woods to reconnoiter the position and strength of the enemy in our front, and General Kane decided to come along. We encountered a heavy force and had to fall back to our main line, and fearing the little general would be taken prisoner, Sergeant John Hughes picked him up and shouldered him and carried him back. [63]

God knows how, but I survived Chancellorsville safe and sound, with most of the same notions which James states in his letters. Over the years, though, I have learned a few things.

Joe Hooker's plan for getting the drop on Lee was a durn good one. It's not just me saying that; anybody who ever studied the battle agrees.

Lee's army was spread out for several score miles along the Rappahannock. In and around Fredericksburg it was packed tight, but toward the flanks its line petered out to a string of picket posts. Burnside's mistake was that he had piled right in on the strongest part of the enemy's line. Hooker decided to go around the main enemy strength and cross the river where the picket line about ended.

Leaving a strong enough force to keep Lee guessing, we headed northwest from our camps around Fredericksburg on the 28th and 29th of April, cut sharply left across the Rappahannock and the Rapidan, and swung around so that we were moving east and southeast toward Lee's rear. After crossing the rivers, the country we had to pass through was second growth saplings of scrub oak and pine. Originally there was no plan to halt in that jungle which a year later would be called the "Wilderness." We were to pass into more open country and it was presumed we would catch the rebs as they tried to retreat.

But we stopped. Right in the middle of that jungle, we stopped. On May 1st, as our division on the Plank Road had stepped out of the woods, Lee had not obliged us by retreating. He shook out a few regiments to develop our situation and, of a sudden, Joe Hooker began to have doubts. He pulled us back into the woods, bringing howls from some of his generals at the madness of retreating from a thin line of skirmishers. But we pulled back and dug in, using bayonets and tin plates and frying pans to dig with because there were not enough tools to go around.

Camp near Aquia Creek, Va May the 10th, 1863

"...We left this camp on the 27th of April and on the 29th crossed the Rappahannock at Kelly's Ford and the Rapidan the same day. On the 30th, we skirmished with the enemy a little and about three o'clock p.m. arrived at Chancellorsville. The next day we (that is our brigade) was sent out on the Gordonsville Road to feel the rebs."

(Now, James calls it the "Gordonsville Road." I don't know where he got that, being as how Gordonsville was in the opposite direction.)

"We went two miles and the rebs threw shells at us quite brisk but that did not hurt anyone. We got orders to come back and our regiment was the rear guard. Some one mile from our camp, the rebel sharpshooters opened on our column and killed two or three of our regiment, but two pieces of our artillery gave them three or four doses of canister which effectually quelled them as far as we were concerned. But to our right they forced a column through the woods to within musket range of our lines and for half an hour the fighting was heavy and sharp. But the rebs found it too hot and broke and run, and they bothered our part of the line but very little after that. They had got enough of us and they did not like our bite a bit..."

(Anyway, there we sat, in woods so thick and close that you could have marched Joshua and all his trumpets past us but a few rods away and we would have neither seen nor heard him. In this case, instead of Joshua it was Stonewall Jackson, with twenty-five thousand men, who marched across our front and around to our right rear, where he attacked the Dutchmen of the Eleventh Corps late on the afternoon of May 2nd.)

James continues:

"...The same evening they attacked the Eleventh Corps who broke and run like a parcel of sheep and the rebs came on, yelling like devils let loose. But the First Division of our Corps and one division of the Third Corps checked the foe and drove them back. The next morning they came on in full force and after some four hours of as awful fighting as the world ever saw, they succeeded in forcing our first line back, but our artillery made terrible slaughter among their masses of infantry. Although our losses cannot fall short of ten thousand in killed and wounded, from the very nature of the ground the loss of the rebs must have been double that of our own...Our regiment lost twenty-eight in killed and wounded.

...Please to tell George Henry that I did not intend to scold him personally but I meant what I said for a certain class in the North that are a disgrace to the name of men. I hope he will never do anything to deserve that most damnable of names: a traitor to the best government that God in His mercy ever allowed for the benefit of man..." [64]

The last thing I told you last week was how Stonewall Jackson had stampeded Howard's Eleventh Corps on the evening of May 2nd, 1863. Remember General Sigel, the man who had borrowed Colonel Cobham's horse and didn't want to give him back? General Sigel had raised many of the regiments in the Eleventh from amongst the immigrant Germans, who all we just labeled as "The Dutch," and it was looked upon as having a strong odor of sauerkraut about it. Sigel had quit in the spring over some perceived slight and the corps had gone to Major General Oliver Otis Howard. Howard was a deeply religious New Englander who had lost an arm in the battles around Richmond.

How we despised the Eleventh Corps for breaking for the rear that Saturday night! They were Dutchmen! Furriners who folded at the first fire. Fact is, there were lots of true-blue Yankees in the Eleventh. The 154th New York of that corps had been recruited in Chautauqua and Cattaraugus counties, just over the state line from Warren. On the other hand in all outfits, including ours, there was a share of fellers who had no little trouble speaking English. But I reckon it was easier to unpack a few prejudices for to explain their rout than to give credit to the rebs or to blame the high command for what happened.

To give the devil his due, the Dutch never had a chance. Picture a long line of men, all facing south. Jackson came bowling in from the west and hit the right flank of that line with all his force. Regiments and brigades tried, each in their turn, to face around to resist, but they were overwhelmed, one after another.

I'm not one to overrate the importance of one man in the scheme of history, but the rebs lost one that evening that they could never replace: Stonewall Jackson, mortally wounded by his own men as he scouted in front of his lines in the dusk. It is useless to contemplate whether his loss made any difference in the final outcome of the war, but it is certain that his skill and tenacity were sorely missed in battles yet to come. It was some time later that we learned that it was a Confederate regiment from North Carolina that accidentally fired the fatal volley into old Stonewall and his party. Even as late as July James talked about how *we* had killed him. I must admit, we did congratulate ourselves at the time for bringing him down. But no matter. He was dead, and it really don't matter who killed him.

With that surprise attack on the Dutch, Hooker's last aggressive inclination faded. The army coiled into a tight semicircle with both flanks bent back to anchor on the Rappahannock. Our division was situated right on the bend of the bow, what you would call a salient, and we proceeded for two days to fend off an endless succession of attacks. We were smack in the center of the whirlwind of the battle, but we were dug in most of the time and so did not lose many men.

For the White Stars, our biggest fight was on the 3rd of May. With Jackson down, the reb assault was under none other than Jeb Stuart, brought over from their cavalry to try his hand at running an infantry corps.

First thing that morning, Hooker had ordered the evacuation of a piece of high ground called Hazel Grove, which was held by Sickles' Third Corps. That was a big mistake. Even though it stuck out to the south of our semicircle like a sore thumb, it was an admirable position for artillery. If our artillery held it, they could shoot right down the line of any enemy attacking either face of our salient. After we gave it over to the Johnnies, they rushed in about fifty or so cannon, and were able to shoot down our lines as a support for their infantry assault. We could do nothing but hug the earth as the air seemed to be black with cannonballs.

In our company, from Barnes, was a man by the name of James Donaldson who was a real character. A good-sized book could be written of the stunts he pulled off. Old Fort, as we called him, was an original lovable fellow. He had been detailed for duty with the pioneers, and he led a mule packed with tools—picks, shovels, axes, and such. On this day, as he stood holding the mule by the halter rope, a shell from a rebel battery struck the mule amidship and exploded—picks, shovels, and mule meat everywhere—and Old Fort, still holding the halter rope with only the mule's head attached, shook his fist in the direction of the battery and said, "Johnny Reb, I'll get even with you for busting my mule!" To spell it out, remember Fort Donelson, taken by Grant whilst we were still in Erie? He was "Old Fort—Donaldson."

That same barrage came near to costing James Miller a foot. A shell exploded amongst the ranks and James went down in a heap, but before I could go to him he was up again, hopping on one foot and holding the other. A piece of shell had bruised his instep and ruined half a pair of brogan shoes. He dusted himself off and limped along with us.

Stuart sent in three divisions, attacking one after the other. They hit the line off to our right and rear. First A.P. Hill's men came in. Rifle volleys from our infantry and canister from our artillery tore them apart.

Over their piles of dead came Jackson's old division, now under a General Colston. They did not fare much better, but the strain was beginning to weaken our lines. Finally, the last wave, Rodes' division, came a-charging in, and things started to fall apart. Troops to our right fell back, and three regiments from Alabama poured right into our trenches.

Colonel Cobham had missed Cedar Mountain and Antietam, so this was our first opportunity to see our commander in the heat of the action. He did not disappoint us. He was a brave and decisive leader, with common sense to boot. A musket ball passed through a bill book and some greenbacks in his coat pocket and lodged in his gold hunting case watch in his vest pocket. The colonel remarked that Chancellorsville cost him seven hundred dollars. Must have been quite a watch.

Those three regiments were alone. We beat off the brigade which was on their left, and got on the flank and rear of them that had already planted their flags on our line. We came storming back in, this being one of the few times during the whole war that I saw bayonets used for their true purpose—that, and rifle butts, and fists, and the officers with their swords and pistols out and using them freely. I saw the reb colors waving, then they went down, and back up again in the hands of a captain. Then Colonel Cobham and a mass of men swarmed in and the colonel personally grabbed the flag, the colors of the 5th Alabama Regiment, away from that captain. About a hundred rebs, including most of their color company, surrendered along with him. We cheered and tossed our caps in the air and fired at the survivors skedaddling back to their lines. It was a grand day to be in the infantry.

The reb captain, on the other hand, looked to be on his last legs, exhausted and sick. He handed his sword to Cobham and collapsed. The colonel stood there for a moment encumbered with the flag, with the names of nine battles inscribed on it, and the sword, but then he passed them along to Cap'n Alexander for safekeeping. Then he knelt down by the captain, gave him a drink of water and got his name, which was Moseley, and then detailed two men to get the poor fellow back to the doctors in the rear. Years later, Alexander sent the sword back to Captain Moseley, earning the eternal gratitude of that former foe.

This is a part of a letter wrote by Captain Moseley to our old Cap Alexander on November 19th, 1878: ***"...Does Col. Geo. A. Cobham live? I often remember with gratitude his kindness to me on that eventful*** *day of my life. When captured, if you remember, I was quite ill, and but for the Col. kindness in forwarding me to the Surgeon I must have died* [65]

Well, we had retaken our line, but we could not stay long. We had really been fighting for time while a new line was set up about a mile to the rear, and with the rebs coming on again it was time to leave. We marched out as orderly as we could under the circumstances, leaving the old trench line littered with the enemy's killed and wounded and with the leaves and underbrush on fire. Some of those fellers would die in the flames, but there was nothing we could do to help them. Such is war: Glory one minute, and the next the awful pop-pop-pop of the cartridges in their cartridge boxes as the flames got to them.

Camp near Aquia Creek, Va May the 12th, 1863

"...For three hours on Sunday morning, the {third} *of May, the rebs forced their columns against our lines in masses and for the whole of that time from twenty to fifty pieces of our cannon poured their double-shotted contents of canister at short range right into the faces of the foe. In a great many places, the butternuts were literally piled three and four deep. It is the opinion of all the officers that it was the most desperate hand-to-hand battle of the war, and I don't believe the world ever saw a more obstinate and bloody fight for the length of time it lasted than that which took place in front of Chancellorsville on Sunday forenoon, the* {third} *of May.*

Our division had but very little do but look on, for our part of the line was not pressed very hard. But about ten o'clock the rebs took four of our guns on our right and for an hour they poured the shells into us like the very devil, and we could do nothing but lay still and take it. That is the hardest part of a battle--to lay still and be shelled and not be able to do anything in return. It was there that the piece of a shell hit me on the left foot, bruising it some so that it bothered me a good deal to walk for two or three days but it is all right now. If I never get hurt any worse than I did that time, I can fight the traitors every day in the week and Sundays to boot.

It is my candid belief that if the Dutch troops that compose the Eleventh Corps had only stood up to the work as well as the rest of the troops did, we should have flogged the rebs all to pieces. But although the Eleventh is one of the largest corps in the army and under Sigel they have done some good fighting, in the last fight they were panic-stricken and run like a parcel of scared sheep. The loss of twenty thousand right in the line of battle and when we needed them the most was a bad go, but even with that bad luck the rebels were terribly cut to pieces. But I can tell you that for the present we think but very little of the Dutch sons of bitches that used to brag that they "fight mit Sigel." I don't know but what they might have fought well with Sigel, but they did not fight worth shit under Howard. On Saturday night, when they broke and run, the rebs drove us back nearly a mile but Sickles, with his old division and parts of two others, drove them back with the bayonet to their first position....

I hear but one opinion expressed by men in regard to our leader, Fighting Joe Hooker, and that is one of unbounded confidence in him. To have seen him as I saw him on Sunday, riding bareheaded right into the thickest of the fight, cheering his men by his voice, and steadying them by his example--at that point our men did fight more like devils incarnate than men, for they clubbed their muskets and drove the foe back for some distance by a clean, hard pounding." [66]

So back across the river we went, defeated by an army half our size, back to the camps we thought we would never see again. Well, there had been a few pessimists who were industrious enough to not wreck everything when we had left at the end of April, and they just pitched their tent halves back over the roof poles of our winter shanties and went back to regular housekeeping.

A great city stood for a while on the banks of the Rappahannock River. It was only a tent city, but in population it was a rival of some of the great cities of the country, 140,000 soldiers plus all the teamsters, washerwomen, sutlers, and riffraff who supported or leeched off of them. Our city was laid out pretty regular, and there was signs directing the traveler from one outfit to another. The roads were broad enough in most places to allow two-way traffic by wagons and artillery plus room enough for troops to march along the berms. Depending on the weather, the roads were usually either sloughs of mud or troughs of dust. Telegraph wire was strung liberally 'longside the roads, linking all the headquarters, but we soldiers had our own system for spreading the word that was damned near as efficient as those little wires with their flashes of electricity.

Chancellorsville having sputtered to a merciful conclusion, there was a flurry of visiting between units. It was all regulated, of course; you needed a pass just to leave the regimental area if not on duty. Anytime the passes were not forthcoming it was a sure sign of an imminent move. Well, by the middle of May we were not going anywhere fast. If you saw a body of troops marching along most likely they were headed to be mustered out. More about that later.

Anyway, like I said, there was a heap of neighboring right after the battle. Now that it was over, we spent our time hashing and rehashing the fight and trying to figure out what had happened and why. My friends, near seventy-four years have passed and I still have not figured out the *WHY* entirely, but by dropping in on friends in the other corps we soon had a pretty good idea of how the thing went, and there was a lot of foot-scraping and line-drawing in the dirt as the privates tried to second-guess the generals.

On May 10th a few of us got a pass and went to visit the 151st Pennsylvania. It was James and me and Calvin, and a few others with kin or friends in that outfit. James would not settle down until he saw with his own eyes that brother Robert was safe, even though his bruised foot still bothered him some. The weather was fine; it had rained enough lately to lay the dust but not to wash the bottom out of the road, and so we had a pleasant hike of about thirteen miles. We found the 151st, still pulling provost guard duty and quite comfortably fixed.

This is a continuation of the letter that James wrote to his brother Will on May 12th:

"...I found Frank Lyon, David Peck, Pierson Phillips, and Dan Porter there. They all felt well and seemed to enjoy themselves first rate. Their corps was not in the battle at all. I had quite a visit with Colonel Allen. Found Colonel Roy Stone there, acting Brigadier for one of the brigades in Doubleday's Division.

The same day that we recrossed the river I saw Lieutenant Finch of Stultz's Company in the 145th Pennsylvania Volunteers, and he told me that Charley Todd was among the missing in his company and is in all probability a prisoner. That regiment had 119 men missing--no doubt but what the most of them were taken though some of them may possibly be killed. But the chances are ten to one in favor of their being prisoners. Lieutenant Finch told me that when their line of skirmishers

began to fire, there was a call for volunteers to go out and strengthen the line and Charley Todd was one of the very first to volunteer. He told him not to go, but Charley gallantly told him that he came there to fight and thought he would have a better chance for a fair shot at the butternuts in the skirmishers than he would in the line. I say bully for him. Boy though he be, he showed the qualities of a true soldier and if he fell, he fell doing his duty like a man and the sorrow I feel on his account is lightened by the glorious truth that he did his duty. (And if I fall on the battlefield, my highest ambition is to leave behind me as bright a record of danger nobly faced and duty gallantly done.) But I think we shall hear more of him (Charley) after a while as a prisoner.

I saw Sam McKelvey and his brother George. They belong to the 49th New York Volunteers. They told me that they had a very sharp fight on our left. They belong to the Sixth Corps under Sedgwick..."

The aftermath of Chancellorsville was a strange thing. On May 10th, the same day we took our stroll, Hooker put out a broadside to the army complimenting us on the fight we put up and saying that although we had retreated across the river we had won, and just in case that was not so, and we had lost, that it was not anybody's fault, presumably including his. After other fiascoes under his predecessors, there had been recriminations all the way down from the top, but Hooker somehow was spared all of that. Knowing what I know now, and if I had been in Lincoln's shoes, I would have fired him in a minute.

For a fiasco is what it was. When we pulled back into the woods on May 1st we were only up against one division—Anderson's. When Lee split his army on May 2nd, sending Jackson around to our right and rear, he stood with Anderson and McLaws, sixteen thousand men, confronting about seventy thousand. On the 3rd, when we fought Rodes' division, at least two corps sat in their trenches and did not fire a gun. On the 4th and 5th, Lee left twenty thousand men to confront us while he took the rest of his army back to attack Sedgwick who was advancing on his rear from Fredericksburg. That was the severe fight that Sam McKelvey and the boys of the 49th New York told James about. Lee druv Sedgwick pell-mell across the Rappahannock whilst we sat in our strong position and prayed that Lee would attack us. And it is not as if this was not known, at least in broad terms, to Hooker and his commanders at the time.

Nobody, least of all Abe Lincoln, was yet able to accept that we could lose battles like this and still win the war. When he got the news that we had retreated he wrung his hands and paced the floor, muttering in anguish, "My God, my God. What will the country say!" The fact is that we lost about seventeen thousand men, while Lee lost thirteen thousand. Based on looking at those figures and nothing else, you would conclude that we had come out the losers again. But if you think about it, that was only about twelve percent of our force but well over twenty percent for Lee. May be you will grow weary of my arithmetic, but I'll say that Lee was the loser overall, and of course he also lost Thomas J. Jackson who, after the successful amputation of his left arm, died on May 10th of pneumonia. Even though several of our corps was thoroughly mauled during the campaign, there was others that had hardly been touched.

General Couch of the Second Corps was so disgusted by the lack of moral fiber and intestinal fortitude in his commander that he got himself transferred out from under Hooker. The main purpose of all of those hell-for-leather attacks on our lines was to scare Fighting Joe, and it worked. After the war a biographer said that Hooker folded under the pressure as many braggarts and blow-hards will do when pushed. When he was asked once it was his drinking that caused him to fold, Hooker said no, that he just lost confidence in Joe Hooker and that was all there was to it. Lee had done it again.

We did not know it at the time, but there was a spell on the 3rd of May when we were pretty much without a commander. Like I told you, in pulling back that morning Hooker had given up a piece of high ground called Hazel Grove, and the rebs quickly took advantage and rushed a bunch of artillery onto the position. From there they commenced to shell us, and some of the shells landed around Hooker's headquarters at the Chancellor House. Hooker happened to be leaning against a porch pillar when a shell struck it and he was thrown to the ground, stunned and shaken. For several hours he was "horse de combat," as they say, but he would come around now and then and forbid General Couch, second in command, from doing anything at all which would be considered offensive. Couch and some of the other generals debated taking advantage of the situation and attacking while Hooker was out of this world, but decided against it.

Pity.

CHAPTER TEN
TO THE POTOMAC

In spite of all that had happened, morale was still high, and the campfire strategists—which was most of us—started predicting Hooker's next move. After all, it was only May, with a whole summer of campaigning ahead of us. The more thoughtful and discerning may have foretold that the next move would be Lee's, and they would have been right. Things were building toward the greatest battle of the war.

It is about now that things began to get grimmer, if you can make a case that things weren't grim before. Conscription—the draft—began to tear the country apart. Long gone were the days when a politician could get up a street corner audience, make a speech, and induce men enough to enlist to make a company. Homes were being emptied of their menfolk, gone forever to their eternal reward. Others came limping back, minus a limb, ravaged by camp diseases, or cracked a little in the head from the awful sights they had seen and been a part of. Not many men—certainly not enough men—were flocking to the colors in mid-1863, so the government had to resort to the draft. The Copperhead Movement flourished, especially out in the Midwest where folks had a lot of ties to the Old South. Peace, peace at almost any price, held an allure for a great many people. Rascals like Clement Vallandigham were beginning to collect followers.

Aquia Creek, Va May the 15th

"...I am very sorry to hear that mother has been so sick but I hope she will get well again soon now that she has heard of the safety of her sons through the last short but terrible campaign. I am afraid that her over-anxiousness for our safety has been one cause for her last illness. I do wish that she would not fret so much on our account but I suppose she can't help it, for I found that in the last campaign the thoughts of Robert's safety and health caused me a good deal of uneasiness and I could not be satisfied until I went and saw him. I had to travel some thirteen to fifteen miles to find him but am happy to say that I found him well, and in good health and spirits.

...if possible we have more faith in Hooker for he showed all the qualities of a great general and if we did not do all that was expected of us or all that we thought we should we are satisfied. The failure was not in any way his fault but was caused by things that no human sagacity could provide for, and the army officers and men are confident that he did all that man could do to achieve success. It is my candid opinion that the whole army would follow him tomorrow into another death struggle for the existence of the government confident in his ability to do the best that could be done under the circumstances..." [67]

Ahem! I must apologize for my friend James Miller. He wrote that letter just a few days after Hooker's proclamation was read to us at morning formation. You may notice that his opinion of Hooker varies greatly with that of posterity, as well as my own, but we badly needed to believe in something—in *someone*—who would lead us to victory. We had to put the best face possible on the battle just passed, with all that spilt blood and missed opportunities.

And I must admit that Hooker did indeed present a pretty image of the bold warrior as he led us into the fight on that Sunday morning at Chancellorsville. Bareheaded, sword in hand, facing the enemy's bullets on his big white charger...that was the kind of stuff that had made Fighting Joe's reputation. It required a kind of courage that he possessed in spades, which was different and easier to come by than the moral courage required to lead an army out of the wilderness against the legendary Lee.

Camp near Aquia Creek, Va, May the 15th [17th], 1863

"...I answered your last letter on the 5th instant in the rifle pits some three miles from the United States Ford with the rebs in sight and a heavy skirmish going on at the time about one mile to the right of the position where our brigade was stationed. Although there had been four days of fighting, that was the first and only time that I as an individual really wanted to see a fight, for from the strength of our position and the temper of the troops defending that part of the line, I felt perfectly confident of our ability to maintain our ground against any force the rebels could bring to bear against us. But they evidently were satisfied that to attack us was a job it would not pay them to undertake and so they did not give us a show for a fight at that time."

(This refers to that situation I told you about where Lee left a skeleton force against our main body, instructed to yell and shoot and make a lot of threatening gestures while he swung over to boot Sedgwick's Sixth Corps back across the Rappahannock. Lee had actually planned to attack our main body again until he found that Sedgwick required his attention, and it is unfortunate in this case that Sedgwick was a threat, because if the Johnnies had attacked our line we would have butchered them as likely as not, just as James said.)

He goes on:

"As I am sitting in the tent on this pleasant Sunday morning with nothing to disturb me and nothing going on, I can hardly make it seem possible that three short weeks ago I was right in the thickest of a terrible battle. But such is a soldier's life. For a brave, reckless man who has no family, wartime has a good many charms and I think I can begin to understand something of the love an old sailor has for his ship and dangers of the ocean..." [68]

Camp near Aquia Creek, Va, June the 6th, 1863

"...Although I cannot blame {Mother} for feeling uneasy about us during such a terrible and murderous campaign as the last was, still she ought to remember that her health is one great cause of uneasiness to us both, and try and not let anxiety for us and our welfare make her sick. I at least would much rather face the hottest rebel fire or charge artillery to the cannon's mouthes than to have the thought that she who gave me birth was fretting herself to death on account of her often erring (but with all his faults her ever loving) son.

...Last evening just before dark there was very sharp artillery firing on our front and to the left of Falmouth, as near as I could judge from the sound of the guns, not more than two miles from the place where Robert was encamped when I went to see him some four weeks since. But I have heard since that time that they have moved this way about one mile so there is but little danger of his company having any fighting to do so long as they are provost guard. The artillery fight last night in all probability was just close enough to them to make them stick out their eyes and think of fun in earnest and the more they are brought in close contact with artillery fighting (so long as they do not suffer from its effects) the better it will be for them if ever it should be their luck to get into a fight in earnest for they will have gotten used to

the noise and be more apt to be steady under its murderous effect. And steadiness under fire is the great beauty of a soldier.

From all I can learn, Robert is very popular with the boys in the company and that will make it a great deal easier for him to get along and do his duty. As for Judge Lott, every man in the company seems to hate him as they would a snake. The position of Orderly Sergeant is the hardest-worked, poorest-paid, and altogether most disagreeable position in the service, and I am glad that Robert did not get it for the three dollars per month difference in the pay would not begin to pay him for the extra work he would have had to do--to say nothing about the curses he would have been sure to get."

Our rations are good in quality and plenty in quantity. Since the last fight we have drawn fresh, soft bread almost all the time, having drawn only three days' rations of hard bread in five weeks. Each division has a bakery of its own and the boss of ours told me that he issued about 8,000 loaves per day, each loaf being a day's ration. But there are not that many men in the Division for the Corps Hospital is situated close by the bakery and that takes some 2,000 loaves per day, and then there are always some outsiders to be furnished."

(See how easy it is for to be a spy? James just got a good approximation of the strength of the division just by asking the boss at the bakery. After the battle we had about six thousand men. Then he gives an account of our losses, which was published for each of the divisions, which made a spy's work even easier.)

"...you will get a better account in the papers than I could give you. The loss of our Division in the battles at Chancellorsville was 1,005 in killed, wounded and missing; of that number 124 were killed, 448 were missing, and 433 were wounded..."

I reckon I'll pick up on the rest of that letter next Sunday. In case you don't know, what we called the "Orderly Sergeant" was also called "First Sergeant" which is a term you may be more familiar with. Top Sergeant, Top Kick, and a few other names that ain't repeatable. Back then there was also a "Second Sergeant" and a "Third Sergeant," etcetera. A good first sergeant actually ran the day to day work of the company, leaving the company commander free to do whatever it is that officers do.

***

CONSCRIPTION AND COPPERHEADS

As if we hadn't enough problems, another flawed government policy caught up with us that spring. Here it was, May-June, 1863. The war had started two years before, and many of our original tried and true regiments had enlisted back then for two years, which seemed like plenty of time in which to have a war and get it done. Other regiments had enlisted in the fall of '62, during the scare of the Maryland invasion, for nine months. Joe Hooker had put together an army of 140,000 men, called us "The finest army on the planet," but now both the two-year regiments and the nine-month regiments was a-going home and mustering out at about the same time. We still needed them, but their time was up and no power possessed by the government, at least none that it was inclined to use, could keep them in the army. Rob's regiment, a nine-month outfit, was due to go home in July; many others went sooner. Between casualties and discharges, Hooker's army lost over fifty thousand men in May and June, 1863. Nigh forty regiments went back north, including two from our brigade. The Army of the Potomac would end up fighting the most important battle in its history at the lowest strength it would ever see. As far as numbers went, the next battle would be a fair fight.

Here's the rest of James's letter that I was reading last Sunday:

"I cannot tell when I have been more pleased with a bit of news than I was to read in your letter that Charley Todd was safe for I was afraid he had got hurt. I feel proud of him for although a boy in size and years he has proved that he is a man in all the qualities of a good soldier. Lieutenant Finch of his company told me that he volunteered to go and assist the pickets, and when he advised him not to go, Charley proudly told him that he came there to fight and he thought he could get a better chance at a fair shot at the rebs on picket than he could in the ranks and he went. Anyone who will face the music in that way, boy though he be, has all the best qualities of a soldier. It was his first time under fire at that!" [69]

Our division commander was John White Geary, Major General of Volunteers. Big man, with ego and ambition to match his physicality, but we all esteemed him very highly. He was governor of Pennsylvania after the war until a heart attack brought him down. I'd say he was one of the better division commanders in the army, and James talks about him in this next letter here:

Aquia Creek, Va June the 8th

"...General Geary is one of those that believe it is best to be ready for the worst and if the enemy ever catch him napping, they will have caught a weasel asleep.

The troops almost idolize him for they know that he will do the best for them he can. He is the beau ideal of a soldier--a large powerful man with black hair and eyes as dark as midnight and as sharp and piercing as an eagle's. When roused by anger or the excitement of the battlefield, his voice and looks have a depth and power that is strange to see, and to hear him at such a time and then to see him in camp when everything goes to suit him and to listen to his voice almost feminine in its softness, one can hardly believe it is the same person. But a close observer will in his most pleasant looks see at once the slumbering tiger that only needs the slightest occasion to rouse. When he is roused, he will swear like a sailor and kick an officer's ass just as quick as he would look at him...as some of the officers in the Division have found to their cost. But he is a good general and brave as steel. There is no such word as 'fail' in his dictionary and the word 'can't' he tore out long ago. In my opinion, if all the officers in the army did their duty as well as he does his, we should not have such scenes to blush for and be ashamed of as the panic in the Eleventh Corps at Chancellorsville.

...If you can imagine how a lot of crockery crates would look, with cotton cloth for rooves, you will have a good idea how our present camp looks. But they are airy and cool and I think very healthy.

As for the conscription, the sooner it comes the better. We in the army will be suited, but I will bet if you have the luck to be drafted that you will find that going on a reconnaissance to find the rebs in Virginia (with hardtack and salt pork for rations and those miserable roads to travel over), is harder work than it was for you and Rob Love to take a horse and buggy and go to Chautauqua Lake with a lot of gay lads and pretty girls to praise you for your success and cover your retreat.. Still, it is a gay life the most of the time, at least so I have found it." [70]

It turns out the Confederacy debated long and hard about what to do with Lee's army that spring, specially after they whipped Hooker at Chancellorsville. Out west, old Grant was getting the cinch on Vicksburg and the Confederate army that defended it, which was commanded by a

Pennsylvanian by the name of John Pemberton. Vicksburg was important. It controlled the Mississippi, and once it was lost the Confederacy would be split in two. The Johnnies started raising another army to go to the aid of the Vicksburg army. That army was under General Joe Johnston, the very same that had been wounded down by Richmond and replaced by Lee. He was only now recovered from his wounds enough to take to the field again. Some of their leaders wanted part of Lee's army to reinforce Johnston. Some even wanted Lee himself to go, but Lee had other ideas, and his prevailed: Put the final twist on the Army of the Potomac. Smash it, and the North will sue for peace.

As you may recall, Stonewall Jackson had went to his eternal reward on May 10th. With Jackson gone, Lee had to find a replacement, and that turned out to be Richard S. Ewell, who was sometimes called "Old Bird Head" due to his quirky appearance. Ewell had been a division commander under Jackson. He'd lost a leg at Second Bull Run and was only just now able to take to the field again, strapped to his saddle with a cork leg sticking out. Jackson and James Longstreet (now returned from his excursion down to Suffolk) had each had themselves half an army in their corps and both were extremely capable at maneuvering and fighting a mass of four or five divisions each, but there were no more Jacksons or Longstreets waiting in the wings.

So what they did was to split the Army of Northern Virginia into three corps instead of two. Each corps would be smaller and easier to handle, so the theory went. Lee took a division each from Jackson's and Longstreet's and made a third division by drawing two brigades from Ambrose P. Hill's big division and tacking on two green brigades just arrived. Hill was given command of the new corps. He had been Lee's best division commander. It remained to be seen how he would do with his increased responsibility. Anyway, each corps now had three divisions. It was all very symmetrical, and looked good on paper. The newly cobbled division was commanded by Major General Harry Heth.

Lee and his army seemed invincible. I mean, we knew we were good soldiers, as good as Lee's, but we just couldn't get a win. Y'know, that Lee, famous and respected by North and South throughout history, had one trait you may not know of: He was the most aggressive soldier America has ever produced. He wasn't content to sit on the defensive. He figured that the rebs could only win with offensive strategy. So, guess what he did after Joe Hooker pulled us back acrosst the Rappahannock? He repeated his 1862 maneuver: He invaded the North, and General Hooker would have to drive us hard to catch up.

First, Lee sent Jackson's old corps, now under Ewell, on a slant to the northwest into their old stomping grounds, the Shenandoah Valley. As Hooker detected movement, he sent our cavalry out on a big scout and they ended up fighting the biggest cavalry battle of the war at Brandy Station. That delayed the rebs a day or two, but our cavalry pulled back, and Lee sent Longstreet's corps out to catch up with Ewell.

About here was where Joe Hooker started having problems with his government. All that was left around Fredericksburg now was A.P. Hill's corps, and Hooker had some notion about going through Hill toward Richmond as a way to get Lee to recall Ewell and Longstreet. But Lincoln said, "No, your objective is Lee's army. Go chase it," (or words to that effect.) I'm not so sure but what Hooker's idea would have been a good move, because Lee's army would have come back quick enough. The consequences of another battle in Virginia under Joe Hooker? That's another thing entirely.

***

ON THE MARCH

We left Aquia Creek at 7 a.m., June 13th. We finally took our tents off our shanties for good. By most accounts—and memories—June 13th was the start date of the momentous 1863 summer campaign. Colonel Cobham was now in temporary command of the brigade because General Kane was sick, but we only had three regiments—the 29th, 109th, and 111th—and we barely mustered nine hundred men. Tom Walker, in turn, temporarily commanded the regiment again.

Sometimes we marched all night, as well as day, to close with our enemies. Soon all of Lee's army was in the Shenandoah, where it flat-out mauled a division under General Shields at Winchester. As it moved northeast toward Pennsylvania its cavalry blocked all the gaps in the Blue Ridge so we could not get at it. There was a leapfrog series of fights along those gaps as everybody sidled, us to the right, the rebs to their left, toward the Potomac River.

Eight days later found us at Leesburg, Virginia, three miles from the Potomac.

On Picket two miles south of Leesburg, Va June the 21st 63

"...I am much obliged to you for sending me your likeness although I must say that it looks older than I expected...as yet we have not done any fighting. How it will be before we shall meet the enemy I can't tell, but in my opinion we will not attack the enemy at present and if they attack us we will do the best we can to give them a warm reception. Our brigade is stationed near an old rebel fort; we have repaired it and I think we are good for three times our number at least. Colonel Cobham, who is Acting Brigadier, told me the night before last that he thought we should have to fight and fight in our present position, but I can't make it seem so to me. Still, it may be for there is heavy cannonading to the southwest of us all day today and we think we can hear musketry but it is so far off that we can't tell for certain. But the cannonade is very plain and I should think it about ten or twelve miles off..."

The cannonading James mentioned was from one of those leapfrog fights I just mentioned. Most likely it was between Jeb Stuart's cavalry and ours, backed up by infantry.

Up til now in the war our cavalry had been a joke compared to the enemy's. The reb cavalrymen were country boys led by the gentry, used to the saddle, what with those high-faluting fox hunts and other horsey activities of the idle rich in the South. Our cavalry was made from scratch, with farm boys and city fellers getting their first introduction to Mister Horse when they reported for training. The first month or two in a cavalry regiment was like a non-stop rodeo, with boys getting throwed, kicked, and generally abused by their mounts. Incidentally, I referred to a young lieutenant once as a "shavetail" and Tommy wanted to know what that meant, and here's a good place to explain. When an outfit would have a mule or horse that warn't broke yet, they would shave its tail, so that all would know, and not walk up behind it and get kicked. So, a shavetail lieutenant was one that warn't broke, and was to be watched closely, not for a propensity for kicking, but just for doing generally stupid things.

Plus, for some reason, our generals had not known how to use cavalry. Instead of keeping it compact and using it as a unit, they scattered it out amongst the infantry divisions and used it for picket duty and messenger service and such. But our boys were learning how to ride, and Hooker had brought them all together as a corps.

This is the rest of the letter that James wrote to his father on June 21st. I wanted to make sure I covered it because he makes a very prophetic statement about the rebs having to come out in the open in the next fight. If you know anything about it you will agree that he was on the mark exactly:

"I was glad to hear that you had been to see Susan and the children. That she needed the money I have no doubt...

If we have got to fight the traitors I don't know but what I would just as leave do it here as at any other place I have been in the state: The country is quite open and the foe will have to come out in the open field so we can see them, and they don't like to do that if they can help it.

I have not heard from Robert since the 7th. He was at White Oak Church, four miles to the left of Falmouth at that time, but said he was under marching orders. From what I hear I am inclined to think that the firing today is in their neighborhood and I am anxious to hear from him.

I suppose that the rebels are or have been in our state and if they would only plunder and rob the copperheads I would care but very little how much they took--just to let the cowardly skunks feel a little foretaste of the realities of war in earnest. I got a letter from sister Jane some time since and I have written one to her that I don't believe she and G. H. will like very well. I can't help it if they don't, for I can't—and won't—listen to anyone that says anything in sympathy with the rebellion and against our government. If they feel that way, I would much rather they not write their feelings in letters to me. From what John said, there is some prospect of trouble with the conscription and that if that should be the case I wish that they would send our old regiment back to enforce it. I bet that we would bring some of them to their milk in short order, for I know our boys would put a bullet or a bayonet through a Copperhead with as good a will as they ever did through a rebel." [71]

We were four or five days around Leesburg until it became obvious that Lee had passed us by. In fact, by the time we crossed the Potomac, on June the 26th, the rebels were within a few miles of Harrisburg, far beyond the Mason-Dixon, and living off the fat of our land. We moved on to Frederick, Maryland. The entire army was now in Maryland, but there was still a lot of country between us and the Johnnies.

This letter I have here is unusual in the collection, because it is from Father Miller to son Robert. It is also interesting for several reasons. First, old Mr. Miller gives the civilian point of view of this invasion business, and a mighty accurate prediction of the final outcome. It shows that James did not have a monopoly on intuition in the Miller clan. Second, I would only say that men who were married or lame were not prime material for the draft, and observe that within the space of a week or so two of James's brothers had managed to disqualify themselves somewhat. You have to watch out for them axes, and cupid's arrows, too.

The letter was wrote and mailed on the 4th of July, addressed in care of the 151st Pennsylvania Volunteers. Mr. Miller's remarks about the $5 put me in mind of an old joke: "I was going to send you five dollars in this letter, but by the time I thought of it I had already sealed the envelope." Anyway, here it is:

Robert Miller, Senior, to his son Robert, July 4th 1863

My Dear son

I write to inform you that we got your letter of the 19th and was very glad to hear from you, that your health was as good as it is and that you were able to stand the long marches so well in that hot country. If it is as much hotter with you in proportion to the distance south that it is here, for my part I pity you for it is very hot and dry here and has been for some time. There is not a day that Mother and myself is not talking about you and James--how you stand the heat. Your mother is as well as we can expect for her, but she is very much troubled about you and James and moreso as we have had information that there is another big battle expected. But if it comes, my prayer is that you may be spared and that you may be successful. There is a great deal of excitement all over the country about the rebels being in Pennsylvania, but the general opinion is that they will be sorry for the day they came over the line. A little time will tell how it will turn out.

We have had a very dry season--less rain than I think I ever saw in May and June. We will have very light crops of hay and oats, and corn is backward. There is plenty of strawberries and there will be considerable apples and peaches if the dry weather don't affect them.

I have to inform you that Joseph was married to Miss Ballard on the 17th of June and he is going to house keeping in Paul Brown's old house down below the meeting house and we hope he will prosper. I am

sorry to tell you that John cut his foot very badly about two weeks since. He is not able to do anything and I am afraid he will not be able to work in haying. It is some better. The way he cut it is he commenced to slash back on the brook and his axe glanced and went into his right foot on the top. It cut about 2 1/2 inches, completely cutting off the main cord to his large toe. He and I went to Warren yesterday. He saw Dr. Strang, who said it is going well. I got 1/2 pound of the best tea and 1/4 pound of pepper and the post master said that he would send it off this morning. I also got a Daily Times of the 1st July and will send it away tonight.

Young Denison of Sugar Grove and a young man by the name of Cook of Warren and Warren Foster of Farmington have got up a company of cavalry of eighty men and left Warren about a week since for the seat of war in Pennsylvania. There is no other efforts making that I hear of to get any more men about here.

I have also to let you know that George B. Gates was buried on Wednesday. He had a very large funeral. Write as soon as you have a chance. We remain your mother and father,

Robert and Jane Miller

N.B. You wanted five dollars. Colonel Allen was gone and if you want us to send it by mail you will let us know in a letter. R.M. [72]

***

FAMILY REUNION

Army life agreed with me and James. We was now lean, hard, sunburned veterans, and we could have marched to Egypt and back. Ol' Bobby—I mean James's brother, not old man Lee—though, after spending all them months in the hospital, was not able to withstand the rigors, especially of the marches ordered by General Hooker to catch up with Lee. The 151st Pennsylvania marched nearly a hundred miles in three days, and by the time we all reached Frederick, Robert was exhausted. We and the 151st camped near each other, and Robert come looking for us. I remember that little reunion very well...

James took one look at his brother and called for the regimental doctor.

Bob sprawled with his back against a tree as the doctor poked at him. He says, "I don't want to quit, James. Eight months with the army and I've yet to stand up to battle. And now, to save Pennsylvania, there's some heavy work to do."

Says James, "Why, you're as weak as a kitten, Bobby. The surgeon here says you'll not make it another five miles."

Doc nodded sagely. "That's right, young man. I'll give you some pills to take, but my best advice to you is to get yourself to the hospital here in Frederick. I'll send a note to your commander advising him so."

Bob gave in. He was real depressed. "Aw, James, I guess you're all the soldier there is in this family."

"Don't worry about it, brother," says James. "It might be a sight better for Mother if we were not both in this next battle."

"Maybe you're right. Pa says she's jest a-wasting away, worrying about the two of us; but you've seen the elephant. It should be my turn."

James handed Bob a cup of coffee from the fire. "It ain't your fault. Your outfit has about a month to go on its term. One of us has to make it home."

(It always depressed me when James talked like that.)

One of the boys showed up at the campfire, all excited. "Say, Miller, did you hear the news? Old Abe just fired Joe Hooker."

"You don't say! Who's top dog now?"

"Why, General Meade is."

"There's a tough customer. We'll catch it now, and maybe so will Bobby Lee."

All the boys started talking amongst themselves about this latest intelligence. "Meade. Ain't the 83rd Pennsylvania is in his corps?"

"Sure enough. He's a Pennsylvanian, too."

"Uh-oh—here comes Colonel Cobham."

Our colonel trudged by, carrying Billy's saddle. "All right there, you men. Better break it up for tonight. We march at sunup."

"Where are we headed, Colonel?"

"Pennsylvania. A place called Gettysburg."

As the boys scattered, each to their own blankets, James said, "You can bunk with us tonight, Bob. Go back to your regiment in the morning."

As I wrapped myself in mine, I found myself asking myself what I knew about this Meade: Hmm... Commanded the Pennsylvania Reserves for awhile, had one of the few fleeting successes at Fredericksburg when he came near to punching in Lee's right flank, only to be druv out by

Jackson and A.P. Hill. They called him a goddamned goggle-eyed snapping turtle, and it was common wisdom that you didn't want to make him mad.

And Gettysburg. It was the Adams County seat. That was all I knew.

CHAPTER ELEVEN
GETTYSBURG

So we left Frederick under a new commander. We had seen them come and go, so there wasn't no carrying on such as when McClellan left. We had big things to do, also, and had no time to lament Hooker's passing.

We marched north. To our right were rolling fields and woodlots, open country, familiar to us from our excursion almost as far up this way about ten months earlier to keep an appointment at Sharpsburg. To our left, innocent looking in their midsummer greenery, loomed the Catoctin Mountains. As we tromped away the miles the mountains assumed a sinister role, at least to our minds, as a cloak screening the moves of that master strategist and wily enemy, Bobby Lee. He was expert at using mountains as a shield, and it was just handy for him that all the mountain ranges hereabouts ran southwest to northeast toward our important cities. If we used them moving the other direction they led away from anything important or strategic for us or them.

But as we got farther and farther north, approaching the Mason-Dixon Line and our good old Pennsylvania, we saw the dawn of a new day, so to speak. A new spirit seemed to set in, for reasons both good and serious. On the good side, crossing the Mason-Dixon meant we were home, back in Pennsylvania. The people were so glad to see us, and we unfurled our flags and bid our bands to play. They gave us fresh milk and butter and other delicacies we had not seen in months. They came sloshing with buckets of cold, fresh well water. They cheered us from every doorway and yard, pretty girls waving their handkerchiefs, young boys trailing us from towns for miles, some wanting to join up, some just wanting to talk to real, live soldiers, and we basked in all the adulation. Ummm...a few of the girls trailed us too, but that is another story.

And sometime during all of this something was reawakened in our hearts and souls, something that had lain dormant for months, to the point where if we had thought about it we would have thought it was dead. It was that magical, mystical something that had brought us, bright-eyed and innocent, into the army in the first place. It was love of country, pure and simple. It was the notion that losing our country to a passel of traitors was unthinkable, and we, every mother's son of us, would fight to the death to prevent that notion from becoming fact. This, multiplied through our regiment, the brigade, the division, the whole Army of the Potomac, was the spirit of the Union Army that filled the roads of Maryland and spilled over onto the soil of my native state. While we did not all become heroes, and we still had our share of cowards, what force could resist an army where the jaded veterans were renewed with the spirit of '61?

But—we feared for Pennsylvania. We had seen the desolation in Virginia and surely did not want our state to go thataway. Some reb strategist should have sat with his feet up for a few hours and realized that the factor that made their army so ferocious down in Virginia would be with us on northern soil: Now it would be us fighting for our homes instead of them.

The Johnnies seemed to be on their best behavior, mostly, but they still requisitioned or confiscated what they wanted, paying for it with worthless Confederate scrip. We heard stories of the Dutch farmers stuffing their big Percheron and Belgian workhorses into their cellars to keep them from being "drafted" into the Confederate Army.

Our army went into Pennsylvania like a man feeling for a lamp in a dark room, arms reaching out, fingers outstretched. We were spread out over a forty-mile front and nobody, including our higher ups, could predict what finger—what corps—would run into the enemy. Information about what the rebs was up to was a lot more plentiful now that we were in our own country, but there were still many unanswered questions about what Lee planned to do. Meade did a good job in covering all the possibilities, I'd say.

Much is made of how the following knock-down-drag-out was the result of us and the Johnnies just blundering into each other. I say few blunders were made, by either side, until the battle was underway. At that point, our blunders and their blunders nearly cancelled each other out. Luck had a part in all of it, too.

Take the story about the shoes, for example. About how a whole division of Confed infantry marched to Gettysburg just for to capture a shoe factory and ended up in a world of shit. By the time Heth's division came marching out of Cashtown, Lee had already gave orders for a concentration somewheres near Gettysburg. He expected a battle, and except for cautionary words to his commanders not to bite off more than they could chew until the whole army was up, he was looking for a fight. He got one, and it was only to his misfortune and our luck that he ran into one of the best outfits in our army: the First Corps, under Major General John Reynolds. Oh, and it didn't help that Heth's division was the newly organized outfit I told you about the other day.

Anyway, I might be stuck as to what to tell you about Gettysburg. It was, history tells us, the turning point of the war. I know we went into it with a do-or-die attitude, and it was a high point for us, but it was a suspenseful three days with no crystal ball to foretell the outcome. History has also told and retold the story many times, and will continue to do so. I don't know that my telling it again, with my limitations regarding the command of the King's English, would add much.

So I'll just tell you where we went and what we did.

When the ball opened we were at a place called Two Taverns—and that was about all that was there. Also moving north, about six miles away to our left, was John Reynolds and the First Corps. The First had three divisions with two brigades to each division, nearly ten thousand men. There was a brigade from the Midwest—Wisconsin and Michigan—under Brigadier General Solomon Meredith. They were called the "Iron Brigade," a moniker going back to their hard-fought battle at Groveton, Virginia, which opened the Second Battle of Bull Run. It was probably the best brigade in our army. (Our brigade was no slouch for fighting; there just wasn't enough of us. Two of our regiments had mustered out, so only about eight hundred men in three regiments marched with me into Pennsylvania.) The First Corps also had a brigade of Pennsylvanians which had not seen much action yet. It contained four regiments, one of which was the green-as-grass 151st Pennsylvania Volunteers. It was minus Sergeant Bob Miller, in the hospital in Frederick, but four hundred men marched under its colors.

John Buford's cavalry division started the battle. Buford fought a delaying action as he waited for Reynolds to come up. Reynolds got there in mid-morning and piled into the Johnnies, who thought they would only be fighting cavalry or militia. The Iron Brigade hit hard, capturing nearly an entire brigade from Tennessee along with its commander, and Lee's words of caution were forgotten. The rebs had themselves a battle against some of our best troops. They had indeed bitten off more than they could chew. Sadly, though, the first attacks cost us our General Reynolds, shot through the head as he cheered the Iron Brigade into action. The rest of the First Corps came up and established a line west of Gettysburg.

The next corps to arrive on our side was not quite so celebrated as the First Corps. It was the Eleventh Corps, the Damned Dutchmen of Chancellorsville's ill fame. While the First Corps faced west, the Dutch came up and faced north, connecting their left with the First's right, to meet two enemy divisions, under Robert Rodes and Jubal Early, coming down from Harrisburg way, and you ended up with a line bent like a piece of angle-iron.

I'll make a sad story short. The Eleventh was attacked, its right flank was turned and caved in, and it was druv from the field again, tumbling through the streets of Gettysburg to the high ground south of town. At the same time, the First Corps was attacked all along its front and at the corner where it adjoined the Eleventh Corps. After the Eleventh gave way, the First had no choice but to follow suit, but not without some stubborn fighting. The stand of the First and Eleventh Corps gave the rest of the Union Army time to get to Gettysburg but the cost was high. In the center of the storm there ended up the 151st Pennsylvania, attacked on all sides as it covered the retreat. Lieutenant Colonel McFarland, acting commander while Harrison Allen was absent, was shot in both legs, one of which had to be amputated. Frank Lyon was badly wounded and would die some weeks later. William Carr, one of James's cousins, was also wounded and died two days after the regiment was discharged on July 27th. Many of the men were captured. Sergeant Paul Brown came through all right, but the regiment was decimated to where barely 120 men out of those four hundred were present for roll call at the end of the day.

You may wonder what WE were doing while all this was going on. Not much, I must admit. It was getting on to noon and we were breaking out our grub when James cocked his ear and motioned for us to shush. We all strained and finally could hear the faint thud-thudding of artillery, far off.

The tricks of wind and air pressure become well known to a soldier on campaign. The whole subject is called "atmospherics," I believe. Not more than six, seven miles away more than thirty thousand men were going at each other tooth and nail, and we could barely hear them.

But the fact is, we heard ***something.*** Certainly our generals could hear it, too. Something momentous, something dead serious, was happening up the road yonder and we slung our equipment and waited for the word to un-stack our muskets and head up that road.

The word did not come for the longest time. The suspense built as we shuffled from one foot to the other, shifted our loads, and checked our guns for the hundredth time. As James said, "it is the danger still to be met that I fear." This was one of those times.

Now, our corps commander, Henry Slocum, was a good commander—not brilliant or flashy, but what you would call "dependable," "solid," and other words that may damn with faint praise when the fate of a nation is at stake. There were some who played on his name after Gettysburg: Slocum...slowcome. For reasons of his own, variously stated, we arrived in the vicinity of Gettysburg after the shooting had ended for the day. It may have been for the best. Whether we could have arrived in time to stay the rout or whether we would have been caught up in it, not even God knows, because neither of those possibilities was meant to be. It ended up that we got there in good order and ready for a fight the next day if that was Lee's intention. And from the east and south, other corps were starting to arrive, ready for action if a little frazzled by the heat.

Our division was sent to the left, down to the Round Tops. Williams's division went to the right and, after poking around and almost getting cut off from the rest of the army, ended up near Culp's Hill, where it spent the night.

The next to arrive was the Third Corps under General Dan Sickles. It gathered on the southern part of Cemetery Ridge. After that came the Second Corps, General Hancock commanding. It, too, was massed on Cemetery Ridge. By dawn five out of our seven infantry corps were up in total, with Sykes' Fifth Corps just starting to arrive. The Sixth Corps under Uncle John Sedgwick had been the farthest east of any corps in the army, so it had the hardest and longest march—near forty mile—and would not arrive until late on July 2nd.

It was rather late by the time we bedded down, near a nameless rocky hill that would gain a name and everlasting fame the next day: Little Round Top. A nearly full moon was rising, casting shafts of light and rippling black shadows across the rough ground. We did not pitch tents but wrapped ourselves in our gum blankets, and I don't know about the other fellows but I slept soundly.

When I woke up, the sky was showing streaks of pink in the east. My blanket and equipments were covered with dew. I sat upright and looked around. Only a few men were up—pickets and a couple of officers and noncoms—the rest were wrapped in their blankets, hundreds of men, filling the little field we had taken for bivouac, and for a sad moment I imagined them all being already dead. After all these miles and the leaden storm that had broken upon our friends the day before, my mind told me that this day, July 2nd, 1863, would likely see the cruelest and most decisive fighting of the war.

The officers and sergeants began going among the groups of sleeping men, shaking them and calling out "sotto voce" to get up and pack up. The corps was to be reunified on Culp's Hill. Hurry or we shall be too late. The Johnnies could attack at any time.

In a few minutes our blankets were rolled, leathers slung into place, and we took our places behind our musket stacks. Considering that we were on a battlefield, in the midst of more than a hundred thousand men, friend and foe, it was deathly quiet. A few lingering camp coughs, the whispered words of commands, the shaking of a horse's bridle, all were hushed by the earliness of the day. A few distant shots from the pickets reminded me of the start of a deer hunt back home.

In the gray light of dawn we headed out cross-lots back to Culp's Hill. The ground behind Cemetery Ridge was a maze of small fields, groves of trees, houses, and small farms. Without the hills to keep a bearing, it was easy to get lost or at least lose direction. Remember I said that.

After a mile or two we started climbing, or rather ascending, the hill. The farther we went, the rougher it got. The plan was to link up with troops of the First Corps—the remnant of the Iron Brigade, as a matter of fact—and form a line to cover the right and rear of the army. Just as Little Round Top would anchor the left, this hill and our corps was to anchor the right.

A long, spiny ridge tapers due south from the summit of Culp's Hill. The ridge is not of uniform slope—it descends and then climbs to a lesser hill before descending again and finally disappearing in the rocky bogs around Spangler's Spring. After much shifting and adjusting, the 111th ended up in the saddle between Culp's Hill and the lesser hill. To our front the ground sloped sharply down toward Rock Creek, but there was higher ground to both our flanks, which meant that we were all right as long as the boys to our left and right would hold fast.

As we filed into line we heard the sounds of axes ringing on the hill above to our left. It was the Iron Brigade, hard at work. They had been sent to Culp's Hill late the day before with an important job: If the rebels had occupied the hill they would have had Cemetery Hill surrounded on three sides and holding it would have been nigh impossible. The Midwesterners, with two-thirds of their men down, had immediately started to fortify their line, using rocks and trees, both of which were in good supply, and then digging where it was possible. When we heard the axes flailing we knew, given the tendencies of General Geary, that we too would be chopping before long.

Our corps also had six brigades, but in only two divisions: Williams's First and us in the Second Division. Greene's brigade of our division held the crest of Culp's Hill, with our brigade to its right. Candy's brigade was in reserve behind us. Later in the day McDougall's brigade of Williams's division took up the line from our right down to the low ground near Spangler's spring.

At first we expected to be attacked at any time. When told to dig in we went to work with a will, and within a short time we had a respectable line scratched out, with rocks and dirt piling higher by the minute. But the hours went by and the sun climbed in the heavens with only an occasional far-off shot from the skirmishers or a few stray artillery rounds to disturb us.

Most folks know of the delays the rebs experienced in getting their attacks under way on July 2nd, and the controversies generated which last even to the present day, so I will not go into them here. Whether it was Longstreet's fault or not, I will only say that for every minute that the rebs delayed, we got stronger and more secure in our positions all along the line. Enough said.

It was well after three in the afternoon before the battle started, and even then it was a long way from us. The army's main line generally faced west, while we faced east, and when the first volleys were fired they were several miles away to our right rear. That was where Longstreet threw in his assault which came near to taking Little Round Top and rolling up our line from the far end. Military history and legends were made down there. The 20th Maine Volunteers under that noble college professor, Joshua Chamberlain, gained immortality. Thousands were killed and wounded, among the killed being Colonel Strong Vincent of Erie, with whom our colonel had had a pleasant conversation as they rode out of Harper's Ferry back in November of the previous year. Vincent commanded the brigade holding Little Round Top. His old regiment, the 83rd Pennsylvania, was next in line to the right of the 20th Maine. We had a lot of friends down there. One of the last divisions to go into the fight on our side was the Pennsylvania Reserves, which included our old friend, Charlie Lyon. They had had six months of rest in the Washington fortifications, and two of their three brigades had rejoined the army just a day or two before.

I can imagine the final discouragement of Longstreet's veterans who had taken on in succession the Third Corps, parts of Hancock's Second and most of the Fifth Corps and whipped them all, suddenly having in their view the three thousand fresh and confident veterans of the Pennsylvania Reserves. When Charlie and the boys rolled forward, just as the sun was setting, they swept most of the ground lost to the Johnnies that afternoon.

***

FIASCO

I said a while back that Geary had us dig even when it was extremely unlikely that we would ever be attacked. It was beginning to look that way there on Culp's Hill, with all the action taking place behind us. The battle rolled from the left to the center, but the northern hills—Cemetery and Culp's—were quiet as yet. I reckon that is why when Meade went looking for more troops to send to the left he naturally decided to send most of our corps.

Most any infantryman knows the frustration of working on his rifle pit and getting it done only to be told to move someplace else. It was nearly dark when the word was passed to pack up and move again. Of where we could be going or what we could possibly do at this late hour, none of us knew, but orders were orders.

Now, General Geary, commanding our division, was one of the best at the business we were now engaged in, so I'll be charitable and say that anyone can have a bad day. Leaving only Greene's brigade to hold a half-mile of entrenchments, he filed us down off the hill and turned us left on some road—turned out to be the Baltimore Pike—and marched *away* from the battle instead of toward it. We were supposed to follow Williams's division, but it had left a good half-hour before us, had left no guide, and was nowhere in sight. We hiked a-ways and came to a bridge over a creek, and that was when we knew we were wrong. We had been down by Round Top the night before and hadn't crossed no creek coming or going. This one we HAD crossed, on approaching the battlefield. This was Rock Creek.

We stood in ranks there in the road while our leaders tried to figure it out. Then they had us form a battle line alongside the road, facing ***away*** from the battle. There was the predictable mutterings and comments about the shortcomings of our officers and the stupidity of all that was transpiring. All but the dullest of soldiers have imagined on occasion that they have superior talents in all aspects of leadership which only fate and unfairness prevent them from being in a position to exercise. Those imaginations were fully voiced by our more talkative soldiers as we were stalled by Rock Creek.

By then it was almost all dark, and all of a sudden a smattering of musketry erupted on the hill we had just vacated. I had been about to tell the croakers to shut the hell up, but that outburst had the desired effect on them. I am about to tell you about the fight in which I fired the most cartridges of any battle of the war and, frankly, had the most fun. Howsoever, it did not start off to be a very promising night.

By luck—bad for us and good for the Johnnies—they attacked just after we had left, finding only Greene's brigade stretched out to cover what four brigades had occupied just a few minutes earlier. Jackson's old division under old "Allegany" Johnson attacked Culp's Hill, while two of Jube Early's brigades attacked Cemetery Hill. After briefly getting a foothold on Cemetery Hill, Early's boys were druv out, but Allegany did a little better.

Very soon we were turned about and heading back to our hill. You may talk of the fog of war. Here on this night it was very real—fog, dust, and smoke conspired with the full moon to play tricks on us. We turned to the right off the road and started back toward our old position in the saddle. I cannot remember EVER being in a situation fraught with such doubt and unknown peril as we were in that night.

We approached our old position. Of what had transpired in our absence we had no idea, but Tom Walker, back in charge while Cobham commanded the brigade, stopped us and had us form line of battle well short of our abandoned earthworks, and from there he sent us by companies up to the line, starting from our left. Two companies had taken their old position when suddenly a volley poured into us from the hill to our right, what I call the lesser hill.

It druv us to cover right quick, I can tell you. We laid there amongst the trees as the regiment redeployed into line facing our old trenches.

Tom Walker came up in a low crouch and knelt down by our company commander. "Did you see them, did you see them?" he asked breathlessly.

"No, just their muzzle flashes," the cap replied.

"It could be Greene's boys, mistaking us for rebs."

Cap nodded. "Could be."

"Well, send out some scouts to see to it."

"Yes, sir. First Sergeant, give me two men."

"Yes, sir. Blanchard, Hodges, come here."

Calvin looked at me and muttered something. Sounded like: "Oh, brother." He crawled up to the little knot of officers.

"I want you boys to go see who is on that hill. Be ready to run for it."

Calvin and Dave Hodges crawled off into the dark. Presently I heard Calvin say, "Who is up there?"

"First Maryland."

Well, damn! We had Maryland troops in our own corps. Ewell's corps had a few of them, too. So Calvin had to ask:

"The First Maryland of what army?"

"Which do you think, Yank?" A few shots zinged past in the dark and we heard the thump-thump-thump of running feet. In a moment our scouts rolled to the ground beside us.

Calvin gasped, "The Johnnies are on the hill, all right. Lots of them!"

About this time Colonel Cobham came up from his place behind us, walking erect.

"Colonel, get down!" said three or four of the boys all at once. Tom Walker shushed them.

"What's going on, Tom?" the colonel asked, rather impatiently.

"Rebs on the hill to the right," replied Walker.

"You're sure?"

"Yes. First Maryland, they said."

"Well, can't you go ahead and reoccupy your line? You're holding up the whole brigade."

Colonel Tom was a little exasperated, and it showed in his testy reply. "Hell, no, I can't reoccupy. With the enemy on that knoll, it would be them shooting fish in a barrel." (Remember when I said that our position was good only so long as the line was held to our left and right? Well, our right was now all rebel territory.)

Now, Walker and Cobham had been soldiering together for a long time now, and I expect there was a mutual respect, regardless of their past intrigues. Cobham was silent for a minute, studying the knoll, peering about. Then he said, "Let's pull back on this little ridge behind us and wait for daylight. I will line up the brigade to your right. Make sure you connect with Greene—if he's still up there."

As it turned out, Greene had been able to hold Culp's, but the few men he had been able to spare for the lesser hill had been druv off. We finally folded back our line from our original left flank along the south slope of Culp's, at a right angle to our old line, and waited for dawn. The Johnnies were right close. Any move which made a sound was immediately answered with shots from the lower hill.

It was a very long night. We laid and watched and waited and sometimes fired at shadows that seemed to move. At about three in the morning Walker tried to move us back, one man at a time, to better link up with Greene's trenches. Even though we were quiet and careful, the Johnnies detected our movement and blazed away in the dark, in a sound and light show that I would have appreciated under other circumstances.

Finally they stopped shooting, and so did we. We completed our movement and waited some more.

Soon the sky in the east began to lighten, and shadows disappeared and shapes took form. As soon as they did, the pickets started shooting, and soon the firing became general. Just before 4 a.m. the Johnnies rose from the earth behind our old entrenchments and charged us, yelling that gawdawful rebel yell.

We had no cover except for that which nature provided, but we manfully stood there and poured it into them. When the smoke cleared we saw that they had taken to the woods and the very trenches that we had built for our own protection, and so we settled into a firefight which, for cartridges expended, equaled no other in the war. Each of us would end up firing about a hundred rounds apiece.

We fired until our guns were fouled and you had to pound the rammer down. At about six o'clock we were relieved by the 29th Pennsylvania and we pulled back out of the line of fire and cleaned our guns. Having no water source to speak of for swabbing out our Enfields, we again had to use what nature provided, if you catch my drift.

We returned to the line and poured in the fire again and were relieved by the 29th again. This kept up until after meridian, when the Johnnies finally called it quits and retreated. It was a few hours later that Pickett made his famous charge, but we were not involved. For us, the battle was over.

Camp near Littlestown, Pa July the 6th

"...The fight, so far as our Corps was concerned, was confined to musketry, the nature of the ground not permitting the use of artillery. For eight or ten hours the roll and roar of the muskets was fearful. During all that time there was not a regiment in our Division and not a man that flinched, but everyone nobly did their duty and stood up to their work like men. In front of our position the loss of the enemy was at least five times as much as ours. Our troops were behind entrenchments while the rebs attacked in the open woods and among the rocks. Three-fourths of the rebs that were killed were shot through the head and the most of them were hit from six to ten times each. In fact, to look at the field it seems as though nothing could have lived, for every tree, twig and stone is all cut up with bullet marks. The heaviest part of the battle was on the left and it was there that the two armies

suffered the most: on the afternoon of the third, we had over 100 pieces of artillery playing on the masses of the foe for four long hours and the rebels were not at all backward in returning the compliment. Shells were screaming and bursting all over the field.

You will doubtless be anxious to hear from Robert, for his regiment and company were almost annihilated. He was not in the fight for I saw him three days before the battle at Frederick and he was sick and said he would go to the hospital. I am afraid he will have the fever again.

I went to see the 151st the day after the battle and saw Colonel Allen. He had just got to the regiment the morning I was there. He told me that there was but fifteen men left fit for duty in Company F. The Lieutenant Colonel lost one leg and was likely to lose the other and the adjutant Sam Allen was wounded in the leg. Judge Lott was hit in the right shoulder in the fight on the first day and so was Frank Lyon. Most of their loss was on that day." [73]

A battlefield after the shooting has stopped is a pitiful thing. All of the grandeur and glory dissolve away like a magician doing tricks, and all that is left is sights and sounds and smells that wrench the most hardened souls. Me and James got permission from Colonel Cobham and strolled around over the portion of the ground where we were engaged. I saw the same strange and pathetic sights that he saw—and more. I saw a Confederate soldier that a ramrod had passed through his body and pinned him to a tree. I marveled at the amount of firepower put out by our brigade's single-shot muzzle loaders.

But the incident most vividly stamped upon my mind happened as we were burying the dead. The weather was hot, the battle had raged all day and into the night of the first and second with thousands of dead men and horses lying in the scorching sun—try and imagine what it would be like. In addition to the Pioneers, details were made from each regiment and even citizens from thereabouts were pressed into service to help with the burying of 180 Confederates put into a single trench. Whiskey had been issued to the Brigade Pioneers, as the stench was almost unbearable. There was a big red-headed chap from the 29th Pennsylvania Regiment, went by the name of Reddy. The last one put in the trench was an orderly sergeant. As long as I live I will remember as a moment frozen in time that second when Reddy, holding by the ankles that bloody dead rag that had used to be a company first sergeant, reared back so that the reb was suspended in mid-air with arms flailing limply before being thrown into the trench. As the body thudded, Reddy said, "There, damn you! Call the roll and see if they are all there!" [74]

I will never forget...

***

AFTERMATH

James turned out a passel of letters after Gettysburg, and you can tell from them that we were all just overjoyed over our certain victory at Gettysburg. Just to tell you before James gives his estimates, we lost a little over twenty-three thousand men at Gettysburg, while Lee's losses was well over the twenty-five thousand that he says.

Camp in the field near Littlestown, Pa ten miles from the battlefield of Gettysburg, July the 6th

"...We have had a long, severe march and a hard fight--and better than all the rest, we have flogged the rebs the most completely that they have been beaten in this war...The loss in our regiment is very light considering the terrible shower of bullets that we had to face on the third of July (the last day of the battle which lasted three days). I think that our loss will amount to 15,000 men in killed, wounded and prisoners. It is my opinion the rebel loss will not fall short of 25,000.

On the morning of the third (and third of the fight) it came our turn to try our luck with them and nobly did the gallant old Twelfth Corps sustain their well-earned reputation for steadiness, and more especially Geary's Division. At daylight, Ewell's Corps--the same one that Jackson used to lead--attacked us with desperation. It came to the luck of our regiment and our company to commence the fight and from that time until noon the fight raged without a moment's cessation. At last the enemy were driven back with at least great loss in killed; they doubtless carried off their wounded or the most of them for we found but few of them on the field, but the dead were thickly scattered over the field. In front of our regiment they were literally piled in heaps, bearing terrible witness to the steadiness and accuracy of our fire.... We had six killed and sixteen wounded and the loss of the graybacks in killed alone was at least ten times as many as ours in killed and wounded together. Our boys fired over 100 rounds to the man...

The 151st Pennsylvania Volunteers were badly cut to pieces and

in Company F there are only fifteen men fit for duty and three days before the battle there were sixty of them. Sam Allen, the adjutant of the regiment, was hit in the leg. The day after the fight I went to see them. Colonel Allen had just got to the regiment that morning. The Lieutenant Colonel (McFarland) lost one leg and was likely to lose the other. Frank Lyon was severely wounded. Ham Sturdevant told me that he saw him; he was hit in the hip but walked some three miles two days after. Brother Robert was not in the fight. I saw him at Frederick three days before it commenced and he said he would go to the hospital as he was quite sick. I am afraid he will have another attack of the fever and I am very anxious to hear from him. He told me that he would write a letter home and if you have any news from him please to let me know where he is.

...Well, William, please to tell Joe that I think he has done it quite young but I hope he and Louisa will have a happy life and plenty of babies. You may take the last part of the wish for yourself and Harriet. You very well know that I wish you good luck in every lane of life..." 75

Camp in the field in front of the enemy near Falling Waters Md July the 12th

"...was sorry to hear of your bad luck in cutting your foot for it is a bad time of the season to be laid up. If help is as scarce as you say, it will be hard to get your grain and hay if you are not able to do it yourself....

Yesterday we came here and have been in line of battle ever since. The pickets of the rebs are not more than one and a half miles from our line and there may be a battle at any hour. But it is my opinion that we will not attack them and if they attack us we will do our best to punish them severely....

July the 14th We have moved some two miles to the right and the news today is that the rebs have all crossed the river. There has been cannonading. All day yesterday we built earthworks; we spoiled one nice farm and it has done no good. Maryland taken all together is the best state for farming I ever saw. The wheat crop is excellent and it seems as though half of the land is covered with wheat and corn. But I am afraid that a great deal of it will be spoiled for I never saw a more catching harvest." [76]

And so the two opposing armies did their damnable business and moved on, leaving the residents of Gettysburg wallowing in gore and dead bodies. And at night we would pitch camp in some farmer's pristine field and leave it in the morning soiled at least for the summer, if not for years. As with most great battles, it started to rain the day after, and it kept up for days. The by-ways we used to chase, or more rightly to try to intercept Lee, became troughs of mud. This normally well-clad and well-shod army was starting to look almost as bad as the rebs.

For a while Lee was trapped at Williamsport with the flooded Potomac River behind him, and it looked like another Antietam was in the works. But our generals dallied while the rebs entrenched up to their eyes, and when the river went down the rebs escaped. I am thankful in a way that they did because the Battle of Williamsport would have been a real barn-burner. I am inclined to think we would have lost if we had not attacked right away, and nobody, from Meade on down, had the stomach for another battle right then.

No stomach should not be interpreted as no guts. Meade came in for piles of criticism for letting Lee get away, but I have to say on his behalf that there is a limit to what human beings can do. More than one out of every four of us was dead, wounded, or captured. Some units were wrecked forever. Only U.S. Grant would not have said that enough is enough for now.

I almost forgot to keep my promise to give you a summing up of what became of the corps and their commanders over the summer. I believe I should, because it will give you an idea of just how deadly was our struggle for Pennsylvania:

First Corps: General Reynolds killed, and his crippled corps disbanded the following spring. Most of the men was assigned to the Fifth Corps.

Second Corps: General Hancock took over when Couch quit, and was himself wounded during Pickett's Charge. He and his corps fought to the end of the war.

Third Corps: General Sickles lost a leg and left active duty, and his corps was also disbanded in the spring, with the men going to the Second Corps. For the rest of his life, Sickles would take friends to visit his leg at the Army Medical Museum in Washington.

Fifth Corps: General Sykes took over when Meade was promoted, but General Warren was given the command in the spring and led the corps almost up to the end of the war. He was fired by Phil Sheridan during the Battle of Five Forks, just nine days before Appomattox, for reasons which would not have even been noted in the war's earlier, more tolerant, days.

Sixth Corps: Little damaged at Gettysburg, it was still the Rock of the Army of the Potomac. In May of '64 its commander, Uncle John Sedgwick, was shot in the head at long range by a sharpshooter at Spotsylvania, Virginia.

Eleventh Corps: Never came out from under the cloud. Howard took over another corps, and the Dutch were consolidated with our Twelfth, and we all became the Twentieth Corps.

General Pleasanton's cavalry corps went to Little Phil Sheridan, who Grant brought with him from Tennessee. General Buford, who along with Reynolds deserves the credit for holding off the rebs on the first day at Gettysburg, died of a heart attack during the fall.

So out of seven corps of infantry only four remained, and only two were under the same commander, at the start of the 1864 campaign.

Camp near Harper's Ferry, July the 16th, 1863

"...Our movements this year are much more rapid than they were last for during this campaign, several days we have marched over twenty miles and that is very hard marching. To go in the column with knapsack, gun, and equipments is as much as it would be to walk forty miles without any load and be allowed to go as you please. One day we marched twenty-eight miles--that is the longest march we ever made in one day.

The rebels I think have got more than they contracted for in their last invasion, being thoroughly beaten at Gettysburg and getting the worst of the bargain in every cavalry fight since. In fact, our cavalry have proved themselves the efficient right arm of the service in all the movements of the army this summer. The rebel cavalry fear and dread ours this season as bad as ours did their last. It is amusing to see the difference in the bearing of our cavalry this summer; at last our boys seem to court an encounter with their foe while last summer they seemed to fear the rebel cavalry worse than they did the devil. Now the thing has changed sides completely.

...if we could only have had 50,000 more men at Gettysburg, we

could have crushed Lee's army. As it is, we have taught him a lesson it will take him some time to forget and if the news from the southwest is only true, I think that the first half of July has been the worst month that the rebellion has ever seen. Now, if our army and fleet under Gilmore and Dahlgren are only successful in taking Charleston, the rebs will begin to shake in their shoes. The quicker it is crushed the better I will be suited. If we could only shoot Lee and Longstreet and Johnston as we did Jackson it would help to finish the war.

I am sorry to hear of the organized resistance to the draft in New York and now that the copperheaded doctrines of Vallandigham, Wood, and Brooks have culminated in resistance to the law, I hope that the government will hang and shoot every one of the leaders--Fernando Wood and Brooks with the rest..." [77]

It was during this time that those nasty draft riots happened that I talked about earlier. They did in fact send troops from the Army of the Potomac to New York City to put them down, but we did not get to go. Fernando Wood was the mayor of New York and he had said and done things which showed he was in some sympathy with the enemy. Some of the worst days of the war happened in New York City.

CHAPTER TWELVE
PURSUIT

Slowly, very slowly, the engine of the Army of the Potomac built up a head of steam to move forward against the Army of Northern Virginia. Lee finally crossed the flooded Potomac River on July 14th, and the only fight, the Battle of Falling Waters, was a rear guard action against our cavalry, led by Kilpatrick, Buford, and George Custer. The rebs lost fifteen hundred men taken prisoner, and one of their better brigade commanders, General Pettigrew, was killed. We did not even start to cross until after the 18th.

Camp in the field near Catelet Station, Va July the 28th, 1863

"...In regard to the future movements of this army I know nothing, but yesterday the pontoons went to the front which looks as though we are going to cross the {Potomac} and feel for the enemy. Today a large force of cavalry went to the front and everything looks like a forward move...Of one thing I am confident and that is if we have a general engagement, thousands of us will fall, but if we do the rebels will remember us for years, for every battle seems to be hotter and more sternly contested than any that have preceded it. And so I expect it will continue to the end of the war.

I have had no letters from Robert since I wrote to you before, but I saw in the papers that Sergt. R. E. Miller of Co. F, 151st P.V. was sent to College Green Hospital, Philadelphia, and I see by the same papers that the 151st Pennsylvania Volunteers had been sent to Camp Curtin to be paid off and mustered out of the service. Although they have been in but one fight, they were almost annihilated and from all I can learn, that regiment suffered the most of any regiment in the whole army.

I got a letter from Susan of the same date of yours. She and the children were well..." [78]

Camp in the field at Kelly's Ford, Fauquier County, Va Sunday morning, August the 2nd, 1863

"...We have marched some three to four hundred miles since the thirteenth of June and fought one of the hardest battles of the war. Better than all the rest, we have thoroughly flogged the best army the rebels ever had--the one with which they boasted that they were going to overrun Maryland and Pennsylvania, take Harrisburg, Philadelphia, Baltimore and Washington, and dictate their own terms of peace on our own soil...

Now after a retreat of two hundred miles they begin to turn at bay and dispute our advance. Yesterday there was heavy cannonading in our front and on our right, and distant (as near as I could judge by the sound) from seven to ten miles, but what it amounted to I have not heard as yet. In all probability you will get the particulars of yesterday's fight in the New York papers sooner than we shall here within ten miles of the action. In fact, we are the most anxious mortals you ever saw to get the papers that give accounts of battles in which we have participated, for in the smoke of a battle field all that we see or know is confined to our own regiment and half of the time we can't see four rods on either side of us.

I am not surprised to hear of your anxiety to hear from me after the battle of Gettysburg for it was a busy place, I can tell you. At our part of the line, the battle commenced at daylight on third of July and became general along the whole of our division in a few minutes. The first three or four shots that were fired on that part of the field were fired by one of the boys in our company at one of the rebel sharp shooters. He hit him at the third shot. Just at that time the rebels showed their line and the fun commenced in earnest, our men being sheltered by log breastworks and the rebs being in the woods behind rocks and trees. Until we fired our sixty rounds of ammunition, we loaded and fired just as fast as we could and then we were relieved by other troops and went out to rest and replenish our cartridge boxes. For one hour we rested and then went in again and fired from sixty to eighty rounds to the man and then were relieved by other troops. About that time the rebels fell back and we took possession of the battle field. For the rest of the day there was skirmishing all along our line and that night the rebs retreated, leaving their dead and a good many of their wounded in our hands.

The next morning it was one of the most awful sights I beheld for where the rebel line was, their dead were literally piled in heaps and there was not a twig, bush, tree, or stone the size of a hen's egg, but what showed the effects of our murderous fire. As a proof of its deadly effects, I saw lots of dead rebels that had been hit ten to twelve times each and our boys found two possums and one young coon that were killed by our fire. The officers of our division said that there was five hundred of the rebels killed and fifteen hundred wounded. Five thousand muskets thrown away by the foe in front of our division were picked up by our men the next day after the battle.

The loss of our division in killed, wounded and missing amounted to three hundred and forty three. The reason for the great difference in our loss and that of the enemy was in the fact that we acted on the defensive and we fought behind breastworks while the rebels had to come out in sight and we butchered them like sheep. The loss in our regiment was six killed and sixteen wounded; of that number our company lost two killed and six wounded, being by far the most exposed of our regiment. But I never saw men go into battle with the recklessness and gaiety that our men displayed on that bloody day. They were laughing and joking all the time while busily engaged in the work of death. Our foe were the very best in Lee's army, being Johnson's Division of Ewell's Corps, and being composed in part of Jackson's old Stonewall Brigade. We took some two hundred of them prisoners and they said that they never withstood anything like such a murderous fire as what we poured into them that day.

...I was very much surprised to hear of Frank Lyon's death, for I heard from him two days after the battle and that he was able to walk some three miles. But I guess that was one thing helped to kill him. I have not heard anything from Brother Robert since he left Frederick and when you write, please to let me know all you can about him as I am very anxious to hear from him. I am in hopes to hear of his being at home when next I hear from home..." [79]

***

GETTYSBURG, VICKSBURG, AND TENNESSEE

So we chased the rebs back into Virginia, doing a pile of marching and almost no fighting, during the hottest, driest summer we ever saw or heard of.

Gettysburg was a turning point in the war. You've heard that before, I am sure. There is a monument where the forlorn hope of Pickett's division, a hundred men with General Armistead leading them, broke through the line on Cemetery Ridge. The monument notes the "High Water Mark" of the Confederacy.

Now, usually history books will tell you some event was decisive or important when to the people involved it was just another day. It is a rare incident when those involved realize that they are in on something big, but it was that way at Gettysburg. We knew at the time that the thing—the war—had reached its high point and would now be on the ebb. In fact, we expected rather more of it than history ended up giving credit for. At the time, we could see the war ending in a very short time, if only the right moves were made to bring Lee up by the short hairs and force him to surrender.

The Army of the Potomac was the glamour army. Its nearness to Washington always kept it in the limelight, and it has always been hard to convince any veteran of that army that other armies made an important contribution to the war. As you will soon understand why, we in the Twelfth Corps developed a more charitable view of the overall picture. That is why I must suspend my account of the activity--or lack of it--in Virginia in August of 1863 and talk about other events.

Being as how I served with the "enlightened" Twelfth Corps, I can tell you without being reluctant that, besides our success at Gettysburg, the doings of other armies flung across the country had at least as much bearing on the outcome of this terrible war. It happened that success was favoring us in other places at the same time. Out west, Grant showed himself to be a thinker as well as a no-holds-barred fighter when he ran a campaign full of bluff and audacity that boxed up a Confederate army in Vicksburg. Joe Johnston's attempt to raise another army, which at first was to reinforce Vicksburg and later tried to raise the siege that developed, was too little, too late.

Can't blame Johnston too much, though. His career was a story of a hard-luck general always tasked to do impossible things. Right or wrong, Lee's insistence that he could win the war his way by invading Pennsylvania deprived Johnston of one source of troops, and in other armies the answer was the same. Whether it was opportunity, as with Lee, or the fear that losing strength would cause bad things to happen, as in Tennessee, there was no overall strategist short of Jeff Davis hisself with the say to move troops from one place to another to influence events. The hard truth for the Johnnie Rebs was that they did not have enough men to cope with all the forces against them, but their lack of overall strategy made it worse.

In Tennessee, the opposing armies of Rosecrans and Bragg had lain in camp since the bitter battle of Stone's River had been fought over New Year's. The rebs had come within a whisker of winning that battle, but Rosecrans had hung on, and Bragg finally had to drag what was left of his army away, with him and his generals brimming with hate and discontent at each other over bungled chances. Rosecrans trooped his line after the fight, saying, "That's all right, boys. Bragg's a good dog, but Holdfast is better." There was no pursuit. The Yankees settled into Murfreesboro for the winter while Bragg retreated about thirty miles and went into winter quarters.

And there they stayed. Winter turned to spring. In Virginia, Hooker and Lee butted heads at Chancellorsville. In Mississippi, Grant doggedly tried different ways to get at Vicksburg. Sometimes our strategy was no great shakes, either. In May, try as they might, our government could not get Rosecrans—Old Rosy—to move at the same time as Grant and Hooker. By June, since nothing much was happening in Tennessee, some of Bragg's army was sent off to Mississippi, putting Bragg's strength down to bare bones. On the 4th of July, as Private Reddy was throwing the orderly sergeant into the ditch, Vicksburg surrendered. Grant's army captured thirty thousand prisoners. That event was the "...news from the southwest..." that James hardly dared to believe in his letter to William on July 16th. Lincoln the poet observed that now the "Father of Waters" moved un-vexed to the sea. In military terms, it meant that the Mississippi was now in our hands and the Confederacy was split in two, with one army captured and Lee's army thought to be mortally wounded. The end, indeed, seemed near.

***

THE RIVER LINE

By August we were back where we'd started in June and we settled into a routine of guarding the river line and lying around the camps, getting fat and lazy, and sometimes getting into trouble.

We got assigned to picket duty, guarding the fords along the north bank of the Rappahannock. The posts were located far enough apart to command a view up and down from one post to the other. I was on that picket post more than a month before being relieved. The Johnnies were on the south bank. They were friendly and by tacit consent there were no hostilities, so that through the daytime it was like a picnic. Through the night we relieved each other on watch, two hours on and four hours off.

Camp in the field near Kemper's Ford, VA, August the 4th, 1863

"...There are three regiments on picket duty at this ford--the 137th New York Volunteers and the 109th and 111th Pennsylvania Veteran Volunteers, but there are not more than 600 men fit for duty. We have five miles of the river to guard and more than half of the men are on duty. The rebel pickets are in sight on the other side of the river but I don't think there is any danger of there being any fighting to do at this point...

Two rebs belonging to the 10th Georgia regiment gave themselves up to our pickets this morning. They just went through our camp under guard to be examined by General Geary, our division commander. They said they were tired of the service and that the whole of their regiment would desert if they had a chance." [80]

In camp near Kemper's Ford, VA, August the 15th, 1863

"...Your kind and most welcome letter of the eighth instant I received today and was happy to hear from you again after so long a time. But I was sorry to hear that your health was so poor. I hope that you will get well again now that you can have the care of home and its food and water. I am still in the enjoyment of the good health I have had all summer and, in fact, ever since I have been in the service.

...it makes very little difference to me where they take me, as long as they don't send us to Charleston: it is hot enough here, God knows, if He knows anything about us. The Paymaster has been to see us and I have just been paid for four months. I would like to send some of my pay to Susan but as far as I know there is no chance to send money by express. I don't see any other way to send it but by mail and I don't like to trust it in that way.

I was sorry to hear of Frank Lyon's death for I heard of him the fourth day after he was hit and heard that he had walked some four miles the day before. I am afraid that he did too much at that time. When you write, please to let me know how William Carr gets along and how Judge Lott's shoulder gets along and whether your adjutant Sam Allen lost his leg as the Colonel told me he was fearful he would at the time I went to see the regiment on the fourth of July.

The 9th New York Cavalry are encamped some three miles from us. I went to see Billy Scranton yesterday; I found that he had been slightly wounded at Gettysburg but had got all over that. Still, he said he had not been very well for a few days but was getting better. Orren Strickland has gone to the hospital. Ham Sturdevant is here and well, and so is Benson Jones...

P.S. I received your letter of the thirtieth of June on the eighth of July when we came to Frederick after the fight. On the tenth I wrote an answer to you and directed it to the U.S. Hospital, Frederick. But I guess you never got it. It makes no difference, only that you might think I was some careless in not answering your letter." [81]

Camp near Kemper's Ford, VA, August the 19th, 1863

"...This summer is the first I have seen in the army but since this last campaign commenced no one (not even the division generals) seem to know anything of what is going on outside of their own commands. If they know so little of the plan of the campaign, you may be sure that the men in the ranks know literally nothing. The health of our regiment is good and has been so all through the last campaign. As soon as two or three men fell sick, they were sent to the hospital and not kept around camp as they were last summer until they were almost dead. In fact, everything seems to go more smooth now than it did then.

...I was glad to hear that you had got your haying so near done, for I want to hear of the draft being enforced and I suppose you will have to stand your chance with the rest...I got Robert's letter of the eighth instant and I need not tell you that I was glad to hear from him again and to hear that he was at home getting better. I hope he will get well for he has had a great deal of sickness since he went to be a soldier.

The Paymaster has been to see us and given us four months pay. I sent thirty-five dollars by express to Father the day before yesterday. Yesterday I wrote a letter to Mother and told her to have Father go and get the money. The drafted men are beginning to arrive at their respective regiments, some 240 having come to our division to fill the ranks of the 28th and 147th regiments of Pennsylvania Volunteers..." [82]

Camp near Kemper's Ford, Va August the 23rd, 1863

"...The rebel pickets and ours are in plain sight of each other and in a great many places so near that they can talk to each other. But there is no firing and in fact yesterday one of our men swam across the river and talked for quite a spell with the rebs. One of the rebs came to our side in the same manner and when they got tired, they went back to their own sides...

I got a letter from Joseph of the same date and at the same time that I got yours. I answered his yesterday as he seemed to be fearful that I would make a mistake and direct his letter to some of the other boys. You can tell him that I directed it to him..." [83]

Predictably, when it came to trouble it was Calvin Blanchard that got into it. It was me, Dave Hodges, Frank Stillson, and Calvin posted together on the picket line that summer day on the Rappahannock. By now you know I'm not one to shirk from telling a tall tale now and then, but I want you to know that this turtle incident really happened.

Calvin had the watch. He was dozily leaning on his musket watching the brown waters of the river pass from right to left. Of a sudden he perked up.

"Say, boys," he says. "Lookit out yonder in the river. Ain't that a turtle?"

"Sure is," says Frank. "Lookit that big ol' slider, headed for Fredericksburg."

Calvin said, "I'd like to take a shot at him."

"You couldn't hit him," said Dave, unintentionally issuing a challenge that a feller like Spoony could not resist.

"I'll bet I could." Calvin's voice rose to the dare.

And, louder, Dave said, "I'll bet you a dollar you can't."

"I don't want to take your last dollar."

"I'll dare you to try it."

That was all it took. "You're on for a dollar," says Calvin. "Watch this."

As Calvin raised his musket Frank said, "I dunno, Spoony, you're gonna upset our neighbors acrosst the river."

It was too late. Calvin blazed away, and that ball hit the turtle and glanced off past the rebs' post.

"Whoo-ee!" shouts Dave, "You got 'im, you got 'im!"

In awe and disappointment Frank said, "Nice shot, Spoony. Pay you payday."

Dave said, a little alarmed, "Except I think the ball bounced over amongst the Johnnies."

They had heard us arguing and saw Spoony shoot and knew it was no hostile act. "Halloa, Yank! What y'all shootin' at? You shootin' at us?"

Frank: "Hell, no. We was just shootin' at a turtle."

Reb: "You get that ol' slider?"

Dave: "Yeah, he got 'im."

Reb: "Well, you'll be making my sergeant awful nervous.

Me: "Yeah, we told him not to shoot."

Reb: "That's well, that's well. We's doin' our darnedest to keep it social around heah. Don't go spoilin' it."

Frank: "Tobacca trade still on for tonight?"

Reb: "You got coffee?"

Frank: "Yep. You got t'bacca?"

Reb: "Yep."

Just about then the sergeants of the guard—ours and theirs—showed up, and we all had to justify our lack of the prosecution of the war. Their man brought four men from the picket reserve with him. Our man was Sergeant Oliver P. Alexander. He came alone.

He says, "Who fired that shot?"

Calvin's reply was noble, but possibly a little insincere, for he stuck his hand into his jacket like Napoleon as he said, "I cannot tell a lie, Sergeant Alexander. I shot at a turtle out there in the river, just to try my gun."

O.P. stammered in disbelief, "You shot at a turtle? B-B-Blanchard, for unauthorized discharge of your gun you may consider yourself under arrest."

Not leaving well enough alone, Calvin said, "Well, I'm not feeling tired, but I could stand a lot of rest."

That done it. "Why you smart puppy—"

Who knows what mayhem O.P. might have inflicted if the officer of the day, Captain Ferguson, had not come puffing up. He had his sword out, and James Miller was trotting after him with his gun at high port. "What was the shooting?" says the captain.

Real quick, before our sergeant could put his two cents in, Calvin said, "I shot at a slider, just to try my gun, sir."

The captain looked around, saw the rebs milling on the far bank and O.P. with red face and clenched fist and not much else to alarm, and I reckon he decided that we had not in fact started the Battle of Summerduck Run. Half amused, he asks, "Did you hit it?"

"Yessir, I did, sir." As proud as if he had just won a gold medal on the rifle range.

Frank and Dave both chimed in, "Oh, yes, sir, it was a splendid shot."

"Well in that case, since you didn't start any racket, we will overlook it."

O.P.'s eyes bugged out. "But sir..."

Soothingly the captain says, "Now, sergeant there doesn't seem to be any harm done. Our friends across the river seem to have taken it well enough."

"B-But sir..."

Dave says, "Oh, yes, sir. We explained it was Spoony done it and they understood complete."

The captain chuckled. "You're becoming somewhat of a legend, eh?" He looked at O.P. getting redder in the face by the second. "All right, Sergeant. Miller here will take Blanchard's place while we straighten this matter out. Now boys, I would point out how much better it is to be on friendly terms with our neighbors across the river than to be shooting at each other."

"Oh, yessir, etc." We all nodded in complete agreement as the captain turned on his heel and headed for camp, followed by Sergeant Alexander. As they disappeared down the path Ferguson and Alexander were in heated discussion and Calvin followed meekly behind with his musket at shoulder arms. But just before he disappeared Calvin turned and, walking backwards, gave us a big shit-eating grin.

***

REUNION

Last week I told you about Calvin's trouble with a certain turtle and the sergeant of the guard. He went with the captain and Sergeant Alexander to get his butt chewed, and James took his place on our picket post.

I was saying, "Ol' Spoony sure got one over on the sergeant, didn't he?"

James leaned his rifle against a tree and unslung his leathers. "He's sure lucky Ferguson is the officer of the day," he said. "Some others would have backed the sergeant."

Dave laughed. "And him and Alexander never agree on anything."

We took our ease and poked at the coals under the coffeepot. Across the river the picket reserve had disappeared and there was just our two original rebs lounging under a pine tree. After a while we heard scuffling on the path and Dave, who had the watch, brought his gun up to port and gave the challenge. "Who goes there!"

A shave-tail lieutenant, at the head of a straggling column of tired and disgusted looking Yankees, gave the reply. "Tenth Pennsylvania Reserves, on foraging expedition up the river."

Dave says, "Well, you're right up close to it, cap'n. This here's the Rappahannock. Don't you suppose you'd ought to be in a-ways, or you'll start collecting rebel minie balls."

The lieutenant (not a "Cap'n" as Dave addressed him; 'course Dave knew it, but it was always fun to talk to new officers as if we thought they would amount to something someday) he had a map which he was turning this way and that, and it was crumpled from much recent misuse, he says, rather puffed up, "Don't be telling me my business, Private. Orders are to go up this way...all right, men. Ten minutes. No fires. Be ready to move at a moment's notice." He went on up the path, trying to figure out where he was.

His platoon crumpled by the wayside, tuckered from the heat and their leader's meanderings. All of a sudden, James gave a start and jumped to his feet. "Tenth Pennsylvania!" He rushed to the third or fourth man in the column. "Charlie! Charlie Lyon!"

James about bowled ol' Charlie right over backwards. For a second Charlie just gaped, but as you might recall, Charlie was never at a loss for words.

"James Miller, you are a sight for sore eyes! Goldangit am I glad to see you! I often wondered why we never ran across each other."

James was patting him on the back and shaking his hand. "Aw, me too, Charlie, you old ruffian. Sit here and rest a spell. Have some coffee. Tell me how it is with you."

"Oh, you know. Same Big Thing. Pennsylvania Reserves out winning the war while you all tag along." That was the first time I ever met Charlie, but James had told me all about him, and the other boys seemed to know him. He exchanged nods and handshakes all around. It was easy to see why James numbered him among his dear friends. He had a sparkle about him, a face capable of a dozen expressions in an instant, a way to be as sober as a judge and make you laugh at the same time. Sorta like Calvin, but Charlie was leaner and lankier, and about a head taller, loose as a new colt.

James says, "Winning the war. Like Antietam, eh, Charlie?"

"Oh, yes! I knew afterward you had to be within a quarter mile of us, but..." he laughed "...I couldn't get a pass."

"Gosh, it's good to see you. How's the war going?

"War? Since Gettysburg, we ain't done nothing but march. Not complaining 'bout the lack of fighting, though. I've had enough of it."

James said thoughtfully, "Well, there's some mighty upset with Meade for letting Lee get away from Gettysburg but, honest to Pete, we fought ourselves to pieces there."

"Amen. It's as if us and the rebs have a mutual agreement to stay out of trouble awhile. 'Til we get more men, it's all the same to me."

Grimly, James said, "It's a matter of time, Charlie. Lee's got as many men as he'll ever get, and we killed a passel of 'em up in Pennsylvania. Meanwhile, the draft will fill us up, and if we can just hammer 'em a time or two more like Gettysburg, it'll be over."

Charlie perked up. "Oh, the draft! A thousand people died in the big riot in New York City, but isn't it a grand joke on the boys who thought they would stay at home?"

"Now, don't get me riled, Charlie. I wish *we'd* got to go to New York with the troops who put the riot down. I fight rebs, but I hate the Copperheads, those cowardly skunks up north who want to quit the war. It pains me considerable that so many back home are doing everything they can do to avoid the draft. Heard about 'The Club?'"

Charlie scratched the sparse stubble on his chin. "Can't say as I have."

"Well, you can pay three hundred dollars and avoid the draft, you know, and all the brave souls back in Farmington are in an insurance club where all of them pay into a fund which pays out if one of the members' names comes up to be drafted. George Cramer and William and John are in it. Makes me sick to admit to it. I call it the 'Farmington Cowards Mutual Insurance Society.' I make no bones about it in my letters home."

Charlie whistled. "They must really look forward to your letters."

"They may think me harsh, but let them. They are no better than you and I and your brothers." Then James remembered how the Lyon family had fared at Gettysburg. "Sorry about Frank, by the way."

"You may be sorry for more than Frank. Brother Henry ain't been heard of since Gettysburg. Edward figures he's still a priz'ner."

"Oh, too bad, Charlie, too bad. A prisoner! If and when my time comes in this war I want to die with my back to the field and my feet to the foe, not die by inches from gangrene or some gut wound, and not to rot in some prison, either."

Charlie slapped James on the back. "You've made quite a soldier, Mister Miller. Just like I always knew you would."

"Charlie, if it were not for my family, I would be content to be a soldier for life, however long that may be."

"Why, then I reckon that's why I'm so content, being footloose and fancy free myself. How is the family?"

"Mother's had another sick spell. It's curious how she gets sicker when we've been in a big battle, but now she's doing a little better. Robert has got home but, poor fellow, he had a rough time of it as a soldier. He's still pretty peaked." He reached into his haversack and pulled out a packet. "Got a letter here from Susan: Johnny don't gain much, she says, he don't walk alone, yet he can push a chair over the floor and walk after it. She wishes I could come home before another winter and help her take care of him. But she don't expect I can. Says there's twenty-five men drafted in Southwest including three of the Goodins, but them that are able to pay three hundred dollars will pay it rather than go, unless they can hunt up a ringbone or spavin or something else to exclude them from the draft. Sam McGee and Cyrus Brown are drafted, for which she's heartily glad. Cy pretends to be blind but his eyes never troubled him till lately!"

We all laughed, ringbone and spavin being horse diseases. The lieutenant came back from his wanderings out ahead and the column began to stir. Charlie stood up. "Well," he said, in a tone especially subdued for such as him. "Guess the reunion's over."

James said with much affection, "Goodbye, Charlie, it's been grand to see you."

"Jim..."

"Yes, Charlie?"

"If you should make it home and I don't..."

"Yes, I'll go see your folks. You'd do the same?"

"Yes. Good luck, James."

"Thanks, and the same to you, but we shall not be killed until our time comes."

As Charlie walked away he said, "I believe that, but I do try to do things to keep the Lord's timetable from getting ahead of schedule. Be careful, goldangit."

And there along the banks of the Rappahannock we passed the last carefree days of summer. For many, they were the last carefree days of our brave young lives.

Susan talks to us from across the years. She was living those long summer days, hearing of battles the like of which the world had never known, which doubtless scared her to death, nursing her children through all the diseases that kids will get and suffering some herself. I know I had the mumps when an older man, and it was no picnic. Then there was Johnny, still hanging on at age two-and-a-half, not able to walk very well even then but able to entertain and please his mother with his child's talk. I expect he would have gained some health if not for getting the mumps.

***

Susan to Robert and Janet Miller, Aug 28th, 1863

Dear Parents, I received your kind letter three weeks ago and was glad to hear from you again but sorry to hear that Mother has had another sick spell. I was in hope she would get well. I am glad that Robert has got home and hope he will get stout and healthy. When I received your letter I was just coming down with the mumps and the children had them one after another. We had them very light--all except Johnny. We was sick with them. I thought I would not write until we got well of them. We are all well as usual...

I got three letters from James last week. In all, he wrote that he was well and enjoying himself. I am glad that he can enjoy himself...

James wrote that they had got four months' pay and he would send me thirty-five dollars. I have seven dollars of the other money yet; I think that I shall get a barrel of flour with it. The wood that you hired Mr. Burns to cut is just gone. I think I have been quite saving of it. I will get him to cut some more if I can. Ellen is learning to read. Robert has not been lame since you was here but is growing tall and slim. I am in hurry for the money. I should be pleased to see you this fall if you can leave Mother. Give my love to all. Please to write soon and write how the folks all are. I remain affectionately, your daughter, Susan Ann Miller [84]

Well, we have finally had a few pleasant days and I've been able to set out on the porch and get a little sun. The other day, whilst I was out there on the porch I had a visitor. A very charming young lady, a descendant of our Cap'n Alexander, stopped by to share some mementos. We had a nice visit. It makes me feel good to see young folks take an interest in our heritage. But, oh, to be sixty-seventy years younger!

I was telling you a while back of how favorable seemed the prospects for the Union in the late summer of '63: Lee defeated and Vicksburg captured. But now, in a case of exquisite bad timing—now that there was no hope for the Confederates to save Vicksburg and therefore Johnston's army was available for work elsewhere—General Rosecrans finally made his move in Tennessee. On August 16th, moving his army on a broad front, Rosecrans flanked Bragg out of his carefully prepared positions, and by September Bragg was in full retreat and the Union Army entered north Georgia. Things looked good, but...

Two months—even six weeks—earlier would have saw Rosecrans moving at the same time as Grant's swing through Mississippi and Lee's march on Pennsylvania. Jeff Davis and his boys would have been faced with some hard choices. In order to reinforce Bragg from Virginia the Pennsylvania business would have had to be cancelled. The reinforcements from Bragg to Johnston for to save Vicksburg may or may not have been sent, which would have improved our prospects in one department or the other.

As it went, by August and September there was lots of unemployed Confederate troops throughout the South. Our Army of the Potomac was too mangled to pressure Lee, and nothing but a sentry force was required in Mississippi. Grant, after capturing half the state, was told to disperse his fine army to hold all that he had taken instead of going after the next objective, which would have been Mobile, Alabama, if he had had his way. For once, the rebs had the potential to vastly outnumber an adversary in a showdown battle, and Rosy and his men entered Georgia like a boy whistling his way through a graveyard.

Now I should get you back to Virginia. I'll tell you about Chickamauga, and the momentous events which that battle set in motion for us, in a little time.

On guard near Ellis's Ford, Fauquier County, Va, Sunday afternoon, September the 6th, 1863

"...I was glad to hear that the draft was over and that cause of excitement removed, in part at least: those that were drafted will have all the diseases in the catalogue. I guess that most of the diseases prevailing at the north among that part of the community liable to military duty are only different parts of that disease which is best expressed by the word 'Coward.'

...I am pleased for your sake that G.H. did not get drafted, but I do hope that the government will fill up the army right off. I don't care by what means, but fill it up and keep it filled if they have to draft every three months from this time until the war is over.

I do pity William Carr, and Margaret Ellen--poor girl--if he should die it will nearly kill her. But such is the fate of war and there is no telling how soon my wife and babes will be left without a husband and father. If such should be the case, I hope it may be my fate to be killed on the field and be spared the agony of dying by inches..." [85]

CHAPTER THIRTEEN
SUMMERDUCK RUN

Sometime toward the end of August I was summoned to Colonel Walker's tent, and the messenger did not say why. Since I could think of nothing in my conduct of late, either good or bad, which would merit said summons, I reported with an open mind.

Upon arriving there, I found Walker, Colonel Cobham, Regimental Sergeant Major Dyke, and a captain who I recognized as being from General Geary's staff, all sitting under the headquarters tent fly.

"...riff-raff is what most of them are," Sergeant Major Dyke was saying as I approached. "Dutchmen and Philadelphia dock scum."

"Nevertheless, Sergeant Major, our job is to make soldiers out of them," said Cobham. "Ah—and here's a man who's going to help do it." I looked behind me to see if he was talking about somebody else, but it soon was evident that I had been volunteered for some important project. Cobham motioned me in and put me at my ease.

Colonel Walker wasted no time. "We are promoting you to sergeant," he said, "and you are to accompany the sergeant major to report back to division headquarters with the good captain here to pick up our first contingent of draftees and substitutes. You will have a detail of six men, which the sergeant major will select, to help you escort them here."

That is how I became a drill sergeant for a time. I would start drawing sergeant's pay but, believe me, I would earn every dime. In a few days I marched a crowd of nearly three hundred of them from division headquarters down to our regimental bivouac. What a bunch they were, all substitutes for the good men and true from about the country who had rather paid three hundred dollars to each of these men in place of putting their own lives in peril. I and my detail felt more like we were guarding prisoners than escorting fellow soldiers.

Incidentally, once I had got my orders and was about to leave, the headquarters captain said, "Now, about this other matter..."

Cobham said, "Miller. He's your man." He turned to me. "When you see him, have James Miller come and see me this afternoon." Well, I did not know what *that* was all about, but James told me about it after his visit. It was, as James said, a compliment to him as a man and a soldier.

I was standing in the company street, chatting with Ham Sturdevant, when James returned from his parley with the colonel. Ham had just got promoted from 1st sergeant to lieutenant, so we were congratulating each other. James was smiling as he sauntered up to us.

First thing he did was congratulate me on my promotion from private to sergeant.

"Well, we'll see how long it lasts," I replied, and I think I sounded a little sour. "What did Colonel George want with you?"

"Secret army mission," James replied. He put his finger to his lips and looked around to see who was in earshot.

"Oh, come now, James. I suppose you could tell me but then you'd have to kill me to keep me from talking."

James laughed. "The colonel tagged me to guard a widow's house a couple of miles from here, outside the pickets."

"Asked for you special, did he?"

"Yes, he did. Seems they had sent an Irishman and he got drunk and spoiled a nice berth for himself, so the colonel sent for me, because he knew I would stay sober."

"Well, now, that's quite an honor," I said, patting him on the back. Lieutenant Sturdevant added his congratulations.

"Seems like things are looking up for all us Warren boys," Ham said, and then he excused himself and went to his tent.

"They tell me I'll sleep in a real bed and get home cooking, which will be a relief from that slumgullion you serve up," says James

I pretended to be hurt. "James, you never complained about my cooking before."

James laughed hearty. "Well, if I did then I'd have to cook, and that would be worse," and then we both laughed. "I am in somewhat of a hurry, though," he says. "I have to be there in an hour."

"I'll help you pack your traps."

Just then Ham reappeared from his tent. "Say, Miller, just a minute before you leave. I want to loan you something." He handed James a brand-new Colt's patent .36-caliber revolver.

"What do I need this for? You just bought this for your officer outfit. I can't take your gun."

Ham insisted. "It's just a loan. You're going to be a mile away from help with a single shot in your Enfield. You may need it."

James shook his head. "I don't know..."

"Look, here," Ham said, smiling. "You may consider this as my first order as a commissioned officer. Take...the...gun."

"Well, if you put it that way..."

So that's how James got a well-deserved rest whilst I beat my head against the wall trying to make soldiers out of bounty jumpers and Dutch immigrants. I could have used him to hold my coat. Our company commander, Captain Wagner, seemed a bit miffed by the whole affair, Colonel Cobham having ignored the chain of command entirely in picking James for the detail. That was to make for some consequences in the future.

But as they say, strange things happen in war.

The folks' name was Mitchell. They lived in a big house overlooking the Rappahannock Valley. It may have been an elegant house in its day, but it had fallen on hard times; slipped, shall I say, into a faded grandeur. I saw that much, having got permission to accompany James over to the place. As for the rest of it, he did not tell me the full story until about May of '64, in the trenches near New Hope Church, Georgia. [86]

The lady of the house, Mrs. Mitchell, met him at the door. She was tall and rather severe looking, but her features softened as she got acquainted. "They tell me your name is Miller, and that you won't get drunk and make trouble like that oaf that they sent before," she said. She showed him into the parlor where two ladies sat on a divan. They were all wearing black, from their losses at Gettysburg, James figured.

"Ladies, may I introduce Mr. Miller," said Mrs. Mitchell. "Mr. Miller, you may sit in that armchair. Make yourself comfortable."

James remembered to whip his cap off his head as he nodded a hello.

The first introduced was frail looking, blonde, with pale, ivory skin. "This is Charlotte, my daughter-in-law."

"Where are you from, Mr. Miller?" Her voice was soft, almost to a whisper.

"Pennsylvania, ma'am. Upstate—but originally from Scotland," he blurted. He threw that fact in figuring it would not hurt to mention a country neutral to their present situation.

"There are Scots in our family. They came here in 1750."

James managed a smile. "That's almost a hundred years before us, ma'am." The second woman had raven hair and dark eyes, and appeared much the hardier of the two. "This is my daughter, Ellen."

James's face brightened. "I have a daughter by that name myself," he said. "She is seven years old."

Ellen smiled. "There are times I feel that is a hundred years after me, Mr. Miller."

Mrs. Mitchell said, "Well, Mr. Miller, please tell us all about yourself..."

James was uncomfortable to be in the presence of women, in such genteel surroundings, after such a long time, but as he made small talk he studied the women and their surroundings.

The furniture was a little threadbare, but passable. The carpet was a faded black and red, patterned with small flowers. The walls was hung with pictures, a stand in the corner sported a bust of Julius Caesar, he thought, only to find out later it was Aristotle.

Later on, after having balanced a cup of tea on his knee for some time, which was an art not often practiced in the 111th, and having to listen to the woes of the Mitchell ladies, Mrs. Mitchell showed him to his room, which was on the first floor at the back of the house.

"This is where you'll sleep," she said busily. "This was—IS—my son's room. I had a mighty job of cleaning it after your predecessor left. I trust you'll keep it tidy. No boots on the bedcovers."

She left, and James stowed his few things and looked around. The room was hung with prints of fox hunts and European castles and such, and there was a painting, probably of some of the Mitchell menfolk. He slipped his dusty brogans off and gave in to the feel of a real featherbed under his bones. He lay there, hands clasped behind his head, and studied the pictures, especially the painting. Hmm...something about that painting...

Anyway, here he was. With a real bed to sleep in, a roof over his head, and three squares a day prepared by an old black woman who knew how to cook. A paid vacation if there ever was one. He had himself a comfortable berth. With little to do but be on the premises in case some foragers tried to take the Mitchells' last cow, he found time to crank out quite a few letters to the folks. Some of those letters were probably hard to take, depending on who read them.

Ellis's Ford, Sept the 7th, 1863

"...I am glad to hear the draft has come off at last. I hope you civilians that dreaded and feared to become soldiers so much will get a short spell to rest without having your dreams disturbed by visions of the provost marshall. In regard to your mutual insurance club, I have a very poor opinion of it but as you had a perfect right to do so according to the letter of the law, I will find no fault with your action in that matter...

From all I can learn, Gilmore and Dahlgren are bound either to take or destroy Charleston. I hope they will not stop their efforts until that hotbed of treason and traitors is entirely destroyed. I rather think that the fire-eaters of that cursed hole don't feel quite as well at present with Gilmore's 200-pounder shells bursting in their streets as they did two years ago the fifteenth of last April, when aided by a traitorous, black-hearted, cowardly Democratic administration, they commenced the war by firing on Anderson in Fort Sumter.

...I don't want to see peace until every slave in the rebel states is free. It is the most abominable institution the world ever saw. I will give one instance of its workings. I am doing guard duty to protect the property of a widow woman who has two sons and one son-in-law in the rebel army. Her nearest neighbor has two slave girls; one of them has five children and the other two, and everyone in the neighborhood says that all of them are the master's. He has sold one woman and four children and the children were his own flesh and blood! The public sentiment is so corrupt that no one seems to think there is anything wrong with such actions. This man has a wife and children that are white, and is a member in good standing in the Baptist Church. I tell you that 'Uncle Tom's Cabin,' bad as it was, fell far short of portraying the evils of slavery in as bad a light as they really exist..." [87]

Charleston, South Carolina, is of course where it all began. There was nothing special that you could call "strategic" or "decisive" about the place, except that it was just another port for the navy to blockade, but we threw a lot of metal and spent hundreds of lives in trying to punish the birthplace of secession. We bombarded old Sumter to smithereens, till the shells merely made the rubble bounce. On a little sand spit guarding the harbor, Colonel Robert Gould Shaw that summer led his all-black 54th Massachusetts Regiment in a doomed attack that earned them all everlasting fame and, for the colonel, a common grave with the former slaves and free blacks that died with him.

Camp in the field near Ellis's Ford, Sept the 7th

"I am glad to hear that the draft is over, but I am sorry to hear that you joined that white-livered thing which you call the Club. I think the best name it could have would be the 'Cowards' Retreat,' for I can't help but think the war is a just one. To pretend to want to see it finished, but then take such a course as that to get rid of doing their share of the duty, shows that they care but very little about their country.

...if those of us that are in the field, and have already borne the war so far, would only go ahead and flog the rebels and crush the rebellion, your friends of the Club would be very much pleased. They would pat us on the back and call us good fellows--as long as you can stay at home and have someone else do the fighting, marching and dying. You are all first-rate, good Union men but just as soon as it comes your turn to do anything to help us end the war, oh no! You all sing a different tune. By your actions you say that you would rather that the rebels would succeed than to help us flog them. You are in favor of the draft if it don't call you from your home and families.

...I know it is like tearing one's eyes out to leave wives and children and friends and the comforts of a good home, to endure the hardships of a soldier's life. Still, your wife is no dearer to you than mine is to me, and you should have the same interest in supporting the government as I have.

...I guess you will think I am quite harsh, but I have written just as I feel on the subject..." [88]

Not that James sat around. Upon request, he made some minor repairs around the place, and volunteered to split firewood just for the exercise.

He was doing that chore early one morning when he realized that one of older Negro hands, Otis by name, was watching him from across the way. James smiled, just to be neighborly, and the old boy must have figured that as an O.K. to come on over.

"You do that right smart, boss," he said as he approached.

"What's that?" says James.

"Splittin' that f'ar-wood. You do that real good." He looked to be about sixty, with graying hair and a wizened face, but James learned later that Otis was not yet forty.

James shrugged. "Least I can do to earn my keep."

"Yassuh. I don' know as I ever seen a white man split wood befo'. We allus do it for the massuh."

James swung at a chunk, splitting it clean. "Well, Otis, you know you're a free man, don't you? Master can cut his own firewood when the war's over."

"Yassuh." Otis laid on a gap-toothed grin. "Thass a fac' He sho' can."

James put the axe down. "As a matter of fact, since you're free, why are you still here? You and the others?"

Otis seemed surprised at the question. "Why, this is our home, suh. We ain' got nowheres else to go. Miz Mitchell, she say we can stay. And the way we sees it, she need us and we needs her."

"Huh! I guess this emancipation idea is not so cut and dried as I supposed," says James.

James did not know if Otis understood his observation. He shuffled away, saying, "No, suh. This my home. Ol' Otis stay here till he die."

A few days later, on a bright morning, with the big old oaks out front shading the sun down to a tolerable coolness, James sat out on the veranda—he'd had the innocent gall to call it a porch, only to be corrected. He had his feet up, and had a pad of paper borrowed from the ladies—he had not seen so much paper in one sheaf in months—and was composing a letter to Susan. He heard a rustle of skirts and looked over to see Miz Ellen come around the corner.

"Writing a letter, I see," she said.

"Yes, ma'am.

"To your wife?"

"Yes, ma'am."

She leaned back against the porch—excuse me—veranda railing, and said, "That man who was here before you, he accused us of spying, and writing letters to our army about what you Yankees were doing." (Of all the southern accents I ever heard, the one of Virginia, when practiced by a lady of some refinement, particularly beguiled me.)

"So I understand," replies James. So far, he had not passed his attention from his letter.

"It's funny, him saying that. Of course, I WOULD write letters to my husband, if I knew where he was, and how to get a letter to him."

James looked up. "That must be very hard," he said. "I write at least a letter a week to my wife, and she the same to me."

"He was in the charge of Pickett's division at Gettysburg. That's where he was captured and made a prisoner. Were you there, Mr. Miller?

"I was."

"Fighting against my husband?"

"No, not exactly. When that charge came in I was facing away from it, fighting your Stonewall Brigade as it came around."

"What a tragedy this all is," she said. "We've convinced ourselves that all you Yankees are monsters. I find you're not that way at all."

James smiled. "Mighty generous of you to say that."

"I am sorry," she blushed, turning on the southern charm. "Mother says that supper is almost ready, and you should wash up."

"I'll be there directly," replied James.

Miz Ellen smiled wistfully. "Mr. Miller, I do hope you won't think me bold for talking to you. It's just that I've had no one for conversation in so long, other than my mother and sister, and especially a man." She made a little curtsy, and went on in the house.

"Nor I a woman," thought James aloud as she left.

Now, now, now, I know what you're thinking: A romantic interlude for James in Virginia, excusable by the circumstances of war. Well, I hope you know James Miller better than that by now. What happened that night was strange enough for James's character. But you might say it was "excusable by the circumstances of war."

Summer Duck Run, Fauquier Co., Va September the 7th, 1863

"...I am on duty 2 1/2 miles from the regiment and outside of the pickets, guarding a widow lady's property. I have a very easy time of it--in fact I have nothing at all to do, only stay here. I have been here some ten days and in all probability shall remain here as long as our army remains in its present position. There is the widow, two daughters, and half a dozen niggers. One of the daughters is married

and her husband is in the 9th Va Cavalry (Rebel), and the old woman has two sons in the rebel service. One of them was wounded and taken prisoner at Gettysburg. He was captain of Co. A, 11th Va infantry. [89]

They are fine folks and use me well. I eat with the family and have a good room to sleep in and, take it all together, I have no reason to find fault although the women are secesh as hell. They say but little to me on the subject but they do groan and wish the war was over. And no wonder, for although in all probability their friends are not more than ten to twenty miles from them they have had no letters from them in six months.

The guard they had here before I came got drunk, went out in the night, and fired off his gun. Told the women that he was fired at and he fired back and broke a man's arm. Then he went and reported in camp that the women were busy writing letters to the rebels and had the house searched. He in fact played hell generally, but the poor fool did not know enough to carry on the fun: the next day after the rumpus, one of the captains on General Geary's staff found him dead drunk in the road and his canteen full of whiskey. They put him under arrest and General Geary sent an order to Colonel Cobham, who is in command of our brigade, to detail a man who would not get drunk and one whom he could trust implicitly. Colonel Cobham sent for me and I think it quite a compliment to me as a man and a soldier. I must say that if I had been Colonel Cobham's brother he could not have used me better than he has...

Our regiment has got 276 conscripts from Philadelphia or more properly substitutes, for as near as I can learn there is only one drafted man among the whole lot...They are a rough, drunken set of mostly Dutch and Irish from the docks and railroads of the cities of Philadelphia and New York. A good many of them were engaged in the New York riots and had to run to Philadelphia and go as substitutes to get rid of being arrested. More than half of them have been soldiers before, either in this country or Europe, and that will make them learn quicker than they would if they were all green recruits. But I shall feel ticklish the first fight we go into, for we won't know how far we can trust them. In our company, the new men are most all Dutch and two or three of them were in the Eleventh Corps at the time of their big skedaddle at Chancellorsville. If they try that trick with us, they will find the old men of our regiment will shoot them like dogs as they will deserve. There is some of our new men that can't speak or understand a word of English and we will have fun teaching them to drill. But if I am left on my present duty, I will not have to drill any for a spell and I hope they will get them broke some before I go back to the company.

Ham Sturdevant has been mustered as a Second Lieutenant. He has had his commission for some time but he could not be mustered until the company was filled up. It would have been two or three hundred dollars in his pocket if the company had been filled up that many months ago.

I am very much obliged to you for the list you sent to me of the drafted and of those who belonged {to} the Club, or to give it its proper name, the Farmington Cowards' Mutual Insurance Society. They may think me harsh in what I have said in my letter to William, but I can't see why those at home are not just as much duty-bound to do a little fighting to help put down this rebellion. Those who are already in the field are expected to do it all. The rebels are conscripting every man from sixteen to sixty and taking them after they have hired a substitute. It all seems to make but little difference to the folks up there. They would like to see the war ended but they are not willing to help do any of the work..." [90]

Left you hanging again, didn't I? I was talking about character and the fortunes of war, and things that go bump in the night.

James awoke from a sound sleep, estimating that it must be two or three in the morning. Something had woke him up, but he knew not what. As he lay there and listened, he felt for the handle of Ham's Colt that he kept under his pillow.

There it was: voices in the garden, barely audible, but James had a very keen sense of hearing, even now not yet spoiled by the crash-bang of battle. He got up and slipped his trousers on. With pistol in hand, he went to the window.

There was not much for moonlight right then, clouds being over the moon, but there in the far corner of the garden were two forms, a man and a woman, talking in low, earnest tones.

It made the hairs on the back of his neck stand up straight. Perhaps the Irishman had not been such a fool, after all. Barefoot, but armed with the pistol, he made his way silently out of the room and to the back door. He crept along a hedge until he was less than a rod from them.

"...hours to get here..." the man was saying. He wore a broad-brimmed hat, and moonlight glinted off his sword scabbard. An officer. An officer with a southern accent! James wasted no time. He stepped out.

"I'll thank you to put your hands up and step away from the lady," he said.

They both gave a start, she a little gasp.

"Oh, Mr. Miller," said Ellen when she had recovered. "Please don't shoot him."

"I'm sorry, my dear," said the officer coolly. "Please step away."

"But, Clayton. Oh, Clay..."

"This is between me and Mr. Miller. What's your game, my friend?"

James had the strangest feeling, of having been through all this before, but that was not possible, of course. He motioned to the right with the pistol. "Over there."

The man obliged. Ellen scurried to James's side. "Oh, Mr. Miller, please don't hurt him!"

James said to the officer, "I was sent here to protect these good people." To Ellen, "It looks like the Irish was not so full of the blarney after all."

"For the love of God," she pleaded. "This is my brother! I have not seen him in a year, oh, please, please..."

I guess you know by now, James was a man with a strong sense of duty, and he knew where his duty lay just then: It was to tie this man up, keep him on ice 'til the morning, and then march him over to the provost marshal. Pretty simple stuff. Why, then, all these contrary notions slamming around inside his head, and why this ridiculous sense of having already been through all of this?

Finally, James says, "Well, if I shoot him I suppose it will wake up your mother, and that would not do."

The reb lieutenant smiled and drawled, "Absolutely not. Mothers need their rest."

"How did you get across the river?"

"Waded it. You should tell your pickets to tend to their knitting. I did it right under their noses."

"Still," James said, "you took an awful chance in doing it. I'd have put a bullet in you."

"Well, now's your chance, Yank—if you don't mind waking up Mother."

"What were your intentions in coming here?" (Now, it sounds like these two are having a pleasant enough conversation, but all the while James had that Colt pointed right at Clay's breadbasket.)

The reb give a short laugh. "What would you do in my place, Yank? I saw my chance to see my family for the first time in a year and I took it. I didn't know they would have their own personal guard, which favor I would normally appreciate, except for these circumstances."

Ellen had stood back, listening to their exchange. At last she said, "Mr. Miller, what are you going to do?"

James looked at her face, and saw her desperation. He thought of his own family, father, mother, brothers, and sisters. I don't know if you approve of his decision, but I did, when he finally told me the story.

"Lieutenant, I'll ask you to hand over your pistol and sword there, and I'm going to sit out here on the veranda with my Enfield, and my pistol—and your pistol—for about an hour. Then I reckon I'll give your arms back to you and I had best not see your face around here come daylight."

The reb hastily unbuckled his sword belt. "Miller, that is fair. That is very fair."

Well, James sat on the porch and listened to the family reunion, Mrs. Mitchell sobbing with joy, and the girls all laughing and happy, for the first since he had been there, and Mitchell finally came out just as the night sky was softening.

"I thank you very kindly, Yank," he said. "I truly hope you survive to go home to your family."

As he handed the weapons over James said, "I took the liberty of removing the charges from your pistol."

The reb strapped on his belt. "I reckon that was the prudent thing to do, but now I'll have to get back across the river by artful dodging instead of fighting."

James shrugged. "It kept me occupied."

They shook hands. "Thanks again, Yank. Take care of my family." The reb walked down the steps.

"Say, Lieutenant, this may sound like a foolish question, but have we ever met before?"

"I should hardly think so," Mitchell replied. He looked out at the pink sky to the east. "Well, good day, my friend." He walked across the garden into the woods and disappeared.

James did not sleep at all in what was left of that long night. After all, this was wartime, and even though he had given quarter to an enemy, he did not disregard the possibility of waking up dead with his throat cut. And the strangest thing happened as the rooster crowed:

With almost a jolt he remembered back to a day in the fifties, when he was setting posts by the road in Southwest. The southern accent. *"All the way from Fauquier County...Good day, my friend."*

Well folks, goodbye for now. Next time, out on the porch—or should I say, "veranda"—rain or shine.

***

Susan to Robert and Janet Miller, Sept 9th, 1863

Dear Parents,

I received your letter one week ago and was pleased to hear that you were all well. I am glad that Robert has got home and is well. Mother won't have so much to worry about.

The reason I did not answer you other letter sooner was because we all had the mumps one after another and I thought I would not write until we got well. Johnny had the dysentery and then the mumps and now he has the dysentery again but is getting better. We are all well except him. Robert is at his Grandpa Main's. The wild plums are ripe. They made him quite sick last year and I thought I would let him stay there until they were gone.

Mr. Evarts thinks he can't have the money for you before the first of November. He said he had forgot when the note was due and the amount. I told him they were eighty dollars each and I thought they were due on the 24th of October. I wish you would send me ten dollars in a letter and I can wait until you come down for the rest. Please to write soon. Give my love to all inquiring friends and accept the same for yourself.

Affectionately yours,

Susan A. Miller [91]

While we were shooting turtles and getting lectures from rebel Baptists and stewing about the draft, those events out west which I mentioned a while back were heading for a big showdown.

***

BLOOD AND FIRE

The Battle of Chickamauga, two days of blood and fire down on the Georgia-Tennessee line, took place on the 19th and 20th of September, five days after James's last letter from Summerduck Run. As battles go, it was second only to Gettysburg in casualties. Seeing as how the armies engaged at Gettysburg were some bigger, and three days were required to tote up the butcher's bill there, Chickamauga may have been the worst of the two. I suppose somebody could work it out in sums.

If there are legions of historians who can tell you who did what at Gettysburg, there is only a corporal's guard who can do the same for Chickamauga. That is for a number of reasons. Gettysburg took place in open country, with definite landmarks, and veterans could go back there years later and show you where they were. Even now, I could take you up on Culp's Hill and show you what part of our wall I helped build. And Gettysburg was handy to civilization.

I am glad I was not at Chickamauga. It was some different. It was fought in primitive woodland with neither side having a real good idea of what was going on. Generals, colonels, and privates went into that hell, men were killed and wounded by the scores, hundreds and thousands, flanked, got flanked, volleyed and thundered, and come back out of the brush with no idea of where they had been, how long they had stayed there, or why they did what they did. They knew only that they had seen the elephant.

When it ended, the only thing that was clear to most of them was that the Yankee Army of the Cumberland had come as close to being obliterated as any army ever did in the whole war.

Our side had been outnumbered. Sixty thousand against seventy thousand is a good guess—nobody knows for sure. Bragg's army contained soldiers from all over the South, some of them getting off the trains and marching straight into battle. The roster included twelve thousand men from the Army of Northern Virginia, under James Longstreet. Finally Lee was forced to send troops west, but if there was ever a chance for a Confederate victory out west, this was it, and the rebels fought with the same do or die spirit which had infected us at Gettysburg.

There was at least one person who was not totally convinced that the rebs had won. Only one man, but his name was Braxton Bragg, and he commanded the rebel army. He saw only the bloody cost and the damnable condition of his own army as the sun finally set over Alabama. There is a story that at some time during the war—I don't know if it was at Chickamauga, though it could have been—a private soldier came to headquarters to report that he had seen a Yankee force in retreat. Bragg, personable feller that he was, said huffily, "How would you know what a retreat looks like?" The private replied, "I oughter know, Gin'ral, I been soldiering with you for two years."

Yes, to tell the God's truth, he had never known victory in this war, and so did not recognize it when it stared him in the face. Instead of getting his enemy by the throat and putting in the coup de grace, as a Grant or a Lee would have done, Bragg contented himself with counting the captured enemy cannon, of which there were scores, and letting the Yanks get away.

It is a cardinal principal that, in war, politicians should do the politicking and soldiers should do the fighting. This principal was forgot, overlooked, or ignored more times than is healthy by both breeds of participants on both sides. You had Old Abe saying that if General So-and-So was not going to use his army then he'd like to borrow it a while. You had them dark fears that McClellan was going to use his popularity with his army to take over the government. At Chickamauga and Chattanooga you had a young assistant secretary of war meddling in military affairs.

Charles Dana was his name. He was Edwin Stanton's snitch, pure and simple. Using the telegraph, Dana sent a blow-by-blow account of the battle to Washington. He was very plain in saying that the battle was lost due to Rosecrans's incompetence, but he himself might have had a hand in losing it.

One of the Yankee units which was not stampeded was the Lightning Brigade, two thousand mounted infantrymen armed with the latest in repeating rifles, under a Colonel Wilder. When Longstreet's assault came pouring through, Wilder was on its flank and saw the opportunity for a hell for leather charge through the middle of it, which probably would have emptied a good many of his saddles, but would have likely wreaked hell and damnation on Longstreet's wing for the rest of the day.

As Wilder was about to do it, up comes Dana, who by then was rattled looser than a bucket of bolts. He does a "Do-you-know-who-I-am?" on Wilder, and insists that the battle is lost and it is Wilder's responsibility to get him safely to Chattanooga. Wilder, not daring to buck the assistant secretary of war, scrubbed his plan and took his outfit, and Dana, to Chattanooga, and Wilder's charge becomes one of them might-have-beens that fascinate those of us who dream. Tennyson's Light Brigade would have had some more competition in the annals of heroism and poetry, I reckon.

Rosecrans, lovable, eccentric Old Rosy, had flat out let the management of the battle get away from him. When Longstreet punched through a hole in his line—a hole which Union mismanagement had helped create—Rosecrans and a third of his army had been druv from the field. The other two-thirds held on by the skin of their teeth, and if Bragg could not be convinced that he had won, Rosy could not see that maybe he had not quite lost. He thought the stampede which had swept him off to Chattanooga was general throughout the army. The part of the army that did hold on, under General George Thomas, was able to fend off the last Confederate attacks and then withdrew to Chattanooga in fairly good order. Thomas became known as the "Rock of Chickamauga."

So the Yankees dragged ass into Chattanooga and started to fortify for a last ditch stand. Bragg followed, and occupied high ground around the town—mainly that of Lookout Mountain and Missionary Ridge. After winning everyplace else all summer, we ended up with a Yankee army in as bad a fix as any we had known since the beginning of the war. It would take some extreme measures to bail them out, and that's where we come in.

Summer Duck Run, Fauquier Co., Va September the 14th '63

"I was sorry to hear that Father's health had been impaired but I hope he will get along without any further trouble. From what Robert and John said in their letters he has worked altogether too hard through haying and I should think he had done hard work enough in his life so that he need not work so hard as to make himself sick in his old age. But there is an old saying that old folks are the most foolish of any, and it does seem to me that both of you are bound to give yourselves more trouble for your children than is needful...

...I hope you will go and see Susan this fall (both of you if you can, that is) for I know she would be glad to see you. God knows that she has a hard time of it all alone with the children but what can't be helped must be endured.

...You may beat a boss to tell just where we are; I will do the best I can to tell you. We are on the east side of the Rappahannock River some ten miles to the southeast of the station of that name, twenty miles to the north and west of Fredericksburg, and some twenty-five miles from Culpeper Courthouse near Ellis's Ford. This is a poor country. The soil is naturally thin and has been plowed to death. It does not look as though it could raise white beans but they do get some very fair crops of corn which seems to be the only crop they try to raise in this part of the country.

I was glad to hear the draft was over although I feel sorry and ashamed to think that so many men showed the coward by joining those clubs. I do hope that the government will make another draft soon and keep on doing so until they get all the men they want. In the letter I wrote to William, I told him what I thought of their actions and they may think me somewhat harsh in the language I made use of. But I can't think {of} the course the men in that section have taken to evade the draft as anything but a white-livered, cowardly piece of poltroonry. For the life of me I can't see why those at home have not just as good a right to part of the fighting and dying to sustain the government and crush the rebellion as those of us that are in the army. But they are more to be pitied than we are, for the coward's fear of dying is worse—a great deal worse—than is brave men's fighting (and dying if need be) in the defense of that which every man worthy of the name values dearer than life: his own honor and that of his country, and his flag." [92]

To his father (Private and Confidential) (Undated)

Dear Father,

You may think me rather harsh in my denunciations of traitors and treason in the North, but I have used the mildest language I could that would even partially express my utter abhorrence and detestation of those false, black-hearted scoundrels in the North who are enticing our men to desert, encouraging the enemy, and giving aid and comfort to the foe by every means in their power. There can be no doubt but what a very large share of the miseries and distress of this war are justly chargeable to the Copperheads of the North and we soldiers hate them a great deal more than we do the rebels in arms. The English language does not furnish terms mean and harsh enough to express the feelings of the army in regard to the traitors at home.

As near as I can find out, some of my relatives in Farmington and Eldred are quite sensitive to things I have said in my letters. But wounded birds almost always flutter, and let the gelded jades wince for all I care. If they felt in regard to this rebellion as I do, they would not be so sensitive. In regard to language: it is not half bad enough to express my opinion of sympathizers with traitors. I hope you will keep this private for I guess they who are so sensitive have enough to make them feel mean without my helping them and I have no particular desire to make hardness with anyone.

There seems to be quite a disposition to find fault with the conscription bill. Although I don't like the 300-dollar part of the bill, the rest of it I do like and it will not be any harder for those who come under the bill than it is for thousands of us that are already in the service. Those who come now will have escaped two years of hard service. The emancipation bill is agoing to ruin Virginia and I suppose it is the same in the other slave states. In Virginia, the niggers have been in the habit of doing all the work. Now there is good prospect of the citizens starving, and I don't care how quick. Although it is hard to think of the women and children suffering, if the men don't want them to suffer let them throw down their arms, go home, and take care of them.

Well, I think I have made out to write quite a long letter, so I will close.

James T. Miller [93]

There is some difference of opinion on when James wrote that letter. Some say it was wrote in the spring of '64, just after our furlough. I say it was wrote about the end of summer of 1863, before we left Virginia. By the spring of 1864 the draft bill was old news, thoroughly discussed in the letters back and forth. James's comments have a here and now ring to them, instead of rehashing old news. I do not believe James wasted his visits to his family in berating the boys, even as strongly as he felt about their dodging their obligations. I think he felt that life is all too short for that sort of thing in a thirty-day furlough. For another thing, he talks about emancipation ruining ***Virginia.*** By March of '64 we had been in Alabama and Tennessee for six months and Virginia was quickly becoming but a dim memory. He also says "as near as he can find out" the boys were quite sensitive to things he had said in his letters. Well, if he had said it to their faces, it was not something he would have had to "find out" and if he had said it to their faces why would he refer to what he had said in his letters?

Nope, late summer, early fall, 1863.

CHAPTER FOURTEEN
TO TENNESSEE

It was probably only a day or two after James had hosted the Mitchell reunion that I showed up, in somewhat of a hurry. James was carrying water to the barn as I rounded the house. "James!" I calls. "Get your stuff. We're moving out quick!"

"Right away, Sergeant. Where are we headed?"

"Don't know for sure. The rumor is, Tennessee."

"Tennessee, of all places. Now there's a bully rumor."

James packed up and said hasty goodbyes to the Mitchell women, and in less than twenty minutes we were stepping out up the road. When we got back to camp it appeared that rumor told the truth. All about was the hustle and bustle of an outfit getting ready to move out, and the shouts were all of "Tennessee!" Tents were coming down, and the quartermasters were directing men here and there with crates and bundles of equipment. We were met by Captain Warner. With all that was going on, our good captain still managed to spare a few moments for James Miller.

A six-by-nine wall tent gives very little room for pacing, but Captain Warner was doing his best. Finally, he said, "I had a visitor this morning, Miller."

"Did you?" James replied innocently.

"Yes. An old black gentleman by the name of Otis stopped by to tell me what a great man you are."

"I see."

"And he told me what made you a great man. It seems you let 'Massa Mitchell' visit at the house and did not detain him. Is that a fact?"

James took a deep breath. "Yes, sir. It is a fact."

"Massa Mitchell is a Confederate officer, is he not?"

"Yes, sir, he is."

"Well, at least you don't deny it. Miller, we are ordered to Tennessee. It is a serious situation and demands our full attention, so I am not going to run this into the ground. Perhaps I shall later, when things calm down. As for now, you may consider yourself reduced back to private. Do you have anything to say?"

James was flushed, feeling himself getting redder by the moment. "No, sir, I do not. You have every right to reduce me."

"Yes, I do. That is all, then. Go pack your equipment."

Well, like I said, it was a long time before James got around to telling me the story of what happened during his guard duty, and I was just about his best friend. Cap Warner got wounded out shortly after we got to Tennessee, so nothing more came of it. James never did know if Otis genuinely wanted our people to know of the kindness he had shown the Mitchells, or if it was revenge for the Mitchells chasing his son all the way to Pennsylvania back about 1858. Your guess is as good as mine, but strange things happen in war, and it sure is a small world.

Do you remember Charlie Lyon inviting James to come with him to see some country and get paid for it? Well, as it turned out, Charlie spent nearly four years marching and fighting in the little space of country between Gettysburg and Richmond, but we were abruptly called away from our idyll along the Rappahannock to make this fateful move. About twelve thousand men from the Eleventh and Twelfth corps were loaded into boxcars, sixty men to a car, and shuttled through Pennsylvania, Ohio, Kentucky, and Tennessee to rescue the desperate Army of the Cumberland.

Why us? Well, we were always the poor relations in the family of the Army of the Potomac, I reckon. Most of the rest of the army had gone with McClellan to the Peninsula in the spring of '62 and became a brotherhood forged in the fires of the Seven Days Battles. The Eleventh and Twelfth had stayed up around the Shenandoah Valley and were rather outside of the family. Whether the decision was made in Washington or by Meade at army headquarters I don't know, and may be my "woe is us" notion had nothing to do with the decision. As far as why the Dutchmen of the Eleventh Corps were sent, after lousing up at Chancellorsville and Gettysburg, I have a theory there, too, and I don't believe I have to tell you what it is. Well, I guess I just did.

Somebody had to command us. For that job the government happened to have a spare major general by the name of "Fighting Joe" Hooker. Now, Hooker had lost at Chancellorsville as the commander of the Army of the Potomac, but he was still one of the best combat leaders around, and Robert E. Lee would not be in Tennessee to put a twist on his head. We still liked Hooker, and there were not a few cheers as we marched by him at the railroad station.

Moving us, lock, stock, and cannon, all the way from the Rappahannock to Murfreesboro, Tennessee, was a feat of logistics that some doubted could be done in the time they said. We left camp on the 24th of September and had to march twenty-five miles to Bealeton Station to load onto flatcars, boxcars, coaches, anything that would roll. The first train took us into Washington, to the relay house. From there we rode the Baltimore and Ohio over the mountains to the Ohio River. From Martinsburg to Wheeling the country was rough and desolate-looking. We marched across the river on a pontoon bridge to Bellaire, Ohio, and stayed there a day while the Ohio Central collected cars enough to haul us through the flat, fertile landscape of Ohio and Indiana, "A paradise for farmers," James said. We went via Columbus and Indianapolis to Jefferson, Indiana, where we were ferried back to the south side of the Ohio River to Louisville, Kentucky.

We got to Nashville on the sixth of October, and two days later we detrained in Murfreesboro. As we got deeper into Tennessee, it was hard to believe that we were on the same continent as the states of Ohio and Indiana. From prosperity, fertility, and a loyal population that lined the tracks as we rolled by, we went to near total desolation: buildings burned down or abandoned, no fences, fields left to weeds and ruin, no commerce, whole towns empty of their white population.

What a war...

Murfreesboro, Tennessee, October the 8th

"The country is--or would be--very pretty, but the moment we crossed the river, the blighting effects of slavery and the rebellion became visible on all sides. We are encamped close to the town on the east side. The battle of Stone's River was fought on the west side of the town and about two to four miles from our camp. This seems to have been a rich valley and resembles the valley of the Shenandoah more than any other place I have seen. The appearance of Murfreesboro indicates a wealthy set of inhabitants, but its glory has departed for you can hardly find a white citizen in the town and there is not a vestige of a fence to be seen in several miles.

The day before we got here the rebel cavalry under Wheeler made a raid on the railroad and succeeded in burning a bridge some four miles when they were driven back towards Shelbyville, Rosecrans's cavalry following them close. After following for four days, they caught up with them and a sharp fight ensued in which our cavalry killed 125 of the rebels and took 150 of them prisoners...and four pieces of artillery.

Christiana, Oct the 10

Well, Robert, I had got so much written on the 8th when the bugle sounded to strike tents. We fell into line and marched some ten miles on the road to Tullahoma. Our Brigade is engaged in guarding the railroad and there is a story in camp that our Division is to be kept guarding it. I hope it may be true for although we will have a great deal of guard duty to do that is not as hard as it is to march with big knapsacks on our backs, to say nothing of the fighting. But we stand more of a chance to be taken prisoners.

We get but very few papers since we came here and I know very little of what is going on. I was very much pleased with the particulars in regard to your old company and regiment. I do hope that there is loyalty enough left in Pennsylvania to re-elect Governor Curtin. If the soldiers had a chance to vote, four-fifths of the votes would go for Curtin. If the Copperheads succeed in electing Woodward, I shall be sorry.... Please to write soon and direct to Co. B, 111th Regiment Pennsylvania Volunteers, 12th Corps, Army of the Cumberland. Yours as ever,

James T. Miller

P.S. Please to drop the 'Corporal' in directing letters to me. The captain had me reduced a few weeks since and so I don't want to be addressed as such." [94]

Camp of the 111th Regt PV Christiana Station ten miles from Murfreesboro Tennessee Oct the 11 '63

"You will probably have heard before this reaches you that our Corps and the Eleventh have left the Army of the Potomac and gone to reinforce the Army of the Cumberland. We left the Army of the Potomac at the Rapidan River on the evening of the twenty-fourth of last month and started on our long journey of twelve hundred miles....

I once thought I would like to live in western Virginia but if the part through which the railroad passes is a fair specimen of that new state, I don't see how anything can live there. But from the time we crossed the Ohio until we got to Louisville, we passed through a most beautiful country. The people cheered us as we passed and at quite a number of towns the people fed us on the best their rich country afforded. We reached Indianapolis one evening and took supper in the Soldiers' Retreat. It was a good, hearty meal, and from what I could see it is a very handsome city. We stayed all night there and the next night stayed at Louisville.

...This place, Christiana, is a few houses and a watering place for the cars. It is very pleasantly situated but I am afraid the ground is too low and wet for the health of the troops. Our Brigade is stretched along the railroad for four miles, the Brigade headquarters being here with our regiment....

I got a letter from Susan dated on the twenty-first of last month. She, Ellen, and Robert were well; John was not very healthy but she said he was better than he had been. I was sorry to hear by William's letter that sister Jane's boy Seymour was sick with the fever. I hope he will get along after a little." [95]

***

WAUHATCHIE

War held charms for us no longer...if it ever did. James may be forgiven for his wishful thinking that the White Stars were going to do nothing but guard a railroad after coming twelve hundred miles. That was not in the cards, and of course we all knew it. The situation was just too serious for to have a first rate outfit like ours sit on our backsides and watch the caboose disappear down the track. Our other division, Williams's Red Stars, ended up doing that.

Just as the rebs had pulled out all the stops to raise up an army strong enough to beat Rosecrans, so the federal government now went to unusual lengths to save him and his army—well, his army, anyway. The government did three things to get the situation turned around.

First, they had us go west. That was an unusual, exciting, and inspiring way to go to war. After walking everywhere we had to go for almost two years, it was a novel experience to see the countryside by rail. It was exciting because we knew we were being called on to do something important, and it was inspiring to see all those thousands of Ohioans pour out their hospitality to us, even lining the tracks in between towns just to wave at us.

Since James didn't mention it, I must admit that I turned out to be pretty much a failure at that drill sergeant business. Of all those men which I had escorted down from division headquarters back on September 3rd, a good many "jumped ship," so to speak, during our trip across the country. But they were no great loss. Many of the bounty men and substitutes who we got courtesy of the draft saw the opportunity—and necessity—to desert. See, they also knew that we were being sent to do something important, which would likely involve getting shot at, and many of them wanted no part of that game, so they elected to desert before they got too far into the Deep South, where getting back north would not be easy. Most probably went to another city, hired on again to be substitutes, and collected their money all over again. Like a land office, that substitute business.

Next, or at the same time, they pulled up an army from Mississippi, totaling up at least as many men as came with us, under Major General William Tecumseh Sherman. Sherman came up the river to Memphis and then headed east along the Memphis and Charleston railroad, fixing it up as he went.

Now and then during my story I have mentioned a man who was getting things done out west, at places like Shiloh and Vicksburg, while we suffered our fools and Fredericksburgs and Chancellorsvilles. The third thing they done was to call him up to head the effort. U.S. Grant met with Secretary Stanton in a hotel room—in Cincinnati, I believe it was—and was given the job of commanding the collection of men from east and west who were to raise the siege of Chattanooga. First thing Grant did was send a wire, firing Rosecrans and putting Thomas in charge of the Army of the Cumberland and telling Thomas to hold Chattanooga. Thomas replied, "We will hold the town till we starve." Then Grant took a train to Bridgeport, Alabama, got on his horse and rode to Chattanooga.

Like most people, when I think of a siege I think of somebody being surrounded. Chattanooga was not like that. (At this point a good map of the area would be in order.)

Chattanooga sits on the south side of the Tennessee River. Stand in the center of town and look up in any direction and you will see that you are surrounded by high mountains and ridges. The railroads that run east from Memphis and south from Nashville meet at Bridgeport and then snake up through the mountain valleys to come into the town from the southwest. Bragg took control of the river and the railroad, right after Chickamauga. It ended up that the only way to get supplies into Chattanooga was by a long, winding treacherous wagon road north of the Tennessee River. That was the route Grant took to get to the scene, and by the time he traveled it, it was well curbed with the carcasses of dead mules and burned wagons. The mules died of overwork, exposure, and starvation, and the wagons had been raided and burned by Joe Wheeler's cavalry. The Army of the Cumberland might as well have been surrounded, because by the time Grant arrived they were on quarter rations and didn't have enough ammunition left for a one day's fight.

Yes, serious. The first thing to do was to open up a practical supply route, and we had a part in that project which ended up getting us into a hell of a fight.

Hooker's job was to get south of the Tennessee River and advance east toward Chattanooga while some of Thomas's boys attacked toward us. There was some dramatic stuff in that enterprise: The Cumberlanders made a night assault by pontoon boat to capture a crossing of the Tennessee, with careful planning and precise timing involved. To make it short, the plan worked. Between Bridgeport and Chattanooga we soon had enough men from the Army of the Potomac to keep the rebs away from the Tennessee River so that eventually the steamboats could pretty much guarantee three squares a day and plenty of bullets for all the Yankees on the scene.

When I said that Bragg had control of the river and the rails into Chattanooga, I did not mean that he had had to string a cable acrosst the river or plant men on the ties. He did it by holding Lookout Mountain.

During our career there were always mountains hanging over us, sometimes being our enemies as much as the flesh and blood rebs: There was Cedar Mountain, where the 111th saw the elephant; South Mountain, which we had to cross on our way to Antietam; the long Catoctin Range that haunted us on our way to Gettysburg. Now we had another mountain to contend with, and this was not just ANY mountain.

Lookout Mountain is the end of a long ridge that is slanty up from the southwest toward Chattanooga. It towered over us, off to our right, the whole way from Bridgeport to Chattanooga. It is high, sure enough, and looks like a challenge to climb even without opposition. After a while, we noticed some familiar enemies, Johnnies from Longstreet's Corps, gawking at us from crags on the mountain as we marched up the Wauhatchie Valley.

You should always remember that your enemy is as human as you. At the same time that we were being awed by the mountain and thinking of the near impossibility of ever capturing it, our enemies were being awed by the seemingly endless length of our column. They recognized us, too. Here, a thousand miles from Virginia, was to be a violent reunion of old adversaries.

The plan had worked to perfection, and the solution ended up being too easy. Those facts added up to a tendency for our generals, particularly Hooker, to become somewhat careless and overconfident. Howard's Eleventh Corps led our column and pushed on until it met up with the Cumberlanders near their Tennessee River crossing, and then they set up camp.

We of Geary's division ended up strung out along the railroad southwest of Chattanooga, with ours and Greene's brigades and division headquarters at Wauhatchie, a little way station 'longside the tracks. The brigade still consisted of the 29th, 109th, and 111th Pennsylvania Regiments under Colonel Cobham. Greene's brigade was made up of the 78th, 102nd, 137th, and 149th New York. We also had Knap's artillery battery, and it was lucky for us that we did. But all told, we had not over fifteen hundred men.

With the nearest of our other troops a couple of miles in either direction, it dawned on the enemy that he could come down off the mountain, isolate us, and capture us in a surprise attack.

If you read about Wauhatchie in the history books, you will see that it was not the battle we made it out to be at the time. The odds were not near as bad as we thought, although they could have been if the rebs' plan hadn't misfired. I won't dwell on correcting the versions which James and Calvin and I put out. Read about it and you'll see. This is just the way it seemed to us.

It was the night of the 29th of October, 1863.

It was about 9 p.m. when I took my shoes off and rolled myself up in my wool blanket and gum blanket. I looked up at the moon. It was about full, sailing across a cloudless sky. You could even see to read. The fields alongside the railroad embankment was covered with men in slumber. In a little house a single candle glowed. All in all, pretty peaceful. I cocked my head up and saw a few officers pacing to and fro. Colonel Cobham was in quiet conversation with Colonel Walker, and now and then one of them would gesture toward the mountain or up the valley toward the rest of the corps. I had felt a certain unease when we filed off the road into our present position, but it is the officers' duty to worry and plan while we get our forty winks. I must say, though, that the concern I detected in them was contagious.

Suddenly there was a smatter of firing from our picket line, which was two companies of the 29th Pennsylvania. "Up, men! Form up on your stacks!" commanded Tom Walker.

There was not much fuss or confusion, as far as I could see, as the regiment seemed to rise out of the ground and we fell in behind our musket stacks. "Take arms! Load!" We seized our guns and there was a rattle of ramrods as we all crammed powder and a minie ball down the barrel.

Then it was quiet again. We stood in ranks facing the looming shadows of Lookout Mountain. Nobody came running back from the pickets to tell us what was going on. After a few minutes Tom Walker said, "Go back to bed, boys, but don't take your brogans off."

We uncapped our rifles, stacked arms, and headed back to our blankets, but before we got into them the firing started again, a crackle of gunfire that fluttered across the entire front of our picket line, and we saw the flashes out among the trees. This time it did not stop, and the shots blended together until it was almost volley fire. We jumped up and threw on our leathers as the drummers beat the long roll.

"Looks like we've got a fight on our hands," said James.

"I think we're in for it, pard," I replied as we ran to fall in.

I never did like to fight at night. In this war, fighting after the sun went down was not in fashion, but we seemed to get more than our share of it. First there was Chancellorsville, and then Gettysburg, and our harrowing night on Culp's Hill. It is everything about it. First the doubt that the darkness stirs up, then the things that it can do in your imagination, such as multiplying and amplifying all the fearsome hazards of the day. And then, when battle is joined, the spectacle of thousands of muskets flashing and roaring is simply awesome. You are not fighting against men; you are fighting fiery spirits which send swarms of death demons humming and buzzing around you. You can see but few of your comrades, but you can hear them scream and cry out. It gets worse as the smoke thickens, and in the night it seems to lie close to the ground, suffocating you in sulfur and brimstone.

But no matter. Whether I liked it or not, the ball had opened, and we all had to dance. What was left of our picket line came in on the run with the Johnnies at their heels, coming from the north, down the road from Chattanooga. As we fell in facing the mountain east of us, it dawned on somebody that we faced the wrong direction. "Change front to the left on the first company, and do it damned quick!" bawled Walker, and we rushed to comply. Our right flank would anchor at the railroad embankment as the 109th Pennsylvania rushed to form up on our left.

In the dark, in the noise and confusion, we executed that maneuver as if on the parade field, and it was a good thing we did, for in an instant they were upon us, swarming out of the dark, filling the field in front of us.

I shot a reb who was coming at me with his bayonet. I cursed him as just another fool who brought a bayonet to a gunfight. To my left, James clubbed a feller I did not see who was also about to stab at me. For a moment it was all animal fury, grunts, groans, and screams, with blood splattering and men cursing. Then they pulled back, but they did not go very far. I was about to thank James for his charitable contribution to my welfare, when he pointed off to the right. "Look there! They're coming around." I looked in time to see a big crowd of them moving to our right, across the tracks. Soon the command was given for the two companies on the right (one of which was us) to change front to the right, and in an instant we rushed to obey the command, so our two companies faced back the way we had faced to begin with.

Knap's battery was both our salvation and our curse. The science of artillery being what it was, they always avoided a position where they had to fire over the infantry, if they could possibly help it. This was one of those times when necessity was the mother of destruction. They swung the guns around on the little knoll they occupied and blazed away with shell and canister. Now, canister was nothing more than a can packed with slugs, which sprayed out of the gun like a giant sawed-off shotgun. It was the most devastating weapon on the field at close range. The problem was that what was left of the can became a ragged piece of metal flying through the air. Shell was fused, and the fuses were not always reliable, so sometimes they exploded too soon. With the guns firing over us, accidents were bound to happen.

The first time the guns fired, they blew my forage cap off, and I never saw it again. Later on, I found a black felt slouch hat, and never again wore a forage cap. Most of the western regiments tended to slouch hats anyway, which were a better protection from the rain and sun.

The fight seemed to go on for hours. My musket got so hot, I wrapped a rag around the barrel so's I could hold it to load. James was still to my left, matching me shot for shot. The rebels withdrew, then came on again, firing as they came. A captain of the 109th Pennsylvania came along bareheaded collecting in his hat the ammunition from the cartridge boxes of the dead and wounded. The captain called out, "Give them hell, boys, I've got another hat full of kill seed!"

Suddenly James let out a little gasp and dropped to one knee. I knelt down.

"Are you hit? I asked.

"Just above the ankle...right leg," James replied.

"Look like you better get out of here," I says, and then Lieutenant Pettit came up from the file closers.

"You hit, Miller?" he says.

"Yes, but not too ba—" At that instant one of Knap's guns fired and a piece of sizzling metal hit the lieutenant in the head, carrying most of it away and splattering us with his blood and brains. Pettit never knew what hit him. We were froze there for a second as his corpse toppled over. James wobbled to his feet.

"Looks like I can give them a few more before I go," he muttered, and he bit the end off a cartridge. After what had just happened, I could not argue with him. I stood beside him, and we each fired three or four more.

James shifted to his wounded leg. "Ugh!" he says.

"Hurt, does it?" I asked.

"Not much, but I'm squishing a shoeful of blood. Reckon I'll go now," he said sheepishly.

"Well, you gave them a few for the Looey. Good luck, James. Have a good rest." James shambled off, using his musket for a crutch.

I chanced to look back at Knap's battery in action while drawing ammunition. The guns stood on that little embattled knoll, silhouetted in the moonlight and the flash of musketry, and I saw men and horses going down steadily. It seemed as if no creature could live long on the knoll. There is a tendency in battle for soldiers to fire high, even moreso at night, and the battery was right up where all of Johnny's "overs" were flying. I saw an officer go down. It turned out to be General Geary's son.

We were outnumbered three to one (or so we thought) and they did have us nearly surrounded, with bullets zinging in from every direction. It was a fact that our two companies fronting on the railroad tracks were not enough to match the two regiments which the rebs sent to flank us, so Geary sent the 78th and 149th New York to extend our right. Colonel Rickards of the 29th Pennsylvania got the idea to have the artillerymen wheel a gun across the tracks to get on the enemy's left flank. Knap's battery had lost so many horses that the 29th had to supply manpower to move the gun, but when it went into action it wreaked havoc on the enemy.

All this time, Howard and Joe Hooker had been trying to move reinforcements down the road to us, but the Johnnies also had men blocking the route, and they fought a little battle of their own, in a state of confusion greater than that which we knew. Finally, the pressure from Howard and Hooker and, if I may say, the fierce resistance of our fight, was too much for the rebs, which turned out to be a South Carolina brigade not much bigger than our force. Their commander called it off, and by three in the morning it was all over.

General Howard and the 33rd Massachusetts arrived at Wauhatchie about dawn. Howard and the "Dutchmen," the ill-famed Eleventh Corps. We never thought we'd be glad to see him—or them—but we sure were... we sure were...

As it was, the loss was heavy throughout the brigade, but the 111th Pennsylvania and the 137th New York suffered the most casualties. Old General Greene, commander of the New Yorkers, was seriously wounded in the mouth. General Geary's son, one of Knap's battery's section leaders, was killed. Nearly all the artillerymen and all the horses were killed or wounded. Colonel Walker was creased over the eye by a minie ball and Major Boyle was killed along with many others of my brave comrades.

Calvin's best friend, Robert Wilson, was also among those killed. Calvin felt mighty blue.

The next day, our commissary sergeant, Lowell, made a rough box for the body of Major Boyle, and I was one of those sent with the box to get it onto the flatboat with some of our wounded, including James Miller. It was a sad sight at the riverbank as our dead and wounded were loaded aboard. General Geary was there, seeing his son's body safely aboard the same boat. That day he was a grieving father rather than a general commanding a division. His face was ashen and strained, and he kept a hand on the coffin up to the last second. I heard him say, in a tortured voice, "This is the price I pay for the pride I had in him."

It would be a sad journey down the river, not without peril from the looks of the current, and sadder still upon arrival at Bridgeport. The officer there, who would be taking charge of Major Boyle's body, was none other than his son, who would not know until the boat pulled in that his father was taking his last ride.

It appeared that James's luck had finally run out, with that leg wound, which he will be telling all at home about. I helped him hobble onto the flatboat and got him situated. He was already tending to some of the more serious wounded as I said, "Goodbye, pard. Have a nice rest." I shook his hand, stepped ashore, and watched as they shoved off.

I would not see him again for near two months.

U.S. General Hospital, Bridgeport, Alabama, Nov the 2nd

"As you will see by the heading of this, I am at last in the place that of all others I have most dreaded: a hospital. But, thank God, I am not sick, only slightly wounded in the right leg three inches above the ankle. I was hit on the morning of the 29th about two o'clock. Our Division was ordered to the front about one week before. We reached a point some six miles from Chattanooga, went into camp, and lay down to sleep in plain sight of the rebs on Lookout Mountain and within range of their guns. Just about midnight, the rebs fired on our pickets and alarmed the camp. The men got into line; two of our companies were sent out as skirmishers and having failed to find the enemy, we got orders to lie down again with our equipments on. In just about fifteen minutes the firing began again and we had just time to get into line when the graybacks came on quite thick and the battle began in earnest.

...The rebels were from five to eight thousand and we had about one thousand men and four pieces of cannon. It was lucky for us that we had the artillery for the rebs did not have any and our guns proved our salvation. The rebs outflanked us on both sides and but for the cannon they would have surrounded us. But when they attempted to do so, the grape and canister from our artillery drove them back with loss. The enemy in our immediate front was Hampton's Legion of South Carolina troops, belonging to Longstreet's Corps. The fight was very sharp and close; our whole loss was 225 in killed and wounded. The rebs did not take a single prisoner and to tell the truth we did not take but a few of them....

The loss in our regiment was seven killed and thirty-four wounded. The largest share fell to the lot of Company B, having four killed and fourteen wounded out of thirty engaged. Our second lieutenant was killed; our first lieutenant was severely hit in the left side; and our major, John A. Boyle, was killed. Our lieutenant colonel, Thomas M. Walker, was slightly wounded but is in command of the regiment again. General G. S. Greene, in command of the third brigade, was quite severely hit through the face and Colonel Cobham was hit with a spent bullet on the side of the head but, thank God, was not hurt. Myron E. Smith has a severe wound on the right arm caused by the premature bursting of one of our own shells. But the Second Division of the Twelfth Corps has every reason to be proud of the White Star, for it has never yet led us to the battle but what we have been victorious.

A son of General Geary, a first lieutenant in Knap's Battery, was killed and the General feels very bad. He was a very promising young man--brave, gallant, accomplished, and considered one of the very best of our young artillery officers. General Geary fought with his usual coolness and gallantry with an eagle eye on the movements of the foe, meeting them with skill and promptitude. Generals Hooker and Howard complimented Geary on the gallantry and success of our defense.

Just after the rebs fell back from our line, a part of the Eleventh Corps attacked the rebels on their flank and had a sharp engagement, losing about as many men as we did. But being compelled to attack their foe, they did not inflict as large a loss on the enemy as we were able to, acting on the defensive and using our artillery with murderous effect. We found over 200 dead rebels in front of our position the morning after the fight. They removed most of their wounded. We found some twenty of the wounded and six or eight of them have died.

This is a very mountainous country. The Tennessee River at this place is a beautiful stream, at least twice as wide as the Allegheny at Warren.

...was glad to hear that your health was good but was sorry to hear that Mother's health was so feeble...Tell {Joseph} that I will answer his letter just as soon as I find out where we are likely to stay long enough {for} your letters to reach me. I rather expect we will be sent to Nashville or Murfreesboro....

In regard to the boys not liking my calling them hard names, I did not much expect they would. But I thought they deserved all I told them--and a good deal more--but I will not provoke them any more unless they broach the subject first. If they do, I shall be compelled to answer them in something of the old style." [96]

U.S. General Hospital, Nashville, Tenn Nov the 7th 63

"...I was in the hospital at Bridgeport, Alabama, when I received your letter and one from Father of the same date, so I answered Father's and as I expected to shift quarters soon, I thought I would not answer yours until I found out where we were to stop. We left Bridgeport on the 5th and got to this place this morning at one o'clock. I like the appearance of things very well but the rules are very strict...my wound is doing as well as could be expected under the circumstances.

We laid in the rain one night in the field hospital after the fight and then were brought to Bridgeport on a flatboat and stayed there three days. They came near starving us and then sent us here in cattle cars. It took them forty hours to run 122 miles. Our wounds were not dressed in that time and feel some sore this morning. Still, I can walk around quite comfortable. There are eight of our regiment in this ward and I think my wound is the lightest of any of them. In fact, I have seen but two or three men that were hit at that battle and rendered unfit for duty whose wounds were lighter than mine...." [97]

***

TO SAVE CHATTANOOGA

For more than two years, the story of James Miller has also been the story of the 111th Pennsylvania Volunteers. Well, after Wauhatchie we lost him for a while, and his experiences were very different from ours and, you will see, much more pleasant. I'll tell his story after I get finished with ours.

After the battle, after we had shipped our wounded off down the Tennessee River and buried all the dead rebels, we went into camp on Raccoon Mountain, not far from the battlefield. We stayed there for nearly a month, while Grant waited for Sherman to come up and for the Army of the Cumberland to recover sufficiently from their hard times. But even when Grant was ready, the Cumberland fellows were not quite what an army ought to be. Most of their artillery was immobile for want of horses; the dozen or so divisions which had fought Chickamauga were consolidated down to seven. Two of the three corps were temporarily disbanded, with their commanders, McCook and Crittenden, removed. The attitude of General Grant and, I must say, the rank and file of our easterners and Sherman's westerners, was that the Cumberlanders were a passel of losers, and we were going to show them how to fight.

For the battles for Chattanooga, the Army of the Cumberland mustered about forty thousand men. Sherman brought with him about twenty thousand in the Army of the Tennessee, and Hooker had about ten thousand engaged. Total for the Union Army was therefore about seventy thousand men. The rebs barely mustered forty thousand, for Bragg had dispatched Longstreet with fifteen thousand men in an ill-conceived expedition to try and recapture Knoxville, Tennessee. Bragg and Longstreet had quarreled over the lost opportunities after Chickamauga, and Bragg mainly sent him off just to get rid of him. Knoxville was held by our old General Burnside with his Ninth Corps. Well, Longstreet failed in his attempt and over the winter he just kept on a-going, cross-country, all the way back to Virginia.

We closed out 1863 with a resounding victory at Chattanooga, becoming famous for taking Lookout Mountain in the "Battle above the Clouds." Them newspapers, I swear, they'll make a to-do out of most anything.

Anyway, Joe Hooker had the job of taking Lookout. He had a division from each of the three armies at Chattanooga. There was us in

Geary's division from Virginia, Cruft's division of the Cumberlanders, and Osterhaus's division from Sherman. We had the rebs vastly outnumbered there on the mountain, but it was no cakewalk. The 111th held the post of honor in the line of battle, so to speak: the extreme right near the summit. Pennsylvania inscribed a tablet to the 111th on the Palisades in memory and recognition of our feat.

On the next day, the 25th of November, we were in the line of battle that stormed Missionary Ridge, but did not meet with much resistance in our front. In the battle, Sherman's men attacked the right flank of the enemy on the ridge and were stalled by fierce resistance from a Confederate division led by a tough Irish rebel by the name of Patrick Cleburne. The battle was finally won by an all out assault on the Confederate center on the ridge by Thomas's supposedly washed-up Army of the Cumberland, who I suppose got just a mite tired of everyone looking down on them and figured that nobody would look down on them if they were on top of Missionary Ridge. It was a glorious day for them. The story goes that nobody ordered the assault; it just happened. Someone said, "When those fellows get started, all hell can't stop them." And Grant growled something to the effect that it had better work or somebody would pay. We learned more of the grit of the Cumberlanders as the war went on.

We had attacked Lookout with three days rations in light marching order. We were out eight days, following the enemy to Ringgold, Georgia, where we had a sharp engagement. Their rear guard, under that Cleburne character again, suckered Joe Hooker in and gave us a bloody nose. The campaign was one of great hardship and suffering, night and day marching and skirmishing. It froze hard at night and if we were fortunate enough to have a few hours in camp, we were not permitted to build fires that would draw the enemy's fire. We were short on rations, shoes, and clothing, but we had been victorious and the morale of the troops was good.

A man was caught in the act of robbing the dead on the battlefield of Lookout Mountain. He was court-martialed and dishonorably dismissed from the service. His head was shaved and the division was formed in open ranks and he was marched between the lines at the point of the bayonet midst the hoots and jeers of his comrades, followed by the drum and fife corps, playing the Rogue's March.

And so 1863 passed into the history books. We had fought at Chancellorsville, Gettysburg, Wauhatchie, and Lookout Mountain. We lost many good men in those battles, but now it seemed that our efforts and their deaths had brought us to a place from which we could see the end of the war, and the view made us feel good. The government did what it could to reward us with some new and enlightened policies, but sooner or later we would have to come down from the heights and get on with the war.

CHAPTER FIFTEEN
HOMECOMING

For Susan, the day was like any other. Chores outside and inside took most of the morning: drawing water from the well, meals for the children, washing and sweeping. Finally, she had a chance to sit awhile, and she pulled a pair of Robbie's trousers, torn at the knee as usual, out of the sewing basket and took up a needle and thread. It was a pleasant November afternoon, chilly but with plenty of sunshine.

The sound of hooves on the road often signaled a visitor, and she always sat by the side window, for the sun and for the view of the road. Most often, within a few moments of hearing a horse coming, she would see who it was as they crested the rise about two hundred yards from the house.

This time it was Mr. White's two-horse wagon. Someone sat beside him, wrapped in an army issue sky-blue winter overcoat. Closer they came, and she slowly lowered her sewing to her lap. Too many times she had imagined this vision only to be sadly mistaken, so she fought the urge to believe what she was seeing. When the wagon was a hundred yards away she stood up and carefully smoothed out her dress, but now her hands were shaking. The man in the blue overcoat was stirring, reaching behind for his bag.

"Oh, my," she whispered, then she dashed to the door and opened it, half expecting the road to be empty when she saw it again, but it was true...it was...

James!

James swinging awkwardly down from the wagon, landing on his good leg and then jabbing his cane into the dirt. "Much obliged, Mr. White. Be seeing you."

When he gained his balance and turned to the house, Susan was standing on the porch.

"You are very welcome, James." Mr. White smiled broadly. "It's good to see you, and truly a pleasure to bring you home." He tipped his hat to James and then to Susan and drove away.

"Oh, James! Children, your father's here! Your father's home!" She ran and met him at the gate, which still stood at the crooked angle that it had two years before. James enclosed her in the heavy overcoat and their embrace was long. They felt each other's hearts beating. Susan reveled in the manly smell of him. Little sighs came from her throat. Her tears of joy disappeared into the heavy woolen fabric. James stroked her hair, ran his fingers across her delicate cheeks. He held her tightly in his arms, and the feeling awakened a remembering which was almost too much to bear.

"Uh…I reckon maybe we ought to go in the house," said Susan. "There's no telling who might pass by and see us like this."

"Well, let them see," James whispered, "but I reckon I could stand to set a spell."

Arm in arm they walked to the house. "Does the wound trouble you much, James?" asked Susan.

"Very little," James replied. "I'm almost to the point of not needing this stick."

"Well, lean on me, my husband, and you can throw the stick away. Does the army know you're here?"

James grinned and swooped that ol' cane far into the bushes. "There's an old doctor in Nashville who told me I wasn't going to be any good to the army for a month or so, and I might as well lay around at home as there. And so here I am."

"For a month, James?"

"Yep. Less travel, of course, and it took me five days to get here."

"Three weeks, then. Oh, how wonderful."

"Praise be, Susan. I guess getting wounded isn't such a bad thing after all."

Susan led him into the house. Robbie was coming in the back door from feeding the cows. Ellen stood up from her doll-play and took a few uncertain steps. Johnny sat up in his bed, looking a little bewildered. "Children, this is your pa. Say hello!"

James knelt down. There was a brief second of silence, and then Robbie stepped forward. "How do you do, sir." He held out his hand manfully.

"Doing very well, son." James took the proffered hand. "My, but you've grown tall."

Susan said, "Ellen, aren't you going to say hello to your daddy?"

Ellen trotted over and looked up at him. "I'm having tea with my dolls. Would you like some?"

"Yes," said James huskily. "I would like that very much."

Susan picked up their youngest. "And this is Johnny. Johnny, can you say hello to your papa?"

"Papa? Papa on the wall."

"Wall?"

"Every day I show Johnny your picture and tell him all about his daddy, so's he won't..." (there was a "ketch" in her voice) "...won't forget."

"Susan, he's so small..."

"Doc says he's gaining," Susan said quickly, her voice strained, almost frantic. "Johnny, how old will you be next month?"

Johnny held up three fingers. "Fwee!" I wiw be fwee nex' monf," he said with a confident nod.

James laughed. "Well, you're a talker, that's for sure." He gathered the three children together in his arms. "Lord, it's good to be home."

All this James told me when he returned from his leave, and not much more. Well, what would you do if you had not seen your wife and family in two years? Although speculating in this narrative on what took place out of my presence has not been above me, I will follow decorum here, and only say that James was yet a young man, and Susan his wife was a most attractive lady. Put another way, I am trying to be a gentleman, in this instance at least. There are only two other episodes that he told me about: His visit to the farm on Miller Hill, and a visit from the Goodin boys.

It was two-three days into his leave at home, a blustery day with sleet coming down. James and Robbie were in the little barn, pitching some hay to the red cow, when James heard a horse nicker. Looking out the door, he saw a rickety buggy, with two gaunt old nags in harness, drawn up by the side of the house, and he was just in time to see the heel of some feller disappear around the front of the house. Well, for some reason as he passed the wood pile he picked up an axe-handle. It had been a while, but he'd seen that old buggy before...

Passing to where he could see the buggy, he noted a jug set up against the dash, and other pieces of broken crockery in the back. At the back door, he heard voices from inside, and stopped to listen.

"...if you spit a chaw on the floor like you did the last time you were here, I'll..."

"Aw...looky here, Miz Miller. Me and Arch are just trying to be neighborly. We figured you'd be in need of wood for the winter, and we'd split some of what you got out back, and it won't cost you but a dollar."

Susan's voice raised defiantly. "MISTER Goodin! I believe the last time you 'helped me' you stole more than you cut."

Then Arch says, "Give it up, brother. She's just being her uppity self, studying to be an old maid widder. He chuckled, a sleazy, likker-lubricated sort of laugh. "'Sides, I'd like to hear just what she WOULD do if we planted a chaw on her nice board floor. Sure wish we had a nice floor like this in our place."

That was enough for James, who stepped in the door and calmly said, "Boys, she'd probably just call me in from the barn and have me bust this hickory handle over your heads."

You talk about jaws dropping. These two sets about hit the floor. Arch stammered, "J-J-Jim!—why, we didn't know..."

"That is pretty obvious, Arch. Now, why don't you boys crawl back in your hole before I forget that I'm only paid to put rebs under the sod?"

"Now, now, now, Jim—J-James—Mr. Miller—we just tryin' to be..."

"...neighborly, I know. I heard it all, Arch. I've got better neighbors in gray in Alabama. Now, git!"

They lit out the door, and James followed them onto the porch. "And if you ever bother her again, I'll bust your heads, and if she's a widow I'll bust your heads in hell!"

Who knew two old nags could run as fast as those were lathered up to? They were out of sight before James got back in the door.

"Oh, James, you sure do speak plain," Susan laughed, but as he reached her she started to sob.

"With everything else, you shouldn't have to put up with that."

She held to him tightly. "Oh, it's nothing, it's nothing. I can handle them."

"I thought those boys were drafted."

Collecting herself, she said, "Only the younger one was. These others got out of it somehow."

"Damn them," James muttered.

"Oh, James, promise me..."

"Promise...oh, that part about a widow?"

"Oh, just hold me, just hold me."

James wasn't one to set around, even while on vacation. He worked mighty hard around the place for about a week. In a perfect snowstorm he straightened the front gate, with Susan pleading with him to come in before he caught his death of cold. He stuffed cracks in the house, mended furniture, played with the younguns (Had that tea party he'd promised Ellen) and got to know his eldest son.

Finally, he faced the next of the duties of his leave: A visit to Miller Hill. He accepted the kind offer of one of Mr. White's saddle horses and set out from Southwest early in the morning of a better day than the one when he set the gate right. It happened to be the last Thursday in November, the day which President Lincoln had just proclaimed to be "a day of thanksgiving and praise to our beneficent Father." The first Thanksgiving Day, 1863.

Twenty-five miles in the saddle is a lot of riding for an infantryman, and James was some sore by the time he started up the hill from Jackson Run. But it had been a pleasant ride, and he was in good spirits when he neared the top of the draw and saw the farm off to the right. It looked right good, and prospering.

His father was coming in from the barn as James rounded the driveway past the house. He stood as if thunderstruck as James rode up to him.

"Saints preserve us!" his father cried, with his Scottish accent pronounced as it always was when he was excited. "Oh, upon my word, lad, it's good to see you!" He reached up and pumped James's hand so hard that James almost fell off the horse.

He dismounted, and the two wrapped in a great bear hug. "How are you, Father," asked James as he blinked tears of joy.

"Oh, fine, fine, especially now."

"And Mother?"

"Oh, James, she has not been well, but this will perk her up! For sure it will. Come in, come in! Mother, look who's here!" James flipped the reins over the back porch rail and followed him in.

The back door led in through the pantry to the kitchen, and the dining room and sitting room were to the right. James led through the doorway into the dimly lit sitting room, where the curtains were drawn. He was appalled when he saw her.

Frail and gaunt, she was. Her hair, once kept up nice and neat in a bun, was frazzled around her face. Seated in a dressing gown, with papers and teacups scattered about, she slowly raised her head as James's bulk filled the doorway.

"Who is it, Robert?" Her voice was shaky and feeble.

James said softly, "It's James, Ma. Your son James."

"James? James, oh can it be?" She started to raise herself up. "Come here, son. Let me take a look at you." She eased herself back into the armchair and he knelt in front of her. She held his face in her hands and whispered, "Oh, James, James, James, my boy James..." She started to cry, and he stroked her hair.

"Don't cry, Ma. Your soldier boy is home."

She held him tightly. "I never thought I'd see the day. Oh, you are so good to hug." She settled back and dabbed her eyes. "You've grown quite thin, lad."

"You should have seen me before the wounding, Ma. I've gained ten pounds since then, what with hospital food and then home cooking."

"Is Susan...?

"With me? Oh, no, no. Johnny is still too poorly to go out, but she sends her love."

Her voice seemed stronger as she said, "Well, let me roust myself, and I'll cook you a supper. Robert, pass the word and get the family together."

That had been the part of his visit that James least looked forward to. In his letters, James had spoken plainly of his disappointment in the conduct of the menfolk back in Farmington, and now it was time to look them in the face.

But it went well enough. Of all the boys, George Henry Cramer was the most reserved, for he had the strongest political leanings against the Republicans and the war effort, but I reckon his wife, James's sister Jane, had gave him a talking to before they arrived, for he was courteous, polite, and respectful.

Robert, as the ravaged soldier home from the wars, was the most relaxed, and he and James had quite a visit. William seemed the most pained by the reunion. It seemed as if he would have liked to have joined up, but he seemed to lack backbone. This attitude would affect him deeply in the future. John, the youngest, had got married quite young, back in June. They were expecting a baby, and that was his protection. For a while, all of the disagreement was put aside, and the Miller house was full of laughter, like in the old days. In the future, you will notice that, even though James has not changed his opinion, he refrains from criticizing in his letters. Thanksgiving Day did everybody some good, it seems.

All things come to an end, and soon it was time for James to take the train back to Tennessee. At the time, it looked as if it would be a long time before he saw the folks again, but events proceeded otherwise.

Hospital No. 19, Ward No. 1, Nashville, Tenn Dec the 25th, 1863

Dear Brother and Sister,

I thought I would write a few lines to you this pleasant Christmas morning and I hope it may be a happy Christmas to you all. My health is good and my spirits buoyant and I hope that this may find you enjoying the same blessing. I don't know as I have any news to write as that is a scarce article at this time. My wound is healing slowly and it does not and has not bothered me but very little. Myron Smith is here and his wound is getting well very fast.

I have not heard anything direct from the regiment since I got back, only that a large share of them have reenlisted for three years more. They get 402 dollars bounty and thirty days furlough. From what I see and hear, I think quite a large part of the old troops will reenter the service. I am sure that if it was not for my family, I should be one of them--and even then I am not sure but {what} I shall. As it is, I have seen two regiments from our Division reenlist: the 29th Pennsylvania Volunteers and the 66th Ohio. It is my candid belief that more of the old troops who have borne the brunt of the conflict so far will enlist than that we shall get volunteers of those what have not yet been in the field.

This is a very busy place but most of the business is on government account. A very large amount of army supplies are stored here and the city is very strongly fortified and guarded. The post is under the command of General Garfield. General Grant has his headquarters here at present.

There is but little prospect of much being done by our army this winter--only hold what we have got unless Hardee tries the offensive. Then we will try to give him and his gang of traitors such a reception that they will not care to have the dose repeated. There is a large number of refugees from Georgia and Alabama taking the oath of allegiance and joining our army. They all say they were conscripts in the reb army and there are no men fit to bear arms left in that part of the country, every one being driven into the rebel ranks... [98]

You will recall that we left home in November 1861, thinking that in six months, a year at the most, our work as soldiers would be done and we could come home, if God spared us. Well, the boys of the 111th were stubborn men. Determined, too. Determined not to leave a job half-done.

Sometime before Christmas, with James home on furlough and us snugging down in winter quarters until spring, the proposition of reenlisting for three years more or during the war was put to us. The offer was announced at a special formation on a Sunday afternoon. Lieutenant Colonel Walker, all decked out in his best uniform, sash, sword, and braid, stepped to the fore. He put us at our ease. This is what he said, as I recollect:

"Men, I have been directed to talk to you about reenlisting..."

This was met with a chorus of hoots and choice comments. Sergeant Major Dyke stepped out and shushed us. "Now you boys shut up and let the colonel have his say. Any more of that and I'll lock you at attention."

Colonel Tom waved his hand. "That's all right, Sergeant Major. If they had reacted in any other way I'd have had them all sent to sick call."

We all laughed. When we had settled down he commenced to speak.

"Men, there is a delegation down from Harrisburg to thank us for our service and to encourage us to stay the course. I want to give you some notice of what it's all about before they show up. Now, men, I reckon even the biggest fool among us would have to say that we are a damned sight closer to winning this war than we were a year ago!" We all cheered, and he smiled and waited for us to quiet down.

"Well, this war is being won by men such as yourselves who signed up almost three years ago and expected that we would have it over within that amount of time. Now it appears that maybe we won't. Just think what the army will be if all of the three-year regiments, with our experience and esprit de corps, just pack up and go home. We might not win after all."

Someone spoke up. "That's all right, Colonel. Let some of the stay-at-homes come and get a taste of old dandy." A chorus of agreement came from the ranks, and somebody else said, "Yes, let them do it awhile. They pay a feller right well to sign up nowadays. We had to wait four months just for our first month's pay."

"You are right in what you say," replied Colonel Tom, "but, men, from what I see here they are going to pay YOU right well if you will stick it out."

"How much, Colonel?"

"If you add up all the state and local bounties it comes to over four hundred dollars."

That brought a few whistles from us.

"Also, any man who reenlists gets a month's furlough, starting next month."

That was greeted with a persistent murmur in the formation:

"Jeez, a whole month."

"I've got a youngun I've never seen..."

"I should like to go home and CREATE a young'n."

"To see my wife and babes again. . ."

Colonel Tom held up his hand. Over the murmur he said, "AND...And if the regiment keeps enough men to stay in being, we will be evermore known as the 111th VETERAN Volunteer Infantry Regiment."

"What do we have to do to get all these good things, Colonel?"

"Reenlist for three more years or for the war, whichever comes first."

"Three more years is a long time."

"No one expects that the war will last that much longer."

"Back in '61, nobody would of dreamed that we'd still be putting our friends under the sod in 1864."

"Men, we could stand out here until doomsday and discuss all the whys and wherefores. This is the proposal. Listen to what the gentlemen from Harrisburg have to say. Discuss it among yourselves and each man will let his company commander know his decision. I will be available to answer any question which you may have, or to discuss it further in detail—there are many whys and wherefores in the plan. Now, I think we've stood out here quite long enough, and since it is Sunday I expect every man jack to have a day of rest. Fair enough?"

With three cheers and a tiger we all dispersed to our huts, with lots to ponder. And I will leave you to ponder until next time.

***

Well, folks, it has plumb been just about a year since we started having these visits. I truly thank all of you who have faithfully come to listen to this old man ramble on. We're about done. For better or worse, by the end of summer, it'll all be over.

To reenlist or not to reenlist: That was the question. My mind was in high gear from the time we broke ranks after the proposal was put to us.

Nobody said much as we took our traps off and hung them up. I rousted a fire under the coffeepot and was not much surprised when a half-dozen of the boys showed up at the door, Calvin in the lead.

"Well, Spoony," I says, "what do you think about going back to see the old folks?"

"That's why we're here," he replied. "Reckon we ought to jaw over this awhile."

We all pulled up cracker boxes around the mud stick fireplace and most everyone dipped his tin cup into the coffeepot.

"Well, what do you think?" Calvin asked brightly.

"I dunno, Spoony. Three years is a long time."

"Well, it is," said Calvin, "but just think: You get the pleasure of my company until the year 1867."

"Yes, if some reb minnie don't find one of us."

"Or unless Sergeant Alexander don't kill you first."

"Oh, he's transferred to Company K. I guess he gave up on me..."

And so the debate continued throughout the afternoon. Occasionally we even got down to a serious discussion.

Finally, I said my piece. "Here's the way I figure it," I said. "If we do not reenlist we will be discharged next fall, after a hard summer of campaigning, in which some of us are bound to get killed. We will probably be near the end of the war by then, and we will be out four hundred dollars for not reenlisting. On the other hand, if we do reenlist, and we do not survive, there will be that money for our families." Well, that's the way my reasoning went at the time, and I thought I would bring it to you through a quote. I probably did not say it in quite the cut-and-dried way it is presented here, but that is the same as most other conversations I recall in these recollections after seventy-some years.

At first, I expected that the offer to reenlist would find mighty slim pickings amongst us, but fact is, most of the regiment did reenlist, and even though the enticements were attractive enough, you have to marvel at those men, who had faced death, privation, and disease for over two years, signing up for more of the same. Me included. For many, thirty days at home was the irresistible clincher.

There were only two men in the company who did not re-enlist, and both were killed a few days before their time expired. Pete Sanford was killed at Kennesaw Mountain; Porter Siggins was killed at Peach Tree Creek by a bullet that went through a New Testament he carried in his blouse pocket. It was fate. The entire Bible might have stopped the bullet.

***

TESTIMONIAL

Colonel Cobham also got two leaves that winter. I understand that the first, which got him home for the holidays, was prompted by the need of a dentist. In addition to his tooth trouble, I think things were going to pot in the Cobham household, but with the community he was a bonafide hero.

He arrived in Warren on Christmas Eve. Word got around town of his presence, and a messenger delivered a note on the 28th:

WARREN, DEC. 28, 1863

To Col George A Cobham, Acting Brig. General 2d Brigade, 12th Army Corps:

COLONEL:—The undersigned, your fellow citizens of Warren County, as a slight token of their appreciation of your military service, both in the Army of the Potomac, and later at Wauhatchie, Lookout Mountain and Missionary Ridge, respectfully tender you a public

dinner, to be given at such time as will suit your convenience before your return to active duty.

Trusting it will be convenient for you to accept this invitation, we are, very truly and sincerely yours,

WM D. BROWN	*LEWIS ARNETT*	*RUFUS P. KING*
S.P. JOHNSON	*G.W. SCHOFIELD*	*H. ALLEN*
B.W. LACY	*L.L. LOWREY*	*E.T.F. VALENTINE*
G.B. CURTIS	*H.P. KINNEAR*	*J.D. JAMES*
AND 59 OTHERS		

Colonel Cobham penned the following reply the next day:

To Messrs Allen, Kinnear, Brown, Arnett, and others:

GENTLEMEN:—I have the honor to acknowledge the receipt of your kind letter of this date, tendering me a public dinner, to be given at such time as would be most convenient before my return to active duty.

I assure you, gentlemen, that I fully appreciate the honor thus conferred, and it will afford me much pleasure to accept your kind invitation; and as my stay will be short, I would suggest Thursday, the 31st inst., as a convenient day. I have the honor, gentlemen, to remain,

Very Respectfully,
Your Obedient Servant,
GEORGE A COBHAM, JR.

The banquet was attended by some people who I knew—junior officers and such—but all of the important men in the county were there, and it must have been quite an affair...yessir, quite an affair...

But you don't have to take my word, or theirs, about the occasion. The major accomplishment which recorded the event for all time was an almost word-for-word account in the January 9th edition of the *Warren Mail,* written up by the paper's editor, Ephraim Cowan. I won't give the whole thing here—you can look it up if you want to—but here is how it started:

"On Thursday evening a company of about seventy-five gentlemen assembled at the Carver House, and after a bountiful dinner and being

liberally supplied with champagne, the company was on motion of Judge Johnson, organized by calling Hon. G. W. Scofield to the chair.

We cannot give in a report of this kind near all that was said or done on the occasion, nor can we convey on paper much of an idea of the good feeling and fun which flowed as freely as the sparkling wine. We will attempt, however, to give some idea of the proceedings.

After the organization the toasts were called for, and the committee on toasts, through Mr. McKelvy, presented them..."

Glenni Schofield was our congressman. His was the first of many speeches and toasts which praised our colonel and the goals of the war. I think everybody got pretty drunk. Finally it was the colonel's turn to speak, and this is what he said:

"MR PRESIDENT AND GENTLEMEN:--I appreciate the honor of the occasion and am grateful for the kindness you have shown me. I recognize in this not only a compliment to my own services, but a just tribute to the bravery of the boys whom I have the honor to command. The 111th Regiment have left their blood on nearly every battlefield since they were organized. They have endured long marches without a murmur, have faced the enemy again and again without a sign of fear and stand today with a line of bristling bayonets, which is a barrier to Rebel occupation of East Tennessee. The army are determined that the rebellion shall be put down.

(This was greeted by applause)

I helped to plant the flag on the rugged top of Lookout Mountain, and if God spares my life I will help to make it float from the Potomac to the Gulf.

(Louder applause)

...I will carry back to the boys in the field the report of this reception and there is not one but will clench his musket with a firmer grasp and vow never to lay it down until the rebellion is crushed.

(Applause)

...I again thank you for the honor conferred on me. I have no words to express my gratitude."

They gave him three cheers.

Later on, it was H. Allen's turn to speak. "H. Allen" is of course our old friend, Harrison Allen, out of the army and back into politics. It all went on past the stroke of the new year, into the momentous Year of our

Lord, 1864, and by the time it ended it had deteriorated into a verbal free for all, with everybody trying to get the last word in, but finally order was restored, and a Mr. Babcock made the last toast:

"Mister Chairman, I propose a toast before adjournment: The health of Col. Cobham. May his star never grow dim, nor his sword ever rust until the last rebel in the last ditch smells hell, or submits to the Government!" [99]

When George Cobham left the Carver House in the wee hours it was snowing and cold. As he walked down to the hotel's livery to claim his buggy someone called to him from behind. It was his old colleague, Caleb Wells.

"George! George! Slow down, for goodness sake."

Cobham says, "Oh, Caleb. Say, I'm sorry I didn't get much of a chance to talk to you in there. How are you?"

Caleb caught his breath as he walked alongside. "I'm fine, George. I'm fine. I'm making lots of money. And you, look at you, living life on the saber's edge. But George—"

"Caleb?"

"George, all I can tell you is—at this moment—I wish I were you."

"Why, thank you, Caleb."

"I mean it, George. You are larger than life. You make all of us who care for our wealth or our health more than country feel small. I could not help but notice that your fellow soldier, Allen, never once spoke of you by name."

"I noticed also, Caleb. But that's Harrison's problem, not mine." He put his arm around Caleb's shoulder. "What say we see if the Ludlow House is still open and if maybe we can still get a drink there?"

CHAPTER SIXTEEN
THE CALM BEFORE THE STORM

Robert Miller to his son, James, Farmington, Pennsylvania, January 2nd, 1864

Dear Son James,

I take this opportunity to write a few lines informing you that we received your letter of the 17th December. We were glad to hear from you and to hear that you were in good health and that your leg was no worse, for according to your own statement it is very strange that it did not pain you badly. You must try and keep it clean if you do no more. We are all in tolerable good health here at present. Your mother has been very poorly for the last two or three weeks. I think worse than she has been for the last year. She got a bad cold about the time you were here and had a very bad cough so that she could not rest any at night for about three weeks. She is some better but far from being well.

We have had some very cold weather here but it is more moderate now. We have had a number of days of sleighing and the prospect of more.

The boys all over are in quite a stew about the draft. We had a special town meeting which was well attended. They voted to raise $300 bounty for volunteers to fill the quota of the town which will be about fifteen. So the town will have to raise 4500 dollars. There were over eighty men present and when they called the vote there were only four against it: Peter Burget, James Feterly, Alexander Stewart, and William Wiltsie. So there was not much opposition. I think if they had voted by ballot there would have been more for people didn't like to walk out and show that they were opposed to it in plain sight. The meeting then appointed a committee of five (and William is one of them) to get the money and look for volunteers.

Colonel Allen came up last Saturday evening and made a speech in the Methodist house. It was well attended but there was only one that offered and that was Reuben Cramer. He said that he would be one if they could find the rest, but it is my opinion that they will not get them in town. All that are in the army from this town that reenlist will be entitled to the bounty if they can be counted in our quota.

Lyman Root's wife is dead and buried two weeks since. We had another soldier's funeral last Friday--a young man by the name of Aaron Thompson, son of John Thompson, that enlisted in Aninacote. He died in Washington of chronic diarrhea. The friends brought home his remains and they were interred in the Thompson's graveyard.

I will add no more hoping soon to hear from you again. We remain,
Your father and mother,
Robert and Jane Miller [100]

By the time James returned from the hospital the regiment had reenlisted and had the word "Veteran" inscribed on the colors. At Christmas time he was not thinking of reenlisting, but by the time he returned to us he had decided to stay on. I guess, like me, he wanted to see it through if he could. On the pragmatic side there was that bounty, and the opportunity to turn right around and go back home again for another month. James liked being a soldier and he may have reenlisted even without the enticements. Who knows?

And so it was that the 111th Pennsylvania was loaded up in boxcars in the dead of winter and went home for a month. It was bitter cold, and, even with risky fires lit on the floors of the boxcars, a few came down with frostbite during the trip.

***

FURLOUGH

First stop: Nashville. When we had come down this way in late September, Nashville had looked quite forlorn, a humble looking burg when compared to the likes of Washington. Now, after a few months in the wilderness, it looked like a prosperous city to us. And, in fact it was coming to be. Now that we had the town and the rebs had about given up on taking it back (not quite, but the realists among the secesh probably realized the jig was up) the town was coming alive again. 'Course, as James wrote, most of the business was on the government account but money is money, even to the secesh.

We were quartered in the Zollicoffer House overnight. It was the first building I ever saw with an elevator lift. The building was unfinished and some of the joists and studding was used in the fireplaces to keep us from freezing. There were other troops in the building. In an Illinois regiment, sometime in the night, someone began to pray, repeating over and over, **"Oh, Lord God, Holy Son of the Heavenly Father, deliver me from all my evils before I leave my knees. Make these fiends depart away from me into everlasting fire!"** Of course he awoke everyone and many got up and gathered around him as he knelt stark naked on the floor, raving, and they began to jeer him and once when he said, "Before I leave my knees," someone called out, "Get up, damn you, and take your knees with you!" [101]

Ahem...a word about religion: As James said early on, we were a profane and blasphemous lot, and we pretty much stayed that way, as you can see from the uncharitable way we treated the naked muse. (I think it would have been all right if he had not woke us all up.) However, there is a tendency, when you have "Seen the Elephant" to also "See the Light," and only the most brutish soul will not try to get on good terms with his maker when death may come his way at any time. Revival meetings was pretty popular throughout the war, and always brought in a few souls for the Lord. Some backslid thereafter, but slowly the Lord gained.

Often when we were about to go into battle, some chaplain or officer would step out in front and pray that the Lord would favor our arms with success. I did not put much store in that, because somebody was likely doing the same thing over in the rebel lines. It required the Lord to choose who He favored most on that particular day, and I did not believe the Lord worked thataway. I personally prayed that I would not be killed or wounded, but if it had to be, I wanted it to be quick and painless. (A bullet through the head, Lord, oh, please, let it be.)

So what might happen, win or lose, live or die, was up to fate or providence, or just plain luck. Calvin had a discussion once long after the war, up in Alaska. There was quite a company of men at a roadhouse, and the question of the intervention of providence came up and was argued pro and con. He remarked that it seemed to him that when a man had seven bullet holes made in his pants in one day that it was an intervention of providence that he did not at least lose both legs. Then an Irishman spoke up and said, "Shur that would be aisy when the pants are hanging on the fence." [102] Calvin had seven bullet holes in his pants at Antietam, and if the graybacks hadn't packed them off when they were taken from him, he would have had them cleaned and fumigated and sent them home. My record for one engagement was only two bullet holes in my coat, and I only got shot once but it was not serious—just embarrassing as to its location. I may see the pearly gates one day, and when I do I'll thank the Almighty for letting me survive the war. He'll probably say, "Don't thank me; you were just lucky."

Probably, considering as how we were all offspring of our creator, and if anyone owned a man it was Him, not any southern plantation owner, it is likely that the Lord sided with Abe Lincoln's Army of Emancipation as it went out like a mighty wind to free the slaves. Another unspoken goal of Abe's proclamation of January 1, 1863, I reckon.

And that's about all I dare say about religion. You always get in trouble with somebody if you stay on the subject too long.

After Nashville, our next layover was Louisville, where we were finally paid, and then on to Erie, which we reached on January 14th, 1864.

We were met at the station by our old Colonel Schlaudecker and about half the town. There was an escort of a company of marines, the bells rang out, and the cannon boomed for us. Banners proclaimed, "Gallant Soldiers, Welcome Home." The mayor gave a speech, a banquet was served to us in Wayne Hall, and the next day we all scattered to our respective abodes which most of us had not seen in two years.

This second furlough for James was a blessing. His son Johnny died on February 1st, aged three years one month and eleven days. If some things can be scored up to fate, this circumstance, of him being home at such a time, can be nothing but the stroke of providence. What would Susan have done without his support? James had the sad task of burying his son in the backyard of his little homestead there in Southwest Township. Somewhere down there, unawares to the current residents, a little child rests in the soil of their neat yard or little garden. There are no words I can put together to describe this time for you.

Thirty days at home were a tonic for most, but before half the time was used up I surprised myself by discovering that I actually missed the rough niceties of field service. I felt I had little in common with them who had stayed at home and I set no store in what was important to the home folks. It paled when compared to comradeship, danger, and hardships.

For yours truly, I really don't know where my head was at during that furlough. Most of the girls I had consorted with before the army were set up with some other feller, and I just didn't feel like stealing one of them back just for the month I'd be home. I went to a social with one of my sister's friends, and looking back, I think she liked me a lot, and she was real pretty, but I never called on her again. You would think, after being away for two years, that I would want to, you know, *get layed.* I became bored, restless, and anxious to get back to Alabama. 'Course, once I got back to Alabama, I would wish I was at home.

While home on furlough the regiment drew new state and national colors. The old state banner was sent to Harrisburg, but the old Stars and Stripes was retained, so thereafter we had three stand of colors. Volunteers were called for to carry the extra flag, and among those who volunteered, the colonel gave Sergeant Calvin Blanchard the honor, and he carried our old Star-Spangled Banner from Chattanooga to the sea.

Our camp had been looked after while we were absent by those who did not reenlist and we remained there until the spring campaign opened.

Bridgeport, Ala March the 21st

"...The weather for the first week after we got here was very warm and pleasant and then it (more especially the nights) got a little too cold for comfort. Last night after dark it commenced to snow and kept at it steadily until noon today. The snow is a plumb foot in depth and that is doing pretty well for Alabama on the twenty-first of March. The camps and men look dreary and dismal today but the snow is thawing. A single day's sun and we shall be all right again, for our camps are situated on dry, rolling, gravelly ground. The water is plenty and in good quality. The land in this vicinity is all rolling; some of it is mountainous, rocky, and covered with quite a heavy growth of timber consisting principally of black and white oak and a good deal of gum trees. The gum of the south is the same as the northern pepperidge.

...This is a very important point at present as the railroad from Nashville to Chattanooga crosses the Tennessee River here. It is the only reliable route by which the troops under Thomas get their supplies. The railroad bridge is a wooden one and nearly half a mile in length; its destruction would be a hard blow to us. More than that, there is a boatyard here that employs 200 men. They have built some seven

steamboats, two gunboats, and quite a number of flatboats, and have orders to build eleven more steamboats. There are three steam sawmills with circular saws in each, so you can see it is a matter of the first importance to our cause that this point be held at all hazards....

Our recruits have mostly joined us and the strength of the regiment is nearly 600 effective men. That is, so far as green troops can be considered effective..." [103]

Bridgeport, Alabama April the 10th

"...I had begun to think there must be something the matter for I was at this place almost a month before I got a single line from home. Then I got a letter from Rob and, on the eighth, yours and Joseph's of the same date by the same mail. I have got but one from Susan since I left home, and four letters is a very few when I have written some eighteen in that time. But maybe I will get more after awhile...

...It is currently reported here that the Eleventh and Twelfth Corps are united in one to be called the First Army Corps and to be under the command of General Hooker, but as yet we have received no official notification of the same...Our regiment is in good health and they are putting on a good many airs but the first march will rub that all off.

In regard to the local bounty, I have not been able to find out anything here. I went to Colonel Cobham and he told me that he had not heard anything about it but said if there was anything that he could do to assist any of the men to get their bounty he would willingly do it. It is my opinion that Lieutenant Colonel Walker is the man to blame for as near as I can find out, he tried to have all he could credited to Erie County to save them from a draft. He had no right to credit any of us to any other place but the one where we first enlisted. If he had only let us alone there would not have been any trouble in our getting the bounty. Well, there is no use to fret. Please to do the best you can under the circumstances and let it rip.

...Lieutenant Sturdevant last Sunday wanted me to come back to the company for duty and he would give me a corporal's place. I told him I would rather stay in the Pioneers, for in camp it is easier. We have no guard duty to do which is the hardest part of a soldier's duty...

Direct to Company D instead of B." [104]

It had been an unusually cold winter, north and south. Us Yankees were used to snow, of course. To us it was a nuisance, but for our foe it was a novelty, in March or any time. While we waited for it to thaw, the Johnnies reveled in it, and during the snowfall in March had the jim-dandy of all snowball fights, with brigades and divisions participating, in ranks with regimental colors flying, with their officers mounted and directing the fight.

Besides building forts and training the droves of new men that had enlisted or been drafted, there was not much going on at our level, but at the top big things were happening and changes were being made to prepare for the summer ahead.

Spring came to the land, greening the fields and forests northerly from the rebellious states. But as spring brought leaves to the trees and lifted our spirits, Susan Miller was in a winter of despair. She wrote to James's parents on April 10, 1864.

Dear Parents,

I again sit down to write a few lines to let you know how we get along. We are well, except Robert. He has had the inflammation on the lungs. He was very sick two weeks but he is getting quite smart again. I was at Father's when he was sick. I have been there most of the time since James went back in the army but I was not contented there and I can't feel contented any where. I feel so lonely without my little treasure Johnny, but the Lord saw fit to take him from us to dwell with Him in a brighter world than this, but it was so hard to part with the sweet little darling and he suffered so much the last day and a half, it was enough to make a parent's heart ache. Every time I turn my eyes I see something that reminds me of him in some way. Oh if I could see him alive and well and hear his sweet prattle, it would be worth millions of money to me, and I miss him more since James went away. Oh, if James could have stayed at home, but that could not be. He is bound to be a soldier as long as the war lasts, and I do hope that won't be long. I have not heard from him in two weeks. He was well and in Alabama. He was some homesick. It was harder for me to part with him than ever before. When he went away last fall, I thought in a few months if his life was spared he would be at home to stay, and the thought cheered me. But God only knows when he will come again. Three years seems like an age to me. Some prophesy that the war will be done next spring. I hope they will be true prophets. I hope this will find you all well. Widow Tyrrel lost a little girl some ten days ago. She died with the canker rash. Mrs. Everts has a boy six weeks old.

Enclosed you will find a receipt which you will please hand to John. Please to write soon. I would like to hear from you all, and especially Mother. Tell the girls to write. Give my love to all and reserve a share for yourselves.

I remain
Affectionately your daughter
Susan A. Miller [105]

Spring brought more than the budding of the trees and the deepening of a wife's despair.

In the spring of '64 Lincoln told Grant to put Sherman in charge in Tennessee and come east to take command of all the armies. I remember the overwhelming dread I felt when I heard of it. A man once said that Grant habitually wears an expression as if he'd made up his mind to drive his head through a brick wall and was about to do it. I may have sensed that Grant would win our war for us at any price—a price we would have to pay in blood and treasure.

Our old Twelfth Corps was indeed consolidated with the Eleventh Corps, and of a sudden them damned Dutchmen were our comrades. When we got to know them, we found out they were not such a cowardly lot, after all. Joe Hooker replaced General Slocum as commander. As the Twentieth Corps, we got to keep our corps badge, the star, but the Eleventh's half-moon was no more. Williams and Geary still commanded the first and second divisions, respectively, but we added a third division in the reorganization, and it was under Dan-Dan-Dan Butterfield, the composer of "Taps."

Military protocol gives a command to the senior officer present. For that reason, George Cobham came back to command the regiment, and Colonel David Ireland, who had been a colonel longer than Cobham, took over the brigade. Besides our old 111th and 29th Pennsylvania, the brigade now included the 60th, 78th, 102nd, 137th, and 149th New York regiments. The old 109th Pennsylvania, with which we had been brigaded for nigh two years, was transferred to our Second Brigade. That made seven regiments in the brigade, but we still ventured out on the campaign with only about twenty-six hundred men. With Ireland's various illnesses and injuries, Cobham ended up commanding the brigade more often than not. I personally think that he was the better man to command the brigade, but of course I am prejudiced.

It may surprise you to find out that the preparations for the spring campaign were hardly started before the end of March. Grant got promoted to Lieutenant General on March 9th. Sherman got command in the west on March 12th, and him and Grant did not arrange things until they met in Nashville on March 18th. They had no formal "meetings." In conversations commenced in Nashville and continued on a train to Cincinnati, and finalized in a hotel room there, they came up with the basic strategy. Years later, Sherman summed up the plan by saying, "Grant was to go for Lee and I was to go for Joe Johnston."

Bridgeport, Alabama, April the 12th

[John] "*wrote that Mother's health was not as good as usual and that you were quite hard up with the rheumatism...*

Last night I saw by the Meadville Republican that they have passed a local bounty bill. It was signed by the governor on the twentieth of March. It seems to me that if my name is not on the provost marshal's rolls that under the provisions of Section 12 of the act in question, I might be credited to some town in Warren County. Get the committee to do something in regard to the matter. I do not mean to dictate but as you are there, you are in a better condition to know how the matter stands than I am.

...General Slocum, our old corps commander, bade us farewell yesterday. He is ordered to take command of Vicksburg..." [106]

Camp at Bridgeport, Alabama April the 25th, 1864

"*...The rations are of the best quality; we have a bakery for the post and get fresh bread every day. The water is of good quality. Take our present condition all together, it is as pleasant a position as we have ever held since we have been in the field. I for one will be very well suited if we are allowed to stay here.*

Our division commander, General Geary, is in command of the post and doing all in his power to strengthen the position. The railroad crosses one branch of the river on the top of a trellis frame some twenty feet in height and they are busy laying a plank bridge for teams under the railroad. General Thomas, the commander of this army, made us a visit last week and gave orders to have another fort built. There are no less than seven already, so you can guess that we are doing our best to be ready to give our foe a warm reception if they should give us a call.

You have no doubt seen by the papers that the Eleventh and Twelfth Corps are consolidated under the command of General Hooker, to be the Twentieth Army Corps. At present the Corps is scattered along the railroad from Nashville to Chattanooga. I hope General Sherman will keep us where we are this summer. There are some colored regiments going to the front and they make a very good appearance. The more niggers they get, the better I will be suited, for I would a little rather see a nigger's head blowed off than a white man's.

...In regard to the call for more men, you are right on thinking that I am well suited to see the men called out. As for their being used politically, the only way I want them to influence the fall election is by beating the rebels in the field. If we can lick the rebels, I shall not feel concerned in regard to the elections...." [107]

Bridgeport, Alabama April the 25th 1864

Dear Mother,

I thought as I was not busy today that I could spend a little of the time that hangs heavy on my hands no better than to write a letter to you, for I very well know that you will be anxious to know how your soldier boy is getting along away down in Alabama, so far from home and the loved associations of relatives and friends. Well, I am happy to be able to say that I am in the enjoyment of uninterrupted good health. In fact, my health never was better than it has been since I left home this time. I get plenty to eat and but very little to do; for the last two weeks I have not done more than half a day's work in the whole time and as you can well imagine I am as lazy as I can be and live...

...It seems to me that there is to be some hard fighting this summer but whether our Corps will be sent to the front I can't tell. For the present, our Corps is doing guard duty along the railroad and as far as I can learn it is the intention of General Sherman, who is in command of this Army, to keep us in our present position unless something that we do not expect should happen. For my part, I hope that we may have the luck to be left where we are--it is a good deal easier to do our present duty than to be in the front and have the hard marches and heavy loads to carry that have been our luck in the past, to say nothing

of the chances of battle. We are not entirely free from the chance of getting into a fight at this point but in my opinion the present garrison of this post are able to defend it against any force the enemy can send against us, and punish them severely if they venture to attack us.

I have received but two letters from Susan since I left home. In the last one she says that her health and that of the children is good. I got a letter from G.H. and Jane today that was twenty-one days on the road and I have answered it. I have heard nothing in regard to my local bounty as yet. I wish you have Father write me and if he knows anything about it, tell me. Please to write soon and direct to: James T. Miller, Company D, 111th Regiment Pennsylvania Veteran Volunteers, Second Division, Twentieth army Corps, Army of the Cumberland. No more at present from the soldier, James T. Miller, to his Mother, Jane Miller, written at Bridgeport, Alabama, this 25th day of April, A.D. 1864. [108]

***

THE ARMIES

On May 5th all of the northern armies quit their winter camps and headed south. In Virginia, Generals Grant and Meade moved on Richmond with 120,000 men, including Charlie Lyon's regiment. In Tennessee, General Sherman with his 100,000 men, including we of the 111th Pennsylvania, moved on Atlanta.

I reckon I should explain a little of how the armies was organized for the Atlanta Campaign before me and James talk about generals and corps and divisions in our offhand way. Sherman's army was actually three armies. In modern parley it would be called an "army group." First there was us, now in the Army of the Cumberland, under General Thomas. We called him "Pap." Those who deal in legends know him as the "Rock of Chickamauga," which I told you about some time back. Thomas was from Virginia. In many ways he was like Robert E. Lee, but his sense of duty was some different: He chose to stay under the national banner when the split occurred. Lucky for us that he did, because he was a very good general.

Actually that is an understatement. I believe that he was an excellent general, cut from the same cloth as Lee, but hobbled in reaching his full potential because of his statehood. He was passed over several times for high command until finally his record could not be ignored. Even then, he was not given the full confidence of his boss. Remind me to tell you more about that later.

Thomas's army was the biggest at sixty thousand men: Three full infantry corps of three divisions each. First there was us in the Twentieth, all brought over from the Army of the Potomac. For weeks there was a rumor that we were going to be consolidated with the Eleventh Corps, and it finally happened. I don't know why they gave us a new number—we kept our star insignia and we kept our division commanders—but we became the Twentieth, under Joe Hooker. There was also the Fourth Corps, under one-armed General Howard, who had found himself looking for a job when the Eleventh Corps was disbanded; and last was the Fourteenth under John Palmer. Not much to say about Palmer, except that he really did not want to be there. He was capable enough, but his heart was not into this business anymore.

Our cavalry was no great shakes, compared to the likes of the men who rode with Joe Wheeler and Bedford Forrest. It was organized as a corps under a General Ellett, of three divisions commanded by Edward McCook, Kenner Garrard, and Judson "Kill Cavalry" Kilpatrick. Kilpatrick was a wacko, a glory seeker pure and simple, who, in his blind seeking, sacrificed a fine young general by the name of Farnsworth in a stupid charge on the third day at Gettysburg. His nickname was not complimentary, but he reveled in it. Years ago he lectured at Roscoe Hall Hall in Warren. People paid good money to hear him speak, thinking he was a hero, but I didn't go, because I knew he was a idiot. By the way, I did not misspeak about the name of the hall. It was named after a feller name of Roscoe Hall, making it Roscoe Hall Hall.

Next was the Army of THE Tennessee, not to be confused with the Army of Tennessee, which was the Confederate army we were fighting. It mustered about twenty-five thousand men, mostly Midwesterners, when we started out. This had used to be Sherman's army, but when he moved up it went to another fine young general by the name of James McPherson. To start with, McPherson only had the Fifteenth Corps under "Black Jack" Logan and the Sixteenth under Grenville Dodge, but the Seventeenth Corps under Frank Blair joined us in June.

The third and last army was the Army of the Ohio, commanded by John Schofield, a solid soldier without much going for him as far as looks.

He was rather pudgy, with a big frizzy beard. With less than fourteen thousand men, it was actually just a heavy corps, the Twenty-third, plus a cavalry division under George Stoneman, another mediocre cavalryman. Stoneman had helped raise the 9th New York Cavalry, in which a lot of our friends from Sugar Grove, *Pennsylvania,* were enlisted. To help your memory again, I will say that James referred to them occasionally as the "Westfield Cavalry." Schofield's men were not as experienced as the rest of us.

That's the lot. Most of our wounded who would ever recover had returned to us, and we had been heavily reinforced by new regiments and replacements in the old ones over the winter, so that we started out one-hundred thousand strong on May 5th, 1864.

Facing us was that Army of Tennessee, with maybe fifty thousand soldiers at the beginning of the campaign. Bragg finally was gone, kicked upstairs as advisor to Jeff Davis, and replaced by General Joe Johnston, who I have mentioned in this narrative a few times. He was a talented general, but he was not in favor with Jeff Davis. It would not help Johnston to have Bragg, with axes to grind, at Davis's elbow all summer.

Johnston had just two corps at the start of the campaign. The first one was under General Hardee, William J., the author of that unfathomable book on tactics which we had just about thrown away by 1864. He had four divisions, one of which was under that Irish rebel, Pat Cleburne. The second of three divisions was under John Bell Hood. More about Hood later, too.

Reinforcing Johnston early in the campaign was another corps, brought up from Mississippi, of three divisions under General Leonidas Polk, which would bring their force up to almost seventy thousand. Polk was an Episcopal bishop turned soldier. Too bad for his church, and too bad for his army, for he was not much of a general, may he rest in peace.

Johnston's cavalry was under a little gamecock of a general by the name of Joe Wheeler. Wheeler had a lot of men, but they had been busy all winter and their horses was pretty worn down. As time went on and the grass grew, they recruited their horses and became more and more a threat to us. We had the rebs outnumbered, as usual, but as you have seen—and we knew, all too well—that did not mean we were just going to walk into Atlanta.

Among the steps they took to even the odds a little was issuing special rifles to selected sharpshooters in their infantry. These was mostly Whitworth rifles, imported from England. They had telescopic sights and special rifling which made them deadly accurate at over a half-mile. They were used especially against our gunners in the artillery and officers in all branches, but occasionally against innocent bystanders, as I shall relate to you later on.

Also, before the shooting starts in Georgia, I should mention our old friends, the Army of the Potomac and the Army of Northern Virginia. I will be brief, because they are now outside the purview of my story.

Before the campaign started, one of them pesky reporters got through to Grant somehow and asked him how long it would take to get to Richmond. Well, Grant he took a long pull on his segar, blew a smoke ring and says, "oh, about three days..." The reporter of course was amazed. For over two years, various generals had been battling with no success, and here this scruffy little fellow from Illinois is predicting it will only take three days. Then Grant finished his statement, "...that is, providing Lee doesn't try to stop us."

General Grant was out to win our war for us, but the price would be high, just as I feared. At first he tried to be scientific about it and flank Lee out of his positions, but every time he tried he found Lee's ragged veterans blocking the way. It was then that some started calling him "Butcher Grant." Grant was every bit as aggressive as Lee, and he had the manpower of the North to back him up. Somebody told him that his army and Lee's would be like the Kilkenny cats that devoured each other, and Grant said grimly, "Our cat has the longer tail." In a month's time Grant would lose sixty thousand men, as many men as Lee had in his whole army, at places called "The Wilderness" (which was the same ground where Chancellorsville was fought the previous May) and Spotsylvania and Cold Harbor and Petersburg. But in that deadly arithmetic that I have mentioned before, Lee's losses, something like twenty thousand, were irreplaceable.

A certain bunch of the soldiers in Grant's army longed for the end of May. These were the survivors of the Pennsylvania Reserves, Charlie Lyon's division. Three thousand men remained out of sixteen thousand who had marched off to war in the bright days of 1861, and June 1864 marked the end of their enlistment. Unlike our outfit, not many in

Charlie's outfit reenlisted. But, goldangit, Charlie did, in the brand-new 190th Pennsylvania. A stubborn lot, those Warren County boys.

If you would see Grant and Lee as two heavyweight boxers, brawling and bleeding in Virginia, Sherman and Joe Johnston would be two master swordsmen, Sherman thrusting and Johnston parrying, with hardly any carving, in a campaign that would slowly bring the Union Army closer to Atlanta.

We were ready. We had our orders, and we were the best trained, best organized that we had ever been. We had sent all our extra baggage home—we would travel light in this campaign. We had policed up our camps, tore the shelter tent roofs off our huts and rolled them up for the carry, drawn our ammunition and rations, and cleaned our guns. It was just a matter of awaiting the drum roll.

Some things you never forget. I remember the night before the campaign began, a beautiful night in Alabama with a soft warm breeze wafting up from the south. Everything was green and growing. As far as the eye could see the white tents of our army speckled the countryside and bonfires shone like constellations among the clouds of white, sending columns of smoke high in the sky. I remember the smell of wood smoke and frying meat as we prepared our rations. Near and far, bands were playing, and there were cheers and hollering and laughter. As it got dark, the boys brought out their candles, most stuck in bayonet sockets next to their tents. The thousands of pinpoints of light made for a spectacle unforgettable and grand. Finally, late in the evening, a band struck up "Home Sweet Home," and all the cheering subsided and we just sat there with our candles, singing the sweet refrain, and as I found myself thinking and hoping that this might be the beginning of the end, I felt pangs of regret when I realized that when it was over I would never see another night like this. Spectacle, comradeship, dedication to a cause, it would all be over and gone. All that would be left, for those of us who survived, would be the memories.

But there was much to be done before we could dwell on memories.

Hang on to your hat.

CHAPTER SEVENTEEN
THE ATLANTA CAMPAIGN
-or-
AS WE GO MARCHING THROUGH GEORGIA

Well, we had laid about all winter, getting "fat and lazy," as James would say, so our first hike was a killer after all that repose. The army was spread out, all the way from Knoxville to Bridgeport to Nashville, and it took time to get us all together. We packed up our camp in Bridgeport and retraced the route that we had took to get to Chattanooga the last fall. That included passing through our old battlefield at Wauhatchie, with all its memories of excitement and comrades lost, and then swinging around the north end of Lookout Mountain. We stared at that lofty old crag and wondered how we had ever taken it.

The rebs had had all winter to prepare a reception for us. They were dug in along a ridge near Dalton, Georgia, and any direct attack on it was bound to fail, so Sherman planned to send McPherson to the south, to get behind the enemy's left flank at Resaca, which was on their supply line. By us taking and holding Resaca, Johnston would either be forced to retreat away from his supply, or to attack us, which was just what we wanted.

On May 9th our brigade was split off from the division to accompany Kilpatrick's division on a reconnaissance to Snake Creek Gap, the back door to Resaca. We found it undefended, and McPherson headed down to take Resaca.

McPherson, though, he missed his chance. He got nearly to Resaca and overestimated the force defending it, which was just one skimpy brigade. He pulled back, allowing Johnston to reinforce Resaca and eventually to bring his entire army away from Dalton and into the lines at Resaca.

***

RESACA

With Johnston gone from Dalton, the rest of our army followed McPherson's track through Snake Creek Gap and we ended up with both armies in their entire confronting each other at Resaca. The reb line, to use a Gettysburg cliché was shaped like a fishhook, with Polk and Hardee from left to right, facing west, and Hood on the extreme right, facing north. This confrontation brought on our first real battle, on May 15th, 1864.

Camp near Tilton Station, Georgia May the 14

Dear Wife,

I take this time to write a few lines to let you know that I am well. I got the letter that you wrote on the first of this month and was glad to hear that you were all well. My health is first rate but for the last six days there has been hard fighting in this army. As yet, our regiment has not been engaged... [109]

It was later on the 14th that our corps was sent to the left to counter a flank attack that Hood threw at Howard's corps, and we met it and stopped it cold. Williams's division arrived just in time to save Howard from being outflanked. The Red Stars, led by the 27th Indiana, formed battle lines on the run, and charged. The rebs were about to capture one of our batteries, but when our boys came on they scattered in all directions. It was the first of many times in this campaign that the Twentieth Corps would save the day. Our division came up just after dark and we took over picket duty.

At ten o'clock the next morning, with the battle already roaring, we shifted to the right and massed in a ravine. At noon we were ordered forward to attack Hood's corps. Of all the ground to maneuver on, this was the worst. It was uphill and down, hills and ravines of flinty rock and shale, covered by spindly scrub oak and pine and prickly wait-a-minute brambles. We had started out to be in reserve as the other divisions of the corps assaulted the rebel line, but we soon came up on Butterfield's division, all shot up, men sprawled everywhere, bloody, thirsty, exhausted men who had done all they could that day, and so it was our turn.

I was nearby Spoony as he crawled and tugged his way through the thickets, carrying our old flag. He was still his old magnetic self when it came to attracting enemy bullets, but miraculously none touched him, though the near misses made for a continuous shower of twigs and branches around our heads. We reached the top of a hill and saw the entrenched enemy line on the next hill over, with a four-gun enemy battery a-booming at us.

Just after we reached the top, the battery let out a salvo, the guns firing quickly in sequence. One after the other, the shells exploded in and around our lines, each coming a little nearer. The last cannonball whistled in and buried itself at my feet, but did not explode. I smiled weakly at James and Spoony, who was at my elbows and would have shared my fate. James, ever the philosopher, said, "We shall not be killed until our time comes," and Spoony replied, "Well, it's HELL not knowing when that will be!"

Of a sudden, old Joe Hooker himself was there with us, heedless to the danger as bullets clipped shards of bark from a tree next to him.

Colonel Cobham said, "General, you are wrong to expose yourself like this."

Hooker replied, "I'm not unwilling to share the dangers my men face."

They studied the enemy position a minute and then the colonel said, "You know, general, as yet I have no orders beyond taking this hill, which I have done, and I don't know what is expected of me next."

Hooker mused, as if thinking out loud, "I would like to have you take that battery, but I don't know that it can be done."

That was enough for Colonel George. "I can try," he said, very businesslike. Then in his command voice he called out, "Attention battalion, guide center, forward march!"

We moved out, and I looked up at all that fire and brimstone belching off the hill and said, "Holy smoke," or words to that effect. I thought that this was going to be very bad. It was bad enough.

Down the hill we went, and across a little crick, pushing through the brush with bullets zinging all around. Butterfield's men had actually gotten up to the battery, and the ground was littered with his dead and wounded. As we climbed the hill we discovered that we were in a dead space where the enemy could not hit us with all his guns. This was our salvation, and we made it to the top with only a few more men hit, but one of them was young George Peters, who was the boy the surgeons pulled a thread through his chest to remove the maggots, after Antietam.

We stormed over the works of the battery, killing or driving the gunners off. Captain Woeltge of Company I was shot dead as he put his hand on an enemy cannon. He had helped carry Calvin off the field at Antietam, almost two years earlier. Calvin wrote me once about a "Captain Woolsey" what was killed in Georgia in '64, and for the life of me I did not remember a Woolsey. Then it dawned on me: That's about how Woeltge's name sounded when spoken.

Well, instead of checkmate it was stalemate. The guns, four Napoleons of Corput's Cherokee Battery, were in a sort of fort about thirty yards in advance of their infantry trenches, and when we tried to push beyond the guns we were met by a blizzard of rifle fire that druv us back over the berm. Colonel Ireland had been wounded, so just then it was George Cobham that led our brigade. Rather than persist into that kind of resistance, he had us lie down, and we and the rebs shot up our basic load of cartridges at each other while the guns set betwixt and between in no man's land. We couldn't get at them, but neither could the rebs. The gunfire was so heavy you'd stick your musket up over your head and fire over the breastworks without aiming or exposing yourself.

As it got dark, Cobham was handed the task of getting the guns into our lines, and men from all three brigades of the division were put in his charge. We were relieved by another regiment and they came up and dug notches in the earthworks to drag the guns through. Many officers and men of the division mentioned our colonel's soldierly qualities afterward. I admired his common sense, for there were some commanders who would have tried to drive the infantry support away, and would have used up their outfits in trying to do so. There was much whooping and yelling as the guns were finally rolled down the hill into our lines.

The incident of the stalemate over the Confederate battery is one of the often-told stories of the Atlanta campaign. In their reports, half the officers in the corps claimed to have captured those guns, but it was General Geary who wanted them most. He had political aspirations and saw them as his ticket to the White House.

May the 17th.

"I had got so much written when we got orders to fall in and march to the left and we went, but did not get into any engagement that day or night. But the next morning our brigade went into battle and was under fire all day...

...There was no one hurt in the fight that you knew. George

Chappel, George Goodwill, and Brad are here and in good health and spirits. As is always the case after a victory, the army is in good spirits and although we feel tired and as dirty as hogs, still we can follow the rebs with a good grace after fighting and flogging them as we have this time. After a series of engagements that has lasted twelve days, I think the rebels will not fight if they can help it until they retreat some thirty miles south of here where they are said to have strong earthworks. There is but little doubt that when we get there we shall have another big fight. But I believe we can (and will) flog them at every point in this army this summer.

Our regiment found seventeen boxes of tobacco in the woods this morning and the men of our division got it, so we have plenty of that for the present..." [110]

Camp of the 111th regt PVV, near Pine Chapel and some twelve miles south of Dalton, Georgia May the 17th

"...When daylight came, [on the 16th] *the rebels were all in full retreat to the south...The loss in our regiment was very light considering the place we were in: We had one captain and three privates killed, and twenty-two wounded.*

The next day after the battle we started in pursuit of the retreating foe and that day came to a stream that we had to wade. It gave the most of us a wet ass. A few miles further along we came to a stream called the Coosawattee River. It was some ten rods wide and the same number of feet in depth, but the rebs were kind enough to leave two flatboats for our use and we crossed the men on them and swam the horses over. This morning they have extemporized a bridge over which they are drawing the artillery by hand. The ambulances will be drawn over by hand and the trains will go some other route. Our corps is all the troops that are on this road, the most of the army being on our right along the railroad." [111]

The rebs was forced to retreat because McPherson finally did what he should have done a week earlier, crossing the Oostanaula River south of Resaca to threaten their supplies and communications. I'll pick up on more of James's letter to Brother Bob, as we continue our deadly waltz through Georgia.

Camp of the 111th regt PVV near Kingston, Georgia, May the 20th

"I had got so much written when the order came to fall in. As I have had no chance to send {this} as yet, and there is news that the mail will leave this evening, I thought I would write a little more. The day we left Pine Chapel, we marched to a place called Calhoun {where} the rebel General Polk, who commanded the enemy's rear guard, had his headquarters the night before we got there. The Fourth Corps skirmished with him all over that section and it is said that our men took 1000 prisoners that day. The column under McPherson, which is on our right flank, fought him (Polk) the same day.

The next day we started at daylight and lay some three hours after we went about a mile, to let the 14th Corps train pass. But when we did get under motion we went as though the Devil himself was after us. The day was very hot. When we got to camp, our regiment was sent on picket. Five of our companies lay in line of battle all night, the other five being out on post. The next morning we started and took across the mountains and through the woods. All day we had skirmishers in front and about five o'clock p.m. we got orders to load our guns. We were closed in mass in the woods and lay down for some time. Then we marched by left flank into the fields and our brigade was formed into two lines of battle and marched through a very large corn field. There was a sharp artillery fight going on in our front, our Third Division and a part of the 23rd Corps being engaged. The rebs rapidly left the field. What our loss or that of the foe was I have not heard.

We went into camp just after dark and have lain here since. How long we shall stay here I don't know, but I expect that tomorrow morning will find us on the move to the southward...The country, take it all together since we left Ringgold, is rolling and in some places very hilly. The water is plenty and of good quality. This place shows less of the effects of war than any other I have seen since the first summer we were in Virginia. Where we're encamped shows quite good cultivation and is the best looking soil I have seen in this state. The man on whose farm we are at present is said to have taken his slaves—194 in number—away from here last Monday...

Well, I have written all I can think of. You must tell the rest of our folks that they may read this and excuse me for not writing to each of them separately, for I can't get time. I have written this sitting under

the broad glare of a Georgia sun--and that is as hot as there is any need of...."

***

FROM DALTON TO THE ETOWAH

Yes, we had thrown away the book; at least in Georgia we did. In Virginia they were still standing shoulder to shoulder and blazing away at each other. While we had tastes of that kind of stand-up fighting now and again, more often than not we went to a different style of fighting, which was more spread out, with skirmish lines preceding us that were much heavier, or stronger, than in the early days. Note also that the old custom of going out and having a battle and then going back to camp was discarded. Sherman called it "enlightened war," which for the common soldier meant days and days of danger without end, until the end. We saw the elephant all over again, and he was more fearsome than ever before.

"Joe Hooker is our leader; He drinks his whiskey clear."

So went the song we sang about the commander of the Twentieth Army Corps. Hooker got his nickname, "Fighting Joe," back on the Peninsula in '62 when a reporter filed a story entitled "Fighting—Joe Hooker." The print setter left out the dash (—) and the title became "Fighting Joe Hooker," and as they say the legend was born and the nickname stuck. Robert E. Lee humorously and sarcastically referred to him as Mr. F.J. Hooker. I may have given you the impression back around Chancellorsville time that Hooker was a flash in the pan general who got his comeuppance from Lee and never again amounted to much. To be sure, he was no great shakes as an army commander, but as a corps commander he had few equals.

As a person, well that is a whole another thing. Hooker always looked like he stepped out of a painting: Tailored frock coat, sash, sword, broad-brimmed felt hat, and the rosiest cheeks I ever saw not on a woman. He may have come by the florid complexion because of his fondness for "Clear Whiskey."

He also had a talent for getting people mad at him, his fellow generals and superiors, especially. Sherman had known him before the war and did not like him much. That is why we would have been better off with a less capable fellow in charge of the corps: We paid the price for the dislike. Hooker had to do twice as much—and be twice as good at it—as the other corps commanders, just to be tolerated by Sherman. That translated into more fighting and more loss for the Twentieth Corps. From the 15th of May until the capture of Atlanta on September 2nd we were under fire almost every day.

From Resaca we moved on Calhoun. We could not cross the Coosawattee at Newton's Ferry, so we swung east to McClure's Ford and Fields' Mill and crossed on makeshift bridges on May 17th. Our objective was Adairsville, over twenty miles south of Resaca. Johnston stopped briefly at Adairsville but, finding it not a favorable place to give battle, he continued on by separate roads to Cassville and Kingston. We headed toward Cassville across Gravelly Plateau.

Johnston's army deployed to defend Cassville, all three corps in a line two miles northeast of the town. They were ready on May 19th to pounce on our corps as it approached from Adairsville, with our Third Division, under Butterfield, in the van. The army was widely scattered and the rebs thought they could take out our piece of it before the remainder could arrive. Hood's corps was moving out to attack us when some of our cavalry came in behind his right flank, headed to get at the railroad at Cassville Station. That spooked the rebs and they pulled back to a new defensive position southeast of Cassville, and it looked like a fight.

We opened with artillery, something like forty guns. This was the "sharp artillery fight" that James mentioned, but it was pretty much a one-sided affair. Our guns wreaked such havoc on the new reb position that they decided their whole line was not defensible. It was unusual for artillery to have such an effect. During the night they evacuated and headed for Cartersville, en route to cross the Etowah River.

As we advanced and Johnston retreated, we grew weaker while he grew stronger. He collected in his cavalry and got the last of Polk's corps up from Mississippi, while we had to start dropping off garrisons to hold the places we had captured, especially if they were on our supply line.

We had a short interval of rest on the north side of the Etowah, and James got to finish and send his long letter to Rob. If you pay close attention, you can match his letters up with my account, which is related with the benefit of hindsight.

Susan to Robert and Janet Miller, June 3rd, 1864

Dear Parents,

Your kind letter I received some time ago and was glad to hear that you were all well but sorry that Mother's health was so poor. But

I am in hopes she is better since the weather has become more settled. We are all well. I received a letter from James last Tuesday night; it was commenced on the 14th and finished on the 17th of May. He wrote a few lines and then they had orders to fall in and march to the left. They went, but did not get in any engagements that day. I will send you James's letter and you can read it for yourselves. He came through all right, for which we have great reason to be thankful. I was worrying so about him that I could not rest. When I get a letter, it is not much satisfaction for he might be killed, or wounded and die, before a letter could get here. But I am in hopes this war will end before another summer. There are six soldier's families in this neighborhood. That is nearly enough for one neighborhood. I got one-half of my garden plowed and I planted it last Monday. The other half is too wet. When James draws his pay I wish you would send or fetch me some if Mother's health will admit. Robert says, "tell grandpa that I went to Sunday School, and read, and wore my new clothes that Aunt Delia gave me." Ellen says, "Tell grandpa that I went to Sunday School and got a lesson in reading the testament, and Robby and me is going to school next week." Give my love to all and reserve a share for yourselves.

Write soon.

Affectionately, your daughter,

Susan Ann Miller [112]

Susan Miller was a strong woman. For over two years she had took care of their small farm and family, including 'round the clock nursing for Johnny, but it was starting to take its toll. In a way, it had been good that her concern for Johnny had took the edge of her mind off of James's safety. Now, with little Johnny gone, she had nothing to think about but James. The news from all fronts was all bloody and all bad. Whenever she got a letter, she would pray that there would be another letter in a few weeks. That would mean that he was presently still alive. With every battle he had survived, the odds that he would survive the next got smaller. Like she said, in her neighborhood there was six other women in the same boat, so if misery loved company, she was in good shape.

Anyway, on the 23rd of May we were on the move again, crossing the river on pontoon bridges. Our objective was Dallas, Georgia. We had cut loose from the railroad, the entire army going around Johnston's left flank. We crossed open, rolling country on narrow and dusty roads. The weather was turning hot.

Johnston's army was around Allatoona, on the railroad. As soon as their cavalry reported that we were swinging west and south of them, Johnston sent two of his corps toward Dallas. The next day, the 24th, we entered country a bit rougher than any since that up around Dalton. The "Star Corps" was the vanguard of the Army of the Cumberland. As was customary, Schofield's little army was off to the left, and McPherson was to our right. We marched to Burnt Hickory, a half-dozen miles from Dallas.

I wish I had a bunch of Georgia road maps I could pass amongst you. Sherman had a special map made of northern Georgia, printed and reproduced on linen for all his corps commanders, so's nobody would get lost.

So if YOU are lost, I'll just sum up by saying that by the 20th of May we had covered half the distance to Atlanta. Our supply line stretched back eighty miles to Chattanooga.

***

NEW HOPE CHURCH

Have you ever been out on a limb and heard it crack? If we thought we were going to steal a march on Joe Johnston, we were mistaken. Our division, Geary's own, led the march on the 25th. We left Burnt Hickory, crossed Pumpkinvine Creek, and turned off on a road that our generals thought led to Dallas. It did not. So much for Sherman's fancy map! The rest of the corps stayed on the main road to Dallas. We were under the impression that there were no rebs within miles of us, but as each of our columns were nearing Dallas they were being confronted first by reb cavalry and then by one or another of their infantry divisions. Wily old Johnston had figured us out, and his main force was there to greet us, set up east of Dallas and north of there around a little Methodist place of worship called New Hope Church, which was where our division, all by its lonesome, was heading. We ended up five miles ahead of any other unit of our army, eyeball to eyeball with John B. Hood's entire corps!

We deployed in line of battle and expected the worst as we skirmished forward. The afternoon dragged by and finally Williams and Butterfield came up and deployed their men in front of us. As it turned out, both sides had awaited the attack of the other, and now, with a few hours to sunset, Hooker sent us forward. We still believed (or hoped) that only a small force was in our front. We plunged into the underbrush and briars.

We ran into a hornet's nest. Not only were the rebs in force, but they had even had time to dig in. Although we outnumbered them, they were in their pits dug into the red Georgia clay, and we did not stand a chance. We lost a heap of men and fired off all of our ammunition, making a racket that was heard all the way to Atlanta, twenty-five miles away.

Then it started to rain. Darkness came, and with that our daily nocturnal chore of entrenching, wallowing in the gooey red clay of Georgia.

The next day was spent in digging and ducking sharpshooters' bullets. We could not see the enemy except for brief glimpses through the trees and smoke, and it was the same for them. Our whole army was concentrated again, but for some reason Sherman still thought that maybe only a corps was in front of us. He was wrong. Hood, Polk, and Hardee were all there. Assuming the odds were still heavy in our favor, Sherman made plans to attack both flanks the next day, the 27th of May, after a heavy artillery fire.

The attack from our right fizzled; the one from our left failed. McPherson went in on the right and came up on well-entrenched rebel infantry. He reported that he could neither drive through nor outflank them, and Sherman had him give it up. Not so on our left. There, Howard's corps made a long march to try to get beyond the enemy right flank, but when he turned south he ran right into Pat Cleburne's division and took heavy losses. The next day, the 28th, the rebs attacked Logan's corps on our right and were repulsed handily.

We stayed in the New Hope vicinity for a week, long enough to nickname it the "Hell Hole." Sand and pine trees, bullets and blood. In the previous battles of this war, you could either attack and stand an excellent chance of getting killed, or you could defend, and stand a lesser chance. Here at New Hope, you could get killed anytime for no reason at all, while you were eating, or sleeping, or even while relieving yourself. To go someplace you either ran like hell or crawled along the ground. Captain Todd of Company A was killed. Big Jim Donaldson, whose mule had been blown apart at Chancellorsville, was wounded and never came back to us, and it was here that George Siggins, one of the few who declined to reenlist with the company, was mortally wounded. Our total loss was nine killed, forty-one wounded, and three missing.

After two years in this business, we thought we had seen it all, but now, after a month of this new kind of work, it was beginning to wear on us. We fought and marched all day, and at night we dug trenches. We all developed what is called the "thousand yard stare," a condition in which the eyes are looking through, rather than at, a person or object. We found ourselves going through whole days doing things mechanically, automatically, without thinking. Eating, sleeping, fighting, or marching, it all blurred together. Some of us drew closer during these times; others, particularly the new men, became quiet and withdrawn. Those we watched. We knew when a man needed a break, a chance to escort a wounded comrade back to the aid station, or go somewhere where the sharpshooter's bullets were not whistling overhead. And they called it "enlightened war..."

***

KENESAW

Finally, troops of Logan's Corps relieved us and we pulled out, in a pouring rain, to shift back onto the railroad at Ackworth. In the old days it used to rain after a battle, but now it was one continuous fight, so it rained every day. The rest of the army followed us, while Johnston moved over to get in our way, with a position stretching from Lost Mountain to the railroad.

It had been a hardship for us to be away from the railroad. Rations got pretty skimpy for a while. It was not until June 10th that we got the whole army up from the Hell Hole and were ready to advance again. The Cumberland was in its customary position in the center, but this time Schofield was to our right and McPherson straddled the railroad on our left. On June 8th McPherson had been reinforced by the Seventeenth Corps, under Blair, which more than made up for our losses so far. Our forces moved a very short distance, with the Twentieth Corps not moving at all, before coming up on the rebs' new defensive line.

This was a strong position, anchored on the hills and ridges that were scattered about the countryside in no particular order, Pine Knob, Lost Mountain, Brush Mountain, Kenesaw Mountain, and a dozen other nameless prominences covered with rocks and brush. It was generally accepted in the ranks that once the enemy—or us for that matter—had been in a position for a few hours, our scratch trenches would make the force impossible to dislodge. Rather than attack and be bled white, we would resort to flanking, on a greater or lesser scale, to make the enemy pull out.

All that would be attended by lots of skirmishing. Our regiment was on the skirmish line a great deal. It was customary to leave a company in reserve with the colors when going on the skirmish line, but the colors of the 111th went on the line, one stand on the right, one in the center and one on the left as guides to keep the alignment. It seems to me miraculous that any of the color bearers of the regiment survived the campaign. Calvin always took position on the right of Company D, where he could be in close touch with Lieutenant Sturdevant, who was now the company commander. The lieutenant was always getting on Calvin for not keeping under cover.

Camp in the field near Big Shanty, Georgia June the 17th

"...Your kind and welcome letter of the fifth instant I got this morning. I was very much pleased to hear from you once more but was very sorry to hear that Mother was so feeble. It seems hard to think that her stay with us is in all probability short, but I can't say that I am surprised, for when I left home I felt that I had seen her for the last time.

...Please to give my respects to William and say that I am glad to hear they have a boy and I hope he will live to cheer his parents.

I was sorry to hear that the boys from that section had suffered so much in the late battles in Virginia, but such is war. My health is good and so is the health of the regiment, that is, what is left of it. Our losses have been severe in this campaign. Three days since, our Division moved to the front and built breastworks about one mile from the rebs who held possession of a high hill in our front. The next day after we got our position, we opened on the rebs with artillery from three sides of their position. That night they left and the next morning we followed them some two miles and a sharp battle ensued. The rebs were driven over a mile to another line of works in the woods--which they held in spite of all our efforts to dislodge them. That night, we built a new line of earthworks and yesterday all their skirmishers and ours were hard at work with but small loss on our side. In the afternoon we had quite a brisk artillery duel with the rebs. This morning at daylight we found that they had left their works in our front and when we moved to occupy them we found them situated on top of a ridge. Of all the reb breastworks I ever saw, those are the strongest and best. From their position and strength, I am satisfied that if we had attempted to storm them we would have been all cut to pieces. But our right out-flanked them and compelled them to leave these works and take up another line over a mile to the rear.

This is a hard campaign: so far, there is a great deal of building breastworks so we have to march and fight daytimes and build the works in the night. We all feel tired but there is no prospect at present but what we are to keep up this kind of work for some time to come, unless we get beaten (which I hardly think will be the case.)

But I must say that Johnston is making a splendid retreat, only falling back when we out-flank him, and we have taken but few prisoners so far. From the nature of the ground I think that our losses must be more than those of the enemy. Well, what the next move will be I cant tell but I expect that when there is any fighting done, old Joe Hooker will give us our full share. At least, so far we have done more fighting than any other two Corps in this army, and the rebs know and fear the 20th Corps and General Hooker more than any other part of Sherman's army. I believe that there is none of the boys that have been hit that you knew. Of those that were hit the day before yesterday, one was Reuben Moss (his folks live in Glade Township) and he had his left arm broken near the elbow. The name of the other was John Myers (his folks live in Warren). Please to write soon and as often as you can and not wait for me as there is no telling when I will get another chance to write. I will try to write to some of the folks in Farmington every chance I get. I got a letter from Susan dated June the first and she said that the folks were all well and that she hoped we would get our pay before long as she was almost out of money. Will you please tell father to please lend her ten dollars or if he cannot do so, please do it yourself as there is no telling when we will get our pay. But not, in all probability, while this campaign continues. When it will be over, God only knows..." [113]

And God wasn't telling. It finally stopped raining and the sun came out on June 14th, after eleven straight days of rain. It was on that day that

Sherman happened to be with Howard's Fourth Corps in front of Pine Knob. Through his spyglass he saw a group of Confederate officers on the mountain and he ordered nearby batteries, including one of Geary's, to fire a salvo at them.

The officers were their army commander, Joe Johnston, and corps commanders Hardee (the hat designer and manual writer) and Bishop Polk. When they saw puffs of smoke from our guns, they made for safer places, but Polk, stately and rather rotund Polk, did not move as fast as the others. A three-inch solid shot hit him squarely in the brisket, doing the most complete and hideous job of killing a corps commander that ever happened during the entire war. A vast pool of his blood was still standing when Howard occupied the mountain the next day. (I must say, though, it was a splendid shot.)

We pushed forward to the right of the mountain about one mile in the morning, skirmishing all the way. Then we attacked and gained another mile.

Finally, it was on June 15th, at Pine Knob, that Rueben Moss was wounded. Lieutenant Sturdevant came up and said, "Spoony, it is damned foolishness for you to be here with that flag, exposing yourself unnecessarily. You go and help Rube back where he can get his wound attended to."

James and me had carried John Myers, who was severely wounded and would die in a week or two back in Chattanooga, back to the surgeons, and we met Spoony and Rube there. Rube's arm was broke and he ended up having his arm amputated. Well, we got John situated, then we started back to the skirmish line together, and passed through the ranks of the 46th Pennsylvania. A voice called out, "Say, Calvin, do you remember me?" It was Rudolph Pratt, one of Calvin's schoolmates. Calvin was both surprised and delighted to see him. They had a few words together and he told him the first chance he had he would come and see him. Several days after, as they were near, Calvin ran over to the 46th, only to learn to his sorrow that only a few minutes after he saw Rudolph the regiment advanced into battle and Rudolph was killed. His brother, DeForest Pratt, one of my most beloved chums, was in the 22nd Pennsylvania Cavalry and was killed in action. [114]

CHAPTER EIGHTEEN
A PRIVATE, A COLONEL, AND A GENERAL

Many prayers went up to the Lord during May. But few were praises. When James Miller had returned to Georgia he had had a feeling that he would never see his mother again, in this world anyway.

He disappeared after mail call that morning, the 23rd of June. I found him sitting in the trench, head cradled in his arms, and a sheet of a letter in his hand. His face was dirty, as was everybody's, but tears had streaked two clean furrows down his cheeks to his beard. He didn't say anything as I walked up to him, just handed me his father's letter and turned away.

It was dated June the 11th. "Dear Son James," it began, "I have to inform you that your dear Mother has died..."

"Sorry, pard," was all I could say.

"How do I answer? What do I say to him that would possibly help him at a time like this?"

"James, you'll find the words. You always do..."

Next day he showed me the letter he had written. The first part, though written from a heart hardened by war, was as soft as a woman's touch.

Camp behind the breast works in line of battle near Marietta, Georgia June the 24th

Dear Father,

I take this opportunity to write a few lines to you in answer to your very sad letter of the eleventh instant which I received yesterday and in which you informed me of Mother's death. Oh! how much there is of sadness to all of us in that sentence of a mother's death. Although I thought I had made up my mind that there was but very little chance for me ever to see her again in this life since I got your letter announcing the fact of her death I have felt a bereavement and loneliness that I never before experienced. Oh how things and times that are past and gone come to my mind--scenes of her devotion to our welfare, regardless of her own comfort. My mind is saddened by the many times that that dear friend has been caused to mourn for the actions of her eldest child but it will not do any good to mourn for those things now. And if I feel lonesome and feel her loss you must be worse. But there is this to comfort us: that our loss is her eternal gain and in that clime to which she is gone her sufferings are all over and she will not have any suffering to endure. While we deplore her loss, let us try to emulate her virtues. I hope that I for one may be able to remember that I have one parent in Heaven and so do my duty that the one still spared to me may not have reason to blush for his soldier son.

...We have had a very long, wearisome campaign and there is no telling how long it will last. For the last three weeks it has been one fight all the time--day and night our skirmishers and those of the enemy have been busily engaged. Some of the time there has been very sharp fighting at different points of the line. The rebels are slowly leaving one strong position after another and our army is steadily following them. There is every advantage on their side, except numbers. Our Corps under its gallant leader, Hooker, is doing its full share of the heavy work in this campaign and it seems to be the luck of our Division, when there is sharper work than usual to do, to be the first to go in.

On the twentieth, our regiment and the 137th New York under Cobham's command were sent to the front of our Corps to skirmish with the enemy and find out his position. The skirmish was sharp all day and night but we succeeded in driving the rebel skirmishers over a mile and off from a ridge that we now occupy. The next day we built breastworks and our First Division was forcing their front line up even with ours. The rebels massed part of their forces and charged the First Division four lines deep but the gallant red stars held them sternly to the work and did not yield an inch. After a fight of about one hour, the rebs broke and fell back in discord leaving us masters of the field. At that point, a part of the battle field was not more than half a mile distant from our part of the line and in plain sight from where we were, and when the rebs ran we gave them a good cheer. Ever since, the contest between our skirmishers and those of the enemy has been kept up and although there is no great deal of loss on our side, still at times the bullets come over our heads when we are behind our works in a manner that is more lively than agreeable. The rebs must be at least three quarters of a mile from us...

We can hear the whistle of rebel cars every day and it does not seem to be more than three or four miles distant. But there seems to be a strong ridge between us and the railroad. What the next movement will be I cant tell but I expect that it will be a repetition of the old tactics of extending our right and overlapping the enemys left and thereby compelling him to leave our left free to continue the movement. I think that this campaign will last a good while yet and if we succeed in driving the rebs out of Atlanta it will be with a terrible loss. Still I think we shall do it after a while if we keep on pounding as I think we shall.

I hope that Susan will move there as I think she will be more comfortable with you than where she is. I got a letter from her at the same time I received yours. It was written on the 9th and in that letter she told me that she intended to go to your house to help take care of Mother she not having heard of her death. She said that her health and that of the children was good. I have written all I can think of for this time so will close. Hoping to hear from you soon and often I remain truly and affectionately your son

James T. Miller [115]

***

WE NEVER TRIED IT AGAIN

Towards the end of that letter, James describes the Battle of Kolb's Farm, fought mainly by Hood's Corps against us and Schofield. Hood for some reason thought that Schofield was on the march and vulnerable to be flanked, and proceeded on that assumption. Instead, he ran into solid battle lines just a-waiting for him. Our artillery, and some good regiments set out in front, mowed his men down.

We were around Kenesaw for quite a spell. If we thought that Sherman was so protective of us that we would never make any full-scale attacks, we were disabused of that notion along about the 27th of June. He sent in massive storming columns of the Fourth, Fourteenth, and Fifteenth Corps on that day to try to bull through. Lucky for us, the Twentieth Corps did nothing but skirmish on that day. The boys that did go in took a bloody repulse. Sherman said something about wanting

Johnston to learn that we could and would come at him like that, but the assaults were a mistake, and we never tried it again.

Finally we resorted to flanking moves again and forced Johnston to give up Kenesaw and retire to his last fortified line north of the Chattahoochee.

Camp in the field near Vining's Station, Georgia July the 9th

"...With you I feel lonely and sad after the news of our best of earthly friends. Although I thought I had partially prepared for the sad news still when it came I found the sense of bereavement and loneliness was and is a great deal more than I had prepared for...

...Since the fifteenth of May which was the day we fought the rebs at Resaca there have been only six days but what we have had more or less fighting in our immediate front. Our loss has been very heavy in our regiment it is not far from 150 killed and wounded and we were a little over 500 strong when we left Bridgeport and in addition a large number of our men are sick and in hospitals in the rear. Our present number of men for duty is a little over 200.

The rebs keep falling back from one fortified position to another and we keep following them up until now they have one line north of the Chattahoochee River. Our present line is from one to two miles from that stream... in fact there has not been a general battle since the campaign began it has been one continual skirmish...The rebs seem to be determined not to give a fair fight and so we do the best we can under the circumstances and outflank their position one after another. And so I think it will be to the end of the campaign unless we can force the rebs to a fight in the field, which they will not do if they can help it. I think that we can flog Joe Johnston's army blind if we can only get a fair fight out of them.

...I hope [Susan] *will not be sorry for leaving her log cabin and going to Farmington and I hope you all will endeavor to cheer her for no doubt she will feel bad on my account so long as this campaign lasts..."* [116]

Sometimes during the campaign, when the bullets were flying thick and fast, I felt like Moses, destined never to see the Promised Land. I guess that's why I climbed to the top of the tallest tree on the tallest hill north of the Chattahoochee River. Far below me at the bottom of the tree there stood James, and Calvin and Lieutenant Ham Sturdevant and a score of the other boys.

A thin morning haze covered the panorama of green spread before me. To the north towered old Kenesaw Mountain, which we had finally outflanked in order to reach the Chattahoochee. To the southeast I thought I could make out the bald dome of Stone Mountain.

But my eyes swung to my right, to find what I was really looking for. There to the south, a good eight or ten miles away, were some wispy, spindly spires and dimly formed rooftops, and I made out smoke from some tall smokestacks.

It was Atlanta.

"Do you see it? Do you see it?" the boys called up.

"Yes," I said. "It's a far piece off, but it sure looks like Atlanta to me, just as General Sherman promised."

"Well," says Ham drily, "You better get down before you fall down."

About then I heard a faint "pumm-m-m" from the south and then, a second later, a bullet went tickety-tick through the branches of my tree. Some enemy sharpshooter had seen me and was trying out his Whitworth in my direction. I didn't have to be told three times. Down from that tree I came.

We got plenty of rest along the north bank of the Chattahoochee. It offered an opportunity to cook up some decent meals, catch up on our mail, and boil our uniforms, for to get rid of the graybacks (lice) which had enlisted in the Union Army since we left Bridgeport. If there is a list of records unmatched in history, it should be recorded that there was a world record skinny dip in the river: Thousands of men, butt naked, washing two months of grime from their bodies. Even William T. Sherman took off his drawers and jumped in.

This next is a special letter, so I include it in its entire:

Camp in the woods two miles from the rebs near Chattahoochee River, July the 15th, 1864

Dear Brother

I received your kind and welcome letter of the third inst last night and was glad to hear from you directly once more and was glad to hear that the folks were all well with a fair prospect of an increase of family at Joe's. My health is good and I am enjoying myself as well as I can expect under the circumstances. To say that it is hot here would be a very faint term to express the state of the weather we endure. For the last three days it has been the most oppressively hot weather I

ever endured so far. For the last seven days we have been encamped in this place and have had nothing but picket duty to do and we are getting pretty well rested. This is the longest rest we have had since the campaign began. I have hardly seen a paper since we have been here and I hear but little of what is doing, even in this army.

The rebs are all on the south side of the river. We can see the steeples of Atlanta by climbing to the tops of the trees on the hills where we are encamped. It is seven miles from the river to the city but I expect that the rebs have made the position as strong as engineering skill and the labor of five to ten thousand negroes for the last year can make it. But they have been driven from no less than eight lines of the strongest field works I ever saw since the campaign began and we have had some hard fighting and by far the most skirmishing I ever saw or heard of. Still in the whole campaign so far we have not had what might properly be termed a general battle. The rebs whenever they could not hold their position without giving us a general engagement in the open field have fell back to another line of works all ready for them. In my opinion we could flog Johnston's army all to pieces at any time if we could only get them in an open field fight, but so far this campaign has been a series of flanking operations.

We soldiers are quite anxious to learn whether we are to have the right to vote at the fall elections and in my opinion if Lincoln and Johnson are elected this fall it will do as much to crush this rebellion and end the war as the fighting this summer in the field and if the soldiers have a right to vote at least nine tenths of them will support Abe and Andy. We hear that the rebs are in Maryland at present and if they stay there any length of time some of the one hundred days men will have a chance to see the elephant I guess. I don't know as I care if they do for they are no better than we are.

There is to me something strange in the prices of gold and everything else in the North. We have not had a defeat this campaign and what there is to make prices run up to such heights I can't see but it must be speculation. I am very sorry to hear that there is so poor a prospect of fodder there. We have not got any pay yet and I don't know when we shall. If Sherman intends to rest here any length of time we will in all probability get our pay but if not there is no prospect of when we will get it.

Please to write soon and I will do as well as I can under the circumstances to answer your letters. I remain as ever truly your brother,

James T. Miller [117]

There is an old saying: "Be careful what you wish for—you may get it." For almost three months we had been wishing that the rebs would come out and give us a fair fight, but all of Sherman's maneuvers to bring that about were frustrated by Johnston's generalship.

The southerners despaired as we finally drew within cannon shot of Atlanta. How excited we were to view the steeples, however faint and far-off, of the city that had been our elusive goal for so long.

As James said, it had been a splendid retreat—but that is not what Jeff Davis was after. He wanted Joe Johnston to beat us. Out east, Lee was fighting pitched battles and inflicting awful casualties, but, fact is, he was losing, and retreating as Grant kept trying to get around his right. Here in Georgia, we kept flanking to the right, and Johnston kept avoiding the snare, all the while making us bleed while his losses were comparatively light. The differences were lost on Jeff Davis: The difference was that Lee was Lee, and the numbers that made people call his adversary "Butcher Grant" gave the illusion that Lee was winning. The difference was that Bragg was at Davis's elbow and being sharply critical that Johnston would not stand and fight. The difference was that the Governor of Georgia, Joe Brown, was setting up a howl about the Yankees getting so far into his state. The difference was that there was a tradition in the Army of Tennessee for generals to undermine their superior, a tradition that was unheard of in the Army of Northern Virginia, under the legendary Lee.

And so it was, in desperation, that President Jeff Davis fired Joe Johnston and replaced him with General John B. Hood. It was a case of the outspoken know-it-all getting the ear of President Davis and telling him what he wanted to hear, but people who knew Hood well called him a general with the heart of a lion and a head of wood. Davis gave us a gift in the personage of Hood, and the campaign would now take a decisive turn.

Hood was a heads down, no-holds-barred fighter, and you need men like that in a war, of course. As commander of the Texas Brigade, Hood had stampeded Porter's Fifth Corps at Gaines Mill during the Seven Days Battles, led the assault that had come near to obliterating Pope's army at Second Bull Run, wrecked the offensive of Hooker's corps at Antietam. Promoted to division command, Hood nearly destroyed the Union left flank at Gettysburg, and for his efforts had his arm mangled by a shell fragment. Patched up, he went with Longstreet to Chickamauga and led the assault that split Rosecrans's army in two. There, a bullet in the leg had caused him to lose that limb, amputated almost to the hip. Promoted and patched up again, strapped in his saddle with a cork leg imported from Europe, he led a corps in this campaign, all the while being sharply critical of Johnston's tactics.

Joe Johnston received the telegram from Richmond on July 17th, firing him and putting Hood in charge. Hood's mission was to defeat us, and the only tactic which he knew was Attack!

It was the calm before the storm. It was also on July 17th that the Army of the Cumberland finally packed up and headed for the Chattahoochee, threatening a crossing direct on Atlanta. As we did, McPherson and Schofield went away up river to the left and crossed the river almost unopposed.

On our front, the river was first crossed by an outfit carrying Spencer repeating rifles, which fired the new metallic cartridge. They awed the rebel pickets by rising up out of the water, pouring the water out of their gun barrels, and firing off seven rounds each. "Keep your powder dry" had become an archaic bit of advice.

We advanced from the Chattahoochee three corps abreast, Howard's Fourth to our left and Palmer's Fourteenth to our right. Schofield's little army was to the left of Thomas's army, providing the link with McPherson, who was swinging a wide loop to come in on Atlanta from the east. It was a tried and true formula that had worked many times since the beginning of May.

***

A TERRIBLE LOSS

Between us and Atlanta was a lesser stream which meandered across our front and emptied into the Chattahoochee west of us. Peachtree Creek is not too wide or deep, but foot troops bottlenecked at the fords, and guns and wagons had to cross on bridges. It was behind the creek that the first fortifications protecting Atlanta were encountered.

Hood's plan was to catch us while we straddled the creek, with McPherson and Schofield too far away to help us, drive any of us that had crossed the creek into the corner it made with the Chattahoochee, and destroy us. It was a fair enough plan, but it required perfect timing. If he attacked too soon, not enough of us would be across the creek to make it worth their while; too late, and we would all be across, entrenched to the eyes as was our custom, and ready to defend. Also, the longer the delay the more progress McPherson would make in his left hook.

July 20th was the fateful day. It was dreadful hot. That morning, we went on the skirmish line, driving the enemy's pickets back until about eleven o'clock. Our brigade was then placed in reserve, with our other two brigades in front of us, and we brewed up some coffee and pulled out our hardtack and salt pork. Our rear echelon boys took advantage of the lull and came up to hand out rations and some new uniforms.

Colonel Cobham and our young adjutant, John R. Boyle, sat on a gum blanket under a tree. The air was still and hot. Colonel Cobham says, "What a life, eh, Boyle? I'm almost too lazy to breathe. I'm sure army life has spoiled me for any honest work."

Adjutant Boyle replied, "Yes, colonel, here we are, holding up this tree and being paid to do it."

All of a sudden there was a volley of muskets off to the left, followed closely by the booming of our artillery. There was a stir in our ranks; Cobham and Boyle stood up. "Well," says James, "I was going to write a letter, but I guess there's no time now."

The firing got louder and closer as more reb brigades took up the attack from their right to left. First Newton's division of Howard's corps was hit, then our Third Division, now under General Ward. Finally it was Geary's turn. The Johnnies overran the 33rd New Jersey, which Geary had set up as an outpost, and then they struck our two front brigades, which were set up for attack, not defense. They hit hard, and both brigades wavered. A battery was abandoned as the rebs got around the right flank of the division.

There was a ravine between us and our front lines. On order, we up and grabbed our muskets and charged across that ravine into a whole storm of screaming Confederates, men from Alabama and Louisiana. We barely made the top of the hill when we met them, and the 111th, being on the right flank of the brigade, was hit hardest.

Side by side, me and James went for broke. Colonel Cobham was with the colors, urging us on. His attention was on the enemy in our immediate front, who were not over twenty feet from us. Calvin touched him on the arm and said, "Colonel, they have turned our right flank." Cobham gave orders to change front to the right, and the next instant fell with a bullet in the chest. He saw the reb that had shot him, and from the ground he pointed and gasped, "Shoot that man!" The reb was riddled with bullets. Instant revenge. It was a critical moment but there was no stampede; the line fell back slowly with brave resistance, bayonets and rifle butts used liberally.

I seen George Cobham go down, and then James Miller fell. I remember a strange feeling, of time seeming to slow down, and an awful red tint seeming to color the scene. The Johnnies were all around us. One ragged character yelled out, "Surrender, damn you!" and James answered, "You go to hell!" He shot the Johnny, and then hefted his Enfield for to use it as a club, and then, also at point-blank range, he was shot. He had wished for a quick death on the battlefield, if his time was to come, and he got his wish. I shot his killer and, out of grief, bayoneted him for good measure.

The rage that I felt is frightening to remember, even now after all these years. I lived what the human race was like in its primitive stages, before we got domesticated and "civilized." I fear that for a few minutes along the bank of Peachtree Creek I had no soul. It was there that I got the two bullet holes in my coat. Colonel Cobham, James Miller, the eighty or so men that were killed or wounded, they went down a-fighting, I'll tell you. No quarter was asked, and none was given. Eighty good men lost, out of two hundred, and those of us who survived fought like enraged beasts.

Alonzo Foust and Frank Guy, the other color bearers, and Dick Zirilla carried the colonel to the rear while Calvin took their colors, stuck the flagstaffs in the ground, and we reformed on the flags and druv the enemy back, winning a great "victory."

In a short time it was over. The forest floor was covered with dead and wounded, ours and theirs. I walked over to where James lay. He was on his back, with his feet to the foe, of which there were a dozen sprawled around him. His face was peaceful; he looked like he was sleeping. I folded his hands on his chest, straightened his legs, and said a little prayer. I felt like crying, but I could not. Not then, anyway...

I feel like taking a break, just now, and so I will just have you read a passage from "Soldiers True," describing the ground over which we fought:

"That narrow, muddy ravine between those hills, near Peachtree Creek, was a throat of death to the One Hundred and Eleventh Pennsylvania Regiment. The thirty minutes that the command stood there, like a finger extended in flame, was the most fatal half hour in its history. It is simply marvelous that a single man escaped. The ravine was a hurricane of bullets and a crater of fire. Trees were clipped of their branches, bushes were cut away as by knives, and rails with which the swale was bridged were splintered..." [118]

That night, about 8 p.m., we went back to the place where the wounded were collected. There were no tents or other covering. Mother Earth was their resting place, the sky above their only covering. The colonel was conscious and recognized Calvin and knew he could not live. He gave him his pocketbook, which contained a considerable amount of money, and his watch and requested they be sent to his wife. Calvin gave the pocketbook, money, and watch to the company commander and I understand it was entrusted to Adelbert Page, Mrs. Cobham's brother, who accompanied the body with the colonel's personal effects home to Warren, Pennsylvania. General Joe Hooker and several other generals and staff officers were present while we were with the colonel. Hooker shed tears of sorrow, and each and all spoke in highest praise of him as a brave and efficient officer and noble, kind-hearted man. He passed away about 11 p.m., July 20th, 1864. [119]

After the fight, we buried our dead. We marked their graves as careful as we could. I carved James's name and regiment on a pine board from an ammunition box. We took care of our own, in death as in life. I would like to believe that no member of the 111th lies in an unmarked grave. They shipped Colonel Cobham's body home, but he'd paid for it ahead of time. Them that could afford it, officers mostly, were squared up with the undertaker if not with their savior. Colonel Cobham was a good man, though. We thought a lot of him, and he took good care of us. They buried him over acrosst the river.

General James McPherson commanded the Army of the Tennessee. He was Sherman's protégé, a very capable soldier expected to rise to the top. He was also in love.

He was engaged to a Miss Emily Hoffman, of Baltimore. You may remember the climate of Baltimore when we were there: Held in the Union only by the placing of a fort on every hill in the city. "Hot," in other words. Miss Hoffman's family was secesh to the core. They did not approve of this stalwart young Yankee, general or not, courting their Emily.

McPherson had wanted to get married in the spring before the campaign began. Sherman had even advised him in March to "steal a furlough and run to Baltimore *in cog*, but get back and take part in the next move." That was before the thunderbolts that elevated Sherman and also moved McPherson into his old place. Afterwards, Sherman told him, "Mac, it wrings my heart but you can't go now."

He never would. After failing to stop the right wing of our army under Thomas on July 20th, two days later Hood next attacked the left wing, under McPherson, as it advanced on Atlanta from the east. McPherson's flank was "in the air" supposedly and Hood was always trying to pull a "Chancellorsville" on us.

The rebs got well to the left flank and into the rear of McPherson's front line. McPherson galloped toward the sound of the guns, thinking he was safe to the rear of the fighting, but he ran right into a Confederate skirmish line. Hailed to surrender, he spun his horse to get away and was shot low in the back as he hunched down on his horse. The bullet traveling upward through his body, he was dead before he hit the ground. "Black Jack" Logan took his place temporarily, and after fighting even worse than our Peachtree Creek, the Army of the Tennessee laid on another of those open field whippings we had wanted so much.

A colonel, a private, and now a general. The news reached Baltimore. Miss Emily Hoffman was upstairs when she heard a member of the family say, "I have the most wonderful news: McPherson is dead!" Miss Hoffman retired to her room and stayed there for a whole year. We thought General Sherman to be a real hard case, with ice-water in his veins, but he wrote a very touching letter to Miss Emily, in which he said, "...better the bride of McPherson dead than to be married to the richest merchant of Baltimore..."

The Army of the Tennessee was put under General Howard, because he was a West Point man and Logan wasn't. A week later, at Ezra Church, with General Howard swinging around to the west of Atlanta, Hood tried again. His men were mowed down. In a week and a day, Hood just about destroyed his own army. All the southern assaults failed, but our cost was high. Not more than we could pay, but almost more than we could bear.

CHAPTER NINETEEN
NO MORE DEATH

Susan had gone to the Miller Farm to help take care of Mrs. Miller but had arrived too late. She stayed, and the presence of the children no doubt helped to cheer Mr. Miller. So it was that Susan was at the farm on that day, a rainy day, August 3rd, 1864.

Mr. Miller came barging in the back door into the kitchen, shaking the rain out of his hat. He had a bundle of mail wrapped in an oilskin. Susan sat at the kitchen table, sewing.

"Who-ee! Rain, daughter. The Lord knows we need it." He unwrapped the oilskin. "William just brought the mail up from the Center. Nothing from James...a letter from Sheriff Allen..."

Susan looked up at him, saw his expression change, and fear clouded her eyes even before he began to speak: "***I have just learned***...(a deep, sighing breath)...***I have just learned by a letter from Sheriff Kinnear's son dated on the 21st July, that...your son James was killed on the 20th. No particulars are... given***...Ohh, Susan..."

"Oh, Father Miller..."

They embraced. The feared news, dreaded for more than two years, had finally come.

I was much distressed after Peachtree Creek. So many comrades from the outfit gone to their final reward, including two of the finest men I ever knew: Our colonel and my best friend.

I can not help but think that it is not too much to say that if they had survived that battle they probably would have survived the war, for that was our last big bloodletting and I don't believe it is giving anything away to say that. My story is almost done.

The war took a very decidedly sharp turn after the big battles around Atlanta. Sherman snipped at Hood's supply lines and lines of retreat with infantry and cavalry during the whole month of August, whilst the Twentieth Corps confronted the main enemy works north of the city. Hooker, upset that he did not get command of the Army of the Tennessee after McPherson was killed, tendered his resignation, which Sherman gladly accepted. We got our old General Slocum back as commander of the Twentieth Corps. Colonel Tom Walker finally got command of the 111th Pennsylvania Veteran Volunteers, although the circumstances in which he got it, through the death of our brave colonel, were not the way he would have preferred.

By daily skirmishing our line was advanced to the enemy's main line of defense around Atlanta. A battery of 64-pounder guns was mounted in the position of the line of works occupied by our regiment and threw shells night and day into the city. The booming of the guns did not disturb our slumber, but let the order "fall in" be given in an ordinary tone of voice and every man would be up instantly.

Finally the climax came at Jonesboro south of Atlanta, on the first few days of September. Confederate lines were finally stretched so far that our assault broke through. It sent the Johnnies pell-mell in every direction, gobbling up remnants of regiments that tried to stand.

It had took us a month to go that last five miles to Atlanta, but when the time came, when even Mister **John Bullhead Hood** knew he'd had enough and blew everything up and skedaddled, guess who was the first regiment to march into Atlanta, to raise the Stars and Stripes over the courthouse? Yep, the 111th. And guess who carried that flag? Color Sergeant Calvin Blanchard, that's who. Calvin went from being a kid who fainted at dress parade to flaunting our national colors at the traitors who had first fired on that flag at Fort Sumter.

That was a grand, proud day, the day we entered Atlanta. I'll admit I had a tear in my eye, thinking of all the good men who'd had to die to make it possible, but I'll wager that George Cobham and James Miller raised a cheer in heaven for the grand old flag that day.

Well, sir, after the war all the dead were collected from the battlefield and buried in neat rows with little white crosses in the new national cemetery in Marietta, Georgia. James lies there yet today, seven hundred miles from home. His name is on a stone up at the Foster Cemetery, on the hill that bears his name, but James ain't there.

They had a funeral for him on Sunday, August 21st, 1864. Elder Sharp led the service. It was attended by Alfred Cowles, a local farmer who wrote about the scripture lesson in his diary. It was from Revelation, 21st Chapter, verses 3 and 4:

And I heard a great voice out of heaven saying, Behold, the tabernacle of God is with men, and he will dwell with them, and they shall be his people, and God himself shall be with them, and be their God.

And God shall wipe away all tears from their eyes; and there shall be no more death, neither sorrow, nor crying, neither shall there be any pain; for the former things are passed away. [120]

The words are a lot like the ones James used when he wrote to his father in June about the loss of Mrs. Miller.

I can imagine they were all there: Next to the center aisle, Mr. Miller senior, silent and stoic; then Susan, dressed in black as they all were, with Robby and Ellen; Jane Cramer, comforting Susan and the young ones, with G.H. Cramer, lips grimly pursed, next to her. Then Rob, wearing his old uniform in honor to his brother, with his girl, Martha Ewers. In the next pew back, William sat behind his father, with his wife Harriet and their new baby by his side; then Rachel with her husband, Bill West; then Joe with his new wife, Louisa, and Jane's son, Seymour. Young brother John and his wife Cordelia was next, and last.

Elder Sharp would have said, "We are here to remember James Miller. His child died in February, his mother in June. Now his family mourns him. He died for his country, much as our savior died for us. How many of us would do the same?" And the boys would have cringed while the women cried.

Julia Ward Howe's words, "As He died to make men holy, let us die to make men free," were not just words in a popular song to us back then. From a population of thirty thousand, Warren County sent at least sixteen hundred men and boys to fight in the Union Army. They fought, and some died, so that all men could be free. They fought so that you wouldn't need a passport to go on vacation to Florida. They fought with an unabashed, simple patriotism that is difficult for folks to understand today.

And what happened to all those good folks? Well, I don't know for certain, but I believe it bothered the Millers mightily for the rest of their lives that the boys had stayed home while James went and did the fighting and dying. Robert was in the clear—he had only served nine months but it had almost killed him—but the others, well I just don't know. John's wife, Cordelia, died in May 1867 and John shot himself the following December 5th, at his sister Rachel's house. Suicide? It was awful hard to accidentally shoot yourself with them old guns back then.

Old Mr. Miller remarried in 1867, to a woman by the name of Hannah, and died in 1877.

***

REQUIEM FOR AN ARMY

Well, we took Atlanta, but if we thought our troubles with Hood were over, we were mistaken. "Heart of a lion, head of wood," you may recall. Quite often during this narrative I have referred you to other accounts rather than rehash them here, but I humbly would like to give you a brief summation of what happened in the fall of '64. This I would like to do for justice not only to our side, but also to the worthy foe which we had battled since May 5th, for although they were the enemy, the outcome was tragic enough to pull at some mighty coarse heartstrings.

I can tell you about it firsthand because a chain of unfortunate circumstances put me on the spot.

Now, my first battle was the big eye-opener at Bull Run. I also fought at Cedar Mountain, Antietam, Chancellorsville, Gettysburg, Wauhatchie, Lookout Mountain, and Chattanooga, and all the battles and skirmishes across half the state of Georgia. I never got so much as a scratch. For that reason it was particularly galling that what was probably the last shot of the Atlanta Campaign struck me squarely in the...um...derriere. It was the third of September, 1864...

What happened was, I was talking to Colonel Walker about some trivial thing, standing rather off to his right, when he happened to drop a sheet of paper. "Let me get that for you," says I, and I stepped in front of him and bent over to get it, presenting an excellent target.

I never heard the shot—they say you never do—and I for an instant thought someone with a vicious sense of humor had kicked me in the ass. I fell to the ground, and saw at once from the copious amount of blood in the dust that after all my good luck it was my fate to be spared the vacation instead of the work, and the comedian was somewhere "out there" with a rifle, and mine was the butt (pardon the pun) of his little joke.

Most certainly that bullet was intended for Walker. He sent some boys out to find the sharpshooter but they never did get him. The surgeons dug a .45-caliber Whitworth slug out of my rump, so it was obvious that the shootist was a specialist at his work. Walker was very solicitous for my welfare, making sure I was as comfortable as possible until an ambulance arrived, and giving instructions that I was to be given first-rate care. He even arranged that my rifle should be stored special in the headquarters wagon until I returned. Spoony, always the humorist, looked at my wound and observed that I did not have to worry about amputation.

So the boys would have to make the march to Savannah without me. I was evacuated, subjected to the train ride without end, from Atlanta all the way back to Chattanooga. I had told Spoony as the ambulance pulled out that I would catch up, and I pictured my own period of repose until then. I never expected to have any adventures in the meantime, but I was to be disabused of that notion.

General Sherman drew the army all in around Atlanta to give it a rest—"a period of repose," is what he called it—before the next phase of his plan: The march to Savannah, which would cut the eastern confederacy in two. What was left of the rebs was concentrated about thirty miles south.

The reb army was still a force to be reckoned with. Even after the bloodletting around Atlanta, Hood still scraped up about forty thousand hardened veterans. He hit on the idea that if he could cut our supply line back to Chattanooga we would have to give up Atlanta. All summer, first Johnston and then Hood had been trying to get cavalry to break the railroad, and protecting it had been one of Sherman's big headaches all along. Hood decided to swing his whole army around us, break the railroad, and force us to retreat.

Well, Hood crossed the Chattahoochee and headed north on September 29th and at first Sherman played the game. Leaving our corps, under General Slocum, to hold Atlanta, he and the rest of the boys took up the chase. Hood threatened the big supply depot we had at Allatoona, held by a few thousand Yankees under a General Corse. Here originated an expression which you have probably used and never known where it came from: From a mountain top within flag-signaling distance of Allatoona, General Sherman sent the message to Corse, "Hold the fort; we are coming." Now, the next time you go someplace and tell somebody to "Hold the fort," you will know you are not being original.

I had a very quiet 93rd birthday last Tuesday, a little saddened over having just related the circumstances of James Miller's death, and a little amazed that I have reached such an advanced age, having done none of the things which are supposed to ensure a long life, and having participated in some ventures almost guaranteed to shorten it. But, humble and undeserving, here I still am.

Hood's attack on Allatoona failed. With our side closing in, he moved on to Resaca, and again failed to take the depot there. Sherman kept following, never quite catching up. See, the reb army was small and traveling light, and was as elusive as a greased pig.

Finally Hood swung over Alabama way and Sherman got fed up. "Damn him," he said, "if he will go to the Ohio River I will give him rations." He sent General Thomas back to Tennessee to organize an army to deal with Hood and brought three corps back to Atlanta. Joined up with Slocum's Twentieth, he would have sixty thousand men for the March to the Sea. It was like two duelists walking their ten paces away from each other and then continuing to walk apart. The Fourth and Twenty-third corps, under Schofield, were sent back to reinforce Thomas.

Hood headed for Nashville and Schofield pushed up from Chattanooga to head him off. Hood saw a chance to cut Schofield off from Thomas at Spring Hill, Tennessee, and was disappointed when the whole Yankee force, some five divisions, snuck by his army during the night, within earshot of his pickets. Hood was enraged. To his mind, enfeebled by the opiates he took for the pain of his withered arm and stump of a leg, all of his efforts, at Peachtree, Atlanta, Ezra Church, Jonesboro, Allatoona, and now at Spring Hill, were frustrated by the incompetence and timidity of his army and its generals. He pushed on, now pursuing his pursuers, determined to make his army fight.

Schofield was headed for Nashville, but he stopped at Franklin, Tennessee, and dug in to give his wagon trains time to cross the Harpeth River there. Hood caught up and deployed his army for an attack.

In the annals of the War of the Rebellion, Pickett's Charge stands out as THE example of the forlorn hope attack. For most people, that is. Those who know anything about the Battle of Franklin will tell you that Pickett's Charge, bad as it was for the rebs, was nothing compared to their disaster at Franklin.

Just as Hood was disgusted with his army, so I believe his generals felt that he had assailed and impugned everything about their manhood, their courage, and their military skill. On a beautiful Indian summer day, November 30th, 1864, under Hood's orders, and with him watching from a blanket spread on a hillside to the rear, the gallant remnant of the Army of Tennessee marched with parade ground precision across a mile of open ground against the fieldworks the Yankees had hastily thrown up. With the sun shining brightly, their shot-worn flags flying, they marched into a wall of lead and steel. They gouged gaps in the Yankee line and then the Yankees counter-attacked, and they fought, tooth and nail, until long after the sun went down.

And when it was over, seven thousand Confederates lay dead or wounded, and before dawn Schofield continued his retreat. Daylight showed the awful cost of Hood's anger and his generals' pride. Included in the dead were six Confederate generals. Highest on the list was our poor Irish rebel, Pat Cleburne. The others were H.B. Granbury, O.F. Strahl, States Rights Gist (honest, that was his name), John Adams, and John C. Carter. Five other generals were wounded, and one was captured.

There is nothing in that description of Hood which I gave you a while back that would give you a notion of how stubborn he was. With rather less than thirty thousand men remaining to him, he followed Schofield to Nashville. What followed next has been called the Siege of Nashville, but it was a curious kind of siege. With Schofield safe in the defenses around Nashville and reinforcements coming in steadily, Pap Thomas would have about sixty thousand men. He was not trapped at all. Hood dug in facing the defenses, hoping against hope that he could defeat Thomas in a defensive battle and then follow up by capturing the city and continuing his invasion.

Thomas had to fashion his army out of outfits pulled in from all over west of the Appalachians. Schofield had brought in the Fourth and Twenty-third. A.J. Smith brought three divisions, parts of the Sixteenth and Seventeenth corps, all the way from western Missouri, and a new corps of cavalry, 12,000 men, was organized under General James Wilson.

This is where I come into the picture. Needing more men, Thomas had General James Steedman cull the hospitals and rear areas, and they organized a provisional division under a General Cruft. I was just about recovered, and had started angling for ways to get out of the hospital and back to the front. I missed the old outfit, and, same as James the year before, I did not care for the strict rules of hospital living.

I did not know about Cruft and Steedman, so when an officer came into the ward, asking questions like, "Who's fit? Who can march?" I jumped up, thinking I was about to go to Savannah.

I found myself in a temporary brigade, made up entirely of Twentieth Corps men cut off from Sherman. For the most part we were a sorry lot. Many of the men still belonged in the hospital, instead of sleeping outside in the winter with only one blanket. Others were new recruits, mostly foreigners, who were also not used to field living. The brigade was commanded by Colonel Benjamin Harrison. If that name sounds familiar, it is because he would one day be president of these United States. They put us all on a train and shipped us up to Nashville. Some of us had to ride on top of the cars and, folks, in the latter part of November there is a big difference in climate between Nashville and Savannah.

I told you a while back to remind me to tell you more about Thomas. Well, I remembered without your reminder. Thomas was stolid, slow, and methodical. Another nickname for him was "Old Slow Trot." He had no "dash" but he always got results. A couple of weeks went by, with the Johnnies shivering in their lines with bare feet, not enough blankets or overcoats or food, or men, while Thomas perfected his plans and organization. He had the situation well in hand, but it did not look that way to U.S. Grant, well removed from the situation at his headquarters down by Petersburg, Virginia. Grant kept bombarding Thomas with telegrams telling him to dispatch Hood and do it quick. Thomas would not attack until he was ready, and, besides, the weather was terrible, with rain and ice storms. Finally Grant prepared an order relieving Thomas and was about to set out on a train to take personal command in Nashville, when he got the news that Thomas had attacked and destroyed Hood's army.

Hang it! Grant had a lot of nerve. With the best of armies and all the resources in the world, it still took him near a year to dispatch Bobby Lee, and he had the gall to threaten Thomas with early retirement after only two weeks!

Every time we fought a battle, it was the goal of one side or the other to destroy the other fellow's army, but there are damn few examples of it actually happening. Grant did it at Vicksburg; Bragg almost did it at Chickamauga. Then of course there is Appomattox. Nashville stands out as the one battle during the war, fought in the open field, where an army was obliterated out of existence. Not surrendered, just flat out destroyed. On the 15th of December Thomas smashed at Hood's army, forcing it out of its original defensive line to a second one. We did nothing but man the trenches around Nashville replacing Kimball's division of the Fourth Corps, so we had a front row seat for the battle. The next day, under an all-out assault across the entire front the Johnny Reb line just caved in, with thousands surrendering, dozens of cannons and battle flags captured, and the rabble remnants driven toward the Alabama border.

If you would say they were considerate of us during the battle, letting the experienced troops fight it while we watched, they were downright inconsiderate during the pursuit. I shall not go into detail, but more or less summarize that we marched in mud, rain, and snow, were shuttled about on rail cars in freezing temperatures, went without rations a large part of the time, and although we did almost no fighting, a quarter of the brigade was sent back sick and exhausted. I am proud to say I stuck it out, but to do so called all my stalwart qualities to the fore, for my pride would not let me give in. What was left of the Army of Tennessee was completely run out of Tennessee by the end of the year, but we were kept on the jump until about the 11th of January, when we finally got back to Chattanooga and they started dispersing us to our regular outfits.

General Thomas did not live long after the war—heart attack, I believe it was—and he never got the recognition he deserved. Hood rode off in disgrace, to resign and then spend the rest of his life defending his actions which led to the destruction of the gallant Army of Tennessee. Some of Hood's boys made up a derisive little ditty, sung to the tune of the "Yellow Rose of Texas," which ended thus:

"You can talk about your Beauregard and sing of General Lee
But the gallant Hood of Texas played HELL in Tennessee!"

***

OUR LAST SESSION

While all of this was happening in Tennessee, the old outfit marched to the sea with Sherman. Sherman cut a sixty mile wide path of destruction to Savannah, which he presented to Lincoln as a Christmas present. I caught up with the boys toward the end of January as they hiked up through the Carolinas, and by the time the war ended we was almost back to Virginia, where it all began for us. Our old foe, Joe Johnston, surrendered a remnant of an army to us near Fayetteville, North Carolina, on April 26th, 1865.

In May of '65 we marched in the Grand Review in Washington, D.C., having marched and fought all the way from Bridgeport, Alabama. Abe Lincoln wasn't there to see his armies march. Neither was James, or Frank Lyon, or Colonel Cobham, nor thousands and thousands of others. Wisht they could have seen it, marched beside us, but then a war where everybody lived to go home wouldn't have been much of a war, now would've it? We all knew when we joined up that we might not see the end of it. Even old Abe, who you might say was one of the first soldiers to leave home and one of the last to die, admitted to the folks in Springfield that he might not see them again.

After the war we went home. Spent the rest of our lives thinking about what it all meant. The war defined and changed our lives forever. It was just terrible, just terrible, but I must say that never were we so alive as in those days. By golly, really alive! We lived life! Life was good because it was so precious, and yet, on fields like Antietam and Gettysburg and Peachtree Creek, so cheap. Calvin Blanchard, he said once that the war seemed to claim our best and brightest. When I think about it, Calvin, old Spoony, he'll live to be a hundred. No, no, just kidding—he's a good man, one of the best, if not the brightest.

From the Foster Cemetery, on the north slope of Miller Hill, you can see New York State, just a few miles away across a rolling patchwork of farmland and woods. Lander nestles at the foot of the hill. All in all, a peaceful enough setting in which to spend eternity. I went up there often to remember James, even though his stone was just a memorial.

Others went up there also. I would say this conversation would have taken place about in May of '65, almost four years to the day from when Charlie Lyon rode out to see James Miller in that half-plowed field:

Jane Cramer turned her buggy off Miller Hill road and ascended the little hill to the Foster. As she approached, she saw a figure sitting near to the stone they had placed in memory of James. These days, if you look at it close, you will notice that it is different from other markers—there is no depression indicating an actual grave.

As she got closer she recognized who it was. His crutch was beside him, and an empty trouser leg was pinned up. She climbed down from the buggy and walked over to him.

"Hello, Charlie."

Charlie Lyon had been lost in thought, and was a bit startled. "Oh, hullo, Miz Cramer. Come up to see Jim, did you?"

She smiled to herself at Charlie's way of putting things. "Well, in a way. How are you, Charlie?"

Charlie had a little bunch of wildflowers in his hand. "Tolerable well, ma'am. Did you hear me and Mary Thompson's getting hitched this summer?"

Jane sat down on the bench next to him. "Well, it's about time, Charlie. She's been waiting for you for an awful long time."

"That's the truth." Charlie's gaze wandered to the horizon, and he was quiet for a moment. "I feel real bad that he's gone, Miz Cramer," he blurted out. "Sometimes I can't even believe it."

"Me, too, but you know, he would have told us not to be too sad about it."

"Well, goldangit, ma'am. I wanted him to go with me. He was older than me, I admired and respected him, and maybe if he...He was a good man."

"He thought a lot of you, too, Charlie."

"But he was a man. I wanted to go for the fun of it. Jim, though, he needed something more than excitement for a reason, and he waited 'til he saw that it was a life or death matter for the country before he joined up. When he did get in on it, he gave it everything he had—in the end, his life. Still, maybe if he'd of went with me..."

"Don't let it bother you so, Charlie. He liked being a soldier and said so many times, but he didn't fight because he liked to fight. He fought for his country, a patriot to the end."

"That he was, ma'am. That he was."

"And you, Charlie?"

"Me? The glory and glamour faded fast. You forget about things like that when you realize some Johnny Reb is trying to kill you...and where's the glory about seeing a field so covered thick with dead that you could walk from one end to the other without stepping on the ground?"

"But you stayed, Charlie, long after the rest of us had become sick of it all."

"Well, ma'am, I had got this idea that the country needed me, and I fit until I couldn't fight no more."

"I'm proud to know you, Charlie. It was men like you and my brother that held this country together."

"Yes, but one comes home and the other don't. How do you figger it, ma'am? I guess I was lucky—just wasn't my time, as Jim would say. I came home, and the worst I got was this empty trouser leg. My family as a whole didn't make out so good, though."

"Your brothers, Charlie?"

"Ain't got but one left, Miz Cramer. Yeah, sad to say, of us four Lyon boys, two died. Ol' Frank, the spunk he had was what done him in. He got hit in the hip at Gettysburg and walked three miles to a hospital. Took grit to do that, but it was too much, and he up and died later. Edward got captured once, but got away. Henry got captured and they say he died in prison in Salzbury, North Carolina. But how's your family, ma'am? Li'l Seymour growing like a weed, is he?"

"We've had our loss, too, Charlie. Besides James, I really believe the war killed our mother. And there are other wounds, too. Not visible, like your leg, but real, just the same. Susan stayed with Father for a while, but she's bought a farm in Cherry Creek, up in New York State near her parents, and we don't see her much. Maybe it pains her too much, seeing us and remembering her James and the three long years she waited for him, living on her own with the three children, little Johnny sick all the time...Oh, how my heart goes out to her, even now.

"You know, Charlie, I'm remembering a time, I guess about October of '62, when the boys—my brother Bob, and your Frank, and Paul and

George, and others, I guess—all got together with their ladies one last time before going off with Colonel Allen's regiment, and they all sang and tried so hard to be jolly, but then—I think it was George Merchant with his guitar—started them singing 'Lorena' and then, one by one, each was taken with a deep melancholy until finally only George was singing...

...Twas flow'ry May when up the hilly slope we climbed
To watch the dying of the day
And hear the distant church bell chime...

It was as if they knew somehow that it was of this May, this hill, this somber piece of ground, that they were singing."

"Well, Miz Cramer, better times are ahead. It's a sad talk we've been having, but maybe it's done us both some good. Say, me and Mary would like to have you and G.H. up for supper once we're set up."

"I'd like that. Goodbye, Charlie."

Jane set some flowers next to the stone and climbed into her buggy. As she drove away she looked back. Charlie was still sitting there, watching the clouds drift by.

Charlie Lyon lived a long and fruitful life. He was constable of Farmington Township for many years, raised a big family, and died of old age.

Well, at the rate we've gone it would take another few months to tell you what became of everybody after the war. Susan stayed at the Miller farm for a while, but then one day she just up and left. Packed up the kids and walked twenty miles up to Cherry Creek, in Chautauqua County, New York, where her parents were living. Susan never told me why they left like that, but then again, I never asked.

I paid a call on Susan in 1882. She had bought herself a small farm in Cherry Creek and while she was well past fifty by then, she was still a handsome woman. We had a nice visit, talked about the old days, sharing our memories. She had remarried in 1869. Her new husband had been Cyrenius Hall, a former lieutenant in the 78th New York. Cy Hall had served but six months before being discharged for infirmities of the ankles, and his marriage to Susan did not last much longer. There had been nothing "infirm" about James Miller, but Cy was a scamp and soon she was alone again. Robbie had got married the year before, to a gal named Lydia. They would have a daughter, Edith Pearl, who would grow up to be Edith Miller Gunnell. Ellen still lived at home. She would get married in 1896 to a man the same age her father would have been. Susan's parents had both died in the 1870s. [121]

Susan lived until 1919, becoming a small, frail old lady dressed in black, spending her last days in her rocker, gazing out the window. Perhaps in her mind she was back in her log cabin in Southwest Township, sitting by the side window, for the sun and the view of the road. Waiting, as she had waited so long down in Southwest, to see her James again.

George Cobham's story does not end with his death. His mother and sisters were so totally devastated by his death; they had all idolized him. Well, the good citizens of the town gave him a hero's burial in the new Oakland Cemetery on the south side of the river, but one night his sister had some men dig him up and rebury him up at the family estate. She sat up nights with a pistol to keep him there.

Finally, through legal means, George was moved back over to Oakland and buried in what is called the Veterans Circle. There is no monument to a war hero such as you might expect, but I think my colonel would have wanted it the way it is: He is one of seventy or so Civil War soldiers buried in a circle with individual markers which are weathered and fading. A large stone in the middle gives all their names and units. He sleeps with his comrades. He is one of them. I will join them some day.

Colonel Cobham's wife, Anne, also remarried but the man was a…was a…well, the man was Harrison Allen, who also made general before the war ended, just like he said he would. Annie died in 1896, at the young age of 58. Harrison was a Pennsylvania state senator, auditor general, U.S. marshal in North Dakota, postal official, and he died in 1904. He was a politician to the end. He is buried at Arlington.

Then there's Calvin. He moved out west, took part in the Alaska gold rush back in '98, worked at City Hall in Tacoma, Washington, and presently lives in California. Years back, about 1926 I believe it was, at about eighty years of age, he drove his roadster all the way from California to Pennsylvania. We had quite a visit, and he helped me remember some things which I had almost forgot—some of them for good reason. He helped some of the boys build a hunting camp, keeping up with fellers a quarter his age, and built himself a tree house for his own comfort. Then he drove back to California. [122]

So there you have it: Our part, a small part, of the great events of 1861 to 1865. There's a heap of stories from those days. I could go on, I suppose. It ain't that the Millers and Blanchards and the little town of Farmington Center were something special—it is just the opposite: They were so typical of folks and places back then. I'm pleased and proud to have helped bring those days back to life. Now, I hear the drummer beating the long roll and I'd best be gettin' on. Sonny, it's all yours...

***

EPILOGUE
by John Ferry

Follow Miller Hill Road south, just a mile or two from the Foster Cemetery, and you'll come to a farm now owned by Bill Schumann, my father-in-law. In 1847 Robert and Janet Miller bought the farm and there raised a family of five sons, James, Robert, William, John, and Joseph, and two daughters. Bill and his wife, Theresa, also raised a family of seven. They had three daughters, the youngest of whom would have been named Joseph, had she been a boy. Their four sons, my brothers-in-law, were named James, Robert, William, and John.

When her father passed away, Jane Miller Cramer bundled and saved all of James and Robert's letters, and she later passed them on to her son, Seymour. She knew those letters, so special to her, would be of interest to future generations searching for the essence of their past. They were written by exceptional men living in historic times.

Calvin Blanchard provided legitimacy for the story I wanted to tell. Here are the beginning and ending paragraphs of his letter to a niece, undated but obviously written in one of the last of Calvin's 100 years:

My dear Niece:

Your interesting letter of February 13th was duly received and read with pleasure. I have been so unsettled of late that I have neglected all my correspondence and I beg you to excuse me for not writing sooner. First I want to tell you how much I appreciate your kind letter and the card bearing the coat of arms of mother's ancestors, for which I thank you kindly. I realize you and Blanche have undertaken a big job and I appreciate your efforts in that direction and will be glad to help you in any way I can. I mailed a letter to Blanche a few days ago on the subject sending her all data I can furnish, and as she can put it in much better form, I am sure she will transmit it to you upon request. As I did not speak of my Civil War experience and service, I will try

and comply with your request and tell briefly in detail the story of my enlistment and service much more fully than even my own children have heard it...

And 20 pages later...

...Fearing you may not have the patience to read so much, or more than I have written, I think I will send this along, and if you find it interesting, I will resume the narrative where I now leave it, if you wish me to do so....[123]

Calvin wrote of shooting a turtle, of being wounded (twice), of meeting Abraham Lincoln, of the death of his commander, of taking Atlanta, and Sherman's march to Savannah and on up through the Carolinas. Only time and space kept him from telling more. As he indicated, he meant to, but if he wrote anything further the letter is not to be found. Perhaps his light finally went out before he had a chance to continue. He died in 1946, just five days shy of his 101st birthday. I figured if Calvin could tell his story at his advanced age, so could my old veteran.

Gradually, all the boys came home. Some were sick, some limped from their wounds, some, like Charlie, had lost a limb. I did not know that fact about Charlie until an elderly lady, a descendant of his, told me after a talk I gave, "I knew old Charlie Lyon. Do you know? He only had one leg."

As you read the letters interwoven with the old veteran's story, you'll see the names of James's friends and neighbors and fellow soldiers. I grew up in Warren County, in Farmington Township, and many of the place names and the friends and neighbors of my lifetime share those names. Not many people know that Roystone, a little village on the road from Warren to Barnes—Calvin's home town—is named for Brigadier General Roy Stone, the organizer of the Raftsman's Guards. Scranton Hollow brings to mind Billy Scranton, "tough and hearty as a bear." Sturdevant Hill reminds me of Lieutenant Ham Sturdevant, who was captured at Peachtree Creek, but survived the war. Conrad Rowland was the ancestor of local athlete "Bud" Rowland, who became a member of the Boston Red Sox for a time. Bill Wiltsie, who courageously voted against the Draft Insurance Fund, passed his name down to the Bill Wiltsie I know today. John and James Stanton enlisted in the 151st Pennsylvania along with Bob Miller, and a John Stanton of the present day, whom I am proud to know, was awarded a Silver Star in World War II. Stanton Hill rises behind my house, and Miller Hill Road climbs south out of Lander, old Farmington Center of 1861. And the list goes on. All those who survived the war became men of peace once again, went back to their farms and businesses, content to reside in the shadow of history but always proud and nostalgic of their part in that terrible war. Daily, as I go about my business, I'll meet a familiar face with an old, familiar name.

Throughout the years, the church in Lander has stood as a bulwark in the stormy seas of life. In my story it was in the shade of that church that a military rally first pulled James Miller toward the cause of the Union. They finally purchased a church bell in 1873. This was quite an investment, but it has paid great dividends, for the same bell calls folks to worship, even to this day—and can be clearly heard up at the Foster Cemetery, a mile away. It has tolled the passing of Sundays and dear departed souls for 133 years and counting.

From "Lorena" a song of the Civil War:

...to watch the dying of the day
and hear the distant church bell chime.

Everything changes, evolves. Warren County has grown some since the 1860s. Higher living standards and improved health care have vastly increased life expectancy. We've paved our roads, built schools, churches, and industry. Many of us believe, with good reason, that there is no better place to live than here, in the valleys and hills of northwestern Pennsylvania. Everything changes, and yet nothing changes. Our ancestors across all of America's landscape, north and south, felt the same way about their valleys and hills. They loved them enough to fight and die for them. Nothing changes. Even as we all know someone who fought in Vietnam or Iraq, so it has been that we have seen our loved ones—brothers, husbands, sons—and daughters—march away to Korea, the Pacific, Europe, and, in 1861, to faraway places like Virginia and Georgia and Mississippi. We waited for them, spoke of them in soft tones of tenuous hope, prayed for them, and sometimes we cried out when God answered our prayers in ways we could not understand. A while back I got an audio tape from some living history folks in Ridgway, Pennsylvania. On it was a song called "Brother Green," which I had never heard before. One of the verses really got to me, because I had written that sentence about prayers answered in ways we cannot understand, about seven years before:

Tell her I know / she's prayed for me
And now her prayers are answered:
That I may be / prepared to die
If I should fall in battle.

"Brother Green" had had it all figured out, years before me.

***

The last letter:

H. ALLEN TO ROBERT MILLER SR.

Warren,

August 2nd, 1864

Mr. Miller,

Dear Sir,

I have just learned by a letter from Sheriff Kinnear's son dated on the 21st July, that your son James was killed on the 20th. No particulars are given.

Your most Ob't S'vte,

H. Allen [124]

This cryptic note is last letter in the collection of James Miller's letters. The old veteran's description notwithstanding, there are NO particulars on James's death. When I sat in the library at Ann Arbor with the actual letters before me, looking like they had just come in the mail, I dreaded to turn to this last one.

I cannot let Harrison Allen have the last word. I hope "Servants of the Wind" has pleased you, the reader. If it has amused, or inspired, or caused a tear to flow (which it continually does for me, even as I write) I will feel it is the ultimate tribute to a band of men and women who lived through the ordeal of our nation, more than 140 years ago.

Douglas MacArthur said, "Old soldiers never die; they just fade away." But now, even our Old Veteran would be long gone. He is fictional, of course, but I cannot resist adding a few lines that I wrote one day as I thought about what this time would have been like for Tommy and Suzie and all the rest of the folks if only it had been real. If you have stuck with us, you may almost feel that you know him, so this is your chance to say goodbye:

The old man got up, shook hands all around, then started off across the fields toward his house on the hill. We watched him go. He ambled over a rise, stopping to pick a wildflower in his path, and then went down the other side of the hill. His path would take him down the hill and to the right, along the worm-rail fence with its tangle of blackberries and sumac; and as he descended the hill he seemed to be vanishing into the earth. We loved that old man. We loved his humor, his knowledge and wisdom, his friendship. These afternoons had been more than a flight through time. In season we had consumed large amounts of lemonade, cider, watermelon, popcorn, and maple sugar. The boys had played ball in his backyard with him cheering them all on. He was the town's ace checker player. In a year, Tommy had won two games; the old man had won 27 games—and Tommy had the best record of all of us. If you came early or stayed late the old man would listen to your problems and give you a fair reading afterward. None of us wanted it to be over, but we knew he was tired, his body slowly catching up with his age. One by one, we bid each other goodbye and headed for our own homes in the gathering dusk.

This next was written on the back of the program for "Heritage" when we presented it at the Library Theater in 1995, as a part of the Warren Bicentennial. It is updated for this book. I include it here as my way of asking the reader to please forgive any poetic license I have taken with history. From first page to last, it has been a labor of love:

I first wrote "Heritage" to celebrate the 130th anniversary of our church, the Lander Methodist Church of Farmington Township, founded in 1861. Tradition said that the first function there, even before the church was finished, was a picnic dinner for soldiers about to fight in the Civil War. I also remembered a visit back in 1985 by a historian, Galen Wilson of Ann Arbor, Michigan, to my in-laws' farm on Miller Hill. Galen was then the Manuscript Curator at the University of Michigan, where he had just transcribed the Civil War letters of James and Robert Miller. My in-laws, Bill and Theresa Schumann, owned the farm where James had grown to manhood, and Galen's visit was part of a two-week research trip to Warren and Chautauqua counties. Our church picnic, and the military careers of two remarkable men—one an obscure private, the other a celebrated officer—formed the starting point for "Heritage" which has become "Servants of the Wind." It unavoidably contains a bit of poetic license, but it is very closely based on real people and actual events. Much of the dialogue is based on entries in the Miller letters, Alfred Cowles's diary, and Calvin Blanchard's reminiscences (written when he was over ninety). I must pay tribute to editor Ephraim Cowan of the *Warren Mail,* forerunner of today's *Warren Times Observer*, for documenting a large part of our nineteenth-century history. He attended the picnic; he also wrote a nearly verbatim account of the banquet for George Cobham.

But by far the most eloquent writer on these pages has been James T. Miller. James's letters were written by an unschooled hand, and his spelling and punctuation showed that. In "Bound To Be a Soldier," the published book of his letters, his original spelling and phrasing are preserved, but for this account, I have edited them even as I have been edited. The point being not HOW he wrote, but WHAT he wrote.

I hope I have not been too rough on Harrison Allen. He certainly had a distinguished career, and during the war was instrumental in obtaining volunteers for the armies in the field. Things just happened to work out for him, I guess. I also hope I have not been too rough on my township—although the words are those of James Miller. "The Farmington Cowards Mutual Insurance Society" is pretty strong stuff, but James called them as he saw them. In the Foster Cemetery alone, about a mile south of Lander, lie enough Civil War veterans to attest that my community did more than its share.

Although not listed as an historical figure, our old veteran is an amalgam of Calvin Blanchard in his old age, and a man who was a neighbor of mine when I was growing up. The neighbor's name was Bill Lyon, a veteran of the Spanish-American War. He was a descendent of Charlie Lyon..."

Timeline [125]

December 20, 1860	South Carolina secedes; birth of John Lee (Johnny) Miller
April 12-14, 1861	Siege and surrender of Fort Sumter
July 21, 1861	Battle of Bull Run (Manassas)
August 16, 1861	Rally at the new Methodist Church
November 2, 1861	James enlists in the 111th Pennsylvania Infantry
January 13, 1862	Calvin enlists
February 16, 1862	Fort Donelson surrenders to U.S. Grant
February 25, 1862	Regiment leaves Erie for the "Seat of War"
April 6-7, 1862	Battle of Shiloh (Pittsburgh Landing)
May 24-25, 1862	Regiment departs Baltimore; First Battle of Winchester
August 8, 1862	Battle of Cedar Mountain
August 29-30, 1862	Second Battle of Bull Run (Second Manassas)
September 17, 1862	Battle of Antietam (Sharpsburg)
December 13, 1862	Battle of Fredericksburg
Dec 31-Jan 2 1863	Battle of Stone's River (Murfreesboro)
January 20-23, 1863	Mud March
May 1-4, 1863	Battle of Chancellorsville
July 1-3, 1863	Battle of Gettysburg
September 19-20, 1863	Battle of Chickamauga
September 25, 1863	Eleventh and Twelfth Corps depart Virginia
October 28-29 1863	Battle of Wauhatchie
November 24-25, 1863	Battles of Lookout Mountain & Chattanooga
January 14, 1864	Regiment arrives in Erie at start of Veterans' Furlough
March 9, 1864	Regiment arrives at Bridgport, Alabama
May 7, 1864	Atlanta Campaign commences
May 13-16, 1864	Battle of Resaca
May 25-27, 1864	Battle of New Hope Church

June 22, 1864	Battle of Kolb's Farm
June 27, 1864	Battle of Kenesaw Mtn
July 20, 1864	Battle of Peach Tree Creek
July 22, 1864	Battle of Atlanta
July 28, 1864	Battle of Ezra Church
September 2, 1864	Atlanta falls
November 30, 1864	Battle of Franklin
December 15-16, 1864	Battle of Nashville
December 21, 1864	Confederates evacuate Savannah; Sherman occupies
March 19, 1865	Battle of Bentonville, North Carolina
April 9, 1865	Lee surrenders at Appomattox
April 26, 1865	Johnston surrenders at Durham Station, North Carolina
May 26, 1865	Kirby Smith surrenders west of the Mississippi
May 10, 1919	Susan Miller dies, age 90
1946	Calvin Blanchard dies, age 100

ENDNOTES

[1] Galen Wilson's interview with Edith Miller Gunnell, June 1985.

[2] "Soldiers True," the Regimental History of the 111th Pennsylvania Veteran Volunteers, by John R. Boyle. Boyle became adjutant of the 111th when his father was killed in 1863.

[3] Letter #1 "Bound To Be A Soldier" The Letters of Private James T. Miller 111th Pennsylvania Infantry 1861-1864. Edited by Jedediah Mannis and Galen R. Wilson. University of Tennessee Press. Hereafter referred to as "Bound To Be A Soldier."

[4] Calvin Blanchard's Reminiscences

[5] Letter #3, to Robert and Janet Miller, Bound To Be A Soldier.

[6] Description based on letter, George Cobham to his mother, 4 March 1862. George Ashworth Cobham's wartime letters, Warren County Historical Society (GAC/WCHS)

[7] Letter GAC/WCHS 4 March 1862

[8] Letter #4, to Robert Miller, Sr. Bound To Be A Soldier

[9] Letter #4, to Robert Miller, Sr. Bound To Be A Soldier

[10] Letter #5, to "Brother and Sister" (William and Rachel West) Bound To Be A Soldier

[11] Letter #6, to "Brother" (Robert E Miller) Bound To Be A Soldier

[12] Letter #7, to "Brother" (Robert E Miller) Bound To Be A Soldier

[13] Letter #7, to "Brother" (Robert E Miller) Bound To Be A Soldier

[14] The Loomis Cemetery

[15] Miller Letters, William L. Clements Library, University of Michigan, Ann Arbor Hereafter referred to as Clements Library

[16] Letter #9, to "Brother" (Robert E Miller) Bound To Be A Soldier

[17] Letter #10, to "Brother and Sister" (G.H. and Jane Miller Cramer) Bound To Be A Soldier

[18] Letter #11, to "Brother Robert" (Robert E Miller) Bound To Be A Soldier

[19] Letter #12, to "Father" (Robert Miller, Sr.) Bound To Be A Soldier

[20] Letter #13, to "Brother" (Robert E. Miller) Bound To Be A Soldier

[21] Letter #14, to "Brother" (Robert E. Miller) Bound To Be A Soldier

[22] Letter #15, to "Brother and Sister" (G.H. and Jane Miller Cramer) Bound To Be A Soldier

[23] Letter #15, to "Brother and Sister" (G.H. and Jane Miller Cramer) Bound To Be A Soldier

[24] Miller Letters, Clements Library

[25] Letter #16, to "Brother" (Robert E. Miller) Bound To Be A Soldier

[26] Calvin Blanchard's Reminiscences

[27] Letter #18, to "Brother" (William Miller) Bound To Be A Soldier

[28] Calvin Blanchard's Reminiscences

[29] Letter #17, recipient unknown, Bound To Be A Soldier

[30] Letter #18, to "Brother" (William Miller) Bound To Be A Soldier

[31] Letter #19, to "Parents" (Robert and Janet Miller) Bound To Be A Soldier

[32] Letter #20, to "Brother" (Robert E. Miller) Bound To Be A Soldier

[33] Letter #48, to "Brother" (William Miller) Bound To Be A Soldier

[34] Letter #21, to "Brother" (Robert E. Miller) Bound To Be A Soldier

[35] Letter #22, to "Brother" (William Miller) Bound To Be A Soldier

[36] Calvin Blanchard's Reminiscences

[37] Calvin Blanchard's Reminiscences

[38] This statement, supposedly uttered in 1936, is true to the present time. Not even in the hard-fought battles of World War II would the nation ever lose so many fighting men (north and south) in a single day. Even the total **civilian** losses of September 11, 2001, did not approach those of September 17, 1862 JDF

[39] Calvin Blanchard's Reminiscences

[40] Letter #24, to "Brother and Sister" (William and Rachel West) Bound To Be A Soldier

[41] Calvin Blanchard's Reminscences, ECHS

[42] Letter #26, to "Parents" (Robert and Janet Miller) Bound To Be A Soldier

[43] Letter #27, to "Father" (Robert Miller, Sr.) Bound To Be A Soldier

[44] Letter #28, to "Sister and Brother" (Jane and George Henry Cramer) Bound To Be A Soldier

[45] Letter #25, to "Sister and Brother" (Jane and George Henry Cramer) Bound To Be A Soldier

[46] Miller Letters, Clements Library

[47] Letter #29, to "Parents" (Robert and Janet Miller) Bound To Be A Soldier
[48] Letter #30, to "Parents" (Robert and Janet Miller) Bound To Be A Soldier
[49] Letter #30, to "Parents" (Robert and Janet Miller) Bound To Be A Soldier
[50] Letter #31, to "Sister" (Jane Miller Cramer) Bound To Be A Soldier
[51] Letter #32, to "Sister" (Rachel Miller West) Bound To Be A Soldier
[52] Letter #33, to "Parents" (Robert and Janet Miller) Bound To Be A Soldier
[53] Letter #34, to "Parents" (Robert and Janet Miller) Bound To Be A Soldier
[54] Letter #36, to "Sister" (Rachel Miller West) Bound To Be A Soldier
[55] Letter #35, to "Brother" (Joseph Miller) Bound To Be A Soldier
[56] Letter #37, to "Parents" (Robert and Janet Miller) Bound To Be A Soldier
[57] Letter GAC/WCHS
[58] Letter #38, to "Brother" (William or Joseph Miller) Bound To Be A Soldier
[59] Letter #39, to "Parents" (Robert and Janet Miller) Bound To Be A Soldier
[60] Letter #40, to "Father" (Robert Miller, Sr.) Bound To Be A Soldier
[61] Letter #41, to "Brother" (John Miller) Bound To Be A Soldier
[62] Letter #42, to "Father" (Robert Miller, Sr.) Bound To Be A Soldier
[63] Calvin Blanchard's Reminiscences, ECHS
[64] Letter #43, to "Sister" (Jane Miller Cramer) Bound To Be A Soldier
[65] Cpt W.J. Alexander, His Civil War Diary and Letters., transcribed and edited by Ursula S.B. Bowler.
[66] Letter #44, to "Brother" (William Miller) Bound To Be A Soldier
[67] Letter #45, to "Parents" (Robert and Janet Miller) Bound To Be A Soldier
[68] Letter #46, to "Brother Joseph" Bound To Be A Soldier
[69] Letter #47, to "Parents" (Robert and Janet Miller) Bound To Be A Soldier
[70] Letter #49, to "Brother Joseph" Bound To Be A Soldier
[71] Letter #50, to "Father" (Robert Miller, Sr.) Bound To Be A Soldier
[72] Miller Letters Clements Library

[73] Letter #51 to "Parents" (Robert and Janet Miller) Bound to Be A Soldier
[74] Calvin Blanchard's Reminiscences, ECHS
[75] Letter #52 to "Brother" (William Miller) Bound to Be A Soldier
[76] Letter #53 to "Brother" (John Miller) Bound to Be A Soldier
[77] Letter #54 to "Brother" (William Miller) Bound to Be A Soldier
[78] Letter #55 to "Parents" (Robert and Janet Miller) Bound to Be A Soldier
[79] Letter #56 to "Sister" (Jane Miller Cramer) Bound to Be A Soldier
[80] Letter #57 to "Brother" (William Miller) Bound to Be A Soldier
[81] Letter #58 to "Brother" (Robert E. Miller) Bound to Be A Soldier
[82] Letter #59 to "Brother" (John Miller) Bound to Be A Soldier
[83] Letter #60 to "Father" (Robert Miller, Sr.) Bound to Be A Soldier
[84] Miller Letters Clements Library
[85] Letter #61 to "Sister" (Jane Miller Cramer) Bound to Be A Soldier
[86] No historic credence should be given to the Old Veteran's story of the events at the Mitchell homestead, although James actually did duty there as he says. The actual circumstances behind his reduction to private are unknown. JDF
[87] Letter #62 to "Brother" (Joseph Miller) Bound To Be A Soldier
[88] Letter #63 to "Brother" (William Miller) Bound To Be A Soldier
[89] Captain Robert M. Mitchell. Roster, 11th Virginia Infantry
[90] Letter #64 to "Brother" (Robert E. Miller) Bound To Be A Soldier
[91] Miller Letters Clements Library
[92] Letter #65 to "Parents" (Robert and Janet Miller) Bound To Be A Soldier
[93] Letter #71 to "Father" (Robert Miller, Sr.) Bound To Be A Soldier
[94] Letter #66 to "Brother" (Robert E. Miller) Bound To Be A Soldier
[95] Letter #67 to "Mother" (Janet Miller) Bound To Be A Soldier
[96] Letter #68 to "Father" (Robert Miller, Sr.) Bound To Be A Soldier
[97] Letter #69 "Brother" (Joseph Miller) Bound To Be A Soldier
[98] Letter #70 to "Brother and Sister" (George Henry and Jane Cramer) Bound To Be A Soldier
[99] The Warren Mail, Jan 9th, 1864
[100] Miller Letters, Clements Library
[101] Calvin Blanchard's Reminiscences
[102] Calvin Blanchard's Reminiscences

[103] Letter #72 to "Brother and Sister" (G.H. and Jane Cramer) Bound To Be A Soldier

[104] Letter #73 to "Brother" (John Miller) Bound To Be A Soldier

[105] Miller Letters Clements Library

[106] Letter #74 to "Father" (Robert Miller, Sr.) Bound To Be A Soldier

[107] Letter #75 to "Sister and Brother" (Jane and George Henry Cramer) Bound To Be A Soldier

[108] Letter #76 to "Mother" (Janet Miller) Bound To Be A Soldier

[109] Letter #77 to "Dear Wife" (Susan A. Miller) Bound To Be A Soldier

[110] Letter #77 to "Dear Wife" (Susan A. Miller) Bound To Be A Soldier

[111] Letter #78 to "Brother" (Robert E. Miller) Bound To Be A Soldier

[112] Miller Letters Clements Library

[113] Letter #79 to "Brother Robert" (Robert E. Miller) Bound To Be A Soldier

[114] Calvin Blanchard's Reminiscences

[115] Letter #80 to "Father" (Robert Miller, Sr.) Bound To Be A Soldier

[116] Letter #81 to "Sister" (Jane Miller Cramer) Bound To Be A Soldier

[117] Letter #82 to "Brother" (William ? Miller) Bound To Be A Soldier

[118] Soldiers True—The history of the 111th Pennsylvania Infantry

[119] Calvin Blanchard's Reminiscences

[120] Alfred Cowles' diary, entry for August 21 WCHS

[121] Afterword, "Bound to Be A Soldier."

[122] Stepping Stones Spring Issue,1958 WCHS

[123] Calvin Blanchard's undated reminiscences to his niece, Erie County Pa. Historical Society.

[124] Letter #83 Harrison Allen to Robert Miller, Sr. Bound To Be A Soldier

[125] References: The Civil War Dictionary, by Mark M. Boatner & Bound to be a Soldier.